ARMOR
©2022 C. B. TITUS

This book is protected under the copyright laws of the United States of America. No part of this publication may be reproduced, stored in a retrieval system, or transmitted, in any form or by any means, without the prior permission in writing of the publisher, nor be otherwise circulated in any form of binding or cover other than that in which it is published and without a similar condition including this condition being imposed on the subsequent purchaser. Any reproduction or unauthorized use of the material or artwork contained herein is prohibited without the express written permission of the authors.

Aethon Books supports the right to free expression and the value of copyright. The purpose of copyright is to encourage writers and artists to produce the creative works that enrich our culture.

The scanning, uploading, and distribution of this book without permission is a theft of the author's intellectual property. If you would like to use material from the book (other than for review purposes), please contact editor@aethonbooks.com. Thank you for your support of the author's rights.

Aethon Books
www.aethonbooks.com

Print and eBook formatting by Steve Beaulieu. Artwork provided by Fernando Granea

Published by Aethon Books LLC.

Aethon Books is not responsible for websites (or their content) that are not owned by the publisher.

This book is a work of fiction. Names, characters, places, and incidents are the product of the author's imagination or are used fictitiously. Any resemblance to actual events, locales, or persons, living or dead is coincidental.

All rights reserved.

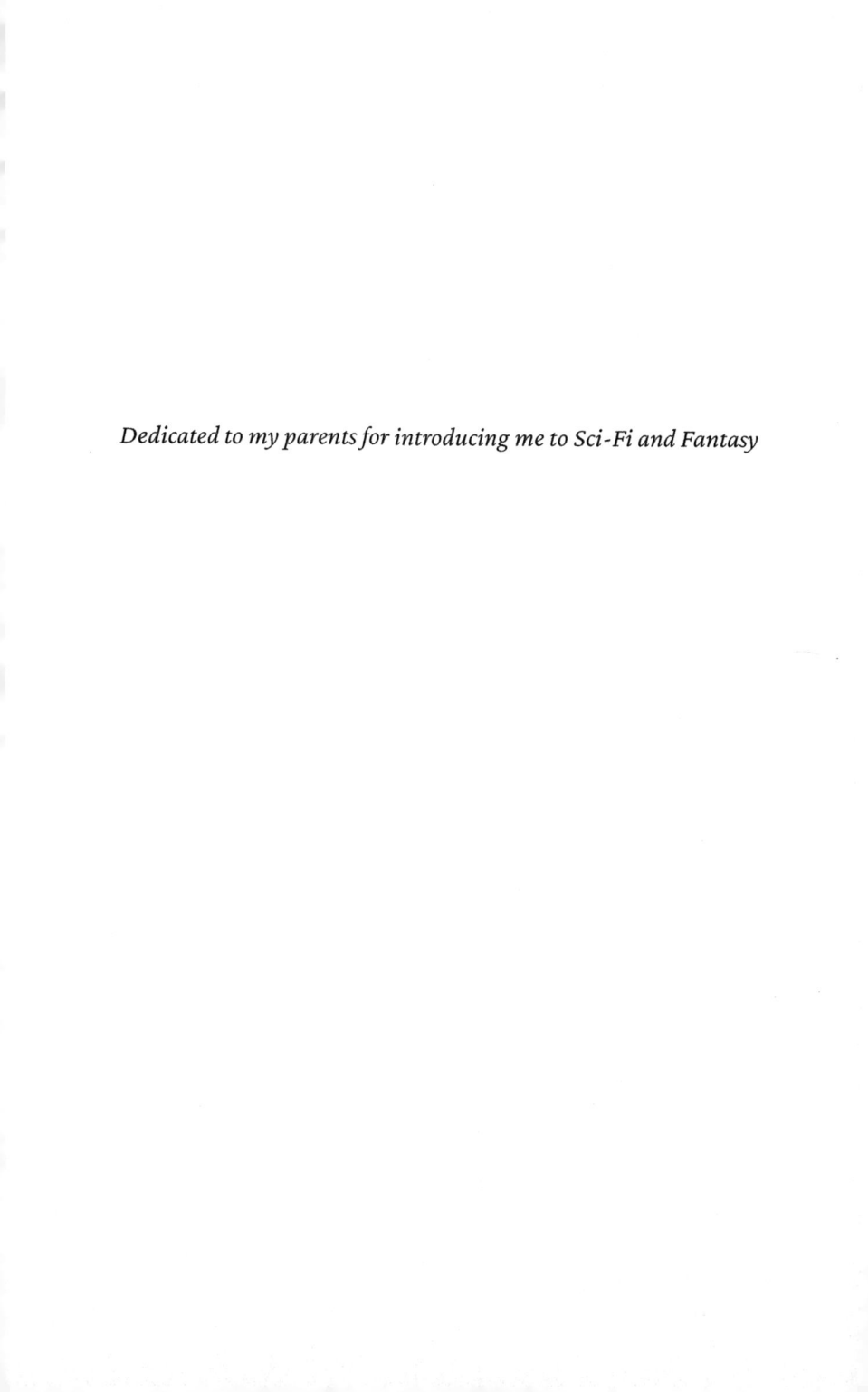

Dedicated to my parents for introducing me to Sci-Fi and Fantasy

1
FOURTH MEAL

The instant the warrior placed my helmet over his head, he was gone, leaving only the suit of full plate that made up my body. He was the fourth adventurer I'd eaten. I stood still for a few moments and savored his essence. I'd been lucky this time; this had been his first quest, and the group he was with didn't know him yet. I lifted his sword and shield with the same practiced ease he would've and went to join his companions farther into the dungeon. I didn't have to go far before encountering a lightly armored dwarf balancing a large hammer carefully on his shoulder.

"Hey lad, looks like a perfect fit," he said.

I searched the memories of my most recent victim. Stone in the River Bed was this one's name, Stone for short. I gave a thumbs-up. I'd be able to mimic my meal's voice, but not his diction or manner. It was best to avoid talking to keep up the ruse.

"I still don't understand why you couldn't wait until we were leaving this forsaken hole to put it on."

I shrugged. I didn't understand either, but all three previous adventurers had immediately donned me after I was found. They'd been understandably excited to find armor so fine as me, but it seemed an unnecessary risk to put me on in the middle of a dungeon. My theory was that my master had placed some sort of glamour upon me that drove them to do it.

"Well, let's rejoin the others."

I nodded and followed him through the dusty halls, my steel feet clanging on the stone floors.

I could've led the way myself, of course. This was my home, after all, but that wouldn't suit my master's game. For now, I had to keep up the façade. As I walked with my faux compatriot, I took note of the lifeless forms of my fellow residents. We passed ten slaughtered goblins, a horribly mutated bear, several large spiders, and a blind cave drake. The drake was new, I noted. My master was always innovating fresh ways to torment adventurers—his favorite form of recreation. I was the crux of that amusement, something I might be proud of...if I were capable of such things.

We crossed into another section of the dungeon and into a large hall. Sconces lit with blue flame lined the walls and illuminated stains of dried blood. A large, muscular woman sat against a wall sharpening a menacing-looking axe while across from her sat another woman, as petite as the other was powerful, wearing a simple white dress that had somehow avoided the myriad potential stains that lurked around them. She was mumbling softly to herself. She would be the biggest risk, both to me and my master. The holy ones were always trouble.

"You done getting all dressed up for the ball?" asked the large woman.

Hrig was her name, according to my last meal. I surprised myself by risking a bow and holding out a hand toward her.

"And would you care to dance?" I asked.

She laughed and took my hand, using it to stand.

"Let's head for the ballroom." She gestured down the hall with her massive axe as if it weighed nothing and tilted her head toward our still mumbling companion. "Coming? Or does your god need you to babble incoherently for a bit longer?"

The other woman stood slowly and sighed.

"You know that prayer is important to my spells, Hrig."

She gave me a once over. "The armor suits you, Sevald. May it protect you in the coming fights."

I tensed momentarily under her gaze, but sensed no attempt to look beneath my surface. She was the trusting type. That suited me fine.

"Thank you, Kyren." I gave a slight nod.

"I'll lead the way this time," said Stone, taking his place in front of us. "I'm tired of being left behind by your overly long legs and lack of consideration for an old dwarf's constitution."

Hrig shrugged and gestured for him to lead the way. I fell in line behind him, with Kyren behind me and Hrig taking up the rear.

After a few winding paths through dimly lit halls, we came to the trapped hallway. Of course, only I knew that's what it was. Stone's foot struck the pressure plate. I waited for the inevitable thud of the arrows into him, but it didn't come. Instead, the crash of armor hitting the ground resounded as I tackled him and the whistle of arrows rang just over my head. Cursing sounded underneath me, and I slowly picked myself back up.

"Yer damned heavy, Sevald. Why the hell did you do that?" asked Stone.

I pointed at the wall to our left. All ten arrows lay in a shattered pile where they'd hit the stone wall.

"Oh, well... thanks. Ye've the keen senses of a dwarf." He gave me a firm pat on my pauldron.

I felt something warm swell in my cuirass as he did so.

Why had I done that? I wasn't meant to interfere with the traps. I'd watched two women and a man be felled by that trap before and had felt nothing. Something was wrong. I'd have to report it to my master after this group was finished.

"We should've expected traps. With everything else we've encountered, it was foolish not to," said Kyren.

"Eh, I say we just push forward and don't worry about it. It was just a few arrows." Hrig flexed as she spoke, as if to say her tremendous biceps made her arrow-proof.

"No, the sorceress is right. I'll handle it." The dwarf began muttering under his breath in ancient dwarven. He closed his eyes, and when he opened them again, they'd changed from blue to slate grey, sclera and all. He looked around the room, into and beyond the walls with his stone sense.

I was familiar with the ability. My second meal had been a dwarf who also possessed it.

"There are four more traps in the room. Follow me close behind and tread carefully. I think I can guide us all through here."

We fell back into formation and followed him. We avoided the pitfall, the pendulum axes, and what my master referred to as the "razzle dazzler," a flamethrower hidden in a wall. I hardly noticed, too focused on determining why I'd saved Stone. Perhaps it was a directive that had been placed into me without me knowing? Master often spoke of his growing boredom; perhaps having more adventurers make it through to the end was a way to increase his pleasure?

The dwarf held up his hand for us to stop. "Everyone quiet down. That's the end of the traps, but there's something in the room up ahead. Something big."

I raised my shield in preparation and readied my sword. The troll was next. I kicked open the door to the dark room and charged.

"Wait, you idio—!"

I ran inside with a roar, doing my best to draw the troll's attention. I succeeded, and after a moment of surprise, he knocked me across the room with an almost casual swing of his massive club.

I slumped against the wall, feigning unconsciousness. This was part of the routine, of course—I rushed in and was struck down, only to miraculously recover after the fight ended and my short-term allies had been softened up.

Stone charged, rolling between the troll's legs at the last moment. Before the troll could turn around, Hrig was in front of him, and he narrowly avoided having his guts exposed by her axe. Already off-balance, he was knocked to his knees by a swift hammer strike to the back of his legs. He swung his club in a wide arc to buy space, but just as he started rising to his feet, chains of light sprang from beneath him and brought him back down to the ground, where they bound his hands and feet. Kyren had entered the room, her eyes ablaze with light, her dark hair a sharp contrast with the halo of white that surrounded her.

Another strike from Stone's hammer caused the troll to let out an animal cry. Hrig closed on him, her axe held high, but she'd made a fatal mistake—she'd forgotten his teeth. Before she could bring down her axe, he stretched out his neck and wrapped his teeth around her waist, biting hard. She dropped her axe. A loud and terrible crunch followed, but she didn't scream; instead, she started striking the troll's head with her bare fists even as she coughed up blood.

I was on my feet and across the room before I knew what was happening. I dropped my shield and leapt the last six feet, taking my sword in both hands and bringing it down on the troll's neck, severing it in a spray of viscera. I realized after a few moments that I'd been yelling. I felt a fire deep in my breastplate, a kind of internal heat I hadn't felt before.

I moved toward Hrig and pulled the troll's jaws from her.

"You're a great dance partner, Sevald. You just need to work on those first few steps," she said as she spat blood from her mouth.

Kyren ran to her, muttering under her breath. The light had not yet left her, and it began to flow over Hrig, stitching her wounds and sealing her innards back into her stomach. By the time she was done, the glow that had surrounded her had faded completely.

As Hrig's wounds healed, I felt yet another new sensation, almost as if I were a clenched fist that was easing its grasp. I searched for an explanation from my previous meals. Relief? Where was that coming from?

"Thank you, Kyren," said Hrig, wiping blood from her mouth.

"You're welcome, but be careful. I can seal your wounds, but you lost a lot of blood. You'll likely feel a bit weak."

Hrig responded by launching herself back to her feet and picking up her massive axe with a single hand before giving it a few test swings.

"Eh, I didn't need that extra blood anyway."

Kyren sighed, Stone chuckled, and I stood there enjoying what my meals told me was a sense of camaraderie.

As we descended down to the final room of the dungeon, I continued to reckon with the new sensations overtaking me. It felt as if heavy stones were rattling around inside me, clanging against my hollow interior. Dread, according to the essences I'd absorbed. This was always my master's favorite part, the conclusion of his grand design.

The room was high-ceilinged, held up by six thick stone pillars. The walls were covered in rich tapestries and lit by a massive chandelier. At the far end of the room sat my master on his throne, draped across it with one foot hanging playfully off one of the arm rests. His right hand held a golden chalice from which he took a generous sip as we entered the room. He smiled at us, but it didn't reach his eyes.

"I see you made it to my inner sanctum." He swirled the wine in his cup. "I'm impressed."

The party was close enough to make him out at this point. He appeared as a young handsome man wearing red silk embroidered with gold thread and covered with jewels.

Instead of responding, we fanned out, readying ourselves for a charge. He wouldn't like that; he always preferred to banter. I'd try some myself, but he wouldn't really consider that satisfying. It would be like a child speaking to their toy.

"Nothing to say? Not, 'stop killing villagers?' Or, 'we're here to end your reign of terror?' Come now, I've been terrorizing this area for years. I'm sure you could come up with something!"

"Oi, I've got something," muttered Stone, hammer held menacingly in his hands.

The lord smiled and nodded for him to continue.

"This!" He charged the throne, raising his hammer to strike.

The lord sighed but didn't move. The hammer fell, cracking the throne, but my master was no longer in it; he now stood behind Stone, facing the rest of the party, wine chalice still in hand, not a drop spilled. He drained it, crushed it with his bare hand, and threw it aside.

"Fine, we'll skip to the part where I kill you."

Hrig threw herself at him, her axe high in the air, but he

raised his hand, and she was thrown by a wall of force. Stone was back on him, sweeping at his knees with his hammer, but he lost his footing as the tiles beneath his feet rose in pillars underneath him, launching him into the air.

Next was my turn. I followed the usual pattern he'd made me practice. Downward strike, left, right, shield bash—he moved the bare minimum necessary to avoid each strike, yawning as he did so to emphasize his overwhelming power. Finally, he gave me a wink as he lightly struck my chestplate with an open palm, and I launched myself backward dramatically.

As I clattered across the floor, an enormous ray of light engulfed the lord, and I was momentarily blinded, despite my lack of eyes. Holy light would do that. When it cleared, the lord was standing, visibly singed. His expression changed from amused to annoyed. Kyren was also standing, surrounded by the light that accompanied her spells, and preparing another one with rapid mutterings under her breath.

He began to move toward her menacingly, but before he could close the distance, both Stone and Hrig attacked him simultaneously. This time, he wasn't prepared, and both strikes were true. He stood there for a moment, unmoved by either blow, but bleeding from a tiny cut where the axe had hit.

"That's enough!" he yelled, and force-propelled his attackers backward. He raised a hand, and the floor beneath Kyren shifted and enclosed around her. He made the same gesture, and both Hrig and Stone were similarly trapped. Now, it was show time.

I stood up and charged my master with a primal yell. He smiled calmly, enjoying the pageantry. Just before I brought my sword down, he raised his hand, and I stopped, seemingly frozen by a spell, but truthfully, stopping out of routine.

"You cannot defeat me, warrior. I'm too powerful."

He clenched his hand in a fist, and I brought my hands to my side as if I were enclosed by an invisible force. I pretended to struggle for a moment before sucking in my armor to give the appearance that I was being crushed. He opened his hand, and I fell to my knees.

"Do you wish to live?"

I stayed there, unmoving, pretending that I had been winded by the force of his spell. He liked this part to be particularly dramatic.

"Yes... I do."

He smiled widely. "I shall let you live... on one condition."

"Anything," I said quietly, but loudly enough for my fellow adventurers to hear.

"Kill your companions."

I pretended to be startled and looked over my shoulder at my allies. Hrig and Stone were furious, but Kyren's face was calm.

"Do it," she said, and that actually did surprise me. My master's face told me it surprised him, too. "He'll kill us all anyway. There's no shame in saving yourself."

In all of the times I'd done this, this hadn't happened. This was new.

"She's right. Do what you need to do." Hrig's expression had changed from angry to sad. "I already owe you my life for earlier."

"As do I, lad. Do what ya need to," said Stone.

I felt in that moment another new feeling building in my empty suit. I looked up at my master. His mouth hung open. He'd never had things go this far off-script. He lived to savor the terror and misery in adventurers' eyes as someone they thought they knew betrayed them and killed them one by one. He enjoyed it so much, he'd created me to ensure it would play out that way every single time.

Unfortunately for him, this change of script would be the second biggest surprise of his day. I raised my sword and drove it hard and fast straight into the small cut he'd received from Hrig's axe. I felt his legs give out as I lifted him above my helmet and let the sword slide up through his chest. The look on his face was one of surprise and fear, two expressions it was completely unused to. I threw him off my sword and watched his body roll across the floor, leaving a trail of blood behind it.

The spell holding my companions was released by my master's death, and before I knew it, Hrig had swept me up in an embrace. I dropped my sword and shield as she twirled me before putting me back on the ground, though not quite letting me go. Stone gave me a firm pat on the pauldron, and Kyren gave my left gauntlet a gentle touch and my helmet a warm smile.

"Now that was spectacular!" said Hrig, smiling ear to ear.

"Y'know, lad, I had my doubts about you when you joined us for this, but you've done a great job addressing them," said Stone as he went over to begin looting my former master's corpse.

"Agreed. You seemed a bit brash and unsure when we met you, but we couldn't have done this without you. You were a real asset," said Kyren.

"Uh, thank you. I... I'm surprised I wound up being so useful," I said.

Hrig looked at each of her companions. "So, shall we have him join us for the next one?"

Stone and Kyren smiled before speaking simultaneously.

"Aye," said Stone with a smile.

"Absolutely," agreed Kyren.

Hrig looked back at me.

"So, what do you say? Want to join us for another one, Sevald?"

I stood silently for a moment and looked over at my master, whose jeweled tunic was already more lightly jeweled than before. I took a moment to try and process what had happened and all the new sensations and feelings I was experiencing.

"Yes... I would like that very much."

2

AN OATH AND A JOKE

I'd never left the dungeon before, and it took me a moment to adjust to the sunlight. I'd only ever experienced the light of torches or the arcane glow some sorcerers could summon for illumination. Sunlight felt different. It felt warm.

We hadn't found much in the way of loot in the dungeon. A small pouch of gems, a smattering of coins, and some old equipment that I knew had belonged to the parties who'd explored the it before. My former master enjoyed the finer things, but his skill in conjuration meant he had no need to carry much wealth, and his raw power had made him feel that enchanted objects were beneath him. Still, in spite of the lack of loot, everyone was in high spirits.

We stood a short way from the dungeon's entrance as Kyren climbed a nearby tree to recover the travel gear she'd hidden there earlier. The sight surprised me, but searching Sevald's memories, I recalled she was a quarter wood elf. Still, the image of a holy woman bounding up a tree in white robes took some adjustment.

"Entden's just a day and half away, right?" I asked.

Sevald's voice had been deep and fine. I took a moment to be grateful it was the one I'd be stuck with.

"Aye, we'll likely travel a bit before making camp for the night. Even if we've cleared the dungeon for now, all sorts of beasties tend to gather around them. Best not to tempt fate."

Stone's words mirrored my own thinking. I'd been awakened more than once to roust goblins that had assumed my master's dungeon was free real estate. Monsters in general are drawn to certain places. I was still feeling a pull to return to the dungeon myself.

Three traveling bags thumped on the ground next to me, followed by Kyren, who had already secured hers over her shoulder.

"Thank you." I grabbed Sevald's bag. It contained a week's travel rations, a bedroll, some travelling clothes, a holy symbol of Dur, and some etchings that I sincerely doubted Dur would have approved of. Sevald had been travelling alone until he'd reached Entden; hard to blame him for a little self-care.

Hrig took her small pack and belted it over her waist. It was the smallest of them. From what I'd seen of her so far, I assumed she preferred to live off the land when she could. Stone added the small amount of loot we'd collected to his own bag.

"Try not to 'lose' any of the loot this time, Stone. I've taken notice of how often your purse seems heavier than mine."

"You wound me, Hrig. You really think I'd ever steal from my companions? I only carry the valuables because I get the best prices from the merchants. Besides, if I ever 'lose' anything, the additional coin I earn you by my haggling more than makes up for it."

Hrig grunted in response, and Kyren rolled her eyes before leading the way back to the trail that led to town.

By their tone, I could tell the argument was a familiar one.

I'd had very little interaction with others, but between the four adventurers I'd eaten, I found that the nuances of people's speech and movement weren't too difficult to discern with a moment's effort. Luckily, Sevald had been quiet when travelling with my new companions, so they wouldn't be expecting me to talk too much. I realized that, at this point, I'd actually spoken more to them than he had. That made them more my companions than they had ever been his.

We stopped along the trail a little before sundown and made camp. We laid out our bedrolls, and Hrig left to see if she could find a rabbit or two to attempt a stew. Kyren set water to boil, and Stone brought out the gems he'd recovered from my dead master's tunic and looked at them with a small magnifying lens. He seemed pleased with their grade.

I took out Sevald's symbol of Dur and pretended to pray. This was where things could go wrong. I didn't eat—well, not anything my comrades would approve of—and when I didn't take off my helmet to eat or my armor to sleep, they would certainly get suspicious. Sevald had changed out of his armor on the night he'd spent with the party and hadn't even worn a helmet until he'd found me. I could simply not address it and keep the armor on, but both Hrig and Stone didn't seem the type to let that go without comment.

If they saw through my ruse, it was quite possible that I would be able to defeat them. Kyren was out of spells, Hrig had lost a lot of blood, and Stone wasn't too strong in a straight-up fight. I wasn't tired—I didn't think I was capable of it—and I was at least as strong as Hrig, though I'd never had any occasion to test myself to my limits. With the element of surprise and a little brutality, I could be free of them, collect the reward from the village, and be on my way.

I didn't want that, though. I wanted to be an adventurer and travel with my newfound party. Wanting was new for me, and I'd prefer not to feel the disappointment of not satisfying it.

I searched the essences I'd collected, trying to think out a solution, when I realized it was already in my hands. I looked down at the symbol of Dur, god of order, balance, and fidelity.

"Kyren... would you do me the honor of bearing witness to a sacred vow?"

She looked up from the boiling water that was now swirling with wild onions and chopped mushrooms.

"Of course. I'm obligated to, in fact. Stone, can you watch the pot for me?"

He nodded and took her place. She approached me, gave a quick prayer in elvish, and nodded for me to start.

"As penance for feeling the temptation to kill my comrades, I take a vow of penance in the name of Dur. I shall not be seen outside of my armor until the weight of my sin is less than that of my armor."

I felt satisfied for a moment; that should give me the cover I needed.

Then something unexpected happened. The symbol of Dur started glowing. Kyren's eyes began glowing, and she spoke in a voice that was not her own.

"Your oath in the name of Dur is witnessed by the servant of Sidi, and accepted." For a moment, the entire camp was bathed in holy light, then it was gone.

That concerned me greatly.

"That was a true godly pact. Those are rare," said Kyren, predicting my question before I asked it. "Gods hear bargains all the time. 'If my crop yield is good, I'll never drink again'; 'I'd give my soul for ten bars of gold'; 'I'd kill to get rid of this headache'. These words are usually spoken jokingly or desperately, but sometimes, a god will answer and bind them to it. Looks like yours was just answered by Dur."

"Well, I suppose I'm honored...though surprised." Being locked into a pact by a god I wasn't even aware of until I ate one of his devout followers was definitely surprising.

"Well, the gods are fickle and often motivated by whimsy, though Dur doesn't seem the type to usually indulge in that. He must be keeping an eye on you."

Her words sent a shiver through the steel of my back. A god of order and balance watching a monster masquerading as a man seemed unlikely to end well.

"Y'know, I made a godly pact once," Stone said, looking up from the soup pot he was still stirring dutifully for Kyren. "I was lost in a deep forest near my hometown. I'd not seen a landmark I'd recognized for two days, and rain had been falling on me constantly. At one point, when I was feeling particularly desperate, I said I'd give my left nut for a mug of ale and a dry chair. I thought I heard someone laughing and went toward the sound. After walking just a short while longer, I came upon a town that neighbored my own. A barmaid took pity on me and gave me a blanket, a corner table, and a tall glass of ale. When the rain cleared, she offered to guide me back home since she was headed that way anyway. I went to help her saddle her mule, when it startled and kicked me square in the jewels. It was the most painful thing I've ever experienced. You can guess what the kick cost me... Anyway, during my long recovery, the barmaid took a liking to me, and that's how I met my first wife. That's also why I only have daughters. Everyone knows that boys come from the left one."

I felt something bubbling up in my breastplate. I tried to hold it in, but before I knew it, the strangest sound was coming from my faceplate. Holding it down only seemed to make it worse.

I was laughing, I realized. The sensation was new to me, but I found I rather liked it.

After a moment, I recovered, then laughed some more, recovered again, and just when I thought I was done, I had a final fit. Stone was looking pleased that he'd elicited such a reaction. and even Kyren had a small smile, though she was doing her best to hide it. I found that the laughter had tremendously relieved my concern for my new godly pact. Whatever it might bring, it was surely worth it for the new experiences I'd be having.

Just then, Hrig emerged into the camp with three fat rabbits dangling from her hand.

"I heard your laughter from a league away. What was so funny?" she asked.

"Stone was just telling Sevald the story of how he met his first wife," responded Kyren.

"Ah, from when the dwarven trickster Jeiri supposedly played matchmaker? I've heard better."

"It always kills in the taverns, Hrig." Stone's voice was filled with indignation.

"Exactly. It's the kind of story that amuses drunks. That isn't really a mark in its favor." She sighed. "I just realized that with Sevald travelling with us, Stone will have an excuse to tell all of his stories again..."

Her and Kyren's expressions grew grave as Stone's eyes started twinkling.

I bluffed my way through a bowl of rabbit stew by gently spooning it into my faceplate and absorbing it the way I had the people that had worn my armor. After that I took the first watch. I didn't sleep or tire, so it made the most sense to me, and my companions were too tired to argue over it.

"Eating" had been interesting. I didn't have a mouth, but I could taste the soup in the same way I could see without eyes, smell without a nose, and hear without ears. I could tell from the lives I'd absorbed that my senses were in some ways keener than theirs had been. I could sense things within a field around myself that let me tell what was going on behind me and even around corners. I could even taste the soup left in the pot if I focused hard enough.

It was going to take a while to get used to. I hadn't ever explored what I was capable of before, as I'd never needed to. I'd only existed to follow my master's script. This was the longest I'd ever even been conscious.

After two hours, I woke Hrig to let her take watch. I could've done it the entire time, but it was best to maintain the illusion that I slept. I lay there, listening to the sounds of owls, and each of my companions taking their turns at watch until I felt the sun start to shine down onto my armor.

3
ODD REUNIONS

After an uneventful night, I feigned waking and stretching with a yawn and helped break down the camp. Once it was cleared, we got our packs and started toward Entden. It wasn't long before we could see it in the distance.

Entden wasn't quite small enough to be a village or large enough to be a town. It was surrounded by a wall of tree trunks that were patrolled by guards. It sat on the border of two kingdoms, wedged near the center of the forest.

Coming through the gates and seeing the buildings gave me an odd sense of familiarity, deeper than the familiarity brought by Sevald's brief time in the town. I thought about it as I continued walking, and something about the sensation of the steel boots that were my feet sinking into the mud of the street sparked something.

My first meal, Byn. He'd been born here to a tanner named Fyn and his wife, Tanda. His memories began to flow uncontrollably through me. His mother holding his hand as they walked to market, his father helping him weave a small bracelet out of leftover strips of leather, an adventuring party offering him a chance to join them to clear a dungeon that had long been a plague on the village.

I started recognizing people in the town. The baker's daughter, Aubrey, now opening the bakery herself, twice as old as Byn's memories recalled. A guard passed by closely—I remembered throwing rocks at squirrels with him as a child. Before I knew it, I was the one leading the party to the town headman's house.

The headman was sitting out front, watching the comings and goings of people through Entden. I recognized him as the same man that had led Entden in Byn's day, though he now sported a head of white hair and a face full of wrinkles.

"Hail, Jusuf!" I said as I approached.

"Hail..." He looked me up and down. "I'm afraid I'm not sure who you are, ser?"

"It's me, B— Sevald. You tasked me and my companions with clearing the dungeon nearby."

"Ah, that's right." He sighed deeply. "You gave up, I suppose? I can't blame you. Dozens of adventurers have tried it, and none have returned. I fear that Entden is doomed to suffer regular terrorizing and harassment by the grim creatures who reside there, and the dark sorcerer who leads them."

Hrig stepped forward, opening a melon-sized bag and removing the head of my former master from it by his hair. "You mean this sorcerer?"

I was starting to sense that she enjoyed dramatic flourishes as much as Stone enjoyed off-color humor. The headman's eyes widened.

"I can't belie— You actually did it!"

"That we did, ser, out of the goodness of our hearts and of your town's generosity with the listed bounty," said Stone, his mind on profit.

"Of course, dear sers. I'll put it together at once! In the

meantime, please make your way to our inn. I'll send word that you are to eat and drink for free for the night and they should provide you rooms."

"Thank you, ser, we shall head there now," said Kyren.

We turned around, and I led the way to the tavern. It was still called "The Thirsty Tree," its sign showing a tree root dipped into a beer mug.

It was early morning, the tavern empty. A few travelers sat eating breakfast in a corner, and a logger sat at the bar enjoying a pint before work. We all sat at a corner table, and Kyren walked up to the bartender.

"Here we go..." said Hrig, letting out a sigh.

"Aye, perhaps we should've timed things so that we arrived later and she couldn't get started so early," said Stone.

"What are you talking about?" I asked.

"Kyren is a bit of a drinker. Being given a free pass to drink 'erfill for free... It's going to be a long day."

"Kyren? Really?"

"Aye, lad. She's devout as anything, but the goddess she worships couldn't care less about vices. Still, she steers clear of most of them—gold, men, women, rich food—but drink is the one she allows herself...and she tends to go a little overboard."

"What's overboard for her? She can't weigh more than eight stone. A pint is almost the size of her head."

"Well, lad, prepare to be surprised," he said as Kyren continued her negotiation at the bar.

"Honestly, I'd have expected you two to be the drinkers," I said.

Hrig smiled. "I only drink wine. I can't stand the taste of beer, and that's usually all there is to be had in a place like this." She paused, her mouth twisting in disgust. "Just because I'm a barbarian doesn't mean I like the taste of piss."

Stone chuckled. "I don't mind drinking just about anything,

but Kyren's soured it a bit for me. She's just drunk me under the table a few too many times."

Just then, Kyren returned to the table balancing four mugs filled to the brim with frothy beer. I expected her to distribute one to each of us, but instead, she put them all in front of herself, lifted the closest one to her lips, and drank it as quickly as I could've consumed someone who'd donned my armor. If I'd had a mouth, it would've been agape. She gently wiped a froth mustache from her upper lip and let out a long, satisfied sigh, then looked up at me.

"Oh, I'm sorry, Sevald, did you want one? Normally, Stone and Hrig aren't up for it this early, so I just assumed you wouldn't."

"You, uh, assumed correctly. Feel free to enjoy those all on your own."

She smiled. "Oh, I will."

———

While bearing witness to Kyren downing more beer than should've been physically possible, I settled in and people-watched while listening to Hrig and Stone snipe at one another. Eventually, the headman arrived with a sturdy pouch of gold coins of which my cut was twenty-five pieces.

"Lad, care to come with me while I go fence the rest of our loot?" said Stone, rolling a single gold piece between his fingers.

"Fence? But we didn't steal anything," I said.

"Oh, yer right. I mean sell. Old habits."

"Sure, but why me?"

"A man in a suit of armor standing behind me may give my negotiations a nice edge."

"If intimidation's the goal, wouldn't Hrig be a better choice?"

"He wants to show off, Sevald. He knows me and Kyren aren't impressed by his haggling anymore." Stone looked a little embarrassed. "We're appreciative, mind you, but not impressed."

"Well, I'll join you. I don't have a lot of experience with merchants."

I had none, in fact. We stood up and left the tavern, which was still relatively empty at just past noon. I let Stone lead the way, though I already knew where the market was. We stopped in at the jeweler's first. The shop owner sat behind a counter carefully polishing a small gold ring. He was a portly fellow, with little hair left on his head, but his eyes were keen as he sized us up.

"Hail. You must be the adventurers who finally cleared up our dungeon problem."

"Aye, that we are. We were just looking to improve your inventory with some of what we found."

"Oh, really? Let's see what you've got."

Stone produced a small pouch from somewhere and started laying out the gemstones we'd found. A few amethysts, a rather large garnet, and two sapphires. Stone then began to lay down the gems he'd taken from my master's tunic, but just after the jeweler had taken notice of them, he put them back into the pouch.

"Ah, not those, actually."

"Wait, ser, those looked...rather interesting."

"Oh, they are, but I'm not sure I'm ready to sell them yet. I feel that for gems of their quality, they may do better in a larger city."

The jeweler frowned. "You'll find no fairer price than what I offer in my own shop, I assure you of that, ser."

"I believe that you believe that, but I've travelled a ways, and it's always been good policy to save the best pieces for the richest cities."

As Stone talked, the shopkeeper was slowly turning red.

"I do not doubt that richer cities seem like they offer better prices, but my shop has stood for one hundred years of family-owned apprenticeship, and in that time, we have never been outdone in terms of the quality of our business and the fairness of our dealings."

"Well, if that's the case, ser, what would you say the gems that I've already laid out are worth?"

The merchant took up a small magnifying lens and began looking through the gemstones. After a few moments, he put them down.

"For this lot, I'll give you sixty gold pieces. And I dare you to find a better price than that in any city."

Stone contemplated the offer for a moment before laying out the remaining gems he'd taken from my master's tunic. They were rubies, I noticed, and seemed very fine to me, though I lacked the skills to truly tell. The jeweler took a few moments with each of them.

"For these, I will offer another hundred."

"Ye've got a deal." Stone held out his hand, and they shook to seal the bargain.

Items were exchanged, and then we were back on the street. Stone let out a satisfied sigh before looking up at me as if he'd just asked a question and was expecting an answer. I thought for a moment, trying to put together the thoughts and memories I had access to in order to figure it out.

"You knew you'd get a better price on the less valuable gemstones if you could distract him with the nicer ones."

"Exactly. I dangled a carrot out of his reach so that he'd give me a higher offer to get to it. Along with a little bit of needling to his pride, I probably managed to make us almost thirty gold more altogether."

I stood there for a moment, thinking over what he said.

"Don't worry about fairness, by the way. I know you're a Durite. He'll be able to sell those gems for almost double what he bought them for once he works them into some jewelry. I just wanted to make sure we got our due after almost dying in that damned dungeon."

"Ah, I understand."

I didn't, but he seemed to know what he was talking about. After that, I watched him sell the equipment we'd found for double its value to a pious man by pretending he was giving away his adventuring gear to join a monastery, and then I watched him convince a man that the foods he was selling were near expiring, but he'd take them off his hands for a steep discount. By the end of it, he was smiling ear to ear, his pockets jingling as we walked.

We reentered the tavern as the sun started to set. The entire atmosphere of The Thirsty Tree had changed. There was dancing, singing, a fight in the corner, and a cow behind the bar. Kyren was sitting in the same spot we'd left her, but the four pints she'd had had multiplied into roughly twenty, and there were four men passed out around her. Hrig was asleep, or more likely passed out, leaning against the table with her thick blond braid as her only pillow.

"She challenged you again, eh?" Stone asked Kyren.

"Yes, it turns out they had wine, too."

Kyren's speech seemed totally unaffected. The only indication that she'd had a drink at all was some redness in her cheeks.

"And these lot challenged you as well?" He gestured at the small pile of men on the floor.

"Yes. And it seems all that led to more drinking in general."

Stone chuckled, shaking his head. "Well, I'll be turning in to count our profits and make sure they're fairly distributed."

"Fairly, eh?" She cocked an eyebrow.

"Fair to me, at least, yes." He smiled and made his way through the tavern-goers and up to the room he'd been provided. I sat quietly, watching Kyren finish yet another pint. As she did, she looked up at me.

"You'll have to be careful, you know."

"Careful about what?"

"About your oath. Some people may take it as a challenge." She gestured meaningfully toward Hrig.

"What do you mean?"

"I mean, some women may enjoy the satisfaction that could come from being enticing enough to make a man break his oath to a god."

"Oh..." Suddenly, the room seemed too hot.

"Don't worry, though. I'm sure you can handle it."

"Will you help me to, uh, avoid such challenges?" I asked.

I was sincerely curious about having that virtue taken, but it wasn't exactly an option for one whose physical form was a void with armor for skin.

"Oh, don't worry, us worshippers have to stick together, and a godly oath in particular should be upheld."

I let out an imitated sigh. "Thank you, Kyren."

She smiled.

"Then again, I also suppose it wouldn't be much of an oath if it wasn't tested now and again." She smiled and returned her attention to the next pint.

She was joking. Probably.

I took a moment to glance around the bar. There were some men playing dice in the corner, the fight had ended with both men being tossed outside, and a few men were asking the cow for another round. A man at the far end of the bar raised his head for a moment, and if I'd had a heart, it might have stopped. It was my, or rather, Byn's father.

He looked much older than Byn's memories of him. His hair had gone white, his skin wrinkled; his face had gone red and irritated in the way of men who drink too much too often, and his clothing was dirty and soiled. It didn't take much to realize how he'd gotten to this state. He'd lost his child.

I suddenly felt very heavy. I hadn't regretted anything before, but a search through my meal's experiences told me that's what was happening.

I didn't care for it. I felt a need to do something to relieve that weight.

I reached deep into myself and slid my hand into the seam between my knee and my thigh plate. Out of that, I pulled a small bracelet of woven leather. It looked the same as it had when I'd eaten its owner. I stood up and approached the man, sliding onto the stool next to him.

He looked up at me into my faceplate, and a sharp pang clanged in my chestplate as memories of him raising Byn flooded through me. I took the leather bracelet and held it out to him.

"He wouldn't have wanted you to suffer this much. He was a man, and he made his own decisions. There's no reason to put yourself through this."

His eyes widened. He took the bracelet and turned it in his hands. Tears welled in his eyes.

"How'd you know?"

"I'm one of the adventurers that cleared out the dungeon. I heard about what had happened to your son when I was investigating what the townsfolk knew about it."

The man looked down at the bracelet. "Thank you, ser. I'll treasure this."

He pushed away his drink and stumbled out of the room. I

felt lighter then. I wasn't sure if it was guilt that I'd felt for eating his son. I didn't know good from bad until yesterday, and I still wasn't clear on the finer points of it. What I definitely felt was indebted to those whose lives I'd eaten. They still lived in a sense, but not in a way that they'd chosen, and their absence from the lives of those that cared for them was my responsibility.

I walked back toward Kyren. She regarded me with a strange look.

"I can see that the gods work through you," she said.

I was profoundly uncomfortable with the implications of that. I went and lifted Hrig. She was light, at least to me.

"I'm going to take her to her bed. This can't be a comfortable way to sleep."

"She's never complained about it before, but it's probably a good idea. If she wakes up on the way, do remember your oath."

Heat built again in my faceplate, and I moved to carry her to her bed. Kyren regarded me with her usual small smile as I made my way up the steps.

4
BRUTALLY CUNNING

I was the last one down to breakfast. My companions were eating and engaging in light chat. Kyren, despite her enormous consumption the previous night, seemed completely fine. Hrig, on the other hand, was squinting and clearly forcing herself to eat any breakfast at all.

"Good morning," I said as I approached the table.

They responded warmly, though Hrig could only really manage an affectionate grunt in my direction. I sat and began the careful dance of pretending to eat breakfast. As we finished, Stone removed a letter from his coat.

"Ye can read, right?" I nodded. "Then 'ave a look at this."

I took it and made a show of holding it in front of my faceplate, though I could've read it even before he handed it to me.

To all Enterprising Adventurers

A Goblin encampment has been discovered halfway between Entden and Cirros
A reward is being offered of 20 gold to assess the threat or 80 gold to end it

Goblin left ears will be accepted as proof of success

"A new quest?" I asked, excited.

"Aye, lad, and we're planning on leaving today." He took the message and rolled it up before placing it in his pack. "We figure we'll head straight for the encampment and then swing up to Cirros to meet our fixer and collect our reward."

"Fixer?"

"The person who sends quests our way. Ours is a woman named Clara. She collects quests and sends them to the adventuring parties that employ her for a small cut of the profits. She sent this letter by raven this morning."

"I've never heard of a fixer before."

"Well, don't worry too much about it. Now that yer with us, Clara is your fixer, too."

"You are still with us, right?" Kyren asked.

"Of course he is. What kind of a man helps to slay a troll and a wizard, then chickens out when it comes to a few goblins?" responded Hrig.

"She's right. Of course I am."

The table grinned.

After a little more breakfast and a divvying up of profits that left a suspicious look on Hrig's face and one of mock innocence on Stone's, we collected our things and headed for the town gates. Entden was just starting to come to life. Stores were opening, men were making their way to their jobs in the logging camp, and the previous night's drunks were being roused by the town guard and told to go home.

I felt a peculiar kind of melancholy as we made our way out of the town and took a moment to place my hand on the outer gate. For a moment, I felt as if I was Entden. I felt people walk across my paths, I knew the names of everyone who lived there, and I could feel the rooftops starting to warm from the morning sun.

I removed my hand from the gate and rejoined my group on the path to Cirros.

After travelling for a few hours, we stopped to rest at the edge of a river. The sun was still high overhead, and we sat in the shade taking a short rest while eating a lunch of travel rations. Kyren went over to the edge of the water for a moment, letting it flow over her hands.

"I think I'll wash in the river."

"What's the point of all that?" Hrig scoffed. "We'll be covered in goblin blood soon anyway."

"I think you probably should, too, and I imagine Sevald is feeling pretty ripe from being in his armor all the time."

"I'm fine, actu—"

"A bit of dirt is good for you, right, Sevald?" said Stone.

"Well, I don'—"

"It's more sweat that he should be concerned about. You can go ahead, Sevald. We'll stay upstream so you don't have to worry about your oath," said Kyren.

"I just don't thin—"

"Unless you need some help washing your back. I'd certainly help with that if you'd like," said Hrig.

Suddenly, bathing at a distance downstream became a good idea.

"No... I'll do that. Thank you, Kyren."

She gave me one of her small smiles. "And next time, maybe we'll let you finish a sentence or two."

I let out a small chuckle. There was a unique satisfaction to a chuckle: different from a laugh, but with a similar flavor to it.

"Shouldn't Stone give you some privacy?"

"Oh, they've got nothing to worry about from me, lad. They're much too young. Besides, only dwarven women are worth looking at."

"He means it, too, and it's nice to have someone nearby with a hammer in case anyone unwelcome comes around," said Kyren.

I nodded at that and made my way downriver.

After I felt I was far enough away, I decided that instead of just standing around for a while and leaving, I should actually give this bathing thing a try. I began walking into the river, letting the water flow over my greaves, then my chestplate, and finally over my helmet. I made my way toward the center and stood there feeling the flow of the water around my steel frame, then watching as curious fish approached before leaving, attracted to the reflection of the sun off my plate.

Remembering the leather bracelet I'd produced the previous night, I decided on a small test. I opened my faceplate and started letting water into myself.

At first, I just let it flow naturally, but after a moment, I started actively sucking it in faster and faster. Eventually, I was creating a small whirlpool at the surface of the water with the force of my inhalation.

After a few moments, I felt myself begin to reach my capacity. I took an inventory. About a small lake's worth of water, twenty fish, a frog, and a particularly unlucky duck. I opened my faceplate again, and this time, I pushed the water back out. It was harder to push out than to suck in, but after a few minutes, I'd managed to put everything back where I'd found it, mostly. The duck kicked furiously back to the surface of the water with a frog clinging to its back for dear life, and I decided I should get out of the river, as well.

As my head surfaced, I noticed my sword and shield weren't

where I'd left them. I moved farther out of the water until it was only waist high.

Suddenly, there was a roar in the distance coming from upriver.

I started to run that way when three arrows shattered against my helmet. As I turned to look for their origin, I found myself surrounded on three sides by goblins. They were armed with crude weapons and armored in worn leather that I could tell, from Byn's memories, was terrible quality.

They clicked and growled at one another in undercommon, displaying rows of sharp teeth, their red eyes emanating hunger and hatred. One of them was wielding my longsword like a claymore, and another had my shield strapped to its back. One of them spoke again in undercommon to the others, and they all chuckled and started to close in. They must've thought I wasn't as much of a threat without my weapon.

How unfortunate for them.

I felt a new sensation bubbling up in me. I was tense, and my senses all felt red. Anger, I realized. Anger at having my weapons stolen, and being delayed in returning to my party.

I let that new emotion guide me and struck the goblin nearest to me with a kick that had all the force I could muster behind it. His face caved in with a crunch, and he spun backward into a nearby tree that shuddered, splintering at the impact.

The other goblins hesitated then, looking at the shattered form of their companion. I took advantage of their surprise, grabbing two of them and smashing their bodies into the ground, where they crumpled like wet rags.

Another of them jumped onto my back, attempting to bite at where my neck would be, but I simply fell backward, crushing him under my weight. Two more jumped at me, swinging crude pickaxes. I rolled under one, grabbed him by his weapon, and threw him into the other one. His pickaxe pierced his fellow ambusher through the skull with his hands still around the handle. I walked to his prone form and crushed him beneath my boot.

The one with my sword attacked next. I simply caught it in my hand and casually shook him off of it. Once he was off, I struck him with the sword's hilt, and he collapsed, dead.

The last goblin made a run for it, likely assuming that I wouldn't be able to catch up running in fullplate through woods. I followed him through the brush for a few seconds then leapt, landing on top of my shield and crushing him beneath it. I dragged my shield off his back and sank my sword into his skull for good measure.

I then took stock. Blood coated my armor, along with thick chunks of viscera, several teeth embedded in my neck plate. I needed another bath.

I started running upriver. When I reached the spot where I'd left my companions, I was greeted by a pile of goblin corpses, their blood running into the river. A quick scan showed that Hrig, Stone, and Kyren weren't among the dead. But they also weren't here. I walked over to a severed head and lifted it by one of its long green ears. I needed more information, and to test how far my ability to absorb could go.

Time for another test. I removed my head and placed it over his, absorbing its essence. What came to me wasn't the usual crystal-clear absorption of memories, skills, and thoughts. It was more like flickers, little impressions of who the goblin was and what he knew.

I sensed brutality and a low cunning. An ambition for more without the capacity to obtain it without violence. I saw a camp, crude to more developed races, but much advanced from what I knew goblins were capable of. There were fences, domesticated dogs for riding, attempts at agriculture and smithing rather than looting.

There was resentment tied to these memories; this wasn't the old way. Things were meant to be taken, looted, and despoiled. I saw a high tent in the center of the camp. With it came a flash of fear and golden eyes.

More recent memories were clearer. A raiding party, *my* raiding party, and a lucky find. A napping dwarf and two women bathing. My first instinct was to kill, to bathe in blood and revel in violence, but I knew I'd be rewarded for capturing them.

We charged, focusing on the dwarf first. He was not a very heavy sleeper, it turned out. His hammer felled one of my group before I knew what was happening. The larger of the two women let out a roar I didn't think a human should be capable of, much less a woman. She charged my men and started striking them with her bare hands and feet, the cracking of bones accompanying each blow.

The smallest of them raised her hands and started muttering something. Suddenly, an axe of pure light was in the larger woman's hands. I directed my party to focus on the smallest one. As I did so, I realized the large woman was standing in front me. Then a moment of being blinded by light and the sight of my own back as my head landed behind me.

I placed my head back onto my shoulders. They'd been captured. The goblin was smart. Disabling Kyren meant the axe she'd summoned would fade, and it would distress Stone and

Hrig. It was exactly the strategy I myself would've chosen when I was thinking with my more monstrous instincts.

I could remember the way back to the goblin's camp, but even if I went, rescuing them would be difficult. It was possible that I could simply charge the camp from the front, slaughter the goblins and free everyone, but that might lead to uncomfortable questions about how strong I was and why even the weapons that slid between my armor plates never seemed to hurt me.

No, I'd need to approach this quietly. I needed a plan.

5
CUNNINGLY BRUTAL

By nightfall, the goblin's memories had led me to the outskirts of the camp. A small fence surrounded it, plus several pikes stuck into the ground with the heads of goblins, wild dogs, and a few humans mounted on top of them. I removed my shield and began sticking several sturdy sharpened sticks into the ground in front of me, along with some daggers, spears, and crude clubs I'd looted from the goblin ambushers.

Finally, I removed my left hand and placed it next to my shield. I focused my attention on it for a few moments, and it stood itself up, balancing on fingers like a five-legged spider. I gently lowered one of the small spears into the gauntlet's opening and stored it where it could be easily accessed. I then placed the sharpened stakes and other weapons into the opening where the gauntlet had been. Finally, I strapped the shield to my arm in such a way that my missing hand was hidden.

Dividing my attention between my main body and my hand proved surprisingly easy. Not like I'd separated myself into two; instead, it simply felt like two parts that were both wholly me. I walked on my fingers under the fence and into the camp. Then, I started working my way in a circle, counting goblins as I went. Eventually, I moved more toward the center. The camp was surprisingly orderly. The outside defenses were patrolled by goblins in pairs, the tents and storage located toward the center of the encampment where they also had a small storehouse of weapons and food.

As I made my way deeper into the camp, staying hidden became more difficult. The center was dense with goblins. Some were fighting, others sleeping, but a few that seemed larger and better equipped than the others were standing guard with far more proficiency than I'd expected from their kind.

After dodging around a group that seemed to be doing their best to pull one another's teeth out, I came to the tent in the center. It was large, made up of thick tan canvas, and capable of holding as many as twenty goblins, though I guessed it was meant only for their leader. Its opening was flanked on both sides by guards wearing genuine chainmail of medium quality. Above the tent flew a banner of a golden dragon on a green field.

Something about it drew my attention. It was familiar to me, but a cursory search of my memories brought only an impression of power and fear.

"What's that?" said a high-pitched voice behind me in undercommon, followed by a few other words I didn't recognize.

I must've picked up a bit of vocabulary from the goblin raider whose head I ate. I looked around and saw two goblins approaching, their eyes wide with curiosity and dripping with malice.

I scurried away, careful to avoid drawing any more attention, and headed down an alley between the lordly tent and two smaller ones. The goblins followed me, arguing over whether they were about to enjoy some fresh rat or fresh spider. I drew them farther away from the center of camp, grateful that the other goblins were ignoring them, too wrapped up in their own petty squabbles and selfish ends.

Once I'd gotten them far enough away, I stopped running and stayed still. The closest of the goblins approached carefully and drew a small dagger to prod me with. After a few pokes, he lifted me, eyeing the hole of the gauntlet.

It was at that moment I extended the spear I'd held in my essence and drove it through his eye and out the back of his head. As he fell, I withdrew the spear and, taking advantage of the other goblin's surprise, I ran between his legs and launched the spear again straight into the back of his neck. He fell, struggling to breathe as he drowned in his own blood.

I decided then that I'd need to accelerate my plans. I made my way quickly back through the camp. Just past the central tent, I found what I was looking for. Stone, Hrig, and Kyren were all caged in the center of the goblin's pen for their riding dogs. They were bruised and bloodied, Kyren and Hrig wearing rough-spun tunics that must've been given to them. They were talking, and I slipped between some sleeping dogs to hear them better.

"Lock is picked, but even if we got out of here, we wouldn't be able to make it out of the camp," said Stone.

"I don't see what other choice we have. We don't know why they've taken us captive. For all we know, it's just an easy way to keep meat fresh. Kyren, would you be able to summon us weapons?" asked Hrig.

"No, I'm too foggy after that blow to the head. Casting spells would be dangerous for us."

"What about Sevald? Do you think there's a chance he's coming?" asked Stone.

"I don't know. They may never have noticed him, and he

couldn't find us when he looked, or they did find him, but had to kill him. I doubt he'd have gone down without a fight," said Kyren.

"Aye, he's a good lad like that," said Stone.

"I think he'll come," said Hrig.

"What makes you think that?" asked Kyren.

"Nothing, it's just a feeling. He seems like a reliable guy."

"Aye, he is that," said Stone.

"Hmm, we should probably prepare for when he arrives, then. That may be our only chance."

I felt something swell beneath my breastplate back at my main body. A new feeling. Pride, I realized. I felt proud that my companions considered me reliable, that they counted on me.

After taking another moment to enjoy the new sensation, I returned my attention to the task at hand. With reconnaissance done, I could begin refining my plan.

There were roughly eighty-seven goblins in the camp, which was manageable. My companions could initiate an escape at any time, but they were in danger due to their lack of armament, the damage they'd suffered, and Kyren's inability to cast spells. If I did rush in and kill everything wantonly, it was possible that the goblins would use them as hostages and block off any method of escape they might have. I would also possibly need to explain the fact that I could slaughter four score goblins without taking any damage beyond some dents in my armor.

I would need more than one distraction. I'd need to create a second diversion that would increase the effectiveness of me charging the gate.

I walked on my five fingers back toward the gate to the dog pen, pausing for a moment to use the spear to push open the latch.

The dogs were asleep, but I was intending to make some noise that would wake them up. I made my way back toward the center of the camp while the rest of me started moving closer to the camp's entrance.

It wasn't long before I found what I needed. One of the camp guards was leaning against a small storage shed, his head downward, snoring. He had one hand holding a spear while the other hung loosely against his side.

I crawled up to him and put myself over his hand. I adjusted myself to fit and flexed his fingers a few times, then his arm. I then firmly grasped his spear and started moving him toward the nearest group of goblins.

He stirred as I did so, but before he could fully rouse himself, I'd reached my target. I lifted his hand and had him drive his spear straight through the nearest goblin. The others looked up in surprise, the one whose hand I was controlling wearing the same expression as his fellows.

I didn't give them a chance to react. Instead, I pulled the spear from the other goblin's chest and threw it, striking another of them through the leg. He let out a cry, and its noise roused his fellows to action. They all jumped on the guard, and I swiftly extracted myself from him, taking his hand with me.

As the goblins started fighting the guard, more of them approached from around the camp. I found a straggler, leapt onto his hand while he was distracted, and had him draw his dagger and stab one of those who'd piled onto the guard before he even knew what was happening, then I dissolved his hand and moved on.

I repeated this pattern several more times as more and more goblins went to investigate. Soon, fights were starting that I had nothing to do with as old factions formed and opportunities to draw blood started putting them into a frenzy.

Then, the dogs came. Drawn by the sounds and the smell of

blood, the wild dogs had burst from their pen and headed into the fray.

That was my cue to leave. I started crawling back to my main body, which was at the same time coming into the camp, right through the front gate.

Two guards stood at the front gate, arguing and making gestures toward the commotion in the center of the camp. I assumed they were deciding whether or not to leave their post.

I lifted my gauntletless arm and fired one of the stakes I'd sharpened from my void. It skewered the guard on the left and stuck him to the fencepost behind him. The other one let out a scream, looking frantically around. When he saw me, he took off down the fenceline.

I waited, taking a moment to adjust my shield and sword. I wanted to be found, so there was no point in moving any deeper into the camp. Besides, I wouldn't want to interrupt the goblin civil war I'd so carefully started. If I could get the exterior guards to engage me, then it would create the perfect opportunity for my companions to escape, but to a certain extent, it was all up to fate and fortune.

When the frightened goblin returned, he brought ten others with him. They all charged me on sight, brandishing wickedly curved daggers and spears. I raised my arm and waited for them to close in.

Just as they were about to reach me, I fired another stake. This one pierced two through the chest and a third in the gut. I moved to the side and deflected a dagger off my shield before kicking another of them, launching him backward. I swept my sword, decapitating another. The remaining goblins all attacked at once, swept up in a mixture of fear and bloodlust.

Two spears shattered against me from the front while two goblins jumped onto my back, attempting to slide their daggers into the spaces between my armor plates. I swung my shield into the spear wielders and heard a crunch as they were knocked back. Then I stabbed my sword into the ground to free up my hand to grab one of the goblins off my back by the ear and haul him off, then I threw him to the ground and stepped on him. The other fell off of me, and I retrieved my sword and ran him through before he regained his footing.

I looked at the remaining goblin. It was the same one who'd run for help—he'd hung back once his allies had reached him. He turned to run, but unfortunately, it was he who was surrounded. He ran right into my returning hand which extended its spear into him as he moved toward it, impaling him. I then waited as my hand returned to me, and I had it hold onto the shield. I didn't know if I'd need the opening to fire more stakes, so I wanted to keep it clear for now.

Something was off, though. I looked around and counted nine dead goblins. The one I'd kicked at the start wasn't there. The kick must not have hit him hard enough to kill him. There was something else wrong, too... I didn't hear barking. What I did hear was footsteps, undercommon, and the clinking of armor, all coming toward me.

They came into view all at once. At least forty of them, far more than I'd expected to make it through the internal spat I'd caused. They'd recovered quicker than I expected, too. Creating internal strife and backstabbing had been my profession not too long ago. I knew they shouldn't have rallied so quickly.

The group parted, and a goblin that could only have been the leader approached. He was the largest of their kind I'd ever seen, standing a head taller than even those riding the dogs. He wore chainmail, over which was a tunic of green with a dragon in gold thread sewn onto the front. Even from a distance, I could tell his eyes were gold, and they shone in the dark like those of a cat.

He was holding Hrig's massive axe in front of himself. Something about him filled me with a strange mixture of unease and comfort. The essences I'd eaten were letting out a kind of instinctual fear, but the monstrous part of myself, the part that made up my core, actually felt drawn to him. Drawn to him in the same way monsters are drawn to dungeons and other places that appeal to their kind.

I couldn't run. If I did, they might send out search parties and find my companions, who were hopefully a safe distance away by this point, but the head goblin left me with a sense that a fight would actually be difficult. I could slay hundreds of the run-of-the-mill goblins without too much effort, but this one had a strange presence that I knew I'd need to take seriously.

Before I could think of a plan, the leader raised Hrig's axe and swung it in my direction, signaling a charge. The goblins that flanked him followed the order with enthusiasm and started toward me with those riding wild dogs in the lead.

I unloaded the remaining stakes and small spears into the onrushing forces before returning my hand to its rightful spot and taking a firm grasp on my shield. I braced myself and rooted to the spot I was in.

When the first of the dog riders hit me head on, I took his attack on my shield and threw him over myself using his momentum. Then I sliced through the side of one of the other dogs, which caused him to tumble across the camp in a flail of limbs. Once they were taken care of, the rest of them descended upon me.

Everything became a blur of teeth, daggers, and blood. Weapons broke against me as I cut them down one after another.

Just as I started to see holes in their attack, something struck me with a force beyond anything I'd experienced before. I was knocked back and rolled through the camp, collapsing two tents as I went. My breastplate dented, and I took a moment to reform it, but it took far more effort than it should have. The strike had hurt me, I realized. It had damaged not just my armor skin, but the essence of what I am.

The golden-eyed goblin could actually kill me.

I rose to my feet and raised my shield, quickly surrounded again. Even if they couldn't hurt me, they provided a tremendous distraction that would make another hit from their leader inevitable. Fate and fortune were no longer on my side, it seemed.

Just as I tensed, ready for another onslaught, one of the goblins surrounding me collapsed. The others stopped, confused, and looked at their fallen comrade. A small rock was lodged in the back of his skull.

Just as I'd realized what had happened, another dropped, his fall accompanied by two battle cries as Hrig and Stone crashed into them.

Stone swiftly smashed two down with his hammer, and Hrig leapt into the center of the fray wielding a massive claymore, her every swipe felling three goblins at a time.

"You focus on the big one, we've got your back," said Kyren.

I looked in the direction of her voice and saw a rock release from her sling, felling yet another of them.

Almost too late, I returned my attention to the goblin leader, ducking just as Hrig's axe swept where my head had been. I slammed my shield into his chest to buy space and followed it with a quick downward strike of my sword, which he blocked with the axe's handle. He pushed my sword away and followed it up with a kick to my knee. I buckled, but used the momentum to roll to the side as he drove the axe into the mud where I'd just been. His kick had hurt me, too, so there wasn't anything special about Hrig's axe—whatever was hurting me had to do with him.

I got to my feet and deflected an axe blow with my shield, risking a look at my companions. They were still actively thinning the goblins, though some of them had rallied from their initial surprise.

I needed to go on the offensive.

I began striking down at the goblin, quickly and without letting up. He blocked my strikes with the handle again, his body shuddering from the impacts. His feet sank deep into the mud as I swung down at him again and again.

He was strong, clever, and capable of harming me, but he was also alive in a way that I wasn't. I could keep striking forever without tiring, but he couldn't, and I began to feel his arms give way from my strikes.

Finally, dropping my shield, I took my blade in both hands and gave a downward strike. He attempted a block, but my sword cut straight through the axe's handle and my blade sliced cleanly through his head and body before it caught too much bone to continue.

His gold eyes looked up at me again from each part of his halved head, and for a moment, I had an overwhelming desire to eat him. I wanted to know why he could hurt me, how he had the same pull as a dungeon, and what lay behind those eyes of his...but even as I felt my faceplate open and the void within my shell start to reach out for him, I heard a cry.

I closed my faceplate and looked in the direction of the cry to see Kyren being attacked by two goblins. I pulled my sword from the leader and threw it at the one closest to her. It flew through his chest, and the other goblin, distracted by what had happened, was readily brained by Kyren using her rock-filled sling as a flail.

I returned my attention to the leader, whose eyes were still somehow alive even as the rest of him remained immobile.

"Interesting," said a voice that felt impossibly large and strong considering the creature it came from. The halves of his mouth curled up in a hideous smile despite his body being nearly cleaved in twain, then he burst into flames, the heat and force of which caused me to step back.

Before I knew it, the body had disintegrated.

6

ONWARD TO CIRROS

It took almost until morning to get back onto the main roads. A night of sifting through the goblins' camp had produced a small cart full of loot and a heavy sack of goblin ears to prove our victory. Hrig was pulling the cart behind her, insisting she be the one to do it, I assume because they all believed I was exhausted from my duel. Everyone wore tired expressions as we moved, though Kyren looked to be deep in thought.

"Draconic," she said, unprompted.

"What?" asked Hrig.

"The last word their leader spoke. You told me it sounded like 'ker'al'fus', right?"

"That was the gist, yeah. Though Sevald was obviously closer." She gestured at me.

"I was…not really paying attention, to be honest. I was distracted at the time."

I'd heard him perfectly, but draconic was a dead language, and the fact I'd understood it so clearly would create questions. Questions I myself didn't have an answer to. None of those I'd consumed had ever even heard the language, so the fact that I could understand it proved troubling.

"Well, I've heard it once or twice. It's used in some of the rituals to honor the gods, but only rarely, and only those higher up in some of the more formal gods' clergy tend to use it. The way it sounds, though, it's very distinct. I'm certain that's the language he used."

"Aye, I've heard a Kobold or two speak their version of it. It's as different from draconic as common is from undercommon, but that word does sound a bit like it. How would a goblin have picked up draconic, though?" asked Stone.

"I'm not sure, but I also don't know how a goblin camp could be that orderly, or how a goblin could farm, or how a goblin could be as large as their leader was. The whole thing was strange."

"'Was' is the key word. They're all dead or routed. It's no longer a problem," said Hrig.

Kyren sighed. "You're probably right, but I think I'll keep fussing over it anyway."

Hrig chuckled. "I'd be worried about the damage that blow to your head did if you didn't."

Kyren smiled, and we continued down the path in silence for a while. My companions were exhausted, and I was doing my best to look like I was, too. I'd even let them pull me in the cart for the first leg of the journey, which they'd insisted was reasonable after watching me attempt to fight all of those goblins myself. Luckily, they'd only seen the parts of the fight that were possible for a human to survive, rather than the portions in which I'd been firing stakes from my arm, kicking goblins across half the camp, and having my hand perform reconnaissance.

Like Kyren, I had a lot of questions about our experience, how the golden-eyed leader could hurt me foremost. I'd always assumed a particularly powerful blow could damage me, but even his lighter strikes had seemed to cut at my essence.

"You owe me a new axe, Sevald," said Hrig, breaking my reverie.

"I do?" I replied.

"You broke the shaft in two. I'd say that warrants buying me a replacement."

"Come on, Hrig, that doesn't seem fair. The boy was fighting for his life," said Stone.

"Are you saying that if he'd broken your hammer, you wouldn't want him to pay for the damages?" asked Hrig.

"That's completely different! You can't compare the elegance of my Lagaetha to that ugly thing!"

"You really think your glorified carpenter's tool is elegant?" Hrig's tone was dryer than the dust we kicked up while we walked.

"Why don't you chop down a tree! That's all a primitive weapon like an axe is good for!"

Their argument, despite how heated it seemed, made me feel like a teapot that just let out all of its steam. Relief, I surmised. We'd had a tough fight, but we were alive and already settling into the easy rhythms I was finding myself growing accustomed to.

After making camp, the others insisted I not take watch for the night. They seemed adamant, so I didn't put up a fight. Since I didn't sleep, I needed to find something to do. Initially, listening to the sounds of the camp at night—bugs skittering, owls hunting, and wind blowing softly through leaves—had been enough to keep me occupied, but I was finding that I needed more stimulation in order to keep myself from getting bored. Instead of observing things happening outside myself, I decided to look within.

The essences I'd eaten were a part of me, their skills, voices, and memories integrated into me the moment I'd consumed them. Some parts of them were easier to access than others. Skills, in particular, became as much mine as they'd been theirs almost instantly. That made sense, based on what my purpose had been. Actual memories and thoughts, however, were another story. They often felt murky and disjointed. I was missing important context for them that only the people who'd made them would have. Only those that were Byn's felt truly clear and accessible. Being jolted to the forefront by my time in Entden must have made them more my own.

Sevald's also felt sharper, though still muddled. He'd been my most recent meal, so it made sense that his would be more readily available. He was a third son of five with a relatively good life who had left home to be an adventurer and spread his name in the hopes that it would increase his inheritance. He was, in a lot of ways, simple and thus easy to understand. Byn was similarly simple, just a tanner's son that wanted to do his part for the village.

The other two were a bit more complex, and I had nothing to anchor myself to when searching their memories. Pebble Under Sand was an older dwarf. His mind was made up of a complex mixture of dwarven and common words arrayed into neat rows, like those of a library. He'd adventured not for his own sake, but for knowledge, both his and what he might be able to teach others. He wielded a crossbow, but his real contribution to his former party had been his insight. Searching his memories felt like wading through his namesake. There was a university, classrooms, the sweet smell of rotting books, and professors whose focus on theory frustrated him, but beyond that, I couldn't produce much in the way of the specifics of his life.

The third of my meals had been Syven, a younger elf. She'd become an adventurer for money more than anything else, but the money had been just a means to an end. She'd wanted to open a restaurant. Those memories of hers that I could access were mostly smells: butter melting in a pan, rich seasoning burning the nostrils, and fresh bread spreading its hearty aroma. If I had a mouth, those memories would have set it watering. She had trained as a monk, her arms already strong from kneading dough and doing all the heavy lifting in a kitchen. For her, my disconnect was more obvious. She was not only rooted in experiences I had no connection to, but she was also very different from the other essences I'd consumed.

I spent the rest of the night trying to delve deeper into those murkier memories and experiences despite how difficult it proved. I was new to feelings and to self-determination, but their lives made for an excellent way to catch up. As I sifted through flashes of memories and experiences, I wondered if what I was doing was at all similar to dreaming.

At dawn, we broke camp and started making our way to Cirros. The closer we got, the more travelers we encountered. Merchants hauling carts full of goods, carriages bringing in local lords, and even the odd adventuring party like my own.

As the sun rose, the city came more and more into view. It was walled in every direction except the riverside, and the stone spires that made up lordly estates, along with the municipal buildings, could be seen clearly, even at a distance.

Cirros was built on the bank of the Cirros River, for which it was named. That river made its way much farther inland and branched off in dozens of other directions with the main body of it being fed by the drainage from snow-capped mountains. Most trade came from the smaller towns and villages and flowed to Cirros, where it was sent by sea to areas that could convert their raw products into manufactured goods. Trade also flowed against the river's currents by chainboat. Over the walls hung a flag of blue and white with a red carp in the center.

Technically, Cirros wasn't the capital, but unofficially, it absolutely was. So much trade went through the town and so many coffers were filled by it, the Dukes of Cirros tended to have a large amount of autonomy and control over their own affairs. As long as the gold and silver flowed, the crown didn't care.

All of this was common knowledge to the essences I'd eaten. They'd all, except Byn, had to travel through Cirros at some point, though Pebble had actually made a point to visit the city's library and found it much wanting compared to those of his university. It did have quite a few volumes on Cirros' history, which he'd made a point to at least skim.

We crossed over the bridge leading into the city, passing through gates manned by disinterested guards and their hounds. Main Street was bustling with activity, and we slowly pushed our way through crowds until we found a small alley in which to regroup. As we settled in and took stock, Kyren looked at Stone and held out her hand, making a small cough in his direction as she did so. Stone sighed and began pulling trinkets, jewelry, and coin pouches from various pockets and handing her every third item. I looked to Hrig for an explanation.

"He was picking pockets on the way in."

That didn't surprise me, but what did was that I hadn't noticed.

"How did Kyren know?" I asked.

"No idea, but she catches him every time and makes him give her some."

"It's my tithe, Hrig. I'm hoping that by donating some of his ill-gotten gains, I might help him keep in the good graces of the gods," said Kyren.

"I need only stay in Jeiri's, and I know for a fact he approves of light theft, blackmail, and even the occasional arson as long as I have fun with it," said Stone.

"No god judges souls entirely alone, not even Jeiri. Consider this a bribe to the other gods if that makes you feel better about it," said Kyren.

Stone looked thoughtful for a moment, and a grin spread across his face. "That's a good way to think of it. You've got a real talent for doctrine."

Kyren gave one of her small smiles. "It's a gift." She turned her attention to me. "Would you like to accompany me to the temple? They have altars to both Dur and Sidi there."

"Sure, I suppose it would only make sense for me to pay respects," I said.

A temple could be interesting. Those I'd eaten had an overall mixed impression of religion. Sevald had feelings somewhere between shame and reverence, Pebble was against it entirely, Byn just worshipped the same way his parents did, and Syven couldn't care less as long as the gods stayed out of her way. My own feelings were a mix of curiosity and fear. I couldn't imagine that the gods had much in the way of favor for one such as myself.

"We'll go ahead and sell the loot from the goblin camp then set up a meeting with Clara at Carp's Flagon by the docks. We'll meet you there at sundown," said Stone.

"I'll keep an eye on his sales and make sure we get our cut, don't worry," said Hrig.

"Ah!" I pulled a small pouch of gold from my pouch and handed it to her. "For your axe shaft."

"Oh, you don't actually have to pay for it, Sevald. I know you were only doing what you needed to," said Hrig.

"Well, consider it a gift, then." I didn't really have as much of a need for gold as my companions, so it made sense to simply give them some when I could.

She took the gold and tied it to her belt. "Well, fine then, but I'll be buying your drinks later at the Flagon."

"Deal," I said, and she and Stone made their way toward the market with their cart full of goblin ears and loot.

7
DEBTS

The temple was near the center of the city, just off the main street, a building of myriad colors and architectural styles meant to reference all of the different gods and goddesses. There were domes of blue, columns of deep burgundy, and rich green walls interspersed with murals of the gods and their servants performing heroic acts. The entire building was surrounded by a garden of old growth trees that looked to be older than the city itself. It was toward those trees that Kyren walked.

"I had assumed you'd want to worship at Sidi's shrine inside?" I asked her.

"Sidi's shrine is the trees, Sevald. She's the goddess of what is ancient and wise. They represent both of those aspects of her, so they act as her shrine here."

"Ah," I said, escorting her to the edge of the treeline. A small group of older women tended to the trees with occasional bows of their heads. A few sat in a circle holding hands and humming softly.

"Is it normal for the priests of Sidi to be so...aged?" I whispered.

Kyren laughed. "It is. Most of her worshippers are converts from other patrons or those who found faith later in life. I'm the youngest of her worshippers that I've ever met."

We walked a short way farther into the garden before an old woman, senior even to the others in the shrine, gestured at Kyren.

"Ah, that's Mother Suthben. She doesn't like to talk to people who aren't within the faith. How about you go on to the shrine of Dur and we'll meet back up at the tavern."

"Works for me. Have a nice visit."

She smiled. "Thank you, Sevald. You, too."

I made my way into the temple proper. I passed Jeiri worshippers in the corner playing dice, a young man laying out flowers for Nevier, the god of love, and two young women making offerings of blood at the altar of Krish, the war goddess. Eventually, I came upon the most orderly shrine, that of Dur.

It took up an entire corner of the temple. Colored light from a stained-glass image of a scale fell over orderly rows of pews in which sat merchants, businessmen, and those who worked in law. They spoke, made deals, and settled differences in this holy place meant to represent fairness and justice. Dur's worshippers tended to believe themselves people of good judgment and reason. This, of course, was often not the case at all. Based on the memories I had of religion, people typically chose their gods based on what they wanted to be or appear as rather than what they actually were.

I approached the altar at the end of the shrine. It was manned by a single mediator, as the priests of Dur called themselves. I approached it as Sevald would have and kneeled, placing a single hand on the symbol of a scale carved into it. I then waited what seemed the appropriate amount of time to offer a silent prayer before standing.

"Would you care for a blessing?" asked the mediator.

"Yes, thank you," I said, defaulting with the choice that seemed the most normal to make.

The mediator held out a hand. I regarded it for a moment before he coughed. I handed him a gold piece, and it quickly vanished into his robes. He then closed his eyes and placed a single hand on my right pauldron. He began muttering under his breath, and his hand glowed.

It...burned. I had to restrain myself from squirming or striking the mediator out of reflex. After a few moments, he removed his hand, leaving me feeling singed where it had been.

"There you go. May you walk tall in the light of Lord Dur... Tips are not necessary, though they are appreciated."

I regarded him with a passive look from my faceplate, wishing I was capable of scowling. Then I brushed past him and headed back toward the shrine of Sidi to check in with Kyren.

Holy energies harmed me. I'd always assumed they were dangerous; it was the only type my master had avoided, after all, but I'd never experienced them myself. It felt similar to the damage I'd sustained fighting the goblin leader. The pain was the same, but it had a different flavor to it.

I entered Sidi's garden but could see no sign of Kyren. One of the shrine attendants approached me.

"Are you Sevald?" she asked. I nodded. "Kyren is engaging in a purification ritual. She received some unpleasant news and is seeking to remove the miasma it brought her."

"What happened?"

"It's not my place to say. She told me to tell you she would meet you at the Flagon."

"Well, thank you."

I left the garden and started making my way through the streets in what I believed was the direction of the harbor. After some time passed without recognizing a single landmark, I realized I was lost. My only experience navigating had been the confines of a dungeon and a village that my first meal had been raised in his entire life. I had absolutely no idea of how to navigate in a city.

I picked a direction, deciding that if I just walked straight long enough, I'd eventually find the outer wall and could follow it to the docks.

After a fourth turn down an alley, I sensed something. Farther along, behind two barrels, were two men lying in wait, clubs ready in their hands to brain an unwary passerby. I could easily dispatch them, but I had a better solution.

"I think we're lost, Byn." I used Sevald's voice.

"No, we're not. We just have to go down a little ways farther," I answered in Byn's voice.

"Will we even get there in time?" Syven's this time.

"We will. They'll wait on our bounty. We slew three trolls for them, after all. It should be obvious that missing our meeting would be hazardous to their health." Pebble's now.

"That's true. I still can't believe you managed to cleave the big one's head off in one strike, Syven." Sevald's.

"Ah, it's a gift. Besides, the way you fired that arrow through the second one's head...now that was truly masterful." Syven's.

"Ah, thank you. Let's be honest, though. Byn and Pebble ripping off the last one's arm and beating him to death with it, now that was truly impressive." Sevald's again.

With that last colorful statement, I sensed the muggers making a hasty but quiet retreat. That would save me a scuffle and possibly save them their lives.

It was night by the time I reached the docks. They were crawling with sailors looking to spend their pay on food, ale, and company. Quite a boisterous crowd, but they gave me a wide berth as I worked my way through them.

The Carp's Flagon was in a seedy area of an already seedy part of the city. Wharf rats scurried about, and old beggars slept dangerously close to the water. The Flagon itself was lit, and sounds of revelry could be heard even at a distance. The tavern's sign was of a bright red fish whose head was completely inside a silver flagon. It wasn't as clever as the sign for The Thirsty Tree, but with the crowd it attracted, simplicity was likely key. I imagined Kyren and Stone were already well into their cups and Hrig might be, as well, though I doubted they had a serviceable wine.

I entered the tavern and took a moment to adjust to the sights and sounds of it. There were men playing cards in one corner, some singing a particularly bawdy song about a mermaid with a fish head and a woman's legs at the bar, and a boisterous crowd at a center table that seemed incapable of speaking at a volume lower than that of a screaming seabird. What wasn't there were my companions. I approached the bar.

"What'll you have?" asked the bartender, a greasy-looking man with narrow features.

"Well, actually, I was looking for my frien—"

"I only help paying customers."

"I'll have an ale, then."

"One gold, please."

"A gold? You charge a gold piece for a mug of ale here?"

"Only for people who have questions."

I mimicked a sigh and handed him a piece. I shouldn't have questioned it to begin with; it was not like I needed money. Stone must've been rubbing off on me. The bartender filled a mug with ale and handed it to me. It tasted watered down, but I feigned a hefty sip to help get his guard down. Kyren had told me once that bartenders didn't trust people that don't drink.

"Yer friends, what do they look like?"

"One is small and wears simple white clothes, with a plain face and dark hair. Her ears are slightly pointed. The other woman is larger than most men, muscular, with blond braids and a nose that's been broken at least once. The last is a dwarf with a mix of grey and white hair. He would have made a point to argue what you charge for drinks here."

"Ah, I remember them. You'll want to speak with that gentleman over there." He pointed at a man sitting at the corner of the bar.

"Can't you just tell me where they went?"

The bartender shook his head and pointed again at the man at the corner.

I approached him and sat in a stool to his right. He turned around and regarded me with a warm smile. He was tall, a head taller than Hrig at least, and lean. He had rust-colored hair and wore a scarlet tunic with black pants and boots. His hair was tied back in a queue, and he wore spectacles with darkened lenses.

"Hello, Sevald. How are you?" His voice was deep but had a kind of raspy quality to it.

"I'm fine, ser. I'm afraid you have me at a disadvantage?" I held out my hand for him to shake. He ignored it.

"Well, that's excellent. I prefer to meet people that way." The corner of his mouth twisted upward. "My name is Talen. I'm a friend of Stone."

"Ah, well, it's nice to meet you." I retrieved my hand. "How do you know Stone?"

"We used to work together. I got him out of some trouble awhile back."

"Do you know where he is?"

"I do, but it may be easier to discuss if it was somewhat quieter."

"Should we go outside?"

"That won't be necessary."

Talen snapped his fingers. The noise in the room immediately stopped. The singing ceased, the card players dropped their hands, and the boisterous group in the center went silent. The entire tavern then quietly left the room. The bartender placed a bottle of gin on the table along with an empty glass in front of Talen. Talen grabbed his hand and muttered something I couldn't quite make out, but the words "playing games within mine" and "your family" had enough emphasis on them that I got the idea. The color drained from the bartender, and before he left, he slid my gold piece back to me with a trembling hand. Talen's genial expression never shifted during the exchange.

"That's better, isn't it?"

Even with my limited understanding, I could tell that the tone of the meeting had shifted considerably.

"My friends, where are they?"

"They're my guests, and it's my preference that you join them."

"Have you taken them prisoner?"

"In a metaphorical sense, yes."

"And in a literal sense?"

"Also yes."

"What do you want?"

His smile widened at the question. "Money, power, and loyalty. Just those three things."

"I mean, what do you want with my friends?" My tone slipped into something more aggressive. I could tell this was a man who enjoyed his own cleverness, but I didn't have the patience to indulge him.

"I want to use them to make a bit more money and accrue a bit more power. I want to use you, too. That's why I decided to meet with you personally. Though initially, you were meant to be brought to me by a couple of my men. They seemed to have lost their nerve, though."

"Go on," I said, wishing he would get to his point. Talen's manner of speaking reminded me an unfortunate amount of my master.

"Stone owes me for the jam I got him out of a few years ago. He owes me his life, in fact. This is his opportunity to repay that debt."

"Why not simply ask him? Why all this skullduggery?"

"Because this is how I prefer to do business, and I wanted to make sure he understood the stakes. I wanted to make sure all of you did."

"How is he going to repay you?"

"By convincing you and your friend Hrig to fight in a little illicit tournament I'm putting together. While you and she do that, he and your other companion will be helping me to put an end to my last competitor here in Cirros."

I didn't hesitate to answer. "I'll do it. I'm sure my companions have already agreed, as well. I also assume that if any of us refuse, you'll likely have us killed."

I could likely fight my way out of the city alone, but I had no idea where my companions were and whether or not they had knives at their throats.

"Oh, yes, it would be quite likely, I think."

"I have a final question, though."

"Go ahead."

"Why meet with me alone? Couldn't you have just met me with the rest of my companions?"

"I suppose I could have, but I wanted to meet you after I had my people dig into Stone's little party's background. You seemed... interesting." He gave another wide smile. A chill ran through my essence as he did. "Anyway, let's return you to your friends, shall we?"

He poured himself some gin and gestured with the glass toward the door.

Outside the Flagon was a simple black carriage. I climbed in, and Talen waved it on. Before I lost sight of him, I watched another man emerge from a nearby alley to stand at his side. He was gigantic, taller than Talen and even more heavily muscled than Hrig. He wore a black cloth over his eyes and simple dark gray clothes otherwise.

I lost sight of them when the carriage rounded a corner. I settled in, grateful that at least this time, my companions and I would be prisoners together.

8
DUCHESS OF DEATH

The carriage arrived at a large warehouse building not too far from the Carp's Flagon. I hopped out and was escorted inside by the driver. The entrance looked nondescript, with no indication it served any particular purpose, but I could tell that the various beggars, men playing dice, and sleeping drunks surrounding the warehouse were armed.

The inside was enormous. After passing through a short hallway, it opened up into an high-ceilinged arena with enough seating for hundreds, all arrayed around a large pit of sand. The sand had a sickly red color to it in some spots, and there was evidence of teeth making it into the seats near where I stood.

I was passed off to a guard who led me deeper into the warehouse where I lost sight of the arena. After a few turns, I was led into a well-appointed room with tables, chairs, couches, fine carpets on the floor, and curtains to give the appearance of windows where none existed.

Kyren, Stone, and Hrig were waiting for me. Stone leapt up, causing the guard who'd escorted me to reach for his weapon, and embraced me. The guard loosened his grip on his weapon.

"I'm glad you're okay, lad," he said.

I felt a by-now-familiar feeling of warmth and returned the hug briefly before separating with the traditional two back pats. "Is everyone okay?"

"We're fine. They haven't tried to hurt us, since we didn't resist," said Kyren.

"It was damned tempting, though," said Hrig.

Stone's expression was pained. "I appreciate yer restraint. I'm truly sorry about this." He turned to me. "Did they tell you everything?"

"Talen did. He said you owed him a debt, and he'd consider it paid if Hrig and I fought in his underground arena and you and Kyren eliminated some of his competition."

"I owe you an explanation," he said.

"Not really. It's fine."

He looked surprised. "Really?"

"You don't owe me anything. I could tell from talking to Talen that his holding this debt over your head was just the most convenient option. Even without it, he'd still pressure you into doing what he wants. He's just that type of man."

He grimaced. "He wasn't always like this. Always a criminal, mind you, but he was never this ruthless before. Hell, he was just middle management when we passed through Cirros last time. He's completely changed. He's destroyed or taken over every other criminal enterprise in the city, bought off lawmen and nobles, and he's even been expanding downriver. Frankly, he didn't used to be smart enough for this. I don't know how he's managed it."

"People change. Not always for the better," said Kyren with a hint of bitterness in her voice.

"Aye, that's true. The gist of it is that he helped me out of an obligation to some very bad people. At the time, I thought it was just him being kind, but now, I wonder if he'd always planned on calling in his chit."

"I understand him wanting to use you to take care of some of his competition, but why does he need Hrig and me in his arena?" I asked.

"Well, as a distraction, lad. Half the city will show up to see the Duchess of Death back in the arena."

"Stone!" yelled Hrig.

"He's going to figure it out when you're in the arena together anyway."

"Duchess of Death?" I asked.

"That was her nickname back when she was a gladiator at the coliseum of Buryn," said Kyren. "She was quite the star. My brothers even went to see her fight once."

"I had no idea," I said.

"That's because I don't like to talk about it, but since a certain dwarf owes a criminal a favor, I guess I'll have to get used to it."

"Yer the best, Hrig."

She snorted and turned her head.

"Okay, so we'll be distracting the criminal element while you and Kyren do what?" I asked.

"We're waiting on some maps and a bit of information, but the gist of it is that I'll be swapping some cooked books and placing some inflammatory evidence so that the last remnants of resistance against Talen eats itself alive."

"Sounds simple enough."

"It's not. The entire plan is very convoluted. That's why Talen needs me to do it."

"You sound proud," said Kyren.

"I am, but only because I earned that reputation."

I turned to Kyren. "And how are you going to help him? This isn't exactly something I'd expect of a priestess."

She smiled. "That's why I'm going to make a great lookout. Also, I can put people to sleep, which Stone has found very convenient in the past."

Stone sat on a couch and took a deep breath. "Thank you all for your help."

I looked over at Hrig and at Kyren. "Don't think that just because we could all die, I'm not waiting on my cut for routing the goblin camp."

"Yeah, I know you did some additional haggling while I was getting my axe repaired. Don't think I'm not expecting my share," said Hrig.

"I will also be expecting my usual tithe for any theft you committed along the way," said Kyren.

Stone looked up and smiled. "Well, assuming we survive, I promise each of you gets your cut...minus perhaps a modest fee."

A couple days later, Hrig and I were standing in the center of the arena surrounded on all sides by a menagerie of warriors, mages, and brutes of all kinds. I counted twenty-six. The crowd was equally diverse—sailors, tradesmen, and nobility all mingled in the stands, hungry for blood and spectacle.

I'd asked Stone how Talen had managed to keep an arena like this secret from the law, and he'd told me that he simply didn't keep it secret. Instead, he gave those in power the best seats, comfortable bribes, and the occasional threat when necessary. The arena had been a part of Talen's responsibilities even before he'd had his meteoric rise.

Talen himself stood on a dais overlooking the pit. He wore a slightly more elegant red tunic, this one with touches of gold thread noticeable even at a distance. He stood, holding up a hand, and the arena quieted. That seemed to be one of his favorite tricks.

"Welcome, my loyal patrons, to another night of bloodsport!" He held for applause and was rewarded enthusiastically. "Tonight, we have a special treat for you all. The legendary Duchess of Death, Champion of the Coliseum of Buryn, is making her Cirros debut!"

The crowd exploded.

Hrig, rather than looking uncomfortable as I'd expected her to, was positively glowing with enthusiasm. She offered up a vicious smile to the crowd, slammed her axe into the ground, and waved, encouraging their applause.

I'd always thought of her as a barbarian. She went into rages, could live off the land, and was as strong as any human I'd encountered. But watching her embrace the crowd, I could tell she was actually a gladiator. She'd been made for the ring.

Talen held up his hand for quiet again, but Hrig encouraged one more round of applause with some flexing. I hoped that bothered him. Talen was perhaps the only human since my master that I truly disliked. He eventually got the crowd to quiet down, though it certainly took him more effort than he liked.

"Now, some of you may be wondering how we'll be organizing the brackets for this tournament. It's going to be very simple. Those in the pit have one minute; after that, it's a mêlée, and the last seven standing will then be paired off to fight one on one." He gestured to the assembled fighters. "Why seven, you ask? Well, because the reigning champion, our very own Donyin, will also be competing!"

The crowd applauded and whooped as the man I'd seen emerge from the shadows at the Carp's Flagon repeated his trick, appearing at Talen's right.

"Now, I think we can all agree he's already earned a spot,

hasn't he?" He took the crowd's enthusiasm for a yes and produced a small hourglass, showing it to the crowd. "One minute, starting... now!" He flipped the hourglass.

The fighters all scattered, taking positions at the edges of the arena and doing their best to position themselves in such a way that they could anticipate incoming attacks. Hrig held out an open hand to me.

"May I have this dance?" she asked.

I wished very much that I could have smiled at that moment.

"Of course." I took her hand, and she led me not to the edge of the arena, but instead to its center. She stretched her arms and legs, and I took position to watch her back. If Talen wanted us to give him a spectacle, we intended to do our damndest to provide one.

The hourglass emptied, and a whistle-blow signaled for the mêlée to begin. A man wielding two swords and leather armor charged me first and swung both of his blades down at my helmet. I raised my shield up, not to block, but to strike at his hands before his blades could build any momentum. I then slammed the hilt of my sword into his exposed stomach. His eyes widened, and he vomited before doubling over and passing out in his own sick.

He was followed by two men, one wielding a club and another a spear. They charged me at the same time, and I dropped my sword to catch the spear by the shaft. I raised my shield to block the club, but the man wielding it moved past me in an attempt to hit Hrig.

I jerked backward, dragging the spearman through the sand, and kicked at the brute with the club's knee. I struck true, and his knee made a sickening popping sound as it bent in the wrong direction. I then dropped my shield, grabbed the spear shaft with both hands, and yanked it toward myself before slamming it back in its wielder's direction, hitting him in the sternum. All the air left his lungs, and he released the spear, dropping to his knees. I then smacked the side of his head with the butt of the spear, and he fell into the sand.

I risked a look in Hrig's direction. She was standing on one squirming man while braining another with the shaft of her axe. Cleary, she didn't need my help. I returned my attention to what was in front of me.

A man was approaching wielding a zwei-hander. I raised my newly acquired spear and gave it a series of twirls before locking it behind my back and raising my other hand to gesture for him to attack. I had no real skills with a spear, but any weapon I touched became a part of me, and that alone gave me some advantages.

The man didn't charge, but instead slowly closed the distance between us. He swung a few exploratory strikes to determine my range, which I sidestepped. He then began to strike in earnest. He swung in such a way that he never lost momentum with his blade; it just continuously moved to strike in dazzling loops. I focused on dodging or deflecting the sword with my spear, careful not to attempt blocking a full-strength blow with it.

I could tell the man was a master duelist, but unfortunately, that didn't count for much in a mêlée. While he was focused on me, a woman in chainmail wielding a buckler and a rapier approached him quietly from behind and ran him through. His eyes widened in surprise for a moment before he hit the ground. The woman bent down, used the man's tunic to clean her blade, offered me a quick smile and wink, then went toward another group locked in a struggle, likely to repeat her winning tactic.

With no one left in front of me, I turned my attention back to Hrig. She was locked in combat with a short man wielding curved daggers. There were several small cuts on her arms and legs, but nothing deep enough to leave a scar. She made a series of axe sweeps that the man dodged under and over before leaving another pair of small cuts on her thigh. She shook her head and dropped the axe. "Damn thing's too slow."

Emboldened by her lack of a weapon, the man charged, attempting to run her through with his knives. Unfortunately for him, her arms were longer than his, even with his daggers, and so she was able to deck him with a straight jab to his face before his blades got close. The man crumpled, clearly better suited to dealing damage than taking it.

I took a quick count. There were eight gladiators left in the arena. Three were locked in combat at the edge, two dueling closer to the center but too focused on one another to involve Hrig or me. The last one was hiding behind a wooden pillar toward the far edge. I lifted my looted spear and threw it with all my strength at the pillar, rewarded with a howl of pain as it embedded itself halfway through the wood and through the man's shoulder.

A whistle rang from the dais.

"Stop!"

Talen's voice cut through the roar of the crowd. Gradually, the remaining combatants stopped their fighting and started shuffling back to the center of the arena. The seven remaining gladiators included me, Hrig, the woman with the rapier, a dwarf wearing full plate, an elf wearing thick steel gauntlets, a man holding two morning stars, and a dwarven woman covered in runic tattoos and wearing clawed gloves.

"Take a good look at our participants, everyone." Talen gestured at us dramatically. "We'll be taking a half hour recess followed by individual fights. Please take this time to place your bets, enjoy our concessions, or perhaps spend some time working off your excitement with one of our many fine escorts."

With that, we were dismissed. Hrig and I gathered our weapons and shuffled out of the pit, making our way back to our preparation room.

9
ROUND ONE

Hrig grabbed a water pitcher and sat down on a bench in the center of the room, drinking from it directly. She was glistening with sweat and panting heavily, but her eyes had that same fire in them they always did when she'd just been in a fight.

"You alright?" she asked, wiping water from her mouth with the back of her hand.

"Fine, just a bit worried about Kyren and Stone." I'd considered following them with one of my gauntlets, but the fact that people in the stands would be able to watch me at all angles meant that my missing hand would've definitely been noticed.

"Me, too." She sighed. "Stone and Kyren are better at that kind of stuff than we are, though. We'll just have to trust them."

I nodded and took a seat next to her on the couch. "How're you? Some of those cuts look pretty deep."

She looked at her arms and legs. Most of the cuts she'd received from the short gladiator were superficial, but some were bleeding.

"I'll be fine. I didn't even notice them, to be honest." She smiled. "I forgot how much I missed the ring. It's easy to lose yourself to it."

I got up and grabbed a small bottle of some type of alcohol someone had left and a scrap of cloth from the table.

"Good idea. I could use a drink."

"It's not to drink, Hrig." I kneeled in front of her, dabbing the cloth in the alcohol, then started moving my hand toward one of the cuts on her leg.

"You don't have to do that."

"I know you don't need me to do it, but humor me."

Sevald had some experience with tending wounds he'd learned from when he was a squire. I started to clean her cuts, carefully moving up her legs to her arms. When I reached her face, I realized she was blushing. It looked pleasant on her, and with that thought, I felt suddenly and uncomfortably warm. She swallowed hard and took the alcohol bottle from my hand. She had a swig of it and I saw that as my cue to give her space.

"Thank you," she said, her eyes focusing on the corner of the room. This was not the brash Hrig I was used to, but it had been a stressful few days.

"So... Why'd you leave the Buryn?" I asked her. "You seemed to really enjoy the arena back there."

She took another swig from the bottle. "I didn't leave Buryn because of the coliseum, I left because it carried too many bad memories for me."

"Is it...something you want to talk about?"

She looked at me and gave me a small smile. "Yes, but not today."

There were two knocks on the door, followed by a man letting himself in. "Break's over, brackets are up."

I was grateful for the break in tension. I hadn't been alone in a room with Hrig, and between the heat of battle and the intimacy of our conversation, I was wrestling with more new feelings at once than I'd had when I first slayed my master.

"Shall we?" I held out my hand to Hrig, who took it and hauled herself off the bench.

"Let's do it."

We returned to our little section on the edge of the sandpit and looked up at the bracket. It wasn't very helpful, as I only knew my name, Hrig's, and Donyin's. Hrig and Donyin were on the opposite side of the bracket as me, but wouldn't fight unless they both made it to the second round. I would be fighting someone named Dorsia in the first fight of the first round.

"I wonder if we'll wind up having to fight in the last round?" I asked.

"Well, that would certainly be interesting." She grinned. "Unfortunate for you, though."

"Yes, I'm sure I'd be no match for the 'Duchess of Death'."

Talen took his place at the dais and motioned for silence. The crowd in the stands shuffled to their seats and turned their attention to the pit.

"For the first fight, we have Sevald, the armored man with the golden throwing arm, versus Dorsia, the backstabbing beauty. Gladiators, enter the ring!"

I walked into the pit. Opposite me was the woman who had stabbed my zwei-hander-using opponent in the melee. She was still wielding her buckler and rapier and wearing a sly smile. A long and lean woman, she wore her short black hair in a topknot and moved with an easy grace that reminded me of a cat Pebble had when he was a child. Her movements were so smooth, it wouldn't surprise me to see her walk on water.

Once we were in position, I drew my sword and adopted a

defensive stance. Dorsia did the same, dropping into a kind of crouch with her rapier pointed downward and her buckler positioned near her chest.

"Fight!" yelled Talen, and we obliged.

Dorsia stepped forward and began stabbing at me fiercely. I deflected the blows with my shield and sword, prioritizing defense and not giving an inch of space. The speed of her blows proved a challenge to deal with. In an unwatched fight, I could simply let her slide the rapier into the gaps of my armor, eat part of it, and then strike at her while she was unarmed, but being watched by a crowd meant I'd have to win in a more "traditional" way.

She continued her attacks. Sparks flew from her rapier as I moved my sword to block it. Suddenly, she ducked down under my defense and slammed her buckler into my chestplate. For a moment, I lost my footing, and she drove the point of her rapier up toward where my neck would be. I let the momentum of my lost footing carry me backwards and fell out of the way of her strike, rolling to create some space between us.

When I brought my head up, I realized she wasn't where I'd left her. I raised my shield above my head just in time, as her boot landed where my shoulders had just been and her rapier skidded off my shield where my head was. If I'd been limited by human eyes, she'd have killed me.

I stood up and pushed her off my shield with all my strength to launch her away. She performed a smooth flip backward, but I took advantage of her inability to change direction in the air and closed the gap between us. This time, I took the offensive, swinging my sword with such force that she could only deflect it with her buckler and so quickly that she couldn't counterattack. Eventually, her defense slipped, and I struck at her with the side of my shield. She lifted her rapier to try and block it, but it snapped from the force of the strike, and she fell backward. She started to stand, but I placed the point of my sword to her chest.

"Do you yield?" I asked.

"I'd be kind of stupid not to." She smirked as she spoke.

I looked up at Talen.

"The first fight is over. Sevald is the winner!"

The crowd yelled.

I felt for a moment as if my armor was tingling all over. Exhilaration, the thrill of the crowd, and the combat. I could see why Hrig enjoyed this.

I reached down and offered Dorsia my hand. She gave a wry smile and took it, standing herself up. We walked toward my exit.

"I knew I wasn't gonna win that one," she said as we walked.

"How?" I asked.

"I could just tell in my gut. I've always been able to tell when an opponent would be too much for me. My mother tells me it's a blessing from Krish."

"Why'd you fight me, then?"

"The challenge, and I knew you wouldn't kill me."

"How did you know that?"

"During the mêlée, you took down four opponents non-lethally. If you wanted to kill them, they'd have been a splatter on your shield."

I thought about that for a moment. It wasn't intentional, but she was absolutely right. I'd gone out of my way to avoid killing since I'd entered the arena. Was it because I didn't consider anyone a threat, or was it just another of the changes I'd had since I killed my master?

"Do you mind if I sit in your section?" she asked.

"No, I suppose not."

We slipped into my viewing section where Hrig was standing looking over the sand arena.

"Well fought." She looked to Dorsia. "Both of you."

Dorsia gave an acknowledging nod.

"Thank you, it was close," I said.

"No reason to lie on my account. It was obvious you were holding back," said Dorsia.

"Good to meet another gladiator that's honest with herself," said Hrig.

"Good to meet one who could kick most men into the sun," replied Dorsia, extending her hand. Hrig returned the gesture, and they locked hands for a moment. "Hope you don't mind me standing in your section. Mine was a bit lonely and a bit too close to Talen after a defeat by forfeit."

"He's not a fan of those?" I asked.

"He'll sometimes forgive it if there's been a good show, but when Donyin is with him, he tends to prefer a little blood spilled. They bring out the worst in each other."

"Bastard." Hrig looked back up at the brackets. "Do you know anything about my next opponent, Vyfell?"

"He's fast, and those gauntlets of his can catch an axe without him getting cut. He tends to work his opponent's body until they drop their guard low, then he goes for their heads. He's a regular, same as me. Used to fight in legit arenas a while back, but got kicked out for some reason."

"Good to know." Her expression turned thoughtful. "I haven't met many elves who focus on hand to hand."

We returned our attention to the arena. Talen was back at the dais.

"For our next match, we have a fight between our reigning champion Donyin, the blind bruiser, and the tattooed wildcat whose claws really leave a mark, the dwarven duelist Jade!"

The crowd erupted into applause as Donyin and Jade took

their positions in the center of the pit. Jade adopted a low crouch and made several quick marks into the sand at her feet. Donyin simply stood passively, not changing his stance at all.

"Fight!"

The runes in the sand and on Jade's skin glowed silver, and for a moment, she actually seemed to vanish, reappearing behind Donyin. Listening, I realized that I couldn't actually hear her movements. She seemed to be taking advantage of Donyin's apparent blindness in order to land a strike. She moved quickly, leaping with her claws outstretched, completely silent, and aimed with deadly precision for the base of his neck.

Donyin made a half step, caught Jade by her head in midair, and slammed her over his head and into the sand. I heard a sickening crunch, and she ceased moving. He then lifted and threw her, sending her tumbling across the sand toward where we were observing from the edge of the pit. Donyin moved toward her, clearly intending to strike her again while she was on the ground.

Hrig and I were moving before I even realized it. I hit him low, and she hit him high. He rolled with the hit and stood up while throwing us off of him. He raised a hand to strike at me, but a whistle rang out from the dais.

"Stop!" said Talen, still wearing his smile, though his tone had a hard edge to it. "Jade is down, and I don't want to throw everyone's bets out of order by letting you three fight. Return to your corners."

Donyin lowered his fists, scowling. "You can have that." He gestured at Jade. His blindness was clearly not an issue for him.

Hrig walked over to her and gently lifted her off the ground. She carried her back to our area and laid her gingerly on the bench.

"Dammit, Jade," said Dorsia as I began examining the

damage. Her back was black with bruising and her face so swollen, it was hard to even tell where to begin.

"Do you know her?" asked Hrig as she watered a cloth and began wiping blood gently away from Jade's face.

"She's a regular, like me. We talked before about what to do if we encountered Donyin. She was so confident she had it figured out, but I told her it was better to be blacklisted and hunted by Talen than to fight him willingly," said Dorsia.

"We'd need a healer to save her at this point. I don't know how to do much more than set a bone or treat an arrow wound," I said, examining her more closely. At the base of her neck on the right side, one of the runes read "sustain" in dwarvish. "I have an idea, but I'll need some help. Dorsia, can I have your hand?"

"I'm flattered, but I don't think this is the time." She gave a wan smile.

"For jokes? I'd agree. This rune on her neck means 'sustain.' It's just a guess, but I'd bet if you invoke it, you could buy her some time at the cost of your own strength. Hrig or I would do it, but we have more fights, and I'd prefer we're both in the best shape possible."

It would also almost certainly lead to a strange reaction if I tried to do it, and I preferred not to risk it, though I would have if there were no other choice.

Dorsia put her hand on the rune.

"Now, say 'duvn'," I said.

"Duvn." The rune lit up in silver and stayed lit. Jade's breathing immediately improved, and I heard her heartbeat strengthen. Dorsia grew pale and sat down.

"We have a friend who is a healer. She just has a few things to do in town, then she's planning on joining us here. You'll only have to hold out until then."

She took a deep breath. "I can do that. Jade owes me a bit of money and a drink. I'd really like to collect."

Hrig gave her a firm pat on the shoulder.

I returned my attention to the arena. While we'd been distracted, the next bout had begun. Rock, the dwarf in full plate, was facing Burias, the man who wielded two morningstars. The sound of the morningstars crashing against Rock's shield was almost like that of rain hitting a metal roof. His speed was incredible, but even from a distance, I could tell his strikes were weakening rapidly.

Within moments, they'd gone from a rain of blows to more of a drizzle, producing only the faintest *tink*-ing noise with each hit on the shield. Burias was dripping with sweat, and his legs actually appeared to be shaking. Rock gave him a firm shove with his shield, and he collapsed, seemingly unable to catch his breath. Rock raised his shield and mace as if embracing the crowd, who responded with a healthy amount of applause and hollering. He was to be my opponent in the next round, and clearly, he had some tricks up his sleeves.

Hrig stood up.

"Keep an eye on them," she said, grabbing her axe and making her way to the arena. I nodded and watched her enter the pit with a smile at the crowd and a few athletic twirls of her axe.

Her opponent Vyfell was as somber with his entrance as she was bombastic, approaching the center of the ring with no fanfare or attempts to woo the crowd. He was tall and wiry with dark hair tied back in a ponytail. The gauntlets on his hands were caked with blood despite the rest of him seeming immaculately clean.

As they approached each other, Talen projected his voice across the stadium. "Ladies and gentlemen, next up is a battle of bruisers. We have on one side our very own Vyfell, the disgraced professional turned battling brawler, and on the other, we have the Duchess of Death, the Beast from Buryn, Hrig!"

The crowd cheered, and the combatants took their positions.

Talen waited for a few moments, letting the tension build before yelling, "Fight!"

Vyfell closed the gap quickly, attempting to remove Hrig's advantage of her weapon's longer reach. She was forced on defense as Vyfell began a series of blows aimed at her stomach, which she managed to deflect with her axe shaft. She attempted a kick at his chest in order to buy space, but he twirled around it and got back inside her defense. He managed a single solid strike to her gut, briefly causing Hrig to lose her footing, but she recovered and managed a half swing of her axe, which bought her some much-needed space.

I recognized his techniques; they reminded me of my third meal Syven's training as a monk. He was a traditional boxer, an exceptional one, his footwork and strikes classic in every way.

Hrig, now that she had some space, took her axe and drove it into the ground next to her before putting her arms up in a boxing stance similar to Vyfell's and rolling her head to stretch her neck. He looked concerned for a moment before he removed his gauntlets as well and placed them on the ground. I was fairly certain I'd seen Hrig use her hands as much as her axe in fights, but going against a trained boxer with them was a bold move.

They approached each other, circling and making probing strikes. Vyfell's hands were a blur outside of the gauntlets, and for a moment, I wondered if Hrig knew what she was doing. They got closer to one another, and their fight began more in earnest. Vyfell was on the offensive, landing blow after blow at Hrig's stomach, but she didn't even flinch, instead attempting her own strikes, though none landed. After several back and forths, Hrig spat, landing a globule of blood in Vyfell's eyes. While he was blinded, she grabbed him by the ponytail and brought his face to her fist. She repeated the motion a few more times until his body went limp and she gently placed him onto the ground.

"That was clever of her," said Dorsia. She'd dragged herself next to me to watch the match, though she was leaning heavily against the wall.

"How so?"

"She could tell he was a trained fighter, so she pretended to act the same so he'd think of it as a fair fight. Problem is, this is an illegal fighting arena, and she never intended to play fair. Poor guy didn't stand a chance."

I nodded. Vyfell was a trained fighter, but Hrig was trained and experienced. There was just too wide a distance between them.

"What a stunning bout, everyone! With the Duchess's victory, we now know the lineup for round two. After a short break, we'll return with a battle between the men of iron, Sevald versus Rock. That'll be followed by a true test of might between our reigning champion Donyin and the champion of Buryn, Hrig!"

10
ROUND TWO

There was another intermission. Hrig looked in on Jade for a moment before finding herself a place to sit. "You holding up okay, Dorsia?"

"I'll be fine. Jade's breathing is staying steady, too," she said, wobbling a little as she sat down.

Hrig shifted her attention to me. "You worried about the next fight?"

"A bit. What I saw of his fight was strange." I shook my helmet. "Burias tired far too quickly."

"He's a strange one. My gut tells me he's pretty harmless, but he won anyway." She rubbed her chin in consideration.

"There's something odd going on with him, but you'll probably have to find out exactly what in the arena," said Dorsia.

"How about you? You worried about Donyin?" I asked.

"Of course. The man's a beast." She gave a wicked grin. "I'd love to cut him down, though."

I chuckled and stood up to pour a cup of water for Dorsia. She accepted it with a nod, still a little color left in her cheeks. I approached Hrig, speaking softly in case Dorsia was listening. "When do you think Kyren and Stone will return?"

"Soon, I'd think. Stone has a real talent for that kind of thing. I'm actually concerned with how long they've taken already. We've certainly been providing them a great distraction."

"I'd agree with that. I'd say the crowd is quite taken with us."

"Of course they are. We're fantastic."

I leaned against the edge of the pit while discreetly repairing small nicks in my armor and taking stock. We'd done our part, kept the arena busy, and had done quite well. I'd even enjoyed it.

The fact that Talen was profiting pained me, though. Something about him unsettled me, even beyond him being a violent and manipulative criminal. Those traits I could deal with. Hrig was violent, and Stone was a criminal, and I was fond of both of them. Talen and his right hand Donyin were different, though, inhuman in a way I recognized both in myself and in my former master.

Perhaps my still relatively new emotions and senses made me particularly sensitive to those like me. The fact that I disliked those that reminded me of myself seemed strange, though. Was that a normal problem for people? It would probably be weird to ask.

I'd already raised enough suspicion with my knowledge of dwarvish and runic magic. Some of that came from Pebble, but the knowledge of how to invoke the rune had been something I knew innately. Between that and draconic, I wondered what else my creator had put into me. Perhaps I was an excellent juggler, or I could perform a perfect pirouette?

The sound of the crowd dipped, and I returned my attention to the arena.

Talen stood to speak. "Everyone, please take your seats and

get ready for the first of our semifinal matches! Sevald and Rock, come to the arena."

"Good luck, not that you'll need it," said Hrig.

I nodded, clanking as I walked into the pit. I met Rock in the center and took an open, easy stance. He flashed a confident grin, raising his tower shield and mace in a defensive stance.

Talen leaned forward as we took position. "Is everyone ready for a fight between our two most heavily armored contenders!?" He held for applause. "Good, then without further ado, let's figure out which of these two contenders is truly made of steel."

If that was the criteria for victory, the battle was already solidly in my favor.

"Fight!"

I took the initiative, approaching Rock's left in order to slip around his shield. I swung my sword, but Rock managed to adjust in time to block. My sword crashed against the shield. I recoiled, taking several steps back.

"What's the matter?" he asked in a nasally voice. "Afraid?"

I ignored him. The strike felt strange. I couldn't tell exactly what happened, but there was an exchange of some kind. I needed more information, so I struck again, aiming for the shield on purpose this time. Rock raised it to meet my sword. The same sensation occurred. I struck again, and again, trying to figure out exactly what was happening.

Rock simply kept up his guard, absorbing my blows. After a few more, I realized what it was doing. The shield was eating my energy, sapping my strength a little with each strike. It was like me; it fed off of people in order to sustain itself. That was how Rock had successfully won battles against those stronger than himself. He only needed to offer up a solid defense, and his shield would slowly eat away at his opponents until they were too exhausted to go on.

Unfortunately for him, I was his worst possible matchup. My energy, as far as I could tell, was infinite, and my strength restored itself as quickly as the shield consumed it.

I placed my sword in the sand and leaned on it heavily, feigning long, heaving breaths. Rock smirked, approaching with his mace gripped firmly in his hand. He raised it and brought it down, aimed for my helmet. I chose that moment to shift my weight, grabbing his arm as he brought it down to strike me.

I flipped him over my head using his momentum, along with some of my own, and smacked him into the sand. He wheezed, unable to breathe, and I crouched over him, letting him recover. Once he'd regained his senses, he started trying to stand, but the weight of his armor made it too difficult for him. He was like a turtle that had been turned upside down.

"It was well fought," I said, offering my hand. He scowled at it but offered up his own. I hauled him up and turned around to retrieve my sword.

There was a hard impact on my back, and I was knocked to my knees.

"I never said I was yielding, idiot."

Another impact rocked me as his mace struck my back again.

There was no third impact.

I stood and twirled, slamming the back of my fist into the side of his helmet. The force spun him once, and he collapsed face first into the sand.

The crowd roared with approval, and Talen rose to speak.

"The winner is Sevald! I guess he's our man of steel, after all."

He didn't know half of it.

"We'll be seeing him again in the final round!"

Some attendants went to drag Rock and his things out of

the pit, but I grabbed his shield before they reached it. I turned my helmet toward them.

"Tell him I took it. If he wants it back, he'll have to take it from me."

They nodded, too apathetic to make a real effort at retrieving it, and continued on their way. I liked the shield; it was like me, though not sentient as far as I could tell. Rock wasn't worthy to wield something that was, in a way, kin to me.

I made my way back to the common area. A flash of golden light told me Kyren had returned. She was standing over Jade, who was slowly coming to. Stone was huddled in conversation with Dorsia, whose color was already returning.

"Spoils of combat?" she asked, gesturing at my new shield.

"It's enchanted. Saps the strength of those that strike it. Someone like Rock shouldn't have it."

Hrig smiled. "Stone and I must be starting to influence you. Knocking a man out and stealing his shield just because you don't like him?"

"He hit me rather hard with that mace. It's hard not to dislike someone after that."

Stone and Kyren moved closer while Dorsia helped Jade stand and started walking her out of the room.

"She's taking her somewhere to rest. She'll certainly need it after suffering injuries that severe," said Kyren.

Her and Stone's return brought me immediate comfort. We were complete again.

"That's understandable. What were you and Dorsia talking about, Stone?" I asked.

"Just trading some information, setting some things up. Dorsia used to pick pockets for me back when I was working here," said Stone.

"Corrupting the youth? You? I'd never have suspected," said Hrig.

"It's important to give children the skills they need to succeed." Stone looked at us both. "There's something I need to tell you. The heist was a success, but I may have done things a bit off script."

"How so?" I asked.

"He's united all the opposition in the city against Talen and set up a series of hits by a mixture of law enforcement and criminal elements at his most sensitive operations to all begin occurring within the next hour," Kyren said matter-of-factly.

I stood silently for a moment, dumbfounded. "Why? I thought all this was to help you pay off a debt."

"This isn't about just me and him anymore. He's changed things, and not for the better. There used to be a way of doing things, rules of a sort. He's thrown all of that out in favor of speed and profit. He's killed entire families to ensure survivors wouldn't rise against him. I can't let someone like that rule the underworld here unopposed."

"Well, how did you do it?" I asked.

"It's not too complicated, lad. Talen's rise was too quick. He jumped over more established organizations, skimped on bribes to certain members of the law, and was too ready to let former opposition kiss the ring, leaving vulnerabilities in his hierarchy. He hasn't actually consolidated his power yet. All I did was create a little network of people that are a bit resentful and slip them the right information. I did it all under the guise of preparing the heist. It was a good excuse to be near his remaining competition's operations, after all."

"That's brilliant," I said.

"Thank you, lad. Unfortunately, he still has plenty of allies, particularly here in the arena. When he gets word of what's happening, we'll be in great danger, but we can't leave until the tournament's over without him stopping us anyway." He sighed heavily. "I'm sorry again for getting everyone into this."

"Don't be, Stone. It's inconvenient, but just from what we've seen and heard here in the arena, Talen needs to be dealt with." Though a bit more honestly, I simply did not like him and would sincerely enjoy tossing him off his little dais. "Will he try to speak with you now that you're back? Ask how things went?"

"I don't think he will. He had men tailing us, and they saw what they needed to see. Besides, I think he likes the attention he gets up there. I doubt he wants that interrupted."

"Donyin and Hrig, please make your way to the arena!" Talen's voice rang out over the crowd.

Hrig looked at the group. "I'm going to finish this quickly. Maybe we can get out of here before there's too much trouble."

"We'll be prepared either way. Just focus on the fight," said Kyren.

"Be careful, Hrig," I said. She was a spectacular fighter, but Donyin's annihilation of Jade showed that he was too strong to be taken lightly.

She nodded and gave me a smile before entering the pit and making her way toward its center. Her opponent was already there, standing a head taller than her, his face still mostly obscured by thick black cloth, his gray tunic clean but worn, and thick cloth wrappings covering his hands.

As they squared up, Dorsia returned.

"Have they started yet?" she asked.

"No, but it should begin soon."

She shook her head. "She should've conceded like I told her to."

"You told her to concede? Why?" I asked.

"That feeling I get. I know she's going to lose. When I think about fighting her, I feel as if there's a raging river between us. I could never beat her. She's just too strong. When I think of fighting Donyin, though, it's like there's an ocean between us. The man doesn't even seem human."

I stood silently for a moment, watching the pit. "What feeling do you get when you think of fighting me?"

"The same as Donyin. The difference feels almost monstrous. If I hadn't seen you act so mercifully in the mêlée, I'd have never stepped into the pit with you."

Being referred to as monstrous gave me a slight uncomfortable twinge, though it was certainly fair in any context. I returned my attention to the arena where Talen seemed to have just finished one of his crowd-pleasing buildups.

"Now let's watch these titans of the arena square off. Fight!"

Hrig and Donyin moved toward one another and began trading blows immediately. They didn't bother feeling one another out or trying to determine the range and speed of each other's strikes. These were professionals, and that showed immediately.

Hrig was raining down blows on Donyin, who was deflecting them with his hands or dodging with deft footwork. Donyin attempted multiple times to switch to the offensive and Hrig would have to dodge his blows, but she always pushed her way into being back on the attack. I could tell she was trying to reduce his movement and avoid letting him pick up any momentum. She was playing it smart, but after several minutes of non-stop striking and dodging, she was tiring. In spite of that, she quickened her pace, pushing even harder until Donyin started losing his ground.

Donyin was slowly pushed back until he was just under Talen's dais, where Talen couldn't observe them. Suddenly, his dodges and blocks grew clumsy, and he stumbled back. Hrig didn't hesitate, and she brought her axe up to his neck with all the might she could muster. As the blade made contact with his throat, instead of the splash of blood I expected, sparks flew, and for a moment, in the spot where the axe had cut the fabric at his neck, I saw a flash of gold. Armor was my first reaction, but gold made for poor protection. I looked closer. They were scales, shining bright and gold.

Hrig hesitated, surprised by the sparks. Donyin took advantage and raised a tree trunk-like leg, slamming it into Hrig's chest and knocking her back toward the center of the arena. He then got out from under the dais and began a series of quick but savage strikes. Hrig couldn't recover, and Donyin's movements regained that same sharpness they'd had before he'd been under the dais.

The impacts were so heavy that I could actually hear them. Hrig took another hit but used the momentum to back away. Her face was bloody, and she was covered in bruises. She spat on the ground.

"I thought this was a fight, not tea in the garden. Why don't you hit me like you mean it?"

Donyin scowled and closed the distance between them. Hrig managed a strike at his chest, but again, where I expected blood was only another rain of sparks and flash of gold scales. He grabbed the blade with his bare hands and hauled it toward himself to strike her, but she moved with the momentum and headbutted him in his mouth, the one area that was exposed.

He stumbled back, roaring in pain and holding his mouth. He pulled away his hand, and several teeth came with it.

Hrig laughed, wiping blood away from her forehead. "Guess you'll be covering your mouth from now on, too, eh?"

He clenched his fist and closed the distance again. Hrig managed a few more strikes, but her strength had clearly left her, the injuries of his previous strikes and the intensity of the combat had taken its toll. He smashed his fist into her gut, making her cough blood, but she held on and spat in his face.

He then grabbed her by the hair, held her up, and began pummeling her with his other hand.

The crowd was completely silent. Their hunger for blood was matched by a hunger for sport, and there wasn't much sport left in this match. After a particularly brutal strike, the hair he'd been holding Hrig up by tore, and she was knocked back several yards.

The railing I was holding shattered under my grip, sending splinters all around me and breaking the silence. Donyin stopped his movement toward Hrig.

"The fight is over!" yelled Talen from his dais. "Donyin is the victor!"

The crowd managed some tepid applause, and I made my way into the pit. I walked over to Hrig and gently lifted her, holding her close.

"Sevald," she coughed out as we made our way out of the arena.

"Save your strength."

"I've got plenty to spare." She smiled in a flash of bloody teeth. "But Talen, Donyin is seeing through Talen somehow. It must be magic of some kind."

That made sense. Under the dais outside of Talen's view was where Donyin had struggled the most during the fight, and he was clearly able to see somehow. Between that and those scales, there was something going on that reminded me very distinctly of my encounter with the goblin leader. Definitely a thread there. I just needed to follow it.

I laid Hrig on Jade's former bench and backed away, letting Kyren tend to her. She grabbed my hand as I moved away.

"Kill that bastard for me, will you? Don't go soft on him like you did the others."

"He's as good as dead."

11
IMMORTAL COMBAT

I moved away from Hrig, giving Kyren space to minister to her in peace, and approached Stone.

"Hrig thinks that Donyin is seeing through Talen's eyes, and I think she's right."

"His movements did seem a bit clumsy when he was under the dais, didn't they?" Stone scratched his beard thoughtfully. "You leave it to me, lad. Distractions and the sort are my specialty."

I nodded and left him to his plotting.

I walked out onto the sand of the arena, my boots leaving imprints as I made my way toward Donyin. He hadn't left since he'd fought Hrig, and her blood was still dripping from the cloth wraps over his hands. I noted with satisfaction that he still had blood running freely from his mouth where she had struck him.

Talen rose to speak. "Ladies and gentlemen! We now come to the final fight of our little tournament. A bout between a classic chivalrous knight and our very own beast of a brawler. Who will be our champion? Who will win this epic test of might? I'll allow an additional two minutes for bets to be placed while you consider those questions for yourselves."

His voice was unencumbered by any worry, but I could tell, even behind his dark glasses, that he was disturbed by Donyin's injury. The fight hadn't been very close, but seeing his favorite toy damaged seemed to distress him.

I looked at Donyin; he was scowling and standing with his arms crossed. This close, I could clearly see that in the areas Hrig's axe had struck, there were golden scales. I could sense him radiating hatred in my direction as I sized him up. I wavered a bit, standing under the weight of his disdain. I hadn't sensed that in his other fights, just contempt and annoyance.

"You're not human, are you?" I asked.

Donyin ignored the question and continued pouring concentrated loathing in my direction.

I took a page from Hrig's book. "What? Did losing a few teeth leave you with a lisp? Embarrassed to talk?"

His nostrils flared, but he didn't answer.

"That's okay, don't answer. I'm sure I'll find out when I run you through."

With that last barb, I stood and waited for Talen to start the fight. I focused on my skin in the same way I did to repair dents and chinks, but instead of repairing it, I was thickening and strengthening it. Unlike the other fights, there was no winning this one without relying on my inhuman abilities. I then left myself in an open position, inviting a strike. I needed him to hit me at least once; it was the only way to confirm he was what I thought he was.

"All bets are in!" Talen's voice rang through the arena. "Let's not test our fighters' patience anymore." He gave one last sweeping look to the audience, raising his hand above his head before bringing it down in a chopping motion. "Fight!"

Donyin smiled. He wasn't missing teeth anymore, and the

replacements were pointed and sharp. He leapt forward and struck me full in the chestplate, launching me backward.

The blow confirmed my suspicions even as it cracked my reinforced armor. It hurt. In the same way the goblin leader's strikes had hurt. I pulled up my shield and blocked his second strike, feeling the shield take a small bite of his energy and strength. I raised my sword and attacked with a flurry of swings. Donyin dodged the first few before blocking the last one with his forearm in a shower of sparks as his scales absorbed the blow.

I changed tactics, aiming my swordpoint at his mouth. He leaned his head to the side to avoid it and kicked at my knee to buy space, but I lowered my shield to block his kick before launching into another stab at his mouth. This time, he caught my sword in his teeth. His lip curled up in a smile. I gave him a kick of my own, and he launched backward, taking the tip of my sword with him.

He spat the sword tip into the sand, and I risked regenerating the nicks and growing breaks in the sword and reinforcing it as much as I could. It took more effort than repairing my skin, but it was doable as long as I was holding it.

He charged again and started attacking without letting up. I managed to block most of his strikes on my shield, but several grazed my helmet, and one blow took me square in the chest. His hits tore at my essence, and before long, I was leaking black ooze from my helmet. I wasn't sure of exactly what it was. I only hoped that from the distance of the stands, everyone would assume it was blood.

Despite my new shield's enchantment, Donyin showed no signs of slowing. His strength must've been as inhuman as my own to be so minimally affected by it. The hits kept coming, and I was losing my footing one step at a time as I recoiled again and again under his blows. I let a particularly strong blow knock me back so I could have a moment to adjust.

I threw down the shield and brought both my hands to the hilt of my sword while planting my feet deep into the sand to steady my footing. I was giving up on blocking Donyin's hits, and shifting my attention to hitting him as much as possible.

He closed the distance and began striking. His fists rocked and dented my armor and cut my essence while my sword crashed down on him in a shower of sparks. No matter where I hit, there was no clear weakness, and since I'd already made a play for the part of his face, I knew he was wary of any strikes in that direction. I could feel my essence draining with every hit, even as my own blows failed to leave any marks.

There was a popping sound from several directions, and smoke began filling the arena. Donyin was distracted, and I took that opportunity to back away, leaving a trail of black bile. Stone's idea, I assumed. The stands were soon filled with it, rendering Talen, and thus Donyin, blind.

I stayed still and circled around him, the sounds of the panicking crowd covering that of my movement. I struck his back, knocking him forward, but not managing to cut him, then I slid away again. I repeated the tactic several more times, but with no luck.

Donyin laughed and ripped away what remained of his gray tunic, revealing a heavily muscled body covered in golden scales.

"Even if you take Talen's sight from me, I cannot be harmed. My father's gifts make me invulnerable to any blow." He started angling his head, listening for my movement. "Eventually, I will catch you. Then I will kill you for what you did to my brother."

His brother? I searched my memories and found no one in my own experience or Sevald's who could possibly be related to Donyin. "I don't know what you're talking about."

Donyin leapt at the sound of my voice, but his fists struck only sand. I'd already moved.

"The leader of the camp. He was noble and strong. Our father had blessed him nearly as much as me and far more than he had Talen."

"The goblin!?"

Another leap, another strike that hit sand. Talen and Donyin being brothers was a stretch, but Donyin and the goblin chief being relatives was, as far as I knew, a biological impossibility.

"He was more than that! Once Father awakens within us, we all become more than what we were. You will die for the death you've brought to a son of Aurum."

I emerged from below him in a shower of red sand and leapt onto his back, wrapping my arms around his neck and squeezing with all of my strength.

"Your skin may be tough, but let's see how strong your lungs are."

He roared, letting out valuable oxygen, and started twisting and turning, trying to throw me off like a wild bull. I didn't shift an inch. He switched to punching at my helmet and trying to pull at my arm, but the only change was another thick clump of black ooze spilling out of my helmet and down his shoulders.

Finally, he threw himself backward onto the sand, trying to crush me. I held fast, squeezing tighter and tighter as the air left his lungs to ensure he couldn't fill them again. His struggling began to grow weaker and weaker until his swings at my helm were down to the strength of a normal man. He stopped moving. I gave one more squeeze with all the effort I had to make sure he was dead.

I removed myself from under him and retrieved my weapons. The crowd was still panicking, and smoke obscured the pit. I needed more information. There were too many unanswered questions. I moved back toward the body, preparing myself for a large meal.

A few feet from him, I hesitated. Donyin was a violent, prideful monster. If I ate his essence, how would it influence me? The goblin hadn't had any impact, but he'd been dead for some time and didn't have a strong personality to begin with. Did I want something like Donyin's essence rattling around in my armor, changing me?

The decision was made for me when Talen burst through the smoke where the dais had been, rolling into the sand and landing just on the other side of Donyin's body. His glasses were off, tears running down his cheeks, flowing from golden eyes. He knelt next to the body.

Before he could turn his attention to me, I ran, returning to where I'd left my companions. I was too injured, inside and out, to attempt another bout with a so-called "Son of Aurum." As I moved, I focused on stopping the black fluid from leaking and consolidating myself as much as possible.

I made it back to find Stone waiting for me. He looked relieved. "Let's go, lad. The others are already waiting for us, but we need to move quickly."

I nodded, falling in behind him. We weaved our way through the panicking crowd for a bit until Stone ducked off into a side passage. I followed him as we slipped our way through until we were out in the open air. We then ducked through several alleys, backtracking a few times.

"Where are we going?" I asked.

"The docks. I'm trying to make sure as few people know where we're headed as possible."

I nodded and fell back in step behind him.

Eventually, we came to the larger part of the docks, where the ships that were meant for the sea were docked. He walked confidently up a plank and onto one of the larger vessels. I followed him. On the deck, we were met by Kyren and, surprisingly, Dorsia. As I boarded, the crew began launching their vessel.

"Hrig?" I asked.

"Down below decks with Jade. She wanted to be up here waiting for you, but I insisted she rest," said Kyren.

"She insisted with a sleep spell, in fact," said Dorsia, a wry smile on her lips.

"I'm surprised to see you here, though I suppose I'm surprised to be here myself," I said.

"I've been thinking of leaving for a long time. When Stone asked me to help him find a way out, I introduced him to the captain." She pointed at a large man with a thick blond beard bellowing orders. "I've known him a long time, helped him with some smuggling here and there."

"And Jade?"

"Well, she heard us talking and asked to join. She'd been looking for a way out, too. Besides, she says she owes us, and I'm in no place to turn down help."

Kyren was looking at me, a concerned look on her face. "You should probably join them below decks. Would you like me to heal you? I should be able to work around your armor."

"No...save it. We don't know what other complications might arise. We should stay as prepared as we can." That was a good enough excuse. If she actually cast a decently powerful healing spell, it might actually kill me. "I think I'll stand on deck for a while. I need to settle a bit after all the excitement."

I walked to the stern and leaned against a railing.

The ship began to shift underfoot and move. It made its way out of the docks, and soon, the city of Cirros began to fade. First the docks, then the stone walls, and finally even the bright flags that dotted the towers were gone. I was grateful to have at least the memories of my meal's tepid exploration of the city; I was unlikely to be able to return and truly experience it for myself.

    I left the railing and let Kyren lead me below decks to our cabins. Hrig lay, snoring peacefully, in a hammock that swayed gently with the motions of the ship. Jade was similarly situated at the other side of the cabin, likely to avoid the noise Hrig was making. I took a spot in the corner and sat, placing my faceplate to my greaves and feigned sleep while I slowly worked to repair my essence and hoped for a peaceful voyage.

12
SUPERSTITIONS AND SUSPICIONS

I lost time. There was blackness, flashes of memories, bits of sights, sounds, and smells followed by a return to my senses. The damage I'd suffered must've put me into a kind of trance. It had likely been the closest I'd ever been to experiencing sleep.

I heard slivers of conversation. Kyren, Hrig, Dorsia, Stone, and Jade were talking in hushed voices, likely to keep from waking me. I strained my senses, trying to eavesdrop.

"—not a scratch. I watched the beginning of his fight. I'm certain his armor cracked," said Dorsia in a hushed tone.

"I don't think his armor has ever had a nick or a scratch, actually. I never really paid attention to it before," said Stone.

"You call yourself a dwarf? Come now, what'll we hold over elves if we can't even notice the condition someone's armor is in?"

That voice was new; Jade, I assumed.

There was a scoff from Stone. "Adhering to stereotypes certainly doesn't help anyone. Besides, we've been a little too busy to care about whether or not his armor has nicks or not."

"What should we do?" asked Hrig.

"Nothing for now," said Kyren. "Let's go back up to the deck. The captain invited us all to dinner. We can talk it over with full stomachs."

There were murmurs of agreement, and they all quietly shuffled out of the cabin.

I felt as if I had a stone inside me and it was rattling around, rebounding all around my interior. I was panicking. Obviously, armor was supposed to wear down over time, but I'd been repairing every nick and scratch almost as soon as I got them. What did they know? Did they realize I wasn't Sevald, or worse, that I wasn't human?

I took a moment to calm myself, trying to settle the rattling sensation I was experiencing. All I knew was that they'd realized my armor was repairing itself. I could only wait and see what they said about it and react from there. At this point, the thought of killing them to protect myself was one I found unconscionable. These were my friends. Aside from that, I'd have to kill the entire crew of the ship, as well. An immoral and impractical option. I'd just have to wait and see what they said. If worst came to worst, I'd leap into the ocean and walk until I found a shore.

I buckled my shield to my back and tied my scabbard about my waist before making my way upstairs. It was awkward, walking while adjusting to the movements of the ship as it rose and fell with the waves. Pebble had fairly well-established sea legs from his long journey from the University at Usalaum, but trying to walk the way he did at Sevald's height just made things worse, so I focused on adjusting based on my own ability.

Up on the deck, I was greeted by a spray of sea air and the sounds of crew deep into their cups. It was evening, and a silver half-moon hung in the sky, lighting the ocean in silver light. For just a moment, the sight caused me to forget my concerns. All of my meals except Byn had seen the ocean, but those memories seemed a poor imitation for the real thing.

I moved toward the nearest group of sailors. When they noticed me, their boisterous and bawdy voices shifted into hushed tones and worried glances in my direction. Had my companions told them something? The panic set in again, but I pushed it down.

"Can you point me to the captain's cabin?"

They exchanged glances until one of them pointed toward the aft. I nodded my thanks and went that way, pushing down more panic and resisting the urge to make a preemptive jump into the ocean.

Light danced under the captain's cabin door, and I could hear the sounds of light conversation drifting from it. I braced myself and opened the door.

"Sevald!" said Stone.

The room was mostly familiar faces, aside from a tall, burly man with a thick, but neatly maintained blond beard at the head of the table. Everyone looked smiling and affable. Some of the tension I'd been feeling melted away.

"Hail, Stone, everyone."

Kyren moved to drag a chair so that I could sit between her and Hrig and across from Stone, Jade, and Dorsia. I sat and turned my attention to the captain, offering my hand. "It's nice to meet you. Thank you for your help, Captain...?"

The man smiled and grasped my hand firmly. "Jase. Welcome to the *Nedra*, and it's no trouble. I'm being paid for it."

"Exorbitantly, in my opinion," muttered Stone.

"Moving you out of the city might cost me business with Talen. You're paying for my assumption of that risk."

"I told you, he's being taken down. His whole operation should be crippled by now."

"I'm not so sure," Dorsia chimed in. "You definitely dealt

him a blow, but you also brought all of his enemies into the open. If he can come back from it, he'll be stronger than ever."

That thought put a damper on the otherwise jovial atmosphere.

"Hmm, perhaps I should've charged even more, then..." said Jase, stroking his beard.

"What will really hurt him is whether or not Donyin is alive." Dorsia turned to me, "Sevald? We never heard how your fight ended, and Stone told us he couldn't tell through all the smoke."

"He killed him, obviously," said Hrig before I could respond. "He promised he would."

I nodded, taking pride in her confidence. "It's true. He's dead."

I took a moment to think about how much of what he'd told me I should mention, but decided they were better off knowing everything. I described what happened. The fight, what Donyin had said about his siblings, how the fight had ended, and Talen's gold eyes. When I was finished, everyone sat in silence for a few moments.

"Aurum?" asked Kyren. "You're sure that's what they said?"

"Yes, Donyin said that he, Talen, and the goblin chief were all 'Sons of Aurum'."

Kyren frowned. "I've heard the name, but it's old. It's only ever mentioned in the rituals I told you about before, the ones that use draconic. It's probably something only those further into their church's mysteries have access to. When we put in at Buryn, I'll visit the cathedral there and make some inquiries."

"Buryn? Is that where we're headed?" I asked.

"Yes, but we should hopefully just be passing through and making our way inland. Clara, or someone who works for her, will have a job for us there," said Kyren. Hrig's expression showed she was thoroughly displeased with the idea. "She was smart to clear out at the first sign of trouble, shame she couldn't have warned us about Talen." He turned to look at me. "There's something else we should probably talk to you about, too."

I felt the mood of the room shift, and panic took hold again. If they all tried to restrain me, it would be very hard to escape without hurting them.

"Dorsia pointed out that we've never seen so much as a dent in your armor," started Stone, "even after your fight with Donyin, in which I'm certain I noticed several cracks. Those are all gone now. You've not had a chance to repair them yourself, besides which I've never noticed you carrying repair tools of any kind."

I managed a nod, too afraid to try and come up with excuses.

Stone looked around the table. "I think," he paused, taking a breath," it's magic, and... I think we should sell it."

My concern turned to a mixture of relief and confusion. "Sell it?"

"Aye, lad, think of the profits! Magical items are rare, and ones as practical as a self-repairing suit of armor are even rarer. A lord would pay an incredible fee for it. We could buy an estate with such a thing." His eyes were alive with excitement at the possibility.

"He took a godly oath to wear it, Stone. You of all people with your own oath should know the value of that. You gave your left nut for your last one," said Kyren.

"Well, I'd give my right nut for the profit from that armor!"

Kyren rolled her eyes. "I told him you wouldn't be interested, but he's been arguing with us about it since Dorsia brought it up."

I laughed, feeling the last bit of tension leave me. "I'm afraid I'll have to decline, Stone. I took an oath, and I intend to keep it."

I'd have to avoid telling him about my new shield.

"Are you sure you can't at least remove it while you're on the ship?" Jase interrupted. "It's a death sentence, you know. If you fall overboard, you'll drown. It's making the men uncomfortable. It's like seeing a dead man walking."

I hadn't considered that, mostly since I didn't need to breathe, and swimming had never been an option for me anyway. "I'm afraid it has to stay on."

Captain Jase shrugged. "I guess there's no helping it, but between that and the women we've brought on board, I've had to ration a bit of extra grog all around to keep the crew from letting superstitious nonsense bother them." He paused. "Honestly, though, seeing a man in heavy armor on a ship even gives me the willies," he said, emphasizing the last word with a shiver.

The rest of the dinner passed uneventfully, but pleasantly, with Stone telling everyone a story about Dorsia botching a pickpocketing attempt that left her with a red face on top of her usual wry expression.

The next morning, I left the cabin later than everyone else. I had no reason to rush and wanted to avoid making the ship's crew uncomfortable as long as possible. When I did make my way to the deck, I was surprised to find Dorsia, Hrig, and Jade locked in combat. They were surrounded by cheering sailors about whom Stone walked, taking small bundles of coins and etching notes on a small clay tablet.

I approached Kyren sitting at the edge of the crowd. "I'd have thought everyone would've been sick of this type of thing after what we just went through."

She let out a heavy sigh. "I would've thought so, too, but

Hrig was up here training alone before anyone else came up. Seeing her swinging that axe of hers around got Jade riled up, and Dorsia joined in once she and Stone realized there was coin to be had with a bit of betting on the side."

"Should Hrig and Jade be doing this with their injuries?"

"Probably not, but after their losses, I think they're just eager to get stronger."

I nodded and watched as Hrig landed a solid blow to Dorsia's leg with an oar she was using in place of her axe.

Training was an interesting thing. I had memories of it from all of my meals. They'd spent hours honing their crafts, learning, and developing. Their abilities were the product of years of diligence, focus, and will. All I'd needed to do was eat them to gain the same mastery. I wondered if I would be able to learn something in that way. I certainly had some innate skills, but whether I could develop something that wasn't given or taken was unknown to me. What would I even choose to learn? I'd been focused on what I could learn from the essences I'd eaten, but eventually, there'd be nothing left to gain from them.

There was a crash followed by groans from more than half of the sailors. I returned my attention to the fight. Dorsia was the only one still standing, holding two short sticks. Hrig was disarmed, and Jade lying on the deck panting.

"That's surprising. She's a great fighter, but I don't think I'd have bet on her over Jade and Hrig."

"It's not that surprising. She's the only one who wasn't severely injured recently. I assume that's why Stone bet so much on her."

I glanced at Stone, who was grinning ear to ear as he collected coins from disappointed sailors and paid out the few that had also bet on Dorsia. He then approached us and handed Kyren a small handful. She'd apparently had the wisdom to bet a few coins herself. He then pulled a small pouch from his belt and handed it to me. I reached out and took it.

"I don't recall placing any bets."

"It's the money from the goblin camp job, minus my fee and your part in paying for our passage. I did promise everyone they'd get their cut, after all."

I nodded, taking the pouch and tying it to my belt.

Hrig, Jade, and Dorsia were preparing for another bout, and the sailors began calling to Stone for their bets. Stone went to return to them, but hesitated, looking back. "I already said this to the others, but thank you, lad. We were all in a jam because of me, but everyone came through, and I just wanted to let you know that I've got your back, always."

I held out my hand, and we grasped each other firmly by the wrist. Friendship was something I'd been lucky enough to be granted only a short while after I'd become capable of it. I would do everything in my power to be worthy of it, even if it had been granted under false pretenses.

13
FIFTH MEAL?

I was the first to notice the commotion. The sounds of men running, orders being shouted, and sails shifting leaked into the cabin from underneath the door. I stood and made my way toward the noise. When I reached the deck, I was greeted by the spray of sea air and the morning sun cresting over the horizon, illuminating three black ships headed directly for us.

"I guess a respite was too much to ask for," I muttered, walking in the direction of Captain Jase, who was bellowing orders to his crew.

"If you bunch of filthy pig-dogs want to live to see your next woman, you better get moving!" His beard was uncharacteristically unkempt, and his eyes had a wild look to them.

"What's happening?" I asked.

He pointed to the approaching ships.

"Privateers," he moved toward the helm, throwing a clearly terrified first mate from it and taking over, "from the Eastlands. You can tell by the ships. Black wood like that only grows there."

The Eastlands were the orcish homeland. They were called

the Eastlands because they acted more as a loose confederation of clans than a united kingdom, so no unifying name existed. They joined together in war and allowed free trade between the separate provinces, but otherwise ruled themselves. Raids on other kingdoms were common, and suspending those raids was often their first move to garner good will when they made a diplomatic effort. Their central desert province was the place Pebble had called home.

"Their ships are small, quick, and meant to take prizes of larger ships. I used to pay them off through Talen, but I figured I'd have time to make a new contact before it became an issue." He furrowed his brow. "How could he have figured out I'm the one who'd smuggled you out and managed to get them a message in just a few days? It shouldn't be possible."

"How many do you think there are?"

"Too many, and their ships are faster than the *Nedra*. I'm having the boys dump some cargo behind us to buy some time, but they'll catch up within two hours anyway. I sent a crewman to wake up Dorsia and your friends."

Hrig, Jade, Stone, Dorsia, and Kyren made their way to the bridge just as I threw a barrel off the stern and into the path of the nearest Eastland ship. After a quick discussion, they made themselves useful in any way they could. Hrig and Jade threw cargo overboard with me, Dorsia and Stone greased the railing to make it harder to climb onto the ship, and Kyren started to prepare a triage area for any wounded.

When the first Eastland ship reached our port side, we were as ready as we could be. The enemy crew was grim-faced and dressed in cream-colored sweaters that bore distinct weaves and patterns, clan markings to help identify them if their bodies fell overboard. Over those, they wore simple blue coats that emphasized the green and grey hues of their skin. They stood a head taller than the mostly human crew that surrounded me, clearly better trained, wielding bladed hooks and light shields. They began laying down planks between the ships, which we quickly kicked off, but it was just a distraction that allowed two of the privateers to climb onto our vessel using their hooks to haul themselves over the railing, completely avoiding the oil Dorsia and Stone had applied.

Hrig moved to intercept them, so I turned my attention to the enemy vessel. Rather than waiting for them to board, I took things into my own gauntlets and leapt down onto the pirate's ship to the gasps of the *Nedra*'s crew. The pirates seemed less surprised, and the two that had engaged Hrig actually leapt back onto their own vessel just moments after I did. The ship itself then shifted under my boots and started moving away from my companions and toward their other ships. I saw looks of surprise on my companions as the vessels separated. This wasn't an attempt on the *Nedra*—this was a trap for me.

I chose not to make it easy for them. I ran through the nearest of the orcs with my sword, knocking another off the side of the boat with my shield. One attempted to trip me with his hooked blade, but was surprised when his hit didn't move me and I severed his arm. I kicked another of them off the deck and heard his ribs crack from the force. After a few more strikes and bodies thrown overboard, there was no one left attacking me, though several of the orc crew were still piloting the vessel.

My break was short-lived as the two other enemy vessels pulled up to the sides of the one I was on, and I found myself again surrounded as the crews of those ships filed on, curved blades in hand. I drew up my sword and shield, preparing for another wave of attackers.

Instead of attacking, they parted, and an orc woman made her way to stand in front of me. Her outfit was more ornate than that of the crew; she wore no sweater, but instead, a simple blue tunic threaded with gold filigree and a black leather bicorn hat.

Her skin was the color of charcoal, and her white teeth were even more pronounced than those of her crew. Above her fanged smile were two golden eyes, a color I was growing far too familiar with.

"Good morning, monster." Her voice came out as a sultry growl.

"It takes one to know one," I responded. I'd been getting a lot of practice with banter.

Her mouth curled up in a wider smile, showing a few more of her teeth. "Talen asked me to take care of you for killing our brother." She let out an exaggerated sigh. "Frankly, I couldn't care less about that brute, but Talen owing me a favor, now that has value."

I added "talking over large distances" to the ever-growing list of talents the children of Aurum possessed.

"More value than your life, apparently. I've already killed two of your siblings."

"A runt of a goblin and a blind beggar. They were nothing without our father's gifts, and so they glutted themselves on them, losing themselves to have more of him. I'm different. I was strong before my father. He didn't build me up from nothing; he just magnified me." She unclasped two hooked blades from her waist. "Keep him occupied. I need to get in as many clean hits as possible."

Her crew closed in, all swinging their blades down at me at once. I lifted my shield and felt it eat a bit of their energies. I then pushed them off of me with enough force to knock them back. I moved toward the heaviest concentration of them, not bothering to be delicate or to act as a mortal knight would. I simply let them hit me while I bludgeoned them with my shield and cut through them with my sword. My friends weren't watching, so there was no reason to pretend to be something I wasn't.

The orc captain's first strike hit me just after I'd left a crater in the skull of one of her crewmen with my sword's pommel. She hooked her blade around my helmet and yanked me backward, knocking me down. I splintered her deck as I landed.

I stood up, swinging my sword in an arc as I did and crippling a row of privateers in front of me. Before I could find my balance, she hit me again, this time hooking my leg and tripping me. I landed faceplate first and felt four pirates pile on, each one grabbing a limb.

I began to push myself up despite their weight, but their captain chose that moment to begin attacking in earnest. Her hooked blades fell onto me, cutting long gashes into my backplate and slipping between my straps and gambeson to strike directly into my essence.

This was a bad matchup for me. Her fighting style relied on keeping her opponents off balance and striking their vitals when they showed openings. It was as if I were fighting Dorsia, but with the strength of the goblin chief.

Since she already knew I wasn't human, I decided to give her a taste of what that meant. I separated my gauntlets from the rest of myself. The orcs that had been straining to hold me down flew backward as the tension they'd been pulling against gave. The surprise let me kick off the remaining two that clutched my legs, and I flung myself upward and backward, slamming my helmet into the captain's face. She recoiled, clutching a bloody eye socket. I let my gauntlets return and retrieved my sword and shield, kicking back a few more orcs as I did so.

I looked over my surroundings. More than a dozen dead around me, the water around the ships tinged red with the blood of those I'd knocked off the deck. "You're running out of crew to hide behind."

She grimaced, removing her hand from her face and picking

up the sword of one of her fallen crew. "He's right. Everyone back away, or we won't have enough men to man the ships!"

"Yes, Captain Vash," said an older-looking orc, and they all made space for us.

I took a defensive stance. Without her crew to hide behind, I'd have the advantage. I wondered where the *Nedra* had gone. I assumed Captain Jase would keep it heading away rather than risk everyone else's lives for me. That suited me— easier this way.

Vash and I moved toward each other. She attacked first, pulling my shield down with one sword and striking at my helmet with the other. I batted away her strike with my blade and lifted my shield and her toward me, attempting another headbutt. She jumped off the shield, leaving one of her blades behind, and swung the other low toward my feet, attempting to trip me. I jumped over it and made a downward strike at her head, but only managed to knock off her bicorn.

She flipped backward, grabbing another of her fallen crew's blades as she did so. We began to charge one another again when the ship rocked. We stopped, looking around. The crew muttered and shuffled on their feet. It rocked again, this time harder.

"Gods, no. The blood and bodies in the water," said Vash, her toothy smile drooping into an equally toothy look of concern, "Move the ships. We have to—"

A massive tentacle shot up from the water and slammed onto the deck, crushing a crewman with a sickening, squelching noise.

"Kraken!" yelled a crewman, running for one of the exterior boats. Just as he was about to leap for it, another tentacle emerged and wrapped itself around him, pulling him down through the murk of his crewmates' blood and into the depths.

Before I could react, more tentacles emerged, and everything devolved into chaos. Crewmen ignored me, and Vash yelled orders to them, trying to regain control. The tentacles began wrapping around the vessels, and I could hear them creaking under enormous pressure. I took that chance to finish the fight, buckling my shield to my back and returning my sword to its sheath.

I charged Vash and tackled her just as the ship gave way and snapped in two. We were launched into the water, and with me holding on to her, she sank like a stone. I risked a look at the kraken as we descended. It was a massive red beast, all tentacles, spines, and dozens of eyes the size of my chestplate.

Vash struggled, bubbles of air escaping from her mouth and making their way toward the surface. I opened my skin and began wrapping myself around her. I couldn't keep dealing with these children of Aurum like this. I had too little information and kept being taken unaware. I needed to risk what her essence would do to me.

I felt her start to fade into me. I sensed the edges of her memories and emotions along with something else. A second presence so massive that to touch it was to feel as if I were pushing on a mountain. As I closed around Vash, a voice rang through my entire body.

"No!" it said, and I felt more strength in that word than in anything else I'd ever experienced.

Vash's essence began burning and exploding inside me. I fought, trying to keep her down, but she broke free and swam out of me, a freshly grown golden tail helping to propel her to the surface.

My essence ached and shuddered, and I lost all sense of the world as I sank down into the depths.

14
FICKLE GODS

I came to my senses amongst the remains of the privateers' ships. Part of a mast lay across my breastplate, orc corpses scattered around being picked apart by skittering creatures with pale white shells. I pushed myself out from under the mast, sending a dozen of the critters scurrying away in surprise.

I was in deep water and could feel the pressure of it pushing down on me. I looked in every direction, but hoping for landmarks proved a stretch, particularly when one wasn't actually on land. I knew the *Nedra* had been travelling parallel to the continent, so I just needed to pick the right direction and move until I hit land. Unfortunately, I had no idea which direction was the correct one. I could wind up walking all the way to the Eastlands if I wasn't careful.

I needed navigation skills, and I was fortunate enough to have a wealth of information decaying all around me. I started approaching the corpses, passed one whose head had already been mostly devoured by the skittering critters, another that was missing half his skull from a swordblow, likely my own, and one with the head crushed by a falling piece of mast.

Finally, I found one that was relatively unscathed. I brushed a few of the pale creatures aside and cut off the orc's head. It was a woman, middle-aged by orc standards, with an intricate tattoo of a fish running under her chin. I removed my helmet and placed it over her head.

I felt a sense of honor and respect that kept a tremendous rage and pride in check. A duty that had been honored by my clan for generations, which eventually fell onto my shoulders. A weight I carried gladly. There was a compass, passed on by my forefathers, that I kept in my pocket to keep my ancestors with me. Then the sensation of rope sliding through callused hands, of drawing back an oar, feeling the resistance of the water, and tying off a ship, making a snapping sound as I pulled the rope taut to check the knot. Every time I performed these tasks, I was echoing my ancestors, building on their legacy.

More recent impressions were clearer. I felt a powerful respect for my captain, a woman like me, but also a captain who came from nothing, who treated her crew with honor and respect. I remembered the day she changed. Her hazel eyes shifted to gold, and her already grand ambitions swelled. Within a year, she wasn't just a captain of our small raiding vessel, but a captain of captains in charge of three. I watched her fight and bleed for us, and I returned the favor. I heard her order to attack, and I charged. A suit of armor stood over the corpses of a dozen of my comrades. He was silver as moonlight, with intricate etchings over his breastplate. His faceplate was drawn down, and the sharp slant of the visor gave the impression of a bird of prey. His dark blue gambeson showed through like midnight peeking through moonlight. He struck me with his shield, and I felt my ribs shatter from the impact, then I felt the cold water hit my back. I couldn't inflate my lungs and sank like a stone. I saw an enormous shadow rising toward the boat as I fell into the depths, all light leaving my sight.

I returned my helmet to my head. My gauntlets were experiencing a slight tremor, and I flexed my fingers to settle them down. The goblin head hadn't been nearly as intense. Lythia had been a thoughtful person possessed of powerful emotions. Even though I only ate a small part of her essence, it left me shaken.

I reached into the corpse's pocket and pulled out the compass, realizing as I did so that if I'd simply searched her first, I could've avoided absorbing any of her essence. Then again, I felt grateful to a certain extent that I had. I would be able to take her skills, passed down for generations, and ensure they would survive. I took note of the pattern on her thick wool sweater—Irontooth clan. I looked over the other corpses, memorizing them, as well. Two from the Viridian Hands, one from the Deadeyes. I likely wouldn't get a chance to inform the clans of their loss, but it felt important to remember them anyway.

I ate the compass, storing it within myself, and began walking west, monitoring it internally as I moved to make sure I didn't deviate from my path. During my trek, I passed by creatures so strange, I found myself questioning if I was still in the same world I'd been in when I'd fallen into the water. They existed in impossible shapes, with little or no coloring to them except occasionally the faintest bit of luminescence. They seemed to float without purpose or move with great haste toward goals unimaginable to me.

After a few hours of walking and observing odd creatures, I saw a light in the distance. At first, I thought it was a larger luminescent creature, but the light didn't move, and only got larger as I moved closer. Eventually, I was able to make out the details and realized it was the wreck of a ship. After walking closer, I realized it wasn't the ship that was glowing, but instead, glowing humanoid figures that were moving among the wreck.

I approached cautiously. The ship was enormous. A royal transport vessel, from what the bit of essence I'd just eaten could tell. I went to the nearest glowing figure—a man, an elvish sailor swabbing a nonexistent deck. I waved at him, but received no response. He faded into nothingness, and a larger group appeared. I moved over to them. A man and a woman dressed in fine clothes and wearing simple crowns. The man was dark-haired with a plain face, the woman tall and beautiful with long blond hair. Across from them stood a man in clothes even finer than theirs. His hair fell in gold ringlets down his back, and his facial features had a predatory but handsome look to them.

"Thank you for allowing me to be a guest on this voyage, Your Majesty," said the man with the golden ringlets, bowing as he spoke.

I was surprised I could hear him, but I supposed that whatever I was seeing wasn't bound to the physical laws that governed the world.

"It's no trouble at all, Count Glint. You're always fine company," said the man in the crown. The woman at his side didn't speak, but the way her eyes worked their way over the count made it clear what she was thinking.

The image faded, and across the ship played another scene. I moved over to it. The count and the queen were wrapped in a lover's embrace. She was clutching at him almost desperately while he lifted her and carried her to a space I presumed had once held a bed. The image faded before things got too interesting, and another vignette appeared, this time at the port side. Count Glint was standing against the railing, surrounded by men with spears. One man was holding back a crying queen, and the king stood stone-faced, regarding the count.

"You're going to die for this!" The king shook his head, facing down, then looked toward his wife. "How could you?"

The count smiled. "She did it with enthusiasm, I'm happy to say."

"Silence! Men, kill this wretch!"

Count Glint widened his eyes in mock surprise before smiling. He opened his mouth, and a burst of flame enveloped the spearman in front of him. He then calmly walked toward the king, speaking as he did so.

"You should be honored. I don't choose just any man's wife to sleep with." He chopped through the neck of two spearmen who attacked him with his left hand, sending a spray of blood across the deck. "Actually—" he smiled. "Come to think of it, I'm not that picky."

The king was cowering against the deck when the count reached him. "My...my Lord, I had no idea it was you. I beg your forgiveness. Please, just spare me and my queen."

Count Glint reached down toward the king and snapped his neck with a single movement of his hand. He looked across the now burning deck over at the queen. "Good luck, Myrdith, and you're welcome."

He launched himself into the air, golden scales covering him as he exploded into a great winged beast and flew into the night.

The image faded, replaced by a woman holding desperately onto a piece of timber, sobs racking her body as she floated slowly west toward the shore. After a few moments, that image faded as well, and I was left in the dark.

The specter of the king appeared, this time alone and

staring directly at me. He looked me up and down, then nodded, seemingly satisfied. I began moving toward him, but he vanished before I'd taken my first step. I stood in the dark for a few moments.

I'd witnessed something important, that much was clear. Count Glint had to be related somehow to the children of Aurum, which meant that they had something to do with dragons. It should have been obvious in retrospect. The goblin chief had flown a banner with a dragon on it and spoken a word of draconic, Donyin had been covered in scales, and Vash had grown a tail of gold. Dragons weren't something that any of my essences knew much about because they'd been extinct for a long time. Pebble only knew that they'd all been killed, but his focus had always been in practical dungeoneering studies, and Sevald's knowledge of them had mostly to do with a childhood dream of slaying one like an ancient knight. Still, it was a place to start.

The coincidence of it was strange. I just happened to fall into the ocean in such a way that my path would cross this sunken ship? That didn't feel like a realistic possibility. I felt a kind of unease in my straps, like I was being pulled in directions without my consent. Considering the effects of divinity on me, that proved deeply unsettling.

I checked my internal compass and began making my way west again. Myrdith had floated in that direction, so with any luck, the debris from the Eastland ships would've also drifted that way. If I was truly fortunate, my companions would already be there searching for me, assuming they'd convinced Jase to take the risk.

After about a day of walking, the ground began to slant in a distinctly upward direction. When I scaled the first sandbar, I could see the beach in the distance, a scattering of debris strewn across it, and a ship anchored at its northern end. I aimed for the southern shore, slowly and carefully making my way in that direction.

I emerged to the sound of screaming seagulls and a firm ocean breeze. I then practiced a kind of rolling stumble as I made my way to the northern part of the beach. When I started getting closer to the boat, a group of men combing the beach pointed at me and hollered back toward the ship.

Soon, a group of people was making their way toward me. Kyren, Stone, and Dorsia were leading a smattering of sailors in my direction. I fell to my knees in front of them as they reached me. Kyren placed her hands on my chestplate, and I screamed internally as she cast a healing spell, but I allowed it to keep up the masquerade.

"Sevald, thank the gods you're okay!" Kyren wrapped her arms around me in a hug.

"Water," I muttered in my raspiest voice.

Dorsia grabbed a flask from her belt, opened it, and handed it to me. I tilted my helmet away from them and swung it back as if I hadn't had fresh water in days, which, as far as they knew, was true.

"Thank you," I said, pushing myself to my feet, faltering slightly to sell the impression I'd been through an ordeal. "I'm surprised you're here. I would've thought you'd be in Buryn by now."

"We couldn't leave you behind, lad," said Stone, clasping as close to my shoulder plate as he could reach.

"How did you convince Captain Jase?" I asked.

"Jade did. She's been holding him at claw point for two days now," said Dorsia.

"She is? I'm surprised she'd do that for me."

"She said that if we found you, it would clear the debt she feels she owes you."

"What about you, how'd you survive? What even happened?" asked Kyren.

"A child of Aurum happened. An orcish sea-captain named Vash. I was her target, not the ship."

"That explains why they trapped you, but not the wreckage."

"A kraken. It came out of nowhere and destroyed the ship. I managed to hold on to a particularly big piece of driftwood, and eventually, I floated to the shore."

"Driftwood? Really?" asked Stone. Kyren and Dorsia looked incredulous, as well.

It was the best I could come up with. By all accounts, I should be dead. "Yeah, it's all a bit of a haze, though."

As I finished speaking, Jade and Hrig arrived. Hrig wrapped me in an embrace, letting out a quiet, "I knew you'd make it." I returned the gesture with a strong squeeze of my own, then turned my attention to Jade. "Thank you. I heard what you did for me."

I held out a hand. She grasped it firmly.

"We're nearly even now, though honestly, I was just the first to act. I'm fairly certain everyone else was moments away from the same. I even saw Kyren start to move toward Jase with a dagger before I made my move."

I looked at Kyren, who simply shrugged in acknowledgement.

"And where is Jase now?" I looked around. "And where are the rest of the sailors, for that matter?"

We all turned our attention to the *Nedra*, which was pulling up a small rowboat filled with the crew off the beach. Jase was standing on the deck making a particularly rude gesture. The *Nedra*'s sails opened, and it began heading back to sea.

"Can't blame him," said Stone, scratching his beard "We did hold him hostage for a while."

"Well," said Hrig. "I guess that means we're walking the rest of the way."

15
BURYN DOWN THE HOUSE

The rest of the day was spent making our way to the main road. Dorsia was carving a path through the forest with a short sword while Hrig dragged me on a sled assembled from the wreckage of the Eastland ships. Once we reached the road, I managed to convince Hrig and Kyren to let me walk some of the way.

Stone was looking around at landmarks, concern showing on his face.

"We're lucky the *Nedra* took us most of the way. It should only be another day or so to Buryn," said Dorsia.

"That's good. We won't miss our meeting with Clara," said Kyren.

"Hopefully, the work she arranged is outside of the city. I'd prefer not to draw too much attention," said Hrig.

"Hmm, perhaps we could cross some more forest to a side road. Might save you some trouble," said Stone.

"No reason to leave the main road for my sake."

"It would only take us another day," Stone insisted, uncharacteristically flustered.

"It's fine, let's just keep moving."

We walked in silence for a while before reaching a small roadside inn. The sign read Nevier's Retreat, and under the lettering was a depiction of a spear piercing a shield that could only be described as...provocative. Everyone in the party came to a stop except for Stone, who kept moving doggedly forward.

"Shall we spend the night here?" asked Dorsia.

"No!" said Stone, startling everyone. "I mean, why spend the gold when we could just camp?"

"Our bedrolls were on the ship. I'd prefer not to sleep on hard ground," said Jade.

"Well, I mean, the inn is clearly a place of ill repute. I can't imagine Kyren would want to spend a night there."

"I don't mind, actually. Such places are important to Nevier's worship. It would be disrespectful for me not to take shelter in such a place based on some type of holier than thou attitude."

"But—"

"Sevald was clinging to a board in the ocean yesterday. Would you really deny him an opportunity to sleep in a bed after that?" asked Hrig.

Stone's mouth opened, but thinking better of speaking, he let out a breath, and with it, all resistance. "Fine, but let me take the lead. I'll have to get something out of the way."

The group parted and let him lead the way up to the entrance. He pushed it open, and we all filed in behind him. The world outside of the inn contrasted so sharply with the inside that it took me several moments to even register what I was seeing. The entire interior was painted a soft shade of pink, and it smelled heavily of perfume and incense. Tapestries along the wall depicted acts that Byn couldn't have imagined, Sevald could only dream of, Pebble could only understand academically, and Syven had actively enjoyed.

Leaning luxuriantly against a bar was a dwarven woman

wearing a loose purple silk robe. She was very well-proportioned, even with her stout frame, her pink hair woven into a large braid down her back. She looked in our direction with heavily made-up eyes and a relaxed expression that shifted into an odd mix of surprise, concern, and disdain as soon as they settled on Stone.

"Dad!?"

Stone smiled sheepishly. "Hi, Sapphire. Been awhile."

"Been awhile?" She stood up and walked over to him until she stood close enough to grab his beard. "Is that really all you have to say to me?"

"No, it's more like that was all I could think to say in the moment."

"Don't try to be clever. What're you doing here? I thought you might be dead!"

"My friends and I are traveling, and we just want a place to sleep for the night."

"Oh, of course, you're here for rooms. That makes more sense than being here to see me."

"That's not fair! I visited just two years ago!"

"For a night! And that was after not seeing you for three years before!"

"Well, excuse me for not wanting to sleep in my daughter's brothel!"

"It's a temple; it just happens to serve multiple purposes. Besides, you didn't seem to have any trouble with brothels after Mom died. Why should this one be any different?"

I stood, stunned, along with the rest of the party as the back and forth continued. As they yelled, a mix of men and women in makeup and various states of undress shuffled into the room to check on the noise. They would see Stone, sigh, and move on to whatever business they'd interrupted. Clearly, as surprising as the situation was for us, it wasn't anything unusual for them.

Kyren moved to stand next to Stone. "Excuse me, I'm sorry to interrupt. I can tell you both have a lot to talk about, but my companion here," she gestured to me, "just spent a day adrift at sea and could use a meal and a soft bed."

Sapphire gained control of her emotions and looked us over. "Since you're friends of my father, I'll give you half-price rooms, but you," she pointed at Stone, "pay double."

"Come on, Sapphire, I'm family!"

"You're lucky I'm letting you stay at all." She returned her attention to the rest of the party. "The rooms and food are half-price, but priests set their own rates if their attention is something you're interested in."

"Thank you." Kyren gave a solemn nod.

Sapphire clapped her hands and attendants came and started guiding us to our rooms. She then began arguing with Stone again in earnest. As I left the room, I heard a complaint from him about her shaving her beard followed up by one from her that he should understand how that would hurt the business she got from elves, which caused him to turn a shade of red that contrasted quite nicely with the pink walls.

The attendant leading me was a half orc. She was pressing herself into me in a way that felt both pleasant and uncomfortable. I looked for something to say in order to distract myself, when her outfit caught my attention. It was made up of leather straps of a fine quality that were somehow dyed a deep blue. From what I understood from Byn, blue was an exceptionally rare shade that needed a special process to create.

The woman gave a sultry smile. "See something you like?"

"That color is interesting. How was it made?"

She looked startled for a moment. "Uh, the blood of cave drake was used to dye it. They bleed blue. My clan developed the technique over a number of years."

"I've used oxblood to achieve a red color, but I didn't realize that shade of blue was possible."

We arrived at the room, and she unlocked the door.

"Here you go." She gestured toward the bed. "And if you'd like any company, I'll give you a special rate. Normally, all I hear is how exotic it is to see an orc girl here. It's nice to talk about my old trade, for a change."

"I, uh, think I'm too tired for that kind of activity, but thank you. It was nice to talk to you, too."

"If you change your mind, feel free to ask for me. My name is Sade." She smiled and left the room.

I sat on the bed for several minutes, noting that the room itself was oddly quiet, considering the activities that were likely going on in the adjacent spaces. Eventually, I stood up and began making my way to the door, thinking I should check in on my companions, but there was a knock before I could reach it. I steeled myself for a polite but firm no to whichever priest of Nevier was waiting on the other side, but when I opened it, I was surprised to see Jade.

"Oh, hi, Jade." I backed away from the door as she let herself into the room. "Is there something I can do for you?"

She took a deep breath and turned to me. "I still owe you. I think I have a way to repay you, but I needed to talk to you alone."

I looked at her, the bed, and the large tapestry above it, and felt a kind of heat wash over me. "Th-that's fine, Jade. You don't owe me anything. You made Jase turn around. I might be dead otherwise."

"No, you wouldn't be. Your friends would've done it if I hadn't. Besides, we both know you would've been fine."

"No, I wouldn't't've. It was sheer luck that I survived. I'd be dead if you hadn't been there to meet me."

"You can drop the act."

I tensed up and maneuvered myself to lean against the doorframe in case I needed to keep her from leaving. "I don't know what you're talking about."

"You knew how to invoke my runes, you fought and killed Donyin, your armor heals itself, and you survived a kraken attack that sank the vessel you were on, and somehow got to shore wearing full plate. I don't know what you are, but I do know you're not human. I assume your companions haven't figured it out because they don't want to. Their affection for you is clouding their judgment."

I tensed, feeling as if the floor itself would fall out from under me next. "You haven't told them, then?"

She shook her head. "No, and with that, you can consider us even."

I moved out of the doorway. "Really?"

"Really." She held out her right hand and showed her palm. The dwarven rune for "deal." I reached out and took her hand, invoking the rune as I did so. I felt something pass between us.

"I can see why your friends are so willing to ignore the obvious. Everything I've seen you do so far makes it clear you care for them. Maybe you should consider telling them yourself?" She opened the door and walked out into the hall.

I stayed in my room the rest of the night, pondering the conversation I'd had with Jade. When it was morning, I made my way out toward the dining area, squeezing past a particularly robust elven woman on the way. None of my companions were there except for Stone, passed out at the bar next to his daughter, who was leaning against him, also unconscious. I watched them for a few moments, listening to them snore, until someone approached from behind.

"This happens every time," said Sade, no longer wearing her blue leather and instead in a simple blouse and skirt. She draped a blanket over the sleeping dwarves.

"Really? They're always like this?"

"Yeah, he'll come here, she'll yell at him, they'll drink and make up."

"Seems...difficult."

"It probably is, but it's also better than never seeing one another. Breakfast?"

I nodded, and she made her way behind the bar to a galley kitchen. I heard a fire start, and rather than sit alone, I went to join her.

"Need any help?"

Sade laughed. "Sweet of you to offer, but I don't want to have to manage you while I'm cooking breakfast for a houseful of exhausted Nevier priests. They build up quite an appetite."

"I promise I won't be underfoot. I've spent a lot of time in kitchens."

"Alright, fine. I'll work on the porridge, you—"

"I'll fry up the bread from dinner, make some rice to thicken the porridge, and throw some slices of ham in with the bread." I eased into the kitchen, leaning hard on Syven's experience.

As I cooked, Sade began making her way into the dining area, speaking with people as they woke up and taking out plates as I finished them. Soon, I was working in the kitchen alone. I could taste the quality of each dish without actually needing to sample it, so I added spices until they all met Syven's strict standards. Eventually, Sade eased back into the kitchen and forced me to leave with a plate of my own in hand. When I entered the dining room, I was met with enthusiastic applause.

"Thank you," I responded, giving a small bow while carefully avoiding spilling the food from my plate. I took a seat next to Hrig at the edge of the table and began the careful dance of pretending to eat.

"Where'd you learn to cook?" asked Kyren.

"Just something I picked up. You'd be surprised at how much you can learn just by paying attention to what you're eating."

Stone and Sapphire were awake and eating at the bar.

"Have you seen that before?" I asked.

"No. I knew Stone had daughters, but I didn't know he had one so close, much less one in service of a god like myself," said Kyren.

"Come to think of it, he's diverted us past this road a number of times. Though usually, he said it was because he owed someone money, which with him was believable and may have been true. I could see him owing his daughter money," said Hrig.

"I've actually been here before, though I met his daughter in a different context," said Dorsia with a smile and no trace of shame.

Hrig chuckled, clasping her on the shoulder. After we finished eating, we collected our things and waited by the door. After he'd finished his breakfast, Stone joined us, with Sapphire close behind.

"I hope you all enjoyed your stay. I know a couple of you did," said Sapphire, her eyes on Dorsia and Jade.

"Thank you for your hospitality," said Kyren with a slight nod.

"Thank you for your being such a good guest." Sapphire turned her attention to me and tossed me a small sack of coins —where she'd retrieved them from was beyond me. "That's for acting as our chef this morning. Come visit again, I'm sure Sade would like to see you."

I nodded, noticing a stare from Hrig as I did so.

"And you—" Sapphire turned to Stone, "—please visit more often. I know you see Ruby twice as much and Diamond three times as often."

"It's hard to visit ya here, and don't pretend you don't know why."

"Well, maybe if you weren't moving around all over the place, I could visit you once in a while."

"That's fair, love. I'll try to do better."

They gave each other a warm embrace, and we walked out of the inn and started back on the road to Buryn.

16

SCARS

The rest of the road was busy as the party started to come into contact with other travelers on their way to the city. Unlike the people on the way to Cirros who were mostly farmers, adventurers, and a few nobles, those on the road to Buryn seemed to be primarily merchants pulling wagons of raw goods and their guards. Buryn was where the majority of manufacturing took place within Caedun. It sat east of the capital, and between the two cities were the estates of the nobility. Sevald had been born in the capital and so had visited Buryn a handful of times.

Everyone seemed refreshed from their night at the Sevier Inn, though Stone was clearly hungover. Hrig was slouching to hide her height and attempting to conceal herself with one of Kyren's cloaks, though due to its size, the cover it provided was almost comically limited.

The city came into view, surrounded by a wall of blue-gray stone over which flew flags of dark green. Passing through the city gates, there were rows upon rows of buildings crammed together tightly. People were equally pressed and walked around with their heads down, avoiding eye contact with one another. We pushed our way through the crowd and found a small pocket free of activity.

"I think this is where I'll take my leave," said Dorsia.

"Are you sure? I don't know about everyone else, but I'd be happy to have you along if you'd like," said Kyren.

"Aye, it's been good to see you again. I'd hate to see it end," said Stone.

"I like you. It's as simple as that for me," agreed Hrig.

"I appreciate it, but I'm no adventurer. A thief, a brawler, a gambler—those are the distinctions I'm most comfortable with."

"I'm going with you," said Jade.

"I figured as much. You still owe me, after all, and an enforcer would certainly help me speed things up while I get settled here." Dorsia started pulling out rings, small coin purses, and a few gold buttons and handed them to Stone. "For old times' sake. Don't be a stranger."

Stone gave her a hug, and for a moment, her usually wry smile turned into a genuine one. We all said our goodbyes, and they faded into the crowd. I shared one final, intense glance with Jade, and then our party was back to its original four members, excepting my replacement of Sevald, of course.

Kyren looked over to Stone, held out her hand, and coughed.

"Really? But they were gifts! Surely, you wouldn't deprive me of all I'll have to remember her by."

"Oh, you can keep what she gave you, but let's not pretend you weren't practicing the skills you taught her on the way in yourself. She learned from you, after all."

Stone obliged with only moderate grumbling, providing every third item he pulled from discreet pockets to her in their little ritual.

"Care to join me while I make this donation in your honor? I may need help putting out a few feelers to see what we can dig up about these 'Sons of Aurum'."

"Aye, I can help you with that." He turned his attention to us. "Clara is going to meet us at the Craven Raven. Do you know it?"

"Know it? I've practically lived there. We'll meet you," said Hrig.

Hrig led the way as we weaved our way through the busy streets of Buryn. The strange smells of the manufacturing district lingered as we crossed into the slums. Tall stacks of buildings that appeared to be almost leaning from their weight cast the streets in shadow despite the sun's height in the sky.

Eventually, those buildings gave way, and in the distance, I could make out a towering circular structure that my meal's memories told me was the coliseum. Hrig was glancing at it, too, a somber expression barely visible under the hood of Kyren's cloak.

Eventually, we reached the Craven Raven, which was signified by a sign depicting a raven hiding behind a mug of ale. Hrig pushed her way in and made a beeline for a booth in the corner. I followed her closely. The tavern was decorated in muted shades of brown, and staff was cleaning floors and repairing furniture. Clearly, they'd had a busy night.

Hrig sat down and pulled off her hood, pulling her blond braids out of it and resting her head on the wall behind her.

"Are you alright?" I asked.

"No, but it's okay. Been awhile since I've been back."

"Did you miss it at all?"

She smiled and pointed at the corner of the table nearest me. It was rounded where every other corner was sharp. "That's from when I cracked a man's head who didn't like hearing no." She pointed at the far wall, which was a slightly lighter shade than the wall around it. "That's where I was thrown for taking liberties with an orcish woman's husband." She gestured toward my chair. "Is it a little uneven?"

"Yeah, the back left leg is short."

"I'm impressed it's together at all. I smashed it over the bartender's back once." Her face became pensive. "My memories of this place are like that, too. They are painful, but time has smoothed them over, covered them up, and sometimes even turned them into something useful. I do miss it, but I also know it isn't home anymore."

I nodded. "Distance makes memories easier to understand, but being in the place they were made can be overwhelming."

"Overwhelming is a good word for it."

A staff member came over with a mug of ale and a cup of wine, setting them down in front of us. "That's from Cole. He says welcome back."

Hrig nodded and raised her cup in the direction of the bartender, who nodded in her direction. She then took a slow, steady sip, which I mimicked. We sat in silence for some time after that. It wasn't an uncomfortable one, just thoughtful. Getting to know people had a kind of intoxicating, warm feeling to it. Having to learn about people piecemeal through their words and actions as well as how other people act and speak with them was an engaging process. I had access to the memories of four people, but those had been taken. The knowledge I had of my companions was earned, and that gave it greater value.

The door to the Craven Raven opened. Stone and Kyren walked in, looked around, and then approached the table.

"Clara been here yet?" asked Stone.

"Not yet," said Hrig.

"Did you find anything at the temple?" I asked.

"Nothing concrete. The elders shut down when I asked anything about the name Aurum or the prayers that use draconic. The only thing I was able to determine is that those rituals and prayers are among the oldest of the church, and they're meant to be used in rituals honoring the major gods as a whole rather than as individuals," said Kyren.

"Could Aurum be a god?"

Kyren looked troubled. "He shouldn't be. I mean, there are lesser gods and even gods that are no longer worshipped, but the idea of there being another of the highest of gods that is unknown? It would be a very difficult thing to hide."

"Donyin said he was a son of Aurum. Is that possible? A god having a mortal child?"

"Jeiri is said to have sired several dwarven heroes. I'm named after one," chimed Stone.

"There are certainly legends of it happening, but all of those are ancient."

"So we have some information, but nothing concrete and nothing truly reliable?" asked Hrig.

"Apparently," said Kyren.

"Then we should just take some jobs and move on. Talen is all the way in Cirros, possibly dead, and we don't know where any more of these children of Aurum are. No reason to get bogged down in it."

"Agreed," I said.

"Seems to me the information will likely come to us anyway, or at least to Sevald," said Stone.

I sighed heavily. "You're probably right."

Kyren patted me on the shoulder. "I'll get you another ale." She went over to the bar.

"One for you and four for her, I'm guessing," said Stone.

We sat drinking and conversing for a while, and as the wine

flowed, Hrig started telling the stories of the life she'd had in Buryn, hunting rats to eat in the slums, raising a brother and sister, and earning a living in the arena.

"I wasn't aware you had siblings. Are they off adventuring, too?"

Hrig's expression turned dour. "They passed away several years ago. The rot took them. If they were alive, I'd have hoped they'd have been married away and safe, but they likely would've made their way to the arena like I had."

The table went quiet, and I took my gauntlet and held it out to her. She looked surprised for a moment, but gave it a firm squeeze and me a small smile.

The tavern door opened, and a woman wearing a dark blue dress with a distinct red cameo brooch walked in. She was tan, with dark hair flowing behind her. She looked over the tavern, which had gotten busier as night began to fall, and her eyes settled on our table.

"Stone! Kyren! Hrig!" She waved as she approached. "How is my favorite group of adventurers?" Her gaze turned to me. "And this must be Sevald. A pleasure."

She held out a white-gloved hand, and I took it.

"Likewise," I said.

Clara sat down and slid one of Kyren's ale mugs over to herself, which drew an eyebrow raise, but no comment. She then took a hearty sip.

"I have a new job for you. A noble requested you all specifically, in fact."

"Details?" asked Stone.

"A noble's family tomb is infested. Skeletons, ghosts, zombies; all the usual suspects."

"A necromancer?" asked Kyren. She had gone from her usual small smile and relaxed expression to leaning forward with an intense look I had only seen her wear in the most dire circumstances.

"Possibly, but it hasn't been confirmed." Clara looked toward the door. "The noble himself actually wanted to be here to tell you the details."

As if on cue, a man entered the tavern. He was tall and lean with long brown hair and pale skin, wearing a simple black satin doublet over a crisp white shirt. Clearly an attempt to dress down, but the quality of the clothes and his bearing signaled him as a noble right away.

Hrig's wine cup shattered in her grip. I turned my attention to her and saw a look of disbelief. The nobleman walked over to the table, his eyes focused on Hrig.

"Hello, Duchess."

Hrig stood up, pushing away from the table. "He's the one that asked for us?" she asked Clara.

"Ah, yes. This is the Duke of Wyther. He's the one who wants to hire you."

"I understand that you don't want to see me, but is this really the proper reaction to seeing your husband again after all these years?"

"Husband!?" I felt the words slide out of my faceplate before I could stop them.

Hrig turned red. "You still didn't divorce me? Just move on!"

"I can't, you know I can't."

"We aren't taking the job. Let's go, everyone." Hrig moved to leave.

"Wait, wait, wait. I really do need help."

"I don't care."

"You have a stake in this, too!"

"How?"

"Where do you think I had your brother and sister buried?"

Hrig stopped, her mouth hanging open in surprise. She sat back down. "Talk."

Clara stole another of Kyren's ales and drank deeply, her forehead now covered with beads of sweat. I couldn't blame her—if I'd been capable of it, I likely would've been in a similar state.

"It started a few months ago. The gravekeeper disappeared while digging a plot for one of the servant staff. I sent some other servants to investigate, and they told me they saw a skeleton walking along the edge of the graveyard. I tried contacting the guard, but apparently, they're short-staffed, as most of them are being drafted by the crown. I need help, Hrig, and you're the only person I could think of to ask for it."

"The pay?" asked Stone.

"One thousand gold pieces, and any treasures you find in the tomb are yours to keep."

Stone turned a pleading look to Hrig. "I'm with you if you refuse, you know I am, but that's a fantastic offer."

"He's good at those," hissed Hrig.

"I'm afraid I have to side with Stone here. It's my duty as a priestess of Sidi to end infestations of undead, particularly if a necromancer is involved."

Hrig sighed. "We'll do it, but I have one more condition."

"Go on," said Duke Wyther.

"A divorce."

The duke looked physically pained for a moment, but managed to spit out, "Deal."

17
WYTHER WITHOUT YOU

We left the tavern, and the duke escorted us to a pair of carriages. He gestured for Hrig to walk ahead and join him in the lead one, but she instead made straight for the second, and we filed in behind her. The carriages began rolling as we settled into our seats. I kept silent as long as I could before my curiosity overwhelmed me. Luckily, Stone beat me to it.

"So, is that why you were the 'duchess' of death?"

Hrig chuckled. "Yes, that's how I got it. Before I married, I was the 'Braided Butcher.' They really liked their alliteration."

"How'd you meet Duke Ellis?" asked Kyren.

I wondered if I'd missed him saying his name.

"He was a fan, my patron, in fact. He'd always throw a single flower onto the arena after each of my fights. One day, he asked me to join him at his estate for dinner, and I didn't want to offend him when the money he was providing was helping to get my siblings and me out of the slums. When we met, he confessed that he loved me and asked me to marry him. I was hesitant, but when he offered to adopt my brother and sister into his family, I agreed." She drew the curtain to glance out the window at the winding streets.

"Why'd you leave?" I asked.

"The rot... My brother and sister didn't get it from the slums; they got it at the estate when a member of the staff got sick. If I hadn't married him... I thought about staying, but the truth was I didn't love him, and everything here reminds me of what happened. So a few nights after they passed, I grabbed my favorite axe and left. I was hoping he'd move on, but clearly, he hasn't."

"Maybe this will be good for him. This could give you a chance to really say goodbye to one another," said Kyren.

Hrig didn't respond, just returned her attention to the window. We sat in silence the rest of the way.

It was evening when we arrived at the duke's estate—an enormous villa situated on an even more enormous piece of land. The leadup to the main building consisted of an elaborate garden filled with flowers and complex hedges, which surrounded everything in neat rows.

The main gate squealed as it opened for us, and the carriages made their way to the front door before coming to a complete stop. We exited, and Duke Ellis was there to meet us.

"Welcome. I wasn't sure whether or not you'd want to head for the tomb immediately or would require lodging for the night, so I had rooms prepared for each of you as well as a dinner, if you'd be so inclined."

"It's best to strike at such places in the daytime. I welcome your hospitality," said Kyren.

"Bed would be fine for me," said Hrig.

"Ah, of course... You know the way I—"

She walked through the doors without another word.

"I could eat," said Stone.

"As could I," said Kyren.

Ellis looked at a loss for a moment, but regained his composure and led the way inside. The manor's interior shared the splendor of its garden, the walls tastefully covered in tapestries and paintings and the floors with rugs of fine quality. Flowers from the garden had been trimmed and potted, giving the home a sweet smell.

We were led through a main dining room with a table that could've sat dozens and into a side room with a much more reasonably-sized dining area.

"I hope you don't mind. Hrig never felt comfortable in the main dining room, so I already had things prepared to eat in here."

"That's fine, lad. We're used to eating around a fire, so this is still a big improvement."

"Ah, of course."

I pulled out Kyren's chair, relying on Sevald's courtly manners to guide me. It may have been a servant's dining room, but it was still a duke's house. She sat, and then, we all joined her. The staff poured wine that I guessed was also likely Hrig's favorite.

The duke put on a smile that didn't meet his eyes, clearly trying to push past his disappointment at Hrig not joining us. I wasn't certain if my companions didn't realize he'd have preferred to be alone or they didn't care and just wanted to learn more about the man Hrig had called "husband." I assumed the latter.

"So, how are things in the south? Clara told me you travelled all the way from Entden."

"Bit of a mess, actually," said Stone, sampling some of the wine.

"Well, that's not surprising. Seems like there are shakeups happening everywhere lately. Caedun is rebuilding its military, the Eastland's raids have gotten more frequent as their clans have joined together, the barbarians to the north have cut off all trade, and two elvish barons to the west have gone independent. Everything seems to be in chaos lately. As soon as you hear one piece of news, there are three more waiting."

I noticed Kyren's ears twitch when the elvish barons were mentioned, but before I could ask her about it, the food arrived, a three-course meal with spiced eggs, roasted pheasant, and a simple soup topped off with a dessert of chilled fruit. I couldn't actually eat, but I could taste, and I appreciated the expertise of the chef.

After dinner, Ellis made a polite excuse to leave and went to his quarters. We were then led to our own separate rooms by members of his staff. I entered my room, not bothering to light any candles, and gently lowered myself onto the too-soft bed.

I lay there for a few hours, going through my memories and those of my essences while trying to sort out my feelings about the duke. He seemed like a nice man. A bit standoffish, clearly used to using some subtle manipulations to get what he wanted, but that was all typical of the nobility. Thinking of him independently didn't muster any strong feelings, but thinking of him with Hrig left a sharp pang that was only dulled by how I'd seen her act around him.

My door opened, and someone eased their way into my room.

"Hello?" I asked. The room was of such a size that I couldn't quite tell who had entered.

"It's me," said Hrig, approaching the bed.

"Is something wrong?"

"Can't sleep."

"Oh, well, I'm sure one of the servants can get you some wine, or Kyren could always knock you out, if you'd like."

"I was hoping for a more 'active' distraction."

I felt her sit down on the edge of the bed.

"M-my vows, Hrig."

"It's pitch black in here, Sevald. I can't see you. Though I assume you're hiding under the covers just in case. That's fine. I'm happy to join you under them."

She couldn't see me, but I could see her. She wore a tight silk robe, and her normally braided hair hung loose down her back. I felt somehow paralyzed and jumpy all at the same time. She slid closer, sliding under the covers next to me, and brought her hand to my chestplate.

She laughed, which wasn't exactly what I expected or preferred to hear.

"You even wear it to bed! Sevald, you're absolutely ridiculous! I have never met a man who takes a vow so seriously in my life." She shook her head and stood up, still lightly laughing. "I'm sorry, Sevald, I shouldn't have surprised you like this. I was just feeling a bit vulnerable."

I sat up, clanking awkwardly as I did so. "It's fine, but I... can't do what you ask of me. At least not under these circumstances." Or any others, unfortunately. "But if you can't sleep, how about I stay up with you? I doubt I'll be able to sleep myself after what just happened."

"I'll take that as a compliment," she said, standing and making her way carefully over to a nearby table to light a candle. She moved suspiciously well for someone who said she couldn't see.

I made my way over to a small table and sat with her.

"So, why can't you sleep?"

"How could anyone with a handsome knight so close by?"

I felt heat in my faceplate but didn't respond.

She chuckled at my discomfort. "I just don't like how I left things here, and the memories I have of this place are...hard to deal with."

"They can't all have been bad. I can't imagine you never had any good times here."

She looked thoughtful. "That's true. I remember once my brother actually managed to set fire to a portion of the hedges."

"Why did he do it?"

"It was an accident. He was attempting to use oil to burn an image into it. He thought the hedge was too green to actually catch fire."

"What was the image?"

"Let's just say it involved a sword and two shields."

I laughed, and Hrig joined me. We spent the rest of the night talking about her brother Gaius, her sister Hrid, and all the little adventures they'd had in the duke's estate.

Hrig slipped out and back to her room before dawn broke to avoid the servants telling Ellis where she'd been. She told me she didn't want to keep hurting him unnecessarily even if she still wanted to be apart from him.

I waited to hear the house wake up and made my way down to the dining area I'd been to before. The servant staff was disturbed that I hadn't waited to be walked down, and that I was still wearing my armor, but I ignored them, though I did make sure my boots were clean before I walked the halls. No reason to make their lives more difficult.

Stone, Kyren, Hrig, and Ellis were already there discussing strategy. I took a seat between Kyren and Stone, returning an acknowledging nod from Ellis as I sat.

"There are definitely traps throughout the tomb. Unfortunately, the only person who knew what and where all of them were was the gravekeeper. I also don't know how extensive the tomb actually is. As family members died, it was common to expand it underground, but I have no record of the size of the expansions or how they were done, not to mention any areas that may have fallen into disrepair. The gravekeepers would just teach their replacements those things."

"I can handle the traps," said Stone.

"Do you have any specifics about the types of undead that have been seen?" asked Kyren.

"Skeletons and zombies are all we've seen outside of the tomb, and only at night. I haven't let the servants out at night since the first sighting, though. There certainly could be more that we aren't aware of."

"Did you get the items I requested?"

"Yes." He gestured to the end of the table where some servants were placing long, heavy crates.

"Hrig, will you do the honors?" asked Kyren.

She nodded and opened the crates. There was a massive warhammer in one, a long-spiked club in another, and a small mace in the third.

"The undead don't stop coming at you due to a missing limb or a stab wound. Crushing has always been the most effective way to stop them," said Kyren.

"Yet another area where the hammer outdoes the axe," said Stone, who was rewarded with a dirty look from Hrig.

I lifted up the club, testing the balance. It weighed significantly more than my sword, but the change wouldn't affect me much. I gave it a few test swipes and was only a little disappointed in the whoosh of the club moving through the air compared to the swish of the sword moving through it.

We finished getting equipped and made our way to the estate's graveyard. It was empty when we arrived, and seemed at a glance to be just another portion of the estate's garden. Flowers bloomed, dripping morning dew, the grass well-trimmed, and the hedges that surrounded the estate bordered one edge of it. But the gray tombstones and large building in the center marked it out for what it was.

Before we entered, Hrig handed Ellis her axe. "I'll be back for this. We'll talk when I return. My conditions are the same, but I think we should clear the air."

"I'd like that," said Ellis, doing his best not to let the weight of the axe cause a dip in his posture.

We entered the graveyard carefully, looking for signs of disturbed graves or any movement. We saw several open graves, but nothing was lying in wait within them.

As we made our way to the mausoleum in the center, I felt something tug at my leg. I looked down, and a skeletal hand had wrapped itself around what would be my ankle. I swung my club downward and crushed the hand with a satisfying crunch. As I did so, five more skeletons rose from the dirt, and the one whose hand I crushed also rose, wrapping itself around me.

I started pulling the skeleton off myself piece by piece, but whatever magic was holding it together simply drew those pieces back to it, so I began crushing the pieces with my hands as I pulled them off.

While I was occupied, Stone was fighting a skeleton to my right. The one he faced wielded a small knife and swung at him wildly. Stone slid between the skeleton's legs, smooth as silk, and brought his hammer down hard on its spine. The skeleton fell, and Stone leveled another strike at its skull, smashing it to dust.

The skeleton facing Hrig was in pieces before I was even done removing one arm of the one that had wrapped around me. Kyren was facing the remaining three who had surrounded her. One closed in on her from behind.

"Kyren, watch out!"

Just as they lunged at her, she held up her hand and gold light flashed around her in a small sphere. The skeletons around her simply collapsed, returning to their previous inert state.

"Wow," I said, crushing the skull that was holding on to my pauldron with its teeth. I'd forgotten how effective Kyren's magic could be.

"Well, I'd say that was a solid warmup," said Hrig.

"The fact that they were lying in wait implies they're being guided somehow, as does the state of the cemetery," said Kyren.

"How do ya mean?" asked Stone.

"The occasional skeleton rising from an unkempt grave is common. They're just dissatisfied with how they're being treated and lashing out. This graveyard is well-tended, though, and the skeletons were waiting here as a trap. I think we have a necromancer on our hands."

"How do you know all of this?" I asked. "I knew that priests as a whole were against undead of any kind, but you seem to know more than is expected."

"Priests of Sidi are tasked with the removal of the undead. Respecting the Ancient includes respecting the dead and the lives they lived. It's our sacred duty to end the type of disrespect a necromancer brings to them."

"Well, let's head on and help you perform your priestly duties," said Stone.

"It's nice to be able to perform a religious rite that involves smashing things. It should be more common," said Hrig.

18

UNDEAD UNDEAD UNDEAD

We entered the tomb, and the doors closed slowly behind us, letting only the smallest amount of daylight in through the cracks. Kyren summoned an orb of light and set it above the group, illuminating our surroundings. The mausoleum was ornate, with marble walls and carvings of the deceased sculpted onto the top of the sarcophagi that contained them.

I ran my hand over one of them. "Why weren't these disturbed?"

"Those who are remembered by the still living are much harder to raise. These are likely some of Ellis's most honored ancestors who are well known by many in Caedun."

I nodded and began leading the way toward a stairway pushing deeper into the tomb.

"Wait, let me take the lead. I'll look out for traps," said Stone.

He began muttering ancient dwarven, and his eyes turned the color of his namesake. He directed his stone sense around and took the lead, navigating the group around a pitfall trap, a falling axe, and an extending spear. Soon, we found ourselves in a portion of the tomb that seemed less well-maintained than the entrance, but still new. We entered and began searching the room.

Two medium-sized statues stood against a wall, behind which I assumed were their remains. The faces of the statues were young and seemed vaguely familiar. Hrig approached them, putting her hammer to the side to gently touch their faces.

"They haven't been disturbed," she said.

"No. I don't believe the necromancer could've used them even if he'd wanted to. Your memories of them are far too strong for that," said Kyren.

Hrig turned and put a hand on her shoulder, smiling in spite of the wetness in her eyes.

"Duck!" yelled Stone.

They obliged, falling forward as a boney creature flew through the entrance and landed against the wall behind them. Hrig rolled forward to grab her hammer as Kyren ran toward me, taking cover behind my bulk.

The monster began to unfurl itself—a snakelike beast made up of human bones. Its teeth were ribs, its eyes hollowed-out skulls, and its body a horrifying amalgamation of everything else. The sound of its movement echoed that of dry bones grinding against each other.

It coiled up again and launched itself in my direction using its tail as a spring. I raised my shield and blocked the strike, but the force of it threw me back into the far wall. I moved forward and struck at it with my club, but it had already coiled and sprung itself at Hrig, so I hit nothing but air.

Hrig struck, attempting to time her blow with the snake's and smack him backward with her hammer, but her timing was off and she took a blow to her side, forcing her to roll with the hit.

Stone called out to it. "Over here, you ugly bastard!"

The creature turned its attention to him and launched itself, but Stone moved at the last moment and the creature slammed into the wall, which broke as it hit, leaving him embedded in it. Before it could extricate itself, Kyren reached the wall and placed her hand on its tail. After a brief golden glow, its pieces all scattered, tumbling out of the hole the creature had made.

"I saw that the wall was weak there," said Stone, gesturing to his still slate-gray eyes. "Figured we'd need to keep the thing from moving."

"Good idea," said Kyren, looking over the now inert pile of bones. "Our necromancer was experimenting when he made this. We'll have to be cautious; looks like it's not just going to be skeletons and zombies, after all."

The group nodded, and we started making our way deeper into the tomb, reaching an area where dirt was beginning to poke through tile and cracks covered the walls. We were about to exit a narrow hallway into a larger room when a low groan drifted from it.

"Zombies," whispered Kyren.

"Can you cast another spell to take care of them all at once?" asked Hrig.

"No, my spells don't work as well on undead who still have flesh. It would damage but not destroy them."

Stone held out a hand for us to wait and moved to the edge of the hallway. I watched him slowly drive a hook into the first wall, tie a rope to it, and then put a hook at the other side and tie the rope again. He then returned to us.

"Let's draw them in," he said, and we all nodded.

Kyren sent out the orb of light she had, following us into the room ahead to an eruption of groans, then she pulled the light back to us. The first zombie came into view, all rotting flesh and exposed bone. It hit Stone's rope and fell. Stone then calmly moved to it and crushed its skull with his hammer, sending bits of viscera flying.

Hrig and I took places next to him as more zombies lumbered in, tripped, and we brained them. After a few waves of this, the zombies were no longer tripping over the rope, but instead were tripping over the corpses of the others.

"This doesn't seem very sporting," said Hrig as she slammed her hammer down onto another of them.

"You'd rather have waded into them and swinging wildly, hoping for the best?" asked Stone.

"Well, yes."

He sighed, looking over to me. "Do I not understand women, or is it that there are only strange ones in my life?"

"Both, I think," I said, stomping on another zombie's head.

After the groans ceased, we climbed over the pile of former undead and made our way into the room they'd come from. It had a high ceiling and rows of opened coffins and mining equipment.

We started moving down another hallway, Stone still leading the way watching for traps. The warm glow of torchlight came into view, and a muttering voice echoed around us. Scraps of words like "tendon," "fresh," and "bled" were all that could be made out of it.

Kyren dismissed her orb, and we all began moving more cautiously forward to peer into the room. First, a large atrium lit by torches. Dozens of skeletons were scattered around the room, lying on tables, the tops of sarcophagi, and sometimes just loosely laid on the floor.

A single man stood on a large white stool in the center of the room. He wore a black robe and was standing over what looked to be an enormous body. Sounds of squelching and tearing could be heard as he shifted his arms through it.

Stone gestured for us to wait and began moving slowly

toward the robed figure while we readied ourselves to charge. Stone moved carefully, his hammer slung low in his hands, the torchlight throwing strange shadows across the floor. The necromancer didn't move, just continued his work, lost in what he was doing.

Stone got within a few steps of him and raised his hammer to strike. He made two swift steps forward and brought the hammer down.

A skeletal arm emerged from the cloak and grabbed the hammer, stalling its advance.

"I'm trying to work!" yelled the robed figure.

His stool moved, and I realized it wasn't a stool, but a platform held up by dozens of skeletal legs, one of which kicked Stone across the room.

We charged to Stone, taking a defensive posture around him as he recovered. As he stood, the various skeletons that had been in the process of being repaired began standing and moving toward us. Unlike the ones we'd encountered before, these paused to pick up shovels, pickaxes, and anything they could use as weapons. The necromancer himself kept working on the massive corpse which, now that we were closer, I could tell was some kind of horrifying amalgamation of multiple bodies.

"Keep them off of me; I have to prepare a spell!" yelled Kyren. She then sat and began muttering

We circled around her as the skeletons closed in. I deflected a pickaxe strike off of my shield and slammed my club into my attacker, smashing through his shoulder. Another of them charged me with a shovel, but I knocked the head of the shovel downward with the club's pommel and drove it into the dirt, then I kicked the skeleton back into two others.

They started attacking more swiftly, and I gave up on being able to block every hit, instead letting anything less than a pickaxe bounce off my armor while making wide sweeping strikes to hold them back. I found myself pushed back as more skeletons pressed into us, using their sheer numbers in an attempt to overwhelm. If I had been alone, I'd have been able to simply wade into them, but with Kyren still preparing her spell behind me, it wasn't an option.

After crushing another of them, I got closer to Kyren and found myself brushing elbows with Hrig and being uncomfortably close to hitting Stone with the bottom of my shield.

"A bit of haste may be in order," he said, kneecapping the nearest skeleton.

"Yeah, I prefer not to be close enough to Stone to smell him," said Hrig.

I slammed my shield into the row of skeletons in front of me, and at that moment, Kyren stood and released a burst of holy energy that erupted outward, slamming into the skeletons and also, unfortunately, into me. The skeletons fell apart into piles of bones, and I collapsed to my knees, my essence reeling from the damage her holy spell had sent outward.

I struggled to my feet quickly, trying to give the appearance that I'd just briefly lost my balance, and heard high-pitched laughter. The necromancer was still standing over his horrifying creation, his arms raised up in elation. The creature began to sit up. The golem of flesh groaned as it brought itself to its full height, which reached almost to the ceiling.

The look on Kyren's face was one of absolute hatred and disgust. She stood from her meditative pose, and a halo of golden light enveloped her head, her eyes sharing the glow.

"Focus on the monster. The necromancer is mine."

Hrig and Stone moved to help me up, and I drew up my club and shield as the flesh beast made its way toward us.

The necromancer threw aside his robe, revealing two more skeletal hands that seemed to be fused with the flesh of his back. His fleshed and unfleshed hands moved in strange motions, creating arcane symbols, and a ghostly hand shot toward Kyren, who dismissed it with a bolt of light from her own hand. They began trading spells, sending energies toward one another, dodging or dismissing them, and starting again in a dazzling display of power.

Just as they were heating up, the flesh golem began its assault. He slammed his fists down at me, forcing me back. Stone and Hrig both landed heavy blows on his legs, but he swept one enormous hand behind himself, forcing them to dodge. He then lifted a sarcophagus lid and threw it at me. It spun through the air, and I ducked, hearing the wall crack as it slammed into it.

I charged, deflecting a heavy strike and slamming my club down on its hand. There was a crunch, but the beast made no indication it felt any pain. His other hand hit me in the back and sent me sparking across the stone floor. I was moving sluggishly, still trying to regain my composure after Kyren's spell.

I looked up to see Hrig and Stone leaping onto the golem's back, embedding pickaxes deep into its flesh. The beast turned and reached for them, but was unable to grab them as they dug the picks deeper.

Kyren was still facing down the necromancer.

"Your spells must be running out, priest," he hissed. "You'll need to stop to pray soon, and then I'll turn you and your friends into something beautiful."

The halo around Kyren grew brighter. "Fighting a necromancer in the name of my god *is* a prayer. When I bind myself to the will of my goddess, my spells are inexhaustible."

Golden chains manifested, wrapping themselves around the necromancer. He struggled against them with all six of his arms, but he couldn't move. She began walking toward him, her new mace in hand. He started casting spells, but they simply faded into nothing as they touched the golden light that surrounded her.

The golem began moving toward Kyren in spite of Stone and Hrig's ongoing attack. I forced myself up and ran to intercept it. I put myself in front of it and held up my shield, bracing myself as much as possible. It reared up to strike, but at that moment, both Hrig and Stone dropped down and swung their pickaxes hard into the creature's heels.

He stumbled, crashing down in front of me. I dropped my shield and raised the club above my head with both hands before bringing it down on his head. I thought it was finished, but the beast's arms began dragging himself toward Kyren.

I moved to the right arm and Hrig and Stone moved to the left one, where we concluded our systematic deconstruction of the golem.

Kyren reached the necromancer, who was screeching incoherently, seeming to have lost all touch with reality at the prospect of his own death.

"For the ancient and wise," she said, raising her mace into the air, then slamming it down onto the necromancer's head.

The blood from the strike evaporated in the heat of the light that surrounded her, which began to fade. Kyren moved to the necromancer's discarded robe, which she gently laid over his now still form.

19
THE LETTER

I moved over to the necromancer's corpse.
"Sorry, I just want to check something," I said to Kyren as I removed the robe from his face. I gently opened one of his eyelids, but saw no hint of gold, only a murky green.
"Comforting, isn't it?" asked Kyren.
"I do appreciate that not all of the evil people in the world are children of Aurum," I said.
We began searching the room and found a small pile of gold, loose gems, and a pair of black leather boots. Stone placed one of the boots next to his own, grunted with approval, and removed his old ones.
"Really, Stone? Boots from a tomb?' asked Hrig.
"You act like you've never worn a dead man's boots before."
"That was different; I'd killed him myself."
"Well, Ellis said we were entitled to whatever treasures we found here, and these seem like damn fine boots." Stone stood up, squatting and taking a few steps to check the fit. He then bent at the knees and pushed off the ground. His eyes widened as he leapt six feet into the air and he just barely managed to land on his feet.

"You...couldn't always have done that, right?" I asked.

"No, lad... I think it was the boots."

Hrig laughed. "Do it again. I don't think I've ever seen a dwarf so high in the air before. Aside from the time I threw you onto that manticore."

"It looks like next time, I won't need to be thrown."

Hrig sighed. "End of an era."

We made our way out of the tomb, taking the time to search any side passages for lingering undead, but finding nothing. We emerged from the tomb into the warm afternoon sunlight, walked out of the graveyard and toward the manor. A servant poked his head out of a slice of hedge and waved at us before hollering back toward the manor that we were safe and on our way back.

Duke Ellis was ready to meet us when we arrived.

"The mission was a success, I presume?" he asked.

"The tomb has been cleansed, but I insist you hire some people to help sort and rebury the newly re-dead. Otherwise, you could have another problem on your hands."

"I've already sent a runner into town to hire some extra help. I'll make sure my ancestors and those of my servants are returned to their proper resting places. Was there a necromancer?"

I unslung the corpse from my shoulder and laid it carefully in front of him before removing the hood obscuring his face.

Ellis's eyes widened in surprise, and the servants all began quietly talking to one another.

"What is it?"

"That's the gravekeeper. The one we thought was missing." He shook his head. "Hrid and Gaius' graves weren't disturbed, right?"

"They were fine. Thank you for treating them with such respect," said Hrig.

"Of course, they were family. Did you find anything else?"

"Just some gold and gems and these." Stone gave a six-foot leap up the steps to stand next to Ellis.

"Great Uncle Jack's boots! I wondered where they'd gone. Well, I'd promised you anything you found was yours." He glanced down at the boots. "I don't think they'd have fit me anyway. Here." He handed Stone a sack that jingled as it landed in his hands.

Stone tested the weight and, satisfied, tied the pouch to his belt.

"And this," said Ellis as he removed a scroll sealed with black ribbon from his cloak and held it toward Hrig, "is for you."

Hrig took it, untied the ribbon, and read the document. "Thank you, Ellis. Before my companions and I leave, let's sit and have some tea. We should say a proper goodbye this time."

"Yes." He gave her a sad but kind smile. "I'd like that. We'll go to the second floor sitting room by my suite." Just as he was starting to head inside, he stopped and turned back toward us. "Oh, Lady Kyren, we received a letter from your brothers. I didn't realize you were a Wyrwind! I'd have put you in our finest rooms had I known."

Kyren's eyes widened, and a blush touched her cheeks. "That wouldn't have been necessary. Your hospitality was generous enough." Her ears twitched, and she regained her composure. "The letter?"

Ellis gestured to a servant who produced a letter sealed with sparkling green wax. She took a small knife from her belt, cut the seal, and began reading.

"Did you know she was Wyrwind?" Stone whispered.

"No." Sevald had been aware of the Wyrwinds—his family's estate only a few over from theirs—but his family moved in different social circles. He hadn't even known the Wyrwinds had a daughter, only two sons.

Kyren finished reading and turned to us. "Well, that's unfortunate."

"What is it?" I asked.

"It would appear that my brothers are going to try to kill me," she said calmly, as if she were discussing the weather.

"What!?" said Stone and I in unison.

"Well, they invited me home for a visit, but it's basically the same thing." She smiled. "Things are...complicated in my family."

"I'm beginning to think things are complicated in all families," I said. My essences hadn't had perfect home lives, but they were never as complicated as a daughter running a brothel, a duke for a husband, and attempts at fratricide. Then again, I suppose I ran my own "father" through with a sword and chopped off his head to prove it.

"Why do they want to kill you?" asked Stone.

"My grandmother died recently and named me as inheritor of her estate. She'd been running the family for fifty years. My brothers likely expected to add her holdings to the ones they inherited from our parents. I asked specifically not to inherit anything. My parents honored that in their wills, but Grandmother never had much time for the wants of other people."

"Is that the news you got in Cirros when we visited the temple?"

She nodded.

"Well... Would you like us to kill them for you?" I asked.

Stone laughed. "I've never heard someone ask to commit a murder so politely before."

Kyren smiled. "I may take you up on that, but I want to see if I can find another solution first."

After that, Kyren spent some time telling the servants how the gravekeeper turned necromancer's body should be disposed of. It involved a mixture of fire, a deep grave, and a stone slab.

Shortly after she was done talking, Hrig exited the manor, holding three packs that she tossed to each of us. She had a lightness to her that I hadn't seen since we'd arrived in Buryn.

"I had Ellis replace our supplies that were left on the boat. I figured we may need them depending on what job Clara has for us next."

"Actually, I was hoping you'd help me with a family matter," said Kyren.

"It would be a little hypocritical of me not to at this point."

"How was your talk?" I asked.

"It was good. We cleared the air about everything. I explained why I left, he explained how that made him feel. We talked about Hrid and Gaius for a while. I didn't realize how much he liked them, too, and how much their death hurt him." She paused, looking away to keep us from noticing her eyes were watering. "I think we'll always be a part of each other's lives. We just have different paths to take now."

Getting everything together for our trip didn't take long. Kyren spoke briefly with Ellis, and he provided with a carriage, as well as several additional bags whose contents she requested. He and Hrig had a short embrace before we got on the road heading west to the estates bordering the capital. The road was well-maintained and free of obstacles, so we made good time.

"So, what should we expect?" asked Hrig.

"Probably poison, or assassins in the night. My brothers can be subtle, but they're also impatient. They'll likely use the most direct methods available."

"They'll probably try to separate us, make us sleep in different rooms. If they don't poison us, that would make it easier for the assassins to kill us," said Stone.

"I have a plan, though it may be a bit uncomfortable for everyone," said Kyren.

"I love a good plan. What're you thinking?" asked Stone.

"We'll have to pretend that you and Hrig are servants. That'll justify me keeping you in the servants' quarters off the guest suite."

"Couldn't we just ignore what they want and just sleep in the same room? Or even just ignore their invite altogether?" asked Hrig.

"No. I've been dealing with them for my whole life. It's time for me to put my house in order, and the best way to do that will be to beat them at their own game so absolutely that they fall in line."

Kyren's voice was as calm as it had always been, but the content of what she was saying was very different from anything I'd ever expected to hear from her.

"Why now?" I asked.

"We're in the neighborhood, and it's what my grandmother would've wanted. It's my job to honor the ancient and wise. She was both."

"And what will I be doing? I can't pose as a servant in full plate."

"Well, we have two options, one practical and another less so, but it would help to put my brothers off-balance."

"Go on."

"You can either be my bodyguard or my betrothed."

"Your betrothed?" I stammered out.

"Yes, it would justify you being in the same room as me even when it's just me and my brothers, and as you're of noble blood, as well, they may have to be wary of upsetting another family by harming me or you."

"But as a bodyguard, he could justify being with you,

sleeping in your quarters, and even eating your food to check it for poison," said Stone.

"Yes, but me having a bodyguard would also alert them to the fact that I'm wary of them and may make them attempt to be more subtle."

"Do they think you won't expect anything of them? Do they really know so little about you?" I asked.

"I was mostly raised by my grandmother. They don't really know me, and what interactions I've had with them, they always tended to get what they wanted from me. They don't understand that I was giving in to their demands out of an attempt to be patient with them rather than any fear."

"I say you tell them he's your betrothed," said Hrig.

"Why?" I asked, incredulousness seeping into my tone.

"I think it would be funny."

"Aye," said Stone with a smile. "Also, keeping them off-balance and making them underestimate you seems the best route to take."

"Well, won't they know who we are? Hrig is the Duchess of Death, Stone is well-known in underground circles, and we've all been travelling with you as adventurers for a while now."

"It won't matter. They don't bother keeping up with tales of adventurers or what I'm doing, and if Hrig and Stone are wearing servants' clothes, they won't look twice at them."

"Wouldn't it be a bit scandalous for a couple that's only betrothed to be in the same room overnight?" asked Stone.

"Not with Sevald's oath. My brothers aren't religious, but it'll be hard to deny his oath once they see how seriously he takes it."

"I'm surprised you left. You seem to be a natural at this type of plotting," said Hrig.

"You should have seen her in Cirros with me. I couldn't have upended Talen's operations without her."

Kyren produced a rare frown. "Just because I'm good at it doesn't mean I enjoy it. Adventuring, helping people, and healing have always felt like my true calling. My service to Sidi has more value than being a Wyrwind."

We spent the rest of the ride discussing plans and contingencies while the carriage took us through the winding country roads that moved people between the lordly estates of Caedun's nobility.

Eventually, we came to what looked like, rather than a lordly estate, a castle built for a siege. A high stone wall surrounded it, with towers in each corner built with small slits to allow archers to fire from it. There looked to be attempts to beautify the structure with flowers and vines being grown over the walls, but they did little to hide the ugly practicality of the structure.

Kyren seemed to predict our questions. "The Wyrwind lands used to border the elvish kingdoms back when there were frequent disputes. Our lands were developed to withstand frequent assaults. The castle itself has hidden passages for escapes, secret dungeons, and even ancient traps built into it. We aren't even sure if we've found all of them, though, because each new lord would build more after assuming lordship, and they didn't tend to be great recordkeepers. That's how my parents passed, actually. About five years ago, they were working on renovating one corner of the estate and got riddled with darts. The darts themselves did nothing, but the poison in them was still active." She paused for a moment. "My grandmother's estate is tucked into the corner of our lands. It's much more modern."

The carriage was waved through the gates and made its way onto the estate proper. The area behind the walls proved much more typical of a lordly estate, with a garden, several sculptures, and the houses built inside in an older style, but which still had a much more inviting look to them than the walls outside. What was less inviting? The large number of rough-looking men patrolling the grounds.

"Mercenaries?" asked Hrig.

"Aye," responded Stone.

With that added wrinkle, we exited the carriage.

20
A FAMILY AFFAIR

Hrig and Stone stepped out of the carriage first, having already donned the servants' attire Kyren had requested of Duke Wyther. I exited next and took Kyren's hand to lead her gently out to the front of the main house.

Two servants awaited, along with two men in regal attire. I'd expected them to actually look evil with foppish overstated attire, sneering smiles, and sallow complexions, but instead, they looked much like Kyren. Slightly pointed ears, dark hair, and quiet smiles, though theirs ended before they touched their eyes. One was taller than the other, but neither had the appearance of being in charge.

"Sister, it's so good to see you," said the taller of the two.

"Yes, welcome home," said the shorter one.

She was wearing an incredibly empty-headed smile.

"Thank you, Byren." She nodded at the taller of them. "Percy," she added, this time at the shorter.

Stone and Hrig had already begun unloading the luggage from the carriage, speaking with the household servants to organize where they'd be going. They moved like they'd been servants their entire life. I was impressed.

"Would you care to join us for tea? At least while your servants and—" Byren gave me a once over, "—fellow adventurer get settled."

"He's my fiancé, actually."

The brothers hid a brief moment of surprise quickly and exchanged a glance.

"Sevald Senturius, son of Gavain and Magda Senturius." I gave a slight bow, not so deep as to admit any inferiority in rank, but deep enough to acknowledge Byren and Percy as hosts.

"Ah, I've heard of your family. Richer in title and deed than anything else," said Percy with a warm smile that somehow veered on a sneer.

"Better than the opposite, I'd think." The backhanded compliment would've rattled Sevald, but I took such things much less personally.

"Well, you'll join us for tea then, as well. After you remove your armor, of course."

"I'm afraid I can't do that. I've made an oath to Dur not to remove my armor until certain conditions are met."

Percy squinted. "And those conditions would be?"

"Between me and Dur. Though I'd like to join you for tea, as long as you don't mind hearing a bit more clanking than usual."

"Of course they wouldn't mind. They understand the importance of faith, right?" She smiled up at them sweetly.

Byren gave another smile that didn't reach his eyes. "Of course. Please join us."

We separated from Hrig and Stone, who would be ensuring that the rooms were secure in their capacity as our "servants."

Percy led us into the house and to a tea room. The interior

had a much more modern sensibility than the exterior. Portraits lined the walls, rich red rugs ran along the floor, and notes of the Wyrwind's signature green were spread liberally throughout the halls. The tea room itself was an intimate space with a small fireplace and a half dozen chairs upholstered with floral patterns.

As we sat, a servant came and began pouring tea and serving it. I gave Kyren's hand two firm squeezes to indicate that it wasn't poisoned. I'd told her my parents were paranoid and had taught me how to smell common poisons, but truthfully, Syven had experimented with the flavors she could create when she introduced small amounts of poison to her dishes, and in the process had developed quite the understanding of dangerous flora.

"So, sister, I'm guessing you're wondering why we've asked you here."

"I just assumed you missed me?" she asked with a warm smile.

"Of course that is the main reason, but there was something else we were concerned about. You've heard of our grandmother's passing, I presume?"

"Yes, I'm still mourning her."

That was the first honest statement of this conversation.

"Of course, I know she favored you," said Percy, a touch of malice in his tone.

Byren spoke up. "Well, aside from seeing you, we also wanted to discuss her estate. We know that in spite of your wishes, she has left you the entirety of her holdings. We were thinking we'd take over management of that property for you, so that you can continue your less earthly pursuits."

Kyren took a steady sip of tea, then another, a guileless smile on her face.

"How kind of you to offer," she said, not letting a hint of displeasure touch her tone like it had her brothers. "While I'd like to have an answer for you now, this really seems like something I should discuss with my soon-to-be husband."

I nodded, letting her play the part of the hapless girl.

"Come now, sister, you know we only have your best interests at heart," said Percy, impatience bleeding through.

"Of course you do, dear brother, but it's just too big of an issue. It would be improper for me to make the decision without Sevy's say so."

"Well, 'Sevy,' what're your thoughts?" asked Byren, taking over as Percy started to grow red in the face.

"My thoughts are that it's impolite to discuss such things over tea, especially after your sister has had such a long journey."

"Ah...of course. Please retire to your rooms and get some rest. We'll put out a dinner call later. I hope to see you there."

"Of course, Byren. What's the point of me visiting if I don't get to spend time with you? Come now, Sevy. I'll show you to the room."

We exited the tea room to find Hrig and Stone waiting outside the door, blending in as well as they could with their surroundings.

"The room is ready, at least as ready as it can be," said Stone with a bow.

"Thank you, Geode. Please lead the way," I said, falling in behind him and Hrig as we made our way deeper into the estate to our suite.

The suite itself was even more ornately decorated than the halls. Hrig and Stone closed the doors behind us as we entered. We exchanged nonchalant pleasantries about the age of the house and the state of the garden until Stone gave the all-clear that there were no longer any servants listening nearby.

I turned to Kyren. "That was very well done. I didn't think you could play dumb so expertly."

"Thank you. I was just playing the role they expect of me."

"They really know so little of you?" asked Hrig.

"My grandmother insisted on having a larger hand in raising me after she had a visit from my brothers and found them...unsatisfactory. She was a bit controlling when it came to the family's future."

"Any poison with the tea?" asked Stone.

"No, I think they were testing to see if they could use a silk glove rather than an iron gauntlet. The good thing is, now they think I need Sevald to make decisions for me. They'll either try to convince you to support their interests, or have you removed thinking that they can control me better without you."

"Well, that's certainly a positive. I'm more equipped to deal with iron gauntlets. Mine are steel, after all."

"How about you? Learn anything from the servants?" asked Kyren.

"Only that they're scared. Apparently, your brothers fired the majordomo, and the mercenaries have been putting everyone on edge. One interesting thing I noticed, though, is that there are at least four different mercenary groups represented here," said Stone.

"Which means either my brothers just hired as many as they could get on short notice, or there are four different interests represented here."

"There are definitely some things that need to be untangled. You sure you don't want to just kill them?" asked Hrig.

"Still sure, though I reserve my right to change my mind. The next thing we'll have to get through is dinner, but before that, I'd like to take you all on a tour."

"To help us have a mental map in case things go wrong?" I asked.

"That, and I want to show my friends my family home. No reason we can't do both."

After getting back into the roles of ingenue, stern but smitten betrothed, and competent, proper servants, Kyren started leading us through the Wyrwind estate. We began by going through the main house, where Kyren showed us the various historical artifacts of her family and the rooms she used as a child, always with the caveat that she spent most of her time at her grandmother's house a fair distance from the main part of the Wyrwind holdings.

She spoke of things with a kind of constant inane rambling that played well into the character of the thoughtless priestess she was playing. I just responded with a lot of quiet nods and by saying "interesting," or "I didn't know that." It was the role I'd been born to play. All the while, Hrig and Stone quietly absorbed everything of value regarding the grounds, counted the number of mercenaries while figuring out who worked for which outfit, and kept an eye out for any potential assassination attempts.

When the sun began to set, we headed back to the rooms to prepare for dinner. Stone gave us the all-clear sign when he was certain no servants were eavesdropping, and Hrig did a quick search of the rooms to make sure no one was lying in wait.

"Things may be more dire than I thought," said Kyren once Hrig had finished her search. "I noticed several heirlooms are missing. My guess is that my brothers sold them."

"Why would they do that?"

"I'm not sure. The estate produces a good amount of money, and we've never had any financial difficulties."

"Could it be gambling?" asked Stone. "It would explain the different merc groups."

"No, my brothers have their vices, but they usually revolve around hoarding money and artifacts, not losing them. There's something else going on, something that could motivate them to go without comforts, which is not an easy thing for them."

"After dinner, Stone and I will see what we can learn from the mercenaries. I've always had good rapport with those types," said Hrig.

"Aye, and if I can learn who they work for, I may get lucky and know a few of their higher-ups."

"Sounds like a plan. I'll knock on the table if I think anything we're served for dinner tonight is poisoned," I said.

"Alright, a servant should be here in a few moments to inform us it's time to join Percy and Byren."

A few minutes later, one such servant arrived, and we were escorted to the main dining hall. Hrig and Stone helped us into our seats and stood at attention against the walls nearest to us. Kyren loudly dragged her chair to be seated more closely to me in a masterful display of feigned stupidity.

"How did you enjoy the tour, Sevald?" asked Byren. "Some of the servants told us our sister was nice enough to escort you around the grounds."

"It was lovely," I responded simply.

"Any questions about our history or lands that you'd like to know?" asked Percy.

"None, thank you." Percy and Byren were looking for a read on me, and I wanted to make it as frustrating for them as possible.

After a few more questions that I did my best to answer just with a yes or no, they decided to fill the conversation with the sound of their opinions on everything, from the food to the weather and all the exciting things in between. This was a talent I knew from Sevald's memories was common among the nobility.

"If you're finished, Sevald, would you care to join Percy and me for a brandy?"

"Alone?" I asked.

"Of course. We'd like to get to know the man our sister wants to marry a bit better."

"Go ahead, Sevy. We'll catch up later," said Kyren. Hrig had to turn a snort into a cough at the name "Sevy."

With that, I followed Percy and Byren back into the tea room we'd first met in when we'd arrived. They each poured a glass and then poured me one. I could immediately tell that the glass itself had been laced heavily with poison. It was rathas root, more deadly to those who became excited after ingesting it. It could also add a fantastic kick to eggs if the quantity was severely limited.

"So, how long have you known our sister?" asked Byren.

"Not long enough," I said, tilting my helmet away and draining half the cup of poisoned brandy, feigning swallowing sounds. I decided to store the poison liquid rather than destroy it. I might need to poison someone or something at some point, and this seemed a convenient time to have some ready.

"You seem quite taken with her," said Percy.

"I am."

"It's a bit surprising then that your family didn't know you were betrothed."

I paused, the brandy glass halfway to my faceplate. "I haven't had a chance to tell them."

"Well, no worries. We made an inquiry to their staff this morning, and they noted they'd not received a message from you in quite some time, though they were sure to mention that wasn't uncommon."

"So you informed them of the engagement?" I asked.

Sevald wasn't on good or bad terms with his parents, but he'd lived his life doing his best to meet their expectations of him. Becoming engaged and not telling them was very out of character, though that might be mitigated by the engagement being to someone of a prominent family like the Wyrwinds."

"Well, we didn't directly inform them, but the questions in the message we sent may have allowed them to infer something."

"Hmm." I finished the brandy and placed the glass gently on a nearby table.

Percy and Byren were eyeing me expectantly. I leaned hard on the table for a moment and watched the hunger in their eyes grow, before standing back up straight. "I think I'll return to my room. Thank you for the drink, gentlemen, it had a very unique flavor."

That got me two pairs of bulging eyeballs as I steadily walked out of the tea room. Before I could round a corner, I heard Percy behind me.

"Would you care to join us on a hunt tomorrow?"

"Sure." I walked the rest of the way to the suite wondering what they'd try next.

21
THE FOOL

The next morning after breakfast, Percy, Byren, and I rode out into their hunting preserve with a half dozen mercenaries. Aside from me with my usual sword and shield, the rest of the hunting party was equipped with crossbows and longswords.

While we were gone, Kyren planned to have more intimate talks with the servants outside her brother's prying eyes, and Hrig and Stone were going to attempt to untangle the mercenaries' circumstances.

"What exactly are we going to be hunting?" I asked as we rode.

"We had two manticores released on the grounds. We're hoping they put up a good fight," said Percy.

Manticores released in an unfamiliar environment being hunted down by nine men were at a distinct disadvantage in my opinion, but I chose not to share that viewpoint. Once we reached the deepest part of the forest, we dismounted from our horses. Byren threw a waterskin in my direction, but it tore as I caught it.

"Sorry about that. Just wanted to make sure you didn't overheat in that armor."

"No problem. Accidents happen." Though the fact that the water smelled suspiciously like manticore musk led me to believe it had been no accident.

Pebble had studied manticore, drakes, goblins, and all manner of creatures at the University of Usulaum as part of his focus on practical dungeoneering. Head of a lion, tail of a scorpion, horns of a goat was the typical configuration, though different regions had different subspecies, including one that actually resided near Usulaum with the head of a man. Pebble had attempted to talk to one on the off-chance he could learn more about them, but unfortunately, they weren't sapient, despite what the human face would indicate.

"Let's spread out, shall we?" suggested Percy.

He took two mercenaries, Byren took two others, and the remaining two went with me. It wasn't long until I heard movement in the forest near me. I didn't attempt to sneak up on it—fullplate tends to render that pointless—so I simply gestured to the mercs to follow me and drew my sword.

Pushing through the woods, I entered a gap in the trees. The manticore was there, gnawing on a deer and letting out low growls. When I stepped into the clearing, it pointed its nose into the air and its nostrils flared, taking in the scent of the musk that covered my armor. I charged it before it could charge me, slamming my pauldron into its face. That knocked it forward, and I slashed downward at its head with my blade, but it deftly moved to the side.

The mercenaries behind me took aim with their crossbows and fired, embedding two bolts into my back. It was a clever plan. Hunting accidents were common, manticores were dangerous, and crossbow bolts would pierce even armor as fine as me. Unfortunately for them, I was unharmed, but now, I was also very much annoyed.

The manticore raised its tail and struck at me, but I deflected the stinger with my shield. It pulled its tail back to prepare another strike, and I dropped the sword and shield. The stinger struck, but this time, I caught it. I could see the mercs behind me quickly working to reload their crossbows, but struggling, distracted by my confrontation.

I pulled on the tail, flipping the beast and causing it to lose its footing. I then dug a single foot into the ground in the direction of the mercs and hauled the manticore by its tail, throwing it in their direction. I heard them cry out in surprise as four hundred pounds of pissed-off monster hit them and began clawing at everything in sight. One mercenary managed to loose a bolt in the beast even as he was torn to shreds, and another managed to pull a dagger out of his belt and started stabbing wildly, hitting his companion as much as he was the beast.

While the three of them struggled, I calmly retrieved my weapon and shield and removed the two bolts from my back, all while taking in the show. Pebble would've loved to see something like this up close. The majesty of a manticore at its most ferocious. By the time they were done, the mercenaries were dead, the manticore mortally wounded. In spite of its injuries, it moved toward me, refusing to even limp. In recognition of a fellow monster, I ended it quickly, driving my sword through its skull.

After removing the manticore's head, I retrieved the crossbows and their bolts, storing them internally for potential future use. I then made my way back to where we'd left the horses, using my internal compass to navigate. Unfortunately, leaving the horses in an area in which a large amount of manticore musk was spilled had been a very poor decision.

The remaining manticore was neck deep in one of the horses when I arrived, two other horses lay spasming on the ground, paralyzed and dying from the venom of its sting. Six horses were missing, the implication of that clear. Rather than disturb what to me was a well-earned meal, I simply melted into the woods and took the long way around the remaining manticore. He may have smelled the musk that hung about me, but with so much food readily available, he likely didn't care.

Toward the entrance to the forest, I picked up the trail of the remaining six horses. Percy and Byren had left with their bodyguards, leaving me covered in manticore musk with two mercenaries whose job it had been to kill me.

I began to make my way back to the Wyrwind estate. Without needing to follow a horse trail, I was able to cut a significant amount of time from my journey.

It was late afternoon by the time I'd made it back. The guards at the main gate were too surprised by the sight of a man carrying a manticore head and covered in blood to question my re-entry. Mercenaries and servants turned their heads as I passed by. Hrig met me at the door to the estate with a smile.

"A good hunt, milord?"

"A little dull, but the result was positive."

"The masters of the house were just sitting down for a late lunch with Kyren. They seem to be under the impression that you'd died. Kyren is in such shock, she doesn't believe them."

"I think I'll join them for lunch. Would you lead me there? I'm a little disoriented after all that walking."

"Of course, milord." She began to lead me to the dining room, dropping her meek stance as we walked outside the gaze of the servants and mercenaries that populated the courtyard. "We weren't too worried, though I'd like you to know that if you hadn't shown up by nightfall, we would've slit their throats. Kyren insisted, in fact."

"It's good to feel loved. Perhaps I should've taken more time to get here, though. I'm not feeling particularly charitable towardthem at this point."

"Neither is Kyren. We think we've got them figured out, and a plan is in place. We'll talk about it once we're back in the room."

I nodded, and Hrig pushed open the door to the dining room. Kyren gave me one of her small smiles, Stone one of his big ones. Percy and Byren looked as if their eyes might leave their heads. I approached them slowly, watching them trying not to squirm, and tossed the manticore head between them. Percy gave a little jump, but Byren managed to keep himself still.

"It was a bit too easy, but thank you for inviting me." I walked over to Kyren, and Stone pulled out the chair next to her for me. I sat and gave Kyren's hand a squeeze, both for comfort and to confirm the food wasn't poisoned, before I started calmly eating a rather well-made vegetable soup. The lunch went on silently for a while before Percy and Byren managed to fully recover themselves.

"We'll have to have this stuffed and mounted," said Percy.

"Yes, it's a fine trophy," agreed Byren.

"The problem with mounting a manticore head is that it just looks like someone killed a lion. It can only really create trophies that are less impressive than the creature itself unless you stuff the whole thing."

Byren and Percy let out stilted chuckles, and Kyren let out a real one.

"I'm sure Sevald would like to rest. We're going to retire to our rooms. We may not be able to join you for dinner."

"Of course, sister."

With that, we walked calmly back to our rooms, making small talk about the hunt and the quality of the lunch. Stone gave the all-clear, and I was immediately assailed with questions regarding my health.

"I'm fine. The mercenaries they sent with me did most of the work, though not until after they tried to kill me with their crossbows. I assume they'd been expecting their return rather than mine."

"So that makes two attempts so far. They're likely to be getting frustrated at this point," said Stone.

"Exactly, especially now that we know why they're so desperate," said Kyren.

"We've solved the mercenary mystery, then?"

"Yes, between the three of us, we managed to pull out the information we needed from the mercs and servants. My brothers owe money to four different people. Two are fellow nobles, and two are less savory merchants from the capital."

"Is it gambling, after all?"

"No, much dumber and more dangerous than that. You remember Duke Wyther talking about those two elven barons who went independent?"

"Yeah."

"Those are my cousins. Our lines intermarried as part of the treaty that created peace between Caedun and Sylfen. Apparently, my brothers have been sending them monetary support for their independence movement. They've been promised princely titles and new lands as soon as the barons have solidified their borders. They don't seem to realize how idiotic they're being."

"Forgive me, I only married into the nobility, so I may not understand. Why is it idiotic?" asked Hrig.

"Because they're nobles of Caedun, a country that has had peace with Sylfen, but not always, and they're supporting two barons who have seceded from that land. If the Sylfen find out, it will look as if Caedun is purposely fomenting rebellion."

"Do your brothers realize how dangerous what they're doing is?" I asked.

"They likely do, but think they can get away with it. They intend to hold lands and titles both here and in the barons' lands at the same time, making them nobility of two kingdoms. They probably think that will make them indispensable to both rather than an enormous liability."

"Why the sudden urgency to take your grandmother's lands?"

"The barons' ploy for independence isn't going smoothly. They need the holdings to buy time with the debtors."

"So, what do we do?"

"Well, I've sent several letters to key allies, legal officials, and a few friends of Stone's in the city. All we need to do now is survive the night and wait."

The first merc to slip into the room used the front door. He wore no boots, but was wrapped in a black cloak with a small dagger in his hand. The first thing he saw when he entered was me, standing with my arms crossed, staring at him. He began to raise his dagger, but I shook my head slowly left to right. He sheathed the dagger, bowed apologetically, and left.

The second merc had actually taken the time to climb a garden trellis up to the balcony near the bed. Unfortunately, his efforts were for naught as Hrig gave him a firm shove, landing him in a particularly thorny rose bush.

The third and final merc attempted to use a servant corridor to make his way into the room, but instead found Stone sitting with two cups of ale. He simply accepted Stone's invitation to sit and enjoy some ale with him, and after hearing a story about Stone out-spitting a troll to cross a bridge, he left, either having forgotten what he'd gone there for, or, more likely, not willing to kill a friendly dwarf servant to get away with it.

After that, the attempts stopped, and everyone was able to get some rest. I had asked why the mercenaries would attack us if Percy and Byren were the ones who owed them money, and Stone had explained that it was simply the easiest way for them to get their money. Still, all we had to do was make it too difficult to go through us, and they would turn their attention back to the Wyrwind brothers.

Breakfast the next morning was quiet. Percy and Byren looked haggard and didn't bother making their usual small talk. A servant entered the room quietly and provided Kyren with a small stack of correspondence.

"I apologize for interrupting, my lady. The courier said these were all urgent."

Kyren thanked her and opened the letters one at a time. Her quiet smile grew ever so slightly with each one read.

"Some good news, sister? Perhaps something from your fellow priests?" asked Byren, suspicion in his voice.

"Oh, something along those lines. I'm sure you'll be receiving your own letters shortly."

By the end of the meal, their own letters had begun to come in, and even just the sight of the names on them turned both Percy and Byren white as sheets.

"I think we'll retire to our rooms. It looks like you two will be busy sorting all of that." Kyren gave a little curtsy, put her arm through mine, and we walked out the door back to the room.

22

REVELATION

"So, what do the letters say?"

"Two are from people my brothers owe, acknowledging that I'd be better at managing their debts than they are and putting their mercenaries under my control. Another is from the office of the king's magistrate declaring my brothers are to be confined to their estate until a thorough investigation can be performed, and a third is from the guard saying they're sending a garrison here to take control of the estate until things are sorted out. Basically, my brothers are now the ones who are in danger here."

"I don't know, Kyren. You've cornered them, but that may just make them more unpredictable," said Hrig.

"True, but it's the strongest hand I have to play. The mercenaries should also be receiving new instructions. Hrig, Stone, you can dress back in your usual clothes if you'd like. There may be some fighting as things shift, and there's no reason to keep up the ruse now that I've shown my hand."

"Really? I was enjoying trying some skullduggery, for a change," said Hrig.

"If you'd like, you can help me blackmail a noble when we get to the capital. The mercenary that tried to kill Kyren last night told me a very interesting story about how he spends his time away from his wife," said Stone.

Hrig perked up at that, nodding agreement, and then she and Stone went to put on their gear.

"Should we barricade ourselves here until the guard shows up, or confront them directly?" I asked.

"Directly, I'd think. They need to know that I beat them and acknowledge it. Otherwise, they could get it in their heads to make another attempt."

"Is it okay if I rough them up a little? I'm a little annoyed with all those attempts to kill me."

She smiled. "Only if they really ask for it."

Hrig and Stone returned in their typical adventurer outfits as there was a knock on the door. Hrig, Kyren, and I took positions around the door while Stone opened it. A rough-looking man with a scar over his right eye and a shaved head was standing in the doorway. He nodded at Stone, then Kyren.

"Ma'am, I'm Mills with the Howling Griffons. I've been told I'll be working with you now."

"What does it look like out there?"

"Well, your brothers have barricaded themselves in the reception hall along with the mercenaries still loyal to them, or at least loyal to the idea of getting their employers paid through them. We were thinking we'd just keep them locked in and wait."

"No, let's see if we can get them to open up. It's possible I can convince them to see reason."

Mills grunted and led us through to the reception hall. The main doors were shut, the mercenaries I assumed were on our side surrounding them.

Kyren approached the doors. "Brothers, there's no reason to keep struggling like this. If you work with me, I can make sure things don't go too poorly for you."

"Poorly for us!?" Percy's voice cracked as he yelled. "You're just Grandma's pet! We're the ones who inherited Wyrwind! Who are close to doubling our holdings!"

"Byren? Are you in there? Can you calm him down and let me in? We should be able to have a civilized conversation. Don't you at least want to hear my terms?"

There was muffled conversation with a few expletives, but eventually, things quieted and Byren's voice rang out. "Alright, we'll let you in to hear terms."

After a few moments, the doors opened. I led the way in, thoughts of crossbow bolts embedded in my armor giving me a healthy sense of paranoia. Our mercenaries followed, taking positions suited to countering those that continued to work with Percy and Byren. We outnumbered them, but only when Kyren, Stone, Hrig, and I were included.

Percy looked almost feral. His long hair was loose, and his eyes had a wild look to them. Byren was less disheveled, but even he had more than a few hairs out of place, and his vest was improperly buttoned.

Kyren walked forward until she stood directly where petitioners would normally stand, and the rest of us stayed close.

"Your terms?" asked Byren.

"You lose all rights to Wyrwind. I marry you off to ensure the continuation of our line, and we use the dowries we receive to help pay off the debts you've accrued. You live the rest of your lives in relative comfort, and I hire back the former majordomo to manage the estate."

"Reasonable."

Percy's eyes bulged at that statement, but rather than say

anything, he held his tongue and moved to the far wall, looking away in anger.

"You got too greedy. If you'd just curbed your ambitions a little, you could have really accomplished some great things. Our parents would've been proud."

"I doubt they would be." Byren lowered his voice so that only Kyren, Stone, Hrig, and I could hear him. "I had them killed, after all."

Kyren went white. "What?"

"Here's my counter offer. Percy!"

Percy pushed in a portion of the wall he'd positioned himself next to, and suddenly, the floor fell out from underneath us. I heard mercenaries unsheathe their swords as we plunged into blackness.

We landed with a crash on hard ground. The fall had been maybe twenty feet, and I could hear groans from Kyren and Hrig. The room was pitch black, but I could see that Stone had landed on his feet.

"Stone? Are you okay?"

"Aye, lad. Looks like my new boots came with an added benefit."

I moved over to Hrig, helping her stand. She tried to put weight on her left leg but collapsed. I caught her gently and let her down. Stone helped up Kyren, who seemed uninjured but shaken.

"Can you make some light, Kyren?" asked Stone.

"Huh?"

"Light, and some healing for Hrig. I can't be sure in the dark, but the noise she made sounded like she broke something."

Kyren spoke a few words in elvish, and an orb of light lit the room. We were in a large cell, surrounded by metal bars less than six inches apart from one another. I held Hrig's hand while Kyren came to her and cast a spell to heal her leg.

Stone moved to the bars, holding his ear to one of them while he rapped a ring on it. The tone of the vibrating metal was high-pitched but oddly musical. He sighed. "It's elyrium."

"Elyrium?" asked Hrig.

"A very rare, very strong metal. Said to be unbendable once forged. It only comes from one mine deep in Sylfen, which has long been exhausted," I said, letting Pebble's knowledge flow out of me.

"It must be one of my ancestor's traps. A trap door in the reception hall, a perfect place to remove some enemies." She ran her hand along one of the bars. "Hrig, Stone, Sevald, I should've taken your advice sooner. Next time we see my brothers, let's just kill them."

We all let out a chuckle.

"What're the chances someone saves us?" asked Stone.

"It doesn't look like there's a gate. Any rescue would have to be from above. If our mercenaries beat theirs, then they'll probably be able to figure something out. If they lose, however... I don't think anyone else knows this exists. I'm guessing my brothers have been mapping the traps here for a while."

She let the implications of that and what happened to her parents hang in the air, and no one felt comfortable filling in those blanks out loud.

Once her leg was healed, Hrig moved toward the bars. She wrapped her hands around them and pulled with all her strength, the muscles on her back exploding with effort as she did so. After a few moments, she stopped, slick with sweat and panting, but the bars hadn't moved an inch.

I stepped forward and tried the same, but the only difference between our efforts was that I wasn't tired afterward. I tried a different tactic, slamming my foot into the bars, but that also didn't have any impact. Eventually, I just sat back down with my companions and waited.

Kyren tried to climb up the bars and push on the ceiling, but was unable to budge anything. She sat back down, too.

After a couple hours, Stone spoke up.

"It doesn't look like anyone is coming."

No one said anything. I had been thinking about our options and had figured out a way to escape. If I shrank myself a bit, and sucked in my armor like I used to when my master would pretend to crush me, then I could escape. I could then make my way back up, open the trapdoor, and throw a rope down for everyone to climb up.

Unfortunately, that would out me as a monster or at least reveal me not to be Sevald. Still, I couldn't just wait around and watch them starve—even the idea of that made my essence knot up. Perhaps I could extinguish Kyren's light long enough to get through without them noticing? Maybe if they went to sleep, I could rescue them before they even awoke and blame divine providence? I thought through all of these possibilities and at one point realized I was physically shaking, my armor making sounds like metal chimes in the wind.

"Sevald," said Kyren. She had placed a hand on my shoulder. Hrig and Stone both looked at me with an expression I'd never seen before. "Do you have some way out of here?"

"I....how could I possibly?"

Kyren kept her gaze on me steady, her features as calm and serene as they ever were. Even when she was dealing with her brothers, she never completely lost that core of calm.

"Sevald, you've gotten us out of quite a few impossible situations and yourself out of even more. Would it help you if we all looked away? Nothing has to change between us; we don't need the truth if you're not comfortable giving it."

I panicked, shaking even more as I realized the implications of what she was saying. I looked at Stone, who was giving me a warm, almost fatherly smile, and Hrig, who was wearing the only look of worry I'd ever seen on her. Worry for me, I realized, concern for how this was impacting me.

"You...you know? You know what I am?"

"Not exactly, lad, but we have a good idea," said Stone.

"How?"

"Well, the first thing is that you're about ten times as strong as I remember Sevald being," said Kyren.

"You're also a fair amount friendlier, though at first I assumed that was because you'd warmed up to us," said Stone.

"You killed an army of goblins single-handedly, survived a shipwreck in full plate armor, and managed to kill Donyin," said Hrig.

"It's not just the big things, lad. You also frequently forget to turn your head towards who you're speaking to, I've never heard you cough or sneeze, you stay completely still without ever shifting the weight of your feet or fidgeting, and you have not once taken the time to relieve yourself in all the time we've travelled together."

Hrig chimed in. "You also resisted my advances, which is a difficult thing for a man to do."

"I thought I was being subtle."

"You were not," said Kyren matter-of-factly.

"We actually had to cover for you several times. We convinced Jade and Dorsia that your armor was enchanted as a way of explaining why it was never damaged, and we went along with your excuses enthusiastically to dim others' suspicions."

"How long have you known?"

"I figured it out before we left the dungeon," said Kyren. "I was going to wait until I could speak to Hrig and Stone privately, but then you went and made a genuine oath to Dur. What really convinced me, though, was what you did for that old man at The Thirsty Tree." She paused. "You killed his son, didn't you?"

"I looked down. "Yes."

"But you still took action to make amends. That told me you wanted to do good, even if you hadn't had the chance to yet."

"What about you, Stone? When did you figure it out?"

He smiled. "About the second week in a row you hadn't left camp to find a tree for yourself. You're good company, though, so eventually, I accepted it as another strange part of adventuring."

"Hrig?"

"When I saw you fight the goblin chieftain. There was a moment when your faceplate was open. I couldn't see exactly, but I knew I saw nothing there. Well, not exactly nothing, just an absence of anything. I assumed it was just my eyes playing tricks, but then there was the other night when I realized you were still wearing your armor even alone in bed. No one takes holy oaths that seriously. Even Dur would probably give you a pass for someone else barging into your room."

Hrig's words raised Stone's and Kyren's eyebrows, but they decided now wasn't the time to go deeper into what she was referring to. Kyren turned to me.

"I have to ask again, Sevald. Do you want us to turn around and let you get out of here without anything changing between us? We can do that if you'd like."

"No... You can watch."

I stood up and moved to the closest set of bars. I squeezed through, sucking myself in order to get through the narrow gap between them. I looked back at them. Their expressions were the same as they always were. A wave of relief washed over me as I returned to my usual shape.

"I'm not sure of exactly what I am, but what I do know is that my master created me to be a dungeon trap. Adventurers are compelled to wear me, at which point I eat them. When I eat them, I also gain all of their memories and skills. I'm meant to use those memories and skills to integrate with the party and play out a specific scenario that ends with me betraying them and killing everyone for my master's amusement. Eating people was automatic for me. I didn't have a perception of right or wrong, only my master's orders. For some reason, eating Sevald was a tipping point of some kind. I started to feel things I hadn't ever felt before."

"How many people have you eaten?" asked Stone.

"Four: a dwarf, an elf, and two men. The elf was a woman. I've also eaten the head of a goblin and the head of an orc I shipwrecked with. I did that for more information. I can get partial memories and skills that way."

"Well, it's not like I've never been friends with killers before," said Hrig.

"Aye, four is actually not that high a number," agreed Stone.

"What all can you, well, do?" asked Kyren.

"Well, I can adjust my size, as you've just seen. I can store things inside myself. I'm bigger on the inside than the outside. I'm stronger and faster than most things, by a pretty significant margin, and I can't grow tired. I can fire things from my void at high velocity. I can separate parts of myself and control them. I can heal myself and repair any scratches to my armor. There may be more, but that's all I know right now."

"That's...a lot for something just meant to be a dungeon trap," remarked Stone.

"I know as much as you do. Well, now we all know what I know." I paused. "Can I...can I keep travelling with you all?"

Surprised looks appeared on each of their faces.

"Of course," said Hrig, "I can't imagine going anywhere without you."

"Aye, lad, you're one of us."

"Well, it's my duty to watch over what's ancient and wise. I don't know how old you are, but I'll assume you're ancient for now," said Kyren with a smile.

23
REBUILDING

I started making my way through the underground passages that ran under the Wyrwind estate. I got lost multiple times, but through a lot of trial and error, I eventually managed to find a set of stairs leading upward.

When I reached the top, I thought I'd found a dead end. I felt along the wall and realized that, unlike the walls of the staircase, the wall in front of me was simply a wood panel. I punched a hole through it and heard a scream from inside. I then tore a me-sized hole and walked through.

A young servant was hiding behind a nearby couch, a metal sconce in his hand with which to defend himself. I gave him an awkward wave, unlocked the door to his room, and found myself in an unfamiliar bedroom. I walked through a few more doors and halls until things began looking familiar, and from there, I made my way back to the receiving hall.

There was blood, a lot of it, spilled on the floor. I recognized the bodies of several of the men who had been with us when we'd entered the throne room. Mills was among the dead.

It took some effort, but eventually, I managed to find the

spot that Percy had pushed on the wall. As it gave way, I heard the creak of the trapdoor swinging open. I released pressure, and the door snapped closed. I pushed it in again, drawing my sword this time. Once it was pushed in and the door was opened, I jammed my sword into the gap between bricks in order to wedge it where it lay. I approached the trapdoor, looking down at my companions.

"I'm going to get a rope from my pack!" I yelled.

"Okay!" responded Hrig.

I ran back to the room and took the fifteen-foot rope I had from my pack, thankful Stone's new boots would spare him the embarrassment of being hauled up to rope by Hrig. I ran back to the opening and threw the rope down, trying to give them as much to work with as possible while still allowing myself decent footing.

Kyren was up first, her natural climbing ability letting her fly up the rope almost before I even felt her weight on it. Next was Stone, who took a bit more time and let out a few choice curses as he made his way to the top.

"I wasn't made for this kind of climbing. Give me a mountain over a rope anytime."

Last was Hrig, who managed to get up the rope in only a few quick motions. I pulled up the rope and went to remove my sword from the brick and return it to my scabbard.

"Let's search the grounds. My brothers may have left a trail."

We began a systematic search of the grounds, finding multiple scared servants and the corpses of several more mercenaries from all the different groups that had been skewered, crushed, or poisoned by traps throughout the fortress.

"Your brothers seem to have used their knowledge of the estate to rid themselves of their mercenaries," said Stone.

"They must have been reactivating them over time." She

shook her head. "After all the effort my ancestors made trying to make this a peaceful place again."

After a bit more searching and a short chat with a very shaken stablemaster, we concluded that Percy and Byren had made their escape, likely toward their cousins, the newly independent elven barons. With half a day's head start, it was unlikely we'd be able to catch them.

We spent the rest of the day cleaning things up as best we could. Stone used his stone sense to locate and disarm as many traps as he could, focusing on the more heavily used areas of the house. Kyren found and organized the servants, doing her best to help them settle. Hrig and I moved to locate all the bodies of the dead and began digging graves. The Wyrwind house already had a sizable graveyard, so the added bodies of the mercenaries did not add to it by a significant degree. After we were done, Kyren performed a blessing over them, and the servants were kind enough to act as mourners.

By the evening, everyone was drained, physically and emotionally. The servants were given the rest of the day off, and Stone made a simple soup for Hrig and Kyren. He went to hand me a bowl as well before smiling and shaking his head.

"Old habits, lad. I wouldn't be surprised if I try to do that a few more times."

"That's fine. I can keep pretending if it makes you more comfortable."

"No, Sevald, you don't have to pretend with us," said Hrig.

"I'll probably pretend if servants offer me food. I don't want to offend them."

Kyren smiled at that. "I appreciate it."

We sat in silence for a while. I could tell everyone still had questions, but there was a certain exhaustion that seemed to come from big revelations.

"I'll have to figure out some other way to pay back the Wyrwind debts."

"I think they'll understand if you need more time. Your brothers killed their mercenaries and trapped you in an inescapable pit, after all," I said.

Stone started laughing. It began as a chuckle, but soon became so intense, he was actually wiping tears from his eyes. "Your brothers are idiots."

Kyren smiled. "True, but it's less funny to me when their idiocy nearly brings my home to ruin."

"No, not because of that. The pit, the one they trapped us in. They clearly knew about it, knew what it was?"

"I would assume so. Why?"

"They had money problems and saved a trap just in case they needed to get rid of someone, but the trap itself has bars made of one of the rarest metals on the continent."

Kyren's eyes widened. "The elyrium... Those idiots! This is exactly why Grandmother thought they were useless. They could never see the forest for the trees."

Stone and Kyren started laughing, and Hrig and I joined in. After we settled down, Stone turned to me.

"So, Sevald, what really happened with the shipwreck?" he asked. "It's been bothering me quite a bit."

"Well, the captain of the enemy ship, a woman named Vash, was a child of Aurum."

"Feels like it's been awhile since we've had to worry about them," said Hrig.

"Aye, though that almost makes me more nervous. What happened to her?"

"She's alive, I believe. She seemed different from Talen and Donyin. More in control. I got the impression she didn't care for them very much. She told me she was there at Talen's request. Wanted him to owe her a favor."

"So they're not a united front, then?"

"That was the impression she gave me. She sent her crew to attack me and struck whenever she found the opportunity. She was skilled, and it was a difficult fight. Eventually, she pulled her crew back to make sure she had enough hands to sail her ships, and we dueled. Shortly after that, the kraken attacked."

"Drawn by the blood and bodies in the water, I'd guess," said Hrig.

"I tried to drown her, and as I did, I went to eat her." That statement drew some brief flashes of concern.

"I wanted more information."

"Of course, Sevald. She was trying to kill you, we understand."

"Well, I couldn't do it. I felt a presence other than her wrapped up in her essence, and it simply said 'no' and she escaped. She used a freshly grown tail to swim to the surface."

"What, then?" asked Stone.

"Then I dropped to the bottom of the sea."

Stone's eyes widened. "You can walk on the bottom of the sea?"

"Yes, it's kind of my only option. I can't swim, after all."

"If I were to tell you the tales of a few lost treasures down there, would you be able to retrieve them?"

"I suppose so."

"Stone," said Kyren in an exasperated tone.

"Ah, we'll come back to that. Go on, lad."

I told the group about the creatures I saw, the state of the shipwreck, and the tale it told me. I ended with how I'd found the group on the beach.

"All of these things happening so close together doesn't feel like coincidence. I wouldn't be surprised if the gods were taking an active hand in things," said Kyren. She then paused with the thought for a moment. "My healing hurts you?"

"Yes. Your healing, a blessing I received from a priest of Dur, and strikes from the children of Aurum. That's what has hurt me so far."

"Interesting. Dur's oath didn't hurt you, though?"

"No."

"Probably because it's not something that affects you directly. So anything from a divine source and the strikes from Aurum's children. That fits with the possibility Aurum is a god of some kind."

"And a dragon, apparently. Gods, a fight with a dragon would be spectacular," said Hrig.

"I don't recall hearing about the king dying in a shipwreck or any such thing," said Stone.

"Well, the wreck was very old, and dragons have been extinct for a thousand years, so it can't have happened recently."

"As always, we need more information. Caedun isn't great about maintaining knowledge unless it's the church, and they seem to be doing their best to hide Aurum's existence."

I thought for a moment. "The University at Usulaum. They have the most complete library in existence."

Everyone looked confused.

"Pebble, my second meal, he was a student there. If there's any information to uncover, it would be there."

"It wasn't Pebble In the Grass, was it?" asked Stone, concern on his face.

"No, it was Pebble Under Sand."

"Oh, thank goodness. I thought you'd eaten my cousin for a moment. I'd've forgiven you, of course, but it's nice that I don't have to."

"Don't worry, none of those I've eaten have any memories of you. I'd tell you if they did."

"So, should we make our way to Usulaum?" asked Kyren. "Sounds like our best bet for more information."

"What about your brothers? I'd certainly understand if you wanted us to try and find them first," I said.

"No. I came here to set my house in order, and I did. I don't forgive my brothers, but I'm not going to hunt them down either."

"We can kill them if we run into them, though, right?" asked Hrig.

"Absolutely."

The night passed uneventfully, and in the morning, we continued our clean-up. Kyren spent much of her time writing letters, giving orders to servants, and drinking inordinate amounts of strong tea. Stone continued the process of finding and disarming traps, in the course of which he realized that many of them had been added recently, likely by Percy and Byren themselves.

Hrig and I helped the servants move the furniture they'd used to barricade various rooms and buried a final mercenary that had fallen into a pit trap, the smell of whom had only been noticeable today. After that, we found ourselves with little to do.

"So, how strong are you really?" she asked after we finished setting a small marker above the mercenary's grave.

"I'm not sure of my limit exactly. I kicked a goblin hard enough that he exploded once. The bars in the trap we were stuck in were the first thing I haven't been able to bend."

She gestured for me to follow her, and I did so. We moved over to an area the mercenaries had clearly set up for card games. She placed one arm on the table, holding her palm toward me.

"Take it."

"You want to arm wrestle?"

"Yeah, it seems like a good way to measure your strength."

I shrugged and took her hand. I felt a small flutter as I did so. Her hand was calloused and strong, and I liked the feel of it.

"Go!"

She took me by surprise, and I lost an inch. I braced my feet on the ground and started pushing back. I considered putting all my force into my hand, but decided to increase my strength gradually instead. I slowly began pushing her hand down. She had a few surges of power, causing me to lose some progress, but eventually, her energy ran out. I gingerly placed her hand on the table.

"Damn."

"Don't feel too bad about it. Your strength was earned. Mine was simply taken or given to me."

"That's true, but losing is losing."

She started to look around, eventually catching sight of the smithy. She moved toward it, and I followed. The blacksmith wasn't in, but a young man that may have been his apprentice was doing some tool maintenance as we entered. He started to say hello, but Hrig moved immediately to the anvil. It was large, not the biggest my meals had seen, but larger than average for sure.

Hrig set herself in a low stance, bent, and with just a grunt of effort, lifted it. She held it there for several seconds, the blacksmith's apprentice staring wide-eyed at her, then put it back down. She then gestured to me to do it, a playful smile on her face.

Taking a similar stance, I lifted it as well without pause or effort. I then shifted my balance and raised it over my head completely. It seemed to be around four-hundred pounds. I could feel my feet sink several inches into the dirt floor as I held it.

"Showoff."

I shrugged while still holding the anvil and then gently placed it back down on the floor.

"Sorry for disturbing you." I nodded at the apprentice, and he managed a feeble nod back.

"No problem, ser."

After that, things just kept escalating. We went to the stables where Hrig managed to lift a colt, followed by me lifting a full-grown horse. We then competed to see who could hold on to a bar the longest before falling, followed by a pushup contest, and finally, a race. In the process, several of the servants began spectating, then a few of them actually began competing, as well. Hrig knew she couldn't beat me, but she still performed incredibly with each feat. At a certain point, I realized she wasn't so much competing with me as seeing how far she herself could go.

The final thing we did was a tug of war. I wrapped a piece of thick rope around my arm and dug my feet into the ground. Hrig anchored the other team along with every servant who had been watching and participating. A few of the servants' children even joined in. I was concerned for a moment that they'd be suspicious of my strength, but decided that suspicion didn't mean much since I was only a visitor.

They started pulling, and I found myself needing to angle my body backwards. Though I didn't give an inch, I found myself moving closer to them, and also, they seemed to be getting taller. I realized that while I wasn't planning on moving, the ground beneath me didn't give me much of a choice.

Soon, I was hip deep in mud, and Hrig's team had successfully moved the center of the rope over the line on their side. There was some cheering, including a roar of victory from Hrig before she moved over to me and offered me a hand. She was smiling ear to ear and had a soft look in her eyes. I took her hand, and she pulled me out of the mud.

24
ROYAL INVITATION

The next day, a contingent of soldiers arrived at the gates. After determining that they were under the orders of the king, they were let in, along with a contingent of servants on loan from Kyren's grandmother's—now Kyren's—estate, and the former majordomo of the Wyrwinds. The captain of the soldiers met Kyren in the reception area, with me, Hrig, and Stone standing behind her small throne.

"Lady Wyrwind," he said, bowing. "I am Captain Tylus. I am here under orders to place your brothers under arrest and investigate their conspiracy with the self-proclaimed independent barons."

The captain was a tall, well-built man who looked to be in his late thirties to early forties. He had a thick mustache the color of pepper. On his shoulder, pinning his cloak in place, was the metal symbol of the army, an eagle's claw, polished to a mirror-like sheen.

"Welcome, Captain Tylus. Unfortunately, my brothers managed to escape, and I no longer know their whereabouts. I do, however, have a record of their correspondences, witnesses to their wrongdoings, and my own testimony to offer in regard to what they've done."

"Thank you, milady Is there a space set aside for my men and me? Aside from the investigation, we've been ordered to garrison here until things along the border are less volatile."

"We have a barracks that I've ordered cleaned and prepared for your arrival. We are less well-staffed than normal, but those that happened to arrive behind you are here to help. Let me know if there's anything we can do for you."

"Thank you. There is one more thing." He reached into a pouch at his side and pulled out a letter. The paper was crisp white and sealed with gold wax. He approached Kyren and handed it to her.

"This seal?" she asked, her eyes wide.

"Yes, milady, it's from the king."

She nodded and took it, turning it over in her hands.

"May we be dismissed?"

"Ah, of course. Luisa, show them to their barracks."

With that, the soldiers left in an orderly fashion, looking slightly comical as they followed a short, elderly maid to their quarters in almost perfect lockstep. After that, Kyren welcomed the arriving servants and gave the returned majordomo, Imiri, an in-depth rundown of what had happened and what she needed from her. Her thoroughness impressed me, especially as she fidgeted with the royal letter, clearly wanting to sate her curiosity as to what was inside.

When the receptions were finally done, we all made our way to the tea room where, with remarkable control, Kyren made a pot of tea and slowly opened and unfolded the letter. She read it quietly while Hrig, Stone, and I did our best not to hover over, or in Stone's case, under, her.

"It's an invitation. It looks like it was written in his own hand." She handed Stone the letter, then Hrig, and finally, it was passed to me

Lady Kyren Wyrwind,

I was incredibly distraught to hear of the recent troubles that have befallen your house. The Wyrwinds have long been honored servants of the kingdom, and to hear of how your brothers plotted and schemed, nearly driving you to ruin, is greatly troubling. Still, I am impressed with your handling of matters, and you should know that I personally will be ensuring there are no issues with your inheritance of all land and titles associated with your house. Furthermore, I am planning a rather large party in honor of a dear friend. As you have had so much trouble recently, I thought that participation in such an activity would allow you a respite from the troubles which have recently plagued you. The event is to be a masquerade two weeks from now here at the palace. You may bring any guests you desire. I look forward to your attendance.

Warmest regards,

His Majesty King Caedus the XXXIV, King of Caedun, Ruler of the Middle Kingdom

Post Scriptum

I never much cared for your brothers, seemed like they had naught but air between their ears, if you catch my meaning.

Post Post Scriptum

I've been informed you're a priestess. Just a warning, my parties are rather tame, but the longer they go on, the more things tend to get a tad more debauched than a holy woman would appreciate. Just a warning.

"He's kind of funny, isn't he?" I asked as I finished reading.

"Aye, he seems a king of good humor. Always a positive thing in a ruler."

"Normally, a royal party would seem boring, but I'm curious to see what our king considers 'debauched'," said Hrig.

"Well, obviously, you're the ones I'm inviting. A masquerade; there hasn't been one of those in quite some time."

"They're out of fashion, right?" I asked, some of Sevald's memories of finding his great-grandparents' masks and wearing them around the manor coming to me.

"Yes, it seems like they encouraged plotting, affairs, and general backstabbing. They weren't banned per se, but they were certainly discouraged by the crown."

"That's a shame. They seem like they were a good time," said Stone.

"I prefer to stab people in the front. It makes me feel better when they can see that I'm enjoying myself while I'm doing it," said Hrig.

"Well, we've got two weeks. We can take one to settle things here and then head for the capital."

After going over the invitation, Kyren went back to work, Hrig decided to do some training, and I was planning on helping the excavation of the elyrium bars. They were going to have to break through large portions of stone in order to remove them, as breaking the bars themselves down would be impossible without ancient elven methods that likely only the oldest living elven blacksmiths were aware of. Still, even as bars, someone could definitely find use for them.

Before I could join the group excavating the bars, I was approached by Stone.

"Hey, lad, I need some help. Are you free?"

"I was going to help with the bars, but what do you need?"

"There's just one section of the palace I haven't been able to disarm the traps in. There's a long corridor running underground that I think leads outside. There was a mechanism for disarming it, but time has made it impossible for me to use. Even beyond that, the traps are layered in such a way that I'm not even sure of what all is there, even with my stone sense."

"How can I help?"

"Would you mind...walking through the corridor and activating all the traps?"

"Sure, I can do that."

"Really? Just like that."

"Yeah, I mean, it probably won't kill me."

"I feel just a wee bit like I'm taking advantage of you."

"Well, it's just something you need done that I'm uniquely suited for. If I needed something stolen or some books cooked, I'd come to you."

"That's true. You don't need that now, do you?" he asked with a twinkle in his eyes. "I could use a break."

"Afraid not, but I'll let you know."

Stone began leading me down some stairs, through a secret passageway, down a short fall, and back through another hidden set of stairs.

"You mentioned you can store things inside yourself?"

"Yes."

"About how much?"

"A small lake's worth of water."

"Really? What're you storing now?"

I did some quick inventory. "Two crossbows and several bolts, a dagger, an axe, some poisoned brandy, thirty-two gold pieces, and some interesting rocks I found."

"So you could have been carrying everything for us this entire time?"

"I, uh, yes. I suppose I could've."

Stone sighed. "The cost of secrets is a sore back for me, it seems. Not to mention lost profit. Do you have any idea how incredible of a pickpocket you could be with that ability? How great a thief you could be?"

"Well, stealth is a bit of an issue for me. I tend to move a bit noisily."

Stone chuckled. "A minor detail, lad. Something we could work on, if you'd like."

We arrived at the corridor Stone had mentioned. It was a long, wide hallway made up of brick and stone. I could see the faintest bit of light toward the end of it.

"The traps start there," he said, pointing a few feet in front of where we stood.

I nodded and began walking calmly in that direction. I saw Stone start to try and stop me before remembering that I'd volunteered to help. I stepped on a slab and felt the floor indent slightly. A wave of darts crashed into my armor, a few of them actually puncturing through it. I pulled those out, stored them, and continued walking. The next trap to activate was a wall of flame that spat out onto me from a statue with the face of a dragon. I walked past it, and the flame stopped.

"Sevald! Stand where you were. We have to make sure it uses up all the oil so it's inactive."

I nodded and moved back to where I had been. The flames licked at my armor, but after about a minute, they fizzled out. I then purposely stepped on a tripwire, which sent an axe swinging at me like a pendulum. This one, I caught before it hit me and held on to until the gears straining to swing it gave, becoming inert. After that, there was a pitfall into spikes, which I took the time to break before throwing slabs of stone into the pit until it was safely covered, then came a mallet that knocked me backward. All I had to do was saw the head of it off, and finally, just at the exit was a guillotine that slashed straight downward and reset itself. I simply took a large rock and placed it in the way of the blade, which shattered as it attempted to cut it. I then stepped outside to a small patch of forest just a short distance from the outer walls.

Stone slowly made his way to me, taking the time to look at each trap and make sure they couldn't be fixed, occasionally making some small additional breaks using his hammer. When he exited, he took a deep breath of the fresh air and clapped me firmly on the back.

"Great work, lad. You've just turned some lunatics' life's work into nothing and saved me a week's effort."

"I was the right person for the job. I used to be part of a lunatic's life's work, after all."

Stone chuckled. "Y'know, I am curious about him."

"The one who made these traps?"

"No, he was probably just some paranoid noble. I've met enough of those. I mean the one who made you."

"Ah, my master."

"You still call him that? I don't know that the name's accurate anymore since you ran him through."

"Well, I don't know his name. He just made me. The only time he spoke to me was to give me orders."

"He was clearly powerful, though. He also seems to have given you quite the suite of powers considering he only wanted to use you as a trap."

"I suppose that's true. I hadn't really thought critically

about him, or myself, to be honest. I've been too busy trying to fit in with you and sort through the memories of my meals. Being a 'person' has seemed more important than knowing more about myself."

"Well, lad, part of being a person is learning about yourself." He smiled. "Don't feel like you need to listen to a self-proclaimed thief, liar, conman, and general scoundrel, though."

"I think more people proclaim you to be those things than just yourself."

He laughed, and after that, we gathered the tools we'd brought and made our way back into the main portion of the estate. Stone might have been all of the things he'd titled himself, but he was also wise. He seemed to be a person who had seen it all, and through doing so, had become eminently comfortable with being himself. It was not that he didn't have issues, just that he approached them directly and honestly as himself.

25
ADJUSTMENTS

The rest of the week passed relatively uneventfully with Kyren ensuring every detail she could possibly manage was handled and the rest of us doing our best to lighten her load. The soldiers were kind enough to help Hrig train, though she had fewer and fewer volunteers to spar with her every day. Eventually, it actually became a punishment that Captain Tylus would liberally dole out to any soldiers he thought were spending too much time with the female staff, or in one female recruit's case, the blacksmith's apprentice.

As we packed and prepared for our journey to the capital, Kyren called me down to the reception hall. I assumed one of the remaining bars needed to be pried loose and they needed my help, but when I arrived, each of the twenty-foot bars had already been laid neatly across the floor.

Kyren waved me over to her.

"Hey, you needed help with something?" I asked.

"I feel a little embarrassed to ask this, but could you... Well, would you mind storing a few of these for me?"

"Sure, I can do that, but why?"

"I want to take them into the city to get an appraisal and confirm to one of the debtors that what I have is genuine. It's a noble my brothers owed money to. If he confirms it, the other debtors will have his word that I have the means to pay them, and I can have more time to find a buyer. I'm going to have Stone hide the rest in hidden areas on the property."

"Makes sense to me." I moved over and lifted one of the bars. Despite it being only two inches in diameter, it was exceptionally heavy, and I found myself needing to adjust my stance to lift it while also holding it steady. I opened my faceplate and gently lowered the bar into myself. Kyren averted her eyes, blushing slightly.

"What's the matter?" I asked as I began lifting the second bar.

"It's just, seeing your faceplate down. The blackness of it. It feels like... Well, it feels like seeing someone naked."

I laughed. "Technically, I'm always naked in a way. I consider this—" I knocked on my chest, "—my skin, though both the armor and what's inside are 'me' if that makes sense."

She shook her head. "It doesn't, but I don't understand why Hrig is so fond of fighting, or why Stone feels the need to steal all the time either." She looked thoughtful. "I guess seeing your, well, let's call it a 'face,' doesn't break your oath to Dur."

"How would we know? Is it not possible that I've broken it already?"

"Oh, no, you'd know if you'd broken an oath like that one. Maybe it's because I'm not seeing you 'outside' the armor since the armor is you. Or perhaps it's because you're not 'outside' the armor, just your face is exposed. Dur is a real stickler for precise wording, and he has a tendency to interpret things in odd ways."

"I'm just hoping he's not paying too close attention to me."

She smiled. "I'm afraid that with how things have been

going for us, I'd be surprised if he wasn't one of many gods keeping their eyes on us."

Hrig and Stone entered the room as the last couple feet of the third bar disappeared. Stone was carrying his usual packs, but along with that, he also had a single large sack.

"I see you had the same idea I did," said Stone

"Which is?"

"To have Sevald here help with the packing." He handed me the sack. I opened it and found multiple faceplate-sized packages with foodstuff or coin. "I figured it would be easier on us if you carry those. I'd understand, though, if you don't want to."

"It's fine, I can do it. Honestly, it'll help me feel less guilty for all the times you guys pulled me on wagons or sleds, thinking I was too hurt to walk." I started to store the packages.

"Not to mention the fact that you could've taken the entirety of every night's watch," said Hrig.

I shrugged; that was true.

Hrig frowned. "Did you still want us to call you Sevald, by the way? I mean, it's not really your name."

"I hadn't thought about it."

"Do you have your own name? One from before?" asked Stone.

"No, my master didn't give me one. Just referred to me as 'armor,' which, while accurate, I don't think counts as a name."

"Would you like to pick a new one?" asked Kyren.

"I think you'd make a great 'Stone,' maybe with your own surname. Something like 'Stone Under Steel'."

"I think people would be confused if I had a dwarven name. Besides, other people already know me as 'Sevald.' I think I'll stick with it for now. It's what I'm used to."

They nodded, seemingly relieved that they wouldn't need to make any major adjustments.

"Are we taking a carriage?"

"No, the capital isn't too far, and it's been awhile since we've actually walked anywhere, and since Sevald can carry everything for us, I don't think we need a wagon either."

"Don't worry. If you get tired, I can carry you," said Hrig with a wink to me. She knew by now that I didn't get tired.

Before we left, Kyren spoke with Imiri one more time about where she could be located while in the capital. Imiri was a middle-aged woman with soft eyes and silvery hair. She projected an air of competent confidence and clearly had been involved with every aspect of managing the house before Percy and Byren had dismissed her. I also got the impression that she'd worked closely with Kyren's grandmother, though I had no concrete proof of that.

We left through the main gate. Between the work of the last week, the soldiers now garrisoned at the estate, and the competent staff running things, Kyren seemed confident that the Wyrwind house was at least in order enough to allow her to return to what she considered her more important work. The fact that her brothers were now wanted men and would be hunted if they ever re-entered Caedun was also a welcome comfort.

The trail to the manor eventually became the road to the capital. It wasn't too busy near the noble estates; the most we ran into for the majority of the day was couriers carrying messages and servants bringing goods to the various manors they served. By evening, the roads were empty, and we set up camp in a small clearing that had clearly been used as a campsite before.

We started a fire, and I pulled a parcel of food out of my faceplate that turned out to contain a plucked chicken, potatoes, and garlic. I went to start cooking, but Stone stopped me.

"Come now, lad, you're already carrying everything and taking the watch tonight. You don't have to cook, too."

"Yeah, you don't even eat. Let us handle it," said Kyren.

"It's okay, I like to cook. One of the people I ate, Syven, was a chef, or at least wanted to be."

"Do you want to cook, though?"

I thought about it, thinking back to the time I cooked at the brothel. "It's not so much that I want to cook as I want to help, and I enjoy it when people like my cooking."

"How about this, lad? We'll take turns. I'll cook tonight. Let me sleep with at least a marginally clear conscience."

"Stealing doesn't bother you, but a friend cooking for you does?" asked Kyren.

"Exactly."

This time, the night didn't pass quietly. Ten men, dressed in dark cloaks and wearing black cloth masks, approached the camp. Three more had bows and hung back preparing them. The rest had a mixture of short swords and daggers and started closing in.

Before they got close enough to see us, I woke Kyren, who woke Hrig and Stone. Stone slipped away before they got too close, and I kept my back to them while Hrig positioned herself to launch out of her bedroll.

The first of them got near enough to reach me with his sword. He raised it, and at the moment he was about to strike, I spun my helmet around one-hundred-and-eighty degrees. He screamed and fell backward into the mud. I stood and turned my body around until it faced the same direction as my head. I then lifted my leg and kicked his face, hearing bones crack as I did.

The dead bandit's scream had caused his companions to rush me, but Hrig caught them by surprise, tackling three to the ground before they had any idea what was happening. I heard an arrow whistle past me and turned my attention to the bowman just as Stone landed heavily on his shoulders, knocking him to the ground and giving himself the perfect angle at which to strike his head with his hammer. Before the other two bowmen could react, he leapt again, driving his heels into the face of one, and on landing, he struck the knee of the other, causing a loud pop.

Two of the bandits charged me, waving their shortswords. I didn't bother drawing my own. Instead, I lifted the man whose face I'd kicked and threw him at their legs. They tripped and rolled forward, but one of them actually used the momentum to roll back to his feet and continue his charge, driving the point of his sword toward my chest. I stepped to the side and grabbed his wrist, squeezing until I heard a crunching sound. He fell to the ground just as his companion had regained his composure and charged me. He was wielding only a dagger, so I prepared a straight right to his face, but before I could throw it, a rock struck him in the temple. I turned back toward Kyren, who was whirling her sling, preparing to fling another stone.

Hrig had four men down and bleeding under her and was fighting three more. She didn't have her axe, but was wielding a short sword she must have taken from one of the attackers. All three of the men were raining down blows at her, but she was deftly dodging and deflecting all of them, a smile on her face. She ducked under an overextended slash and lodged the shortsword into another man's foot before launching herself into an uppercut that took the first man in the chin and threw him several yards.

The last of them tried to strike her face with a mace, but she leaned just a hair out of its reach before closing the distance and punching his throat, which sent him gasping for air to the ground. The man with the sword in his foot managed to remove it just in time for Hrig to bring the other man's mace across his temple. By the end of it, she didn't have a scratch on her. All that training she'd been doing since fighting Donyin seemed to be paying off.

With the last bandit down, we took stock. Thirteen men, most dead or dying. I grabbed the living ones and tied them around a tree using a sailing knot I'd learned from Lythia.

We searched the bodies and found nothing but some coins and a few rings. I decided to keep a few of the nicer weapons and stored them.

"What do we think? Regular bandits or assassins?" I asked.

"Bandits, I'd say. Probably servants trying to make quick gold by robbing people on the roads between estates. The masks are to hide their faces in case they rob their own employers," said Stone.

"Any of yours?" I asked Kyren.

She looked around. "No, but there are a few whose faces aren't really recognizable anymore, so I can't be certain." She shrugged. "I can't blame them. For a lot of servants, the pay is just enough to survive on, and many lords are worse than others when it comes to how they treat people."

"I've had words with more than a few when Ellis got me to attend a party and I saw one of the lords strike a maid. Maybe it wasn't words, so much as fists, but you understand."

"Shall we just leave them like this?" I gestured to the ones who were tied up.

"Aye, it may be some time until someone finds them. I think the scene will speak for itself."

With that, we packed our gear to the occasional moans of pain of the living bandits. There was no chance of getting any more sleep after the scuffle. Kyren insisted on taking a moment to perform last rites over the bodies, but she didn't have us bury them, just cover them with their cloaks. She said that was more than enough for people who'd tried to kill us, at least in Sidi's eyes.

26
THE CAPITAL

By the time the sun rose, we were more than halfway to the capital. The road had widened and become crowded with people moving to and from the city. It wouldn't have felt nearly so congested, however, if not for the inordinate amount of overly ornate carriages that moved on the road.

I watched as a man walked in front of one of them, letting the wheel of the carriage roll over his foot. He screamed at the top of his lungs, stopping most of the traffic. The driver then jumped down, and I could see a heated exchange as a passerby passionately pointed and shouted at the offending carriage. The driver was eventually summoned by the noble inside and a man handed him a small pouch, which he then handed to the hurt man before walking back to the carriage and getting it moving again.

Stone tapped my back. "Watch the man on the ground."

I took his advice and watched as the other man helped him up. They walked a short distance and I saw the "hurt" man pass some money to the "stranger," then they shared a smile, and the man's gait corrected itself from the limp.

"A scam?"

"Aye, lad, a classic. It would never work in a place like Cirros where people are more savvy, but here in the capital, it's still possible to get away with it."

"I'm certain he did have his foot run over, though. How is he not injured?"

"He's wearing shoes about three sizes too big and stuffed with cloth. His actual foot was never in any danger." Stone looked thoughtful for a moment. "I wonder if there's a variation of this you and I could do... It's not like you have a foot that could get hurt."

"Stone..." said Kyren.

"What? I just think we should consider possibilities. It's smart for the lad to keep his options open."

"Thank you, Stone, but I think I'll stick to adventuring as my main source of income for now."

"No reason you can't do both. I do, after all."

I shrugged, and Stone let it drop. I had a feeling he was more interested in passing the time than actually trying to get me to help with a scam.

We reached the capital gates shortly after. Unlike Cirros and Buryn, you couldn't get a very good idea of what Delvus was like until you were actually through one of the gates. There were three of them: one to the east, one south, and one north. The city had been built during the war with Sylfen and so wanted to make entry from their direction as difficult as possible.

When one did enter the city's main gate, the initial impression was wealth and splendor. The main street buildings were owned by the richest merchants and nobles of Caedun, the roads themselves frequently cleaned. Behind those buildings, however, was where the city hid the homes of its servants and laborers. The entryway through the other gates was similar, the idea being that visitors to the city needed to be impressed. Closer to the center of the city was where the nobility and the richest nobles lived behind an interior wall. I had some experiences here through Sevald, but he'd always been with his parents, and they weren't invited into the city often.

Kyren led our way out of Main Street and through several alleys to an inn by the name of The Drunken Monk. She opened the door, and before I was even halfway in, the bartender yelled.

"Kyren!"

"Bruis!" she yelled back, and he stepped around the bar to embrace her. He was a young man with dirty blond hair and a wide smile. After they were done embracing, she turned to us.

"Sevald, Hrig, Stone, this is my friend Bruis. We met at the temple here. He's my mentor's grandson."

"Nice to meet you, lad," said Stone, clasping arms with him.

Hrig and I followed suit. Me with a nod of acknowledgement, and Hrig with a grip that made him wince.

"Nice to meet you all. Any friend of Kyren is welcome here. What can I do for all of you?"

"Rooms, food for three of us, ale for two of us, and wine for one."

"Can do. I'll break out the barrel I keep just in case you visit."

"Thank you, Bruis. You make this place feel like home."

He gave us a wink and disappeared into a room behind the bar. I took a look around. It was a comfortable place. The decoration was sparse, but it had a warm, intimate quality to it. A few other patrons sat tucked into little corners, some with books, others just enjoying a chat, but almost all of them wore priestly vestments of some kind.

"I can see this place is popular with the clergy."

"Yeah, Bruis's first customers were his friends from the

temple, and from there, word of mouth spread mostly through the people they knew, who were also from the temple."

"Is that why it's called the 'Drunken Monk'?"

"Uh, no."

Bruis picked that moment to enter with a tray of five ales and a wine. A smaller robed figure followed behind him with a tray of food.

"Thank you," said Stone eagerly, taking an ale and a plate of food.

"Yes, thank you both," said Hrig, taking her wine.

"First round's on the house, Kyren. That means you owe me for two."

"Do they not all count as first rounds since they all came out at the same time?"

"Sorry, Kyren, if I let you drink for free, I'd go broke." He eyed me, noticing that I had nothing in front me. "Nothing for you, ser?"

"Ah, no. I'm...fasting."

"We get that here pretty often. I'll get you some water."

"Before that, I have to ask. Why is this place called the 'Drunken Monk'?"

Bruis's smile widened even further. "She didn't tell you?"

Kyren hid her face behind a mug of ale, taking a large drink and looking away.

"It's named after Kyren! She won the place in a drinking contest. She gifted it to me after I left the temple."

"Kyren winning a drinking contest? What a surprise," said Hrig with a wry smile.

"I'm concerned about what kind of man would bet their bar. Especially one in such a prime location," said Stone.

"I really don't think he expected to lose. He was a giant of a man. He'd have the contest once a week and hadn't lost for seven years."

"What happened to him?" I asked.

"I got him a job at my grandmother's estate. I felt horrible when I took his bar, but he refused to let me return it to him. I didn't want him to starve, so I sent him to my grandmother with a letter. She was nice enough to hire him on, even though I'd run away from her to join the priesthood just a couple years prior."

"I'm still surprised you didn't consider honoring Jeiri. With your drinking, it seemed an obvious fit," said Bruis.

"You don't choose, Bruis, you know that. You feel a calling. Mine pulled me to Sidi."

"Well, mine pulled me here. Guess I worship the tavern now."

"Few gods are finer," said Stone, raising his mug and taking a deep sip.

Bruis pulled a mug out and raised it in agreement with Stone before also taking a long drink.

The rest of the evening went by smoothly, and before it was too late, everyone was asleep in a communal room above the bar. Everyone but me, of course. I spent the night doing my usual sorting of memories, trying to comb through everything Sevald knew about the capital.

I was the first one downstairs in the morning and ordered everyone breakfast and waited, making small talk with Bruis.

"So why did you leave the temple?"

"It wasn't for me. I had it in my head that I was meant for a life of discipline and quiet contemplation, but I just didn't have it in me."

"Couldn't you have just served Jeiri, Krish, or Nevier? They don't seem particularly dedicated to discipline and quiet contemplation."

"I wanted to be a priest of all the gods. There have been a few, and it's usually the best way to set oneself up for success in the city temples, but I never actually felt a calling or a pull. Not to any of them. I realized at some point that I didn't want to be a priest; I just wanted to be important."

"Does owning a tavern fulfill that for you?"

His eyes twinkled. "Let's just say that the bar the priests all drink at is privy to a surprising amount of information. On top of that, it's a natural place for higher-ups to meet to discuss business. I would never have even spoken to some of those higher up in the mysteries if I'd continued to struggle as a priest, but as a bartender? I see many of them more than once a week."

I chuckled and raised my mug to him. Between Stone and Bruis, Kyren seemed to have a knack for attracting a very peculiar type of person, especially for a holy woman.

Stone and Hrig made their way down from the room and joined me at the table.

"Four plates?" asked Hrig, eyeing the one in front of me.

I looked to make sure Bruis was out of earshot. "I appreciate Kyren not ordering me food so I didn't feel like I had to eat it, but I still want people to feel as comfortable around me as possible, so I'm going to keep pretending to eat."

"Alright, lad, that makes sense, but you know we have your back, right?"

"Of course. I just want to make sure my back stays as light as possible."

With that, Hrig and Stone dug in, tearing through their food quickly. I allowed them to take any of their favorites from my plate that they wanted so I'd be wasting as little as possible as I mimicked eating. Eventually, only Kyren's plate remained.

"I'm surprised she's not down yet," I said.

"I'm not. She's exhausted. Between handling her brothers and cleaning up their mess after they left, she's had barely any time to rest. She's been fueling herself with tea and anxiety," said Hrig.

Tea and anxiety brought forth Pebble's memories of finals. "I didn't realize. She seemed so calm about it all."

"She's good at that. I would've liked to cast a sleep spell on her, but that's really something only she can do. My version tends to involve a concussion."

"Well, we have some time to kill here. Let's let her sleep in," said Stone, picking up her plate and moving it in front of himself. "No reason to let this get cold in the meantime."

Kyren appeared roughly an hour and a half later, during which time Stone and Hrig asked me questions regarding whether or not I could store them and walk across the ocean. My answer was "I don't know," which meant "we definitely shouldn't test it" to me and "we definitely should test it" to them. She seemed to have a bit more force to her steps, her small smile a bit wider.

"Good morning," she said, taking a seat with us.

"Afternoon more like," said Stone.

"Oh, I guess it's time for lunch, then." Kyren ordered something from Bruis and proceeded to show a gusto for eating that had rivaled the gusto with which I'd seen her drink.

I felt bad for not noticing how exhausted she'd been. I'd have to try and be more aware in the future.

"So, what should we do in the city today?" I asked. "We have a few days before the king's masquerade."

"Well, Sevald and I need to meet a noble about the elyrium bars I need to sell, but aside from that, there's only one other thing I can think to do."

"Yes?" I asked.

"There's one thing we'll all need for a masquerade. I figured we'd head to the artisan district and see if we can find a mask maker that can take a job on short notice."

"Been awhile since I wore a mask. Last time I think I was robbing a former business partner who'd gone into the slave trade. Didn't do me much good, though. He recognized my beard. I should've known better, my beard is impossible to miss, after all," said Stone.

"I say masks first. If we are going to bother an artisan for something last minute, I'd like to give him as much time as we can. After that, we can head to the nobleman," said Hrig.

"Agreed," said Kyren, and our first full day in the capital began.

27
MASKS

After Kyren was done eating, we headed out onto the streets, following her as she weaved her way through the city toward the artisan district. It bordered the inner wall of the city and overall seemed nicer than most of the areas we'd been through so far. There were homes with small gardens, stained-glass windowed studios, and people's crafts on display all throughout.

We began looking for anyone who seemed like they could make masks and eventually saw a man working in a small garden to thread several feathers through a dainty porcelain mask painted the colors of a peacock's tail. We approached him, but before we could say anything, Kyren held her hand up to us, and we waited until he was done with the feather he was working with.

"Excuse me, ser," said Kyren.

The man sighed. "Masks, I'm guessing?"

"Yes."

"Then, no."

"Pardon?"

"I can't take another order for masks. Every one of these

frilly nobles has a dozen specific little requests and notes, and every time I do exactly what they ask for they tell me, 'no, I didn't mean like that, I meant like this,' I can't do anymore, okay? You can go ask Dulyn or Creyd a few blocks down. Honestly, though, I think most everyone is booked up at this point."

With remarkable patience, Kyren simply nodded, and we left.

Hrig shrugged as we left. "I can't blame him. Could you imagine having to deal with the nobility all day? I could barely stand the few parties I went to."

"Aye, I can't imagine trying to keep people like that happy all the time. I can manage it until I get what I want from them, but as a day-to-day job? No, thank you."

We had no more luck with Dulyn and Creyd and were heading back through the market when a young man with short curly hair approached us.

"E-excuse me." He paused; he was out of breath and had clearly been running to get to us. "Are you looking for masks?"

"Yes," said Kyren. "Are you alright?"

'I'm fantastic." He paused again, still trying to catch his breath. "I would like to volunteer to help."

"Yer an artist?" asked Stone.

"Yes, well, an artist's apprentice. My master is Dulyn, who you spoke to earlier."

"Shouldn't you be doing whatever work your master assigns you?" I asked, feeling a bit hypocritical as I did so.

"Well, yes, but he's so narrow-minded! He only ever lets me do the most basic of tasks. Not to mention getting him food, pouring him tea, and emptying his chamber pot."

"Why take this risk, then?" I asked.

"Because making masks for the king's masquerade is a chance to get my name out there. If people ask you about them, you can say it was courtesy of Trevlyn Conters, artist extraordinaire. If it goes well enough, I could open my own shop, or maybe even find a patron!"

"Well, it's not like we have much of a choice," said Kyren.

Trevlyn smiled. "Thank you. I only have a couple of conditions. I'll only charge you one gold piece each, but you have to let me design the masks myself."

We all nodded to one another.

"That sounds reasonable," said Kyren.

"Alright!" He began pulling out small white tablets. "I'll just need a face mold for each of you, and I can get started. Where are you staying?"

"The Drunken Monk."

"Excellent, I'll bring them there myself in a couple of days." He began making the molds. It only took a short press for the impression of everyone's faces to be made. Eventually, he got to me.

"I'm afraid I can't remove my armor. I'm bound by an oath to Dur not to."

"Oh, well, in that case." He simply pushed the mold onto my faceplate, startling me for a moment. "I think I'll be able to figure something out for you. I'd hate for you to miss out. Also for me to miss out on more potential customers."

"Thank you."

Once he was done, he simply hopped along the sidewalk, back in the direction of Dulyn.

"The lad forgot to take our money," said Stone, frowning.

"Luckily, artists don't need good business sense to be good artists," said Hrig.

"I suppose that's true," he conceded.

After that was settled, we made our way to a tailor, where everyone but me got themselves fitted for finery. Hrig grumbled a bit at first about it, but when the tailor informed her men's cuts were coming into fashion for women, she was satisfied with a red doublet with silvery sleeves. Stone managed to find a piece of clothing another dwarf had never picked up in his size and so got a deal on a black outfit with touches of light blue and gold buttons. Kyren found a simple but elegant white dress. I spent most of my time nodding yes or no when one of them asked if something looked good or bad. I felt a little left out, but it wasn't anyone's fault. Besides, I was always the best dressed member of the party. It was their turn to shine.

We left the clothes for some last-minute alterations and gave the tailor the location of The Drunken Monk. From there, we headed for the inner gates to meet with the nobleman Percy and Byren had so liberally borrowed from.

The inner city was a place of absolute splendor. The houses, while more modestly-sized than estates, were built upward to make up for it. Gardens of flowers and topiaries in unique shapes proved common, and many were open to the public. People in fine clothes walked and talked, seemingly less weighed down than the people of the outer city. Eventually, we came to the manor of one Lord Phaismis, the man Kyren's brothers had borrowed a hefty sum from.

Unlike the surrounding homes, this one was clearly a new construction, the architecture in a newer style with columns and a kind of downward swooping roof that curved at the edges. It was painted white, which seemed gaudy even in comparison to the splendor that surrounded it. I got the distinct impression that Phaismis was new to being a noble. I certainly didn't recognize the name.

Kyren showed a butler at the front door a letter, and he escorted us into the waiting room. A young woman was cleaning the room as we entered, but she bowed and left. Another young woman came in to offer us tea, which we accepted. A third young woman entered with a small platter of pastries. My first thought was that his house seemed overstaffed, my second was that it seemed odd not to hire more experienced help, and my third simply resulted in me muttering, "Oh."

"It's not too uncommon," said Hrig, hearing me. "I can't blame a man for wanting some eye candy, and I didn't notice any bruises on them. My guess is that these girls knew what they were getting into."

"My grandmother did the same thing. She always called her servants her 'young men'; it made more than a few visiting nobles uncomfortable. I think that was the point as much as prettying up the rooms was."

"An enlightened woman, clearly," said Hrig with a smile.

"You know, I always hear you refer to her as yer grandmother, but what was her actual name?" asked Stone.

She sighed. "It was Kyren, of course."

"Ah," said Stone, dropping it.

A few moments later, we were called into a small reception area, where a man dressed in a purple doublet with gold sleeves and wearing a hat with a jaunty feather poking from it was sitting. He was thin, with a black beard trimmed into a neat goatee, his mustache also thin, sitting just above the top of his lip. He stood as Kyren entered and gestured for us to sit at the chairs arranged in front of him. He had an oddly infectious grin that I would've returned if it had been possible.

"Welcome, Lady Kyren, and company, welcome."

"Thank you for meeting us."

"Of course, of course, it's the least I can do after what happened with your brothers. Besides, it's not smart not to meet with people who owe you money."

Stone chuckled at that.

"I do hope there are no hard feelings. I feel, in many ways, betrayed by your brothers, as well. They seemed like good people, friendly, and capable of paying the debts they accrued. Had I realized that they were sending the money to those damnable barons, I'd never have agreed to it." He had a kind of musical way of speaking, one that made it easy to get lost in his rhythm.

"It's fine, ser. A loan is a loan, and debt is debt. The circumstances are behind us, and it looks like I may be able to pay you off. I will simply need some time to find buyers."

"Yes, the elyrium you found. I have a specialist staying with me. He'll be able to determine if it's genuine, and if so, I will grant you three months without interest to find a buyer and pay in full. The others your brothers borrowed from are willing to take my word and offer the same deal."

Kyren nodded. "Sevald, please go retrieve the sample we brought."

I nodded and left the room. I then made sure there was no one nearby, removed my gauntlet, and began to remove one of the bars from myself. I narrowly missed a vase, three small statues, and a rather low-hanging chandelier, but I managed to extricate it without incident.

I re-entered the meeting room and gently laid the bar down in the center of the room. An older elvish man was standing next to Phaismis with excitement in his eyes.

"May I?" he asked.

I nodded, and he made a beeline for the bar. He lifted it at the end and began inspecting it. He tested the weight a few times before taking a small hammer out of his hand and tapping it. His ears twitched as it rang out that same peculiar sound it had made when we'd struck it in the dungeon. He then licked it.

"Does that really help with identifying it?" asked Phaismis.

"Not really," he responded, not elaborating further. After a few more seconds, he nodded, satisfied. "This is it, this is genuine elyrium. Gods, I haven't seen it since I was a boy."

"Well, Lady Kyren of Wyrwind, it looks like we have a deal." Phaismis removed a piece of parchment from his desk and signed his name.

Kyren then stood and signed the document as well, after which they shook hands.

"Am I to understand that you'll be at the masquerade?"

"Yes, we'll all be attending. The king was very kind to invite us."

"Kind, trying to control the narrative; I suppose he can be both."

"It's often a king's job to be."

After those pointed words, we made our way out to leave. Unfortunately, a maid was escorting us out, so rather than simply storing the elyrium as I had when we entered, I instead had to somehow make it from room to room while holding it. After a few too many close calls with fine antiques, they simply opened a window, and I passed it out to Hrig. Once we were farther away, we ducked into an alleyway, where I quickly stored it again.

After that, we headed back to The Drunken Monk for food and ale. I realized that this was the first time I'd been able to actually enjoy what a city offered. Certainly, I had the memories of moonlit walks in Usulaum, eating street food in Cirros, and going to dinners in the capital, but experiencing it myself had been different, and very enjoyable.

"I'm thinking we should see what research we can do here on Aurum," said Kyren, breaking my reverie.

Stone finished chewing a piece of sausage. "We should.

There may not be much, but maybe we can figure something out."

"I'll check the temple. My mentor may be willing to share what she knows, though I may hit the same walls I did in Buryn."

"I'll see if any of the contacts I used to have here know anything."

"I suppose I could check the library. The recordkeeping in Caedun is terrible, but most places at least have information on their own city's history and that of the ruling line. I may be able to learn more about what happened with that ship," I said.

"I suppose, out of those options, I'll help out at the library," said Hrig.

"Really? I'd have expected you to be more interested in Stone's contacts."

"With Stone, 'meeting old contacts' means two hours of talking about the good old days, and maybe ten minutes of actual discussion. I'd take the silence of a library over listening to old men reminisce about the old times anytime."

28

RESEARCH AND REVENGE

The next day, we went through what had become our morning routine at the tavern before separating. Stone went toward the outer part of the city, and Hrig, Kyren, and I headed through the inner gates before separating. It was a gloomy day, the clouds pregnant with rain, and the sun had only managed brief peeks down on the world below. I didn't particularly mind rain. I liked the sound it made bouncing off me.

We made it into the library just as the first few telltale tings started ringing out from my helmet. The outside of the building was relatively nondescript, stuffed between the magistrate's office and a bank. Inside, it was gloomy, with only candles lighting the building, with any light the windows would've brought in significantly diminished by the storm outside.

It was surprisingly organized, and clean, with only the design of the building itself and the smell of rotting books showing its age. Hrig and I were among the only four people inside, with one man studying, and another standing at a desk at the end of the room, writing something in a ledger.

I began approaching the man at the end of the room,

assuming he was a librarian, and it was at that moment I became distinctly aware of how loud a suit of armor is in a large, echoey room. As I approached him, I watched the man slowly put down his quill, close his ledger, raise an eyebrow, and scowl. By the time I reached him, I understood, even with my limited personal experience with body language, that I was perhaps the most disdained piece of scum he had ever had the displeasure of seeing.

"Ser, I'm afraid you'll find no monster to slay here, no giant rats, or goblins, to run through, and certainly no snipes to hunt."

Hrig approached the desk, as well, much more silently than I had. "Are you sure?" she asked with a cheeky smile. "I've read books full of such things."

"I apologize for my manner of dress. I have made an oath to Dur not to be seen outside of my armor, but I still had some research I needed to do here. I apologize for the noise I'm making, and will, in all honesty, likely continue to make."

The man sighed, and I saw a bit of his contempt for me leave his expression.

"I must be being tested." He pulled an amulet out of the folds of his robe and showed it to me. It was a golden coin engraved with a scale, the symbol of Dur.

"That explains why this place is so well-maintained."

The man managed to turn his scowl into something approximating a smile. "Well, the place isn't too busy today. Honestly, it's not too busy any day. Is there something I can help you find?"

I let Pebble's researching instincts take over. "I need a reference on the lives of the royalty, any older religious texts with information on rituals that honor all gods, and whatever you have on dragons and their extinction. History, preferably not just tales of knights slaying them."

"I, however, will take any books about knights slaying them."

"Hmm, well, I could guide you to some books, but that's a rather eclectic mix, and while I understand your oath, I'd prefer not to listen to you clanging all throughout the room." He thought for a moment. "How about you sit down and I'll bring you the books I think would be most helpful?"

"I'd appreciate that, ser, thank you."

The man nodded and started to weave his way through the shelves. I sat at the nearest desk and waited for him. Hrig returned first, holding a book titled *The Duke's Hammer*. She put her feet up and began flipping through it.

Shortly after that, the librarian came pushing a small cart loaded with books. He put them into two separate piles, with reference materials at the top.

"Unfortunately, we don't have much in regard to church ritual—much of that is oral tradition—but I did find this rather old prayer book." He placed it in a third position in front of me. "Let me know if you need anything else."

I nodded. "Thank you, ser, you've been very accommodating."

He nodded and thumbed his pendant. "Anything in the name of Dur."

After that, I began poring through all of the material in front of me. I started with the prayerbook. It included many prayers I was familiar with through my meals and several I'd never even heard of, including a section for minor mantras to lesser gods. Toward the middle, however, I found something interesting. A short prayer for protection.

> May all the gods
> Lesser and greater
> Protect me from one

Who hears no prayer
Keep his whims at bay
And his flames that slay
From all of those
He sees as his prey

The content of the prayer seemed to indicate something draconic, but it was clear the prayer referred to only a single entity rather than dragonkind as a whole. Aside from that, the prayer book was a bust, so I moved on to the historical books on dragons.

One was simply a list of dragons killed, who'd killed them, and what kingdom they hailed from. I saw no indication of Aurum's name, though there were a few that came close.

Another was a more general history of dragon slaying, and it was there that I found that while the earliest dragon slayings had been commissioned by kingdoms sick of unruly dragons pillaging livestock or destroying villages, the later ones had been issued by the temples. Priests of every god began offering payments to any individual who could kill a dragon, regardless of whether or not they'd been disturbing anyone.

Shortly after that, dragons went to ground, taking the form of humans, elves, and other races in order to blend in and survive, but eventually, even those were found and killed by dedicated hunters until there were none left.

I wondered if perhaps Aurum was one dragon that managed to hide all this time, but based on what I'd seen in the shipwreck, I had a feeling he wasn't much for hiding.

Finally, I moved on to the books on Caedun's royal line. There were many ups and downs throughout its history. Recognized bastards, usurpations, cousins fighting over claims, it was quite a spicy bit of history, but most of it was superfluous to what I was looking for. Eventually, I found it, a small line in one book detailing how a queen, pregnant with the king's child, had been the only survivor of a shipwreck. That had occurred more than eleven hundred years ago.

So, the current king was descended from that queen. Due to the incestuous nature of royal marriages, he was as full-blooded as any other king at this point, but I wondered how cautious I would need to be of him. If he was a descendant of that dragon I'd seen in that vision, it was a concern, but that had also occurred more than a thousand years ago. There were likely many people descended from dragons, who might not even be aware of what lay within their bloodline.

I was snapped from my study by Hrig shaking my arm. I was surprised, as she'd seemed completely absorbed by *The Duke's Hammer*, even seeming to be blushing at times. She gestured around the room with her eyes, and at that moment, I noticed that the library was completely full. There were more than a dozen dwarves all around us, some leafing through books and others looking directly at us. All of them had weapons at their sides.

I calmly closed the book in front of me and placed all of them in front of me back onto the cart the librarian had used. I then simply sat and waited with Hrig, not making any sudden moves. Another dwarf entered the room then, and though he was wearing less armor, I recognized him immediately. It was Rock, the man I'd taken my shield from.

He sat down in front of me, a wide smile on his face.

"Hello, bastard," he said with a sneer on his lips.

"Hello, loser," I responded, wishing I could return his expression.

"I've come for my shield. Give it to me, and I'll spare your friend here."

I noticed then that the men above us began drawing crossbows while the men near us unsheathed their weapons.

"Even if you spare her, I don't think she'd grant you the same kindness."

"You and her may be strong in a one-on-one fight, but come now, you're outnumbered."

Hrig and I laughed.

"We're actually more used to fighting outnumbered," I said.

"Fine. Be that way." Rock snapped his fingers.

Hrig dove under the table as a half dozen bolts shot down at us. I simply turned my back toward the majority of shooters, blocking the bolts with my shield.

Rock's men attacked me while I was sitting. I threw the chair back and rolled under their blows before they could strike, then I threw myself back up. I considered drawing my sword, but I was concerned about knocking over the bookshelves.

Hrig launched herself out from under the table and into Rock's chair, pummeling him with blows that quickly wiped the smile off his face. She only ceased her attack when two of his men attacked her with swords, forcing her back.

The men I was engaging began attacking in earnest. I caught one's shortsword before it gained momentum and threw a swift jab for his face, knocking him out cold. I then used the hilt of the shortsword to club the shoulder of the other dwarf, forcing him to drop the mace he was holding. From there, I dropped my elbow like a hammer into the top of his skull.

It was then that a bookshelf fell on top of me. I heard the librarian cry out as it slammed into me, driving me to my knees. I felt a hammer slam into the shield on my back through several books. I was tempted to simply throw the shelf back toward the dwarf with the hammer, but I didn't want to create a domino effect, and so instead, I rolled forward and let the shelf fall the rest of the way, cringing as I heard a page rip when I rolled over one of the books.

Hrig was finishing up with the two dwarves who had engaged her, knocking one out with the copy of *The Duke's Hammer* I realized she was still holding. From there, she leapt onto the ledge of the second level, pulling herself up just as two more crossbow bolts whizzed by her. The crossbowman nearest to her had his nose broken with the palm of her hand. The farther one went to fire at her again, but didn't have time to as Hrig threw his companion at him, causing them both to roll across the floor and hit a wall of books, which promptly rained its contents down onto them.

I got around the bookshelf, and the dwarf with the hammer took a defensive stance. I decided then to be cheeky and pulled out my shield. He tried to get underneath it with a low swipe, but I dropped it, feeling it take a portion of his energy. He tried a few more times to get around it, but I blocked him every time and could feel his blows growing lighter. Finally, I simply fell onto him, shield first, knocking him straight onto the ground. He didn't get up.

By the time I was done, Hrig had taken down all of the men on the second level. I looked around for Rock and found him behind me, at the librarian's desk, holding a crossbow aimed at me. He went to pull the trigger, but at just that moment, the librarian popped out from behind his desk and slammed a massive book into Rock's head, knocking him flat onto the ground.

The librarian looked at me. "Brigands! In my library! The absolute nerve!"

"I'm, uh, sorry about the mess. I'll help you clean up."

"Don't bother. I'm going to get the city guard. They'll clear this filth out of here. Besides, I don't trust anyone else with putting books in their proper places."

"In that case, do you mind if we leave? I'd prefer not to have to deal with the guard."

"Yes, that's probably wise."

"I will be taking this one, though," I said, lifting Rock and tucking him under my arm.

"Any chance I can keep this?" asked Hrig, holding up her now thoroughly dented book.

"*The Duke's Hammer?*" He laughed. "Go ahead. That romance was last season's great hit. I'm sure someone else will donate a copy soon now that ladies are moving on to *The Barbarian's Sword*."

She nodded her thanks, and we walked out of the library with our prizes in tow.

We moved quickly, not wanting to draw too much attention to ourselves, and we quickly found an alley we could tuck into. Hrig poured some water on Rock's head, and I gave him an open-handed slap, waking him up.

"Wha—"

His eyes were foggy, but as soon as I came into focus, they narrowed, and he spat in my faceplate. I calmly ripped a piece of his tunic and used that to clean myself.

"How did you find us?" I asked.

"It wasn't hard. You left an easy trail to follow."

"Maybe not for someone with a brain, but you? I'm certain you had help."

"Talen told me where to find you, where you were headed."

"Talen!? He's here?" asked Hrig.

"No, he told me in Cirros. I've been on your trail for some time."

"Well, that's a relief, at least," I said to Hrig. "Well, I would appreciate it if you could stop following me and maybe get on with your life."

"Only if you give me the shield. And also die."

I sighed. "I like the shield. Though honestly, if you'd just asked to begin with, I probably would've given it to you. Now I'm fairly certain even if I do give it to you, you'll still try to kill me."

"Liar, you'd never have given it up."

"He really would have," said Hrig. "He doesn't really have the best understanding of the value of things."

"Listen, I could just kill you, but how about instead, you just promise me you'll take a little break from trying to kill me?"

"A break?"

"Yeah, a break. How about in, oh, six months we meet here. From there, we can arrange a time and a place. You can fight me, or I'll even fight a champion of your choice. Whoever wins gets the shield."

Rock frowned. "I'd prefer to catch you unaware."

"Well, I could just kill you now, if you'd prefer."

"What's keeping me from just gathering more men and attacking you?"

"Nothing, I suppose. Though the men you gathered... Not so impressive. I think within six months, you may have better luck either training yourself or finding a suitable champion."

Rock thought on it for a minute. "Deal."

I held out my hand, and he shook it. From there, Hrig and I left the concussed dwarf to figure the rest of it out himself.

"Was that a good idea?" asked Hrig.

"Not at all, but I'd prefer not to kill anyone while we're in the city. Besides, I just don't see him as much of a threat, but if he does bring a legitimate champion for me to fight, that could be interesting."

Hrig chuckled. "I'm starting to rub off on you, I see."

"Yep, you're a terrible influence, I'm afraid."

29
UNFASHIONABLY EARLY

The party regrouped at The Drunken Monk later that day to discuss our findings. We ordered some ale, Hrig got wine, and I began by telling them what I'd uncovered in the library as well as going over Rock's attack.

Stone sighed. "Talen sending Rock your way lines up with what I managed to learn, too. Talen survived what we did to him in Cirros—thrived, even. He's apparently even managed to align himself closely with the Duke. It appears Dorsia's idea that he'd consolidate his power if he wasn't beaten was right. I couldn't turn up anything about dragons, or the damned Children of Aurum, though. Just that there have been a lot of shake-ups up and down the continent, possibly all over the world. Oh, and there's a black market for dragon artifacts, teeth and such, but it's hard to prove fakes, so it didn't seem worth our time."

Kyren nodded. "It took a long conversation, but I managed to learn from my mentor that Aurum is indeed a god. A major one, in fact, but beyond that, I couldn't pry anything else from her. What she did tell me was that the higher levels of all city temples are already involved. She couldn't reveal more, said I'd need to be higher into the mysteries to be allowed that kind of access, and even what I've learned is a closely guarded secret."

"Is that an option?" I asked. "Could you attain the status necessary in your order to learn more?"

"Possibly, but you have to understand that it's as political as it is religious. I'd need backing, the support of priests both within and without my own sect, and most of all, time."

We all sat, sipping absently out of our mugs. Even I took a small sip out of habit.

"Let's remember why we're really here," said Hrig, giving all of a serious look. "To party."

The tension broke as we all shared a laugh. After that, we made small talk for a while.

Later in the evening, we were met at the tavern by Trevlyn, a large box in hand and a wide smile on his face. He had a look in his eyes that I could only describe as a kind of manic delirium.

"Hello, hello, hello, hello," he said to each of us, nodding as he did. "I've completed the masks you requested, and I am absolutely thrilled with how they turned out."

He began opening the box, inside which were four more boxes, and then he began opening those one at a time. He grabbed the first of them, opened it, and handed its contents to Stone.

Stone took it and turned it over in his hands. It was a cross somewhere between a monkey and a goblin. It had an impressive array of sharp teeth, all of the facial features curled up in such a way that it gave the impression of laughter. The piece was masterfully constructed, and when Stone put it on, it fit perfectly. It had a mildly intimidating effect to it when he smiled, as his own teeth made it seem like another mouth hid inside that of the laughing creature.

Hrig was the next to receive her mask. It was simpler than Stone's, but no less impressive—a bear with the tusks of a boar curling out of the side of its mouth. The genuine blond fur woven into it somehow perfectly matched the shade of Hrig's own braids. When she placed it on, it almost looked as if it were her actual head.

Kyren's was third. The first thing I noticed about it was its color. Pure white, matching the tunic she was wearing. At first, it seemed completely unblemished, but on closer inspection, one could actually see incredibly intricate patterns carved throughout the piece. The mask itself had the appearance of a rabbit, ears included. Like Stone's and Hrig's, hers fit perfectly.

Finally, we came to mine. Trevlyn reached into the box. What he pulled out surprised me. The face of a dragon. Unlike the porcelain and leather of the other masks, this one was made of metal, and the silver of it caught the candlelight of the room beautifully. Holding it in my hands, I could tell it was a true masterpiece, even with my limited artistic knowledge.

"I had to consult with a smith friend and a metallurgist for yours, but they were very excited to help. You should be able to simply place the mask against the front of your helmet and it will connect. It uses something called 'magnets'."

I lifted the mask to my face and felt it snap into place. As perfect a fit as I could imagine, and I shook my head a few times to ensure it was truly connected. I then opened and closed the mouth, realizing it was also magnetized.

"This is incredible."

Trevlyn positively beamed. "Thank you, ser. I was up all night working on them."

"The craftsmanship is incredible," said Stone. "Worthy of a dwarf."

Kyren looked over at my mask. "What made you choose the animals?"

"Well, I don't know that I chose them so much as they were chosen for me."

"What do you mean?" asked Hrig, her voice surprisingly unmuffled from within her mask.

"Well, I just went off the impression I received from each of you. I tried to match that impression as closely as possible to the masks themselves."

I nodded, but felt a bit disturbed at the idea that he'd felt I was dragon-like. Perhaps it would be a compliment to some, but from what I'd seen of them, the thought made me distinctly uncomfortable. Still, the mask was incredible, and I didn't want to seem ungrateful, so I made no complaints.

We gathered his payment and each handed him a gold coin, plus a tip of five additional gold coins each, which not even Stone complained about.

"Ye need to charge what you're worth, lad. There's no sense in doing work just for 'exposure'."

He nodded, taking the money and placing it into a pouch tied at his waist. He seemed to be coming down from whatever mania had driven him to complete the masks so quickly, and his eyes were beginning to droop.

"Here, why don't I take you up to my sleeping area upstairs, and you can take a nap."

He yawned and gave a tired nod, and I led him up to my bed, where he immediately collapsed. I gently placed a blanket over him and returned downstairs to find everyone still admiring the masks they'd received.

"That kid has a real gift," said Hrig, running her fingers along the snout of her mask.

"Aye, now once we get the clothes we ordered, we should more than match the fap-about nobles that are attending." He turned in Kyren's and my direction. "No offense."

"None taken," said Kyren. "I'm not always a big fan myself."

"And I'm not actually a noble; I just ate one. It would be

interesting if that's how the government actually worked here, though."

Trevlyn wound up sleeping through the night on my bed, so I made myself comfortable on the floor until he got up, which by dawn, he still hadn't. So I simply slipped out of the room and made my way downstairs to meet with everyone. Kyren was speaking with Bruis, holding a package, and Hrig and Stone sat at a table together cleaning their plates.

"Morning," I said, sitting next to Hrig. I realized I almost always sat next to Hrig. Made the table feel a bit uneven when Kyren and Stone sat across from us.

Hrig and Stone returned the greeting through mouthfuls of food. Kyren finished her conversation with Bruis and came to the table.

"Good morning, Sevald."

"Morning, Kyren. What's in the box?"

"Well, we felt like you maybe wanted to do a little something extra for the masquerade, so we all chipped in at the tailor to get you something." She handed me the box.

"Really? Thank you, I don't know what to say."

"Don't say anything, lad. Just open the box," said Stone.

I did, and inside, I saw a neatly folded bundle of fabric. I stood up and unfurled it, revealing a beautiful cape, primarily burgundy with a border of silver thread. The colors contrasted beautifully with my navy gambeson. I tied it on immediately.

"It's beautiful. Thank you all."

"We just wanted you to meet the rest of the group's standards. Can't have you dragging us down at the party," said Hrig, smiling.

I chuckled. "I was just thinking it would be good for you all to be the ones dressed nicely, for once. Unlike the rest of you, I'm always in my finest clothes."

The rest of the day was spent primarily pacing about and trying to keep ourselves busy while not simply making a beeline for the palace as quickly as possible. When the sun finally began dipping, we all got dressed in the attire we'd prepared for the party. I decided to store the shield that was formerly Rock's within myself and tied a peace knot around my sword. Technically, I could rip right through it, but the gesture was important. After we were ready, we set out toward the palace.

Nighttime in Delvus was very different than it had been in Cirros or Buryn. The streets were lit by lanterns that gave the place a kind of ethereal atmosphere. There were street vendors still out, taverns lit with the noises of revelry pouring out of them as freely as ale, and we regularly encountered city guardsmen on patrol. It seemed like a generally safe and pleasant place to be. This, of course, made Stone uncomfortable.

"I was under the impression you've been here before. Why are you so uncomfortable?" I asked.

"Aye, but that was some time ago back when this place had some edge to it. Yes, there's still some lovely dens of sin here, and it's an easy place to pick a pocket, but there's no real crime, no real vice here. Sure, the nobles plot, have their little 'orgies' and double crosses, but it's just not as fun as a few people from the docks tearing their way through rich people's wallets and spending it all on enough ale to drown auroch."

I gave a solemn nod. "I'm terribly sorry that no one is trying to slit our throats for a few copper."

"Thank you, lad. Your sympathy means a lot to me."

When we got through the inner gate, we began to see other invitees making their way to the palace. The most popular mask type seemed to be lions and other jungle cats for men, and birds for ladies. I had a feeling that we'd stand out as a group, but I supposed that was likely to be the case no matter what we did.

We reached the third and most interior wall of the city where the party attendants had gathered and a man was checking their invitations. We got into the line, but before we even moved up once, a guard approached Kyren.

"Lady Wyrwind?"

"Yes?"

"You and your companions may follow me directly inside. The king has designated you as special guests."

He looked us over for a moment, checking us over. I noticed him paying particular attention to my sword, but once he saw the peace knot, he simply began walking us toward the palace.

The grounds of the palace were stunning, the garden full of white roses that seemed to have been planted just for the party. Servants were taking refreshments out to the line of guests, themselves wearing plain white porcelain masks that contrasted sharply with their black uniforms. The palace itself was built out of what looked to be a kind of black marble with rich details in white stone and a beautiful wooden door that seemed to be carved from a single piece of wood.

I could have spent hours simply staring at all the little details and beautiful materials that had been used in the construction, but there was a party to get to. The guard allowed us a moment to absorb everything, clearly used to the occasional gawking rube, but after what he thought was an appropriate waiting period, he gave a slight cough to get our attention and led us inside.

30
THE MASQUERADE

The party itself was being held in one of the upper levels in a grand ballroom. Everything was ornate to the point of being visually confusing, with the incredibly intricate rug being the standout. It had images of gods, kings, and monsters locked in struggles or simply posing in the most grandiose way imaginable. The weaving of it must have taken a decade.

The guests that had already arrived were mingling and laughing, a general air of cheer all throughout. I had the distinct impression we were earlier than expected, despite arriving very close to the time listed in the king's invitation.

We found a corner and settled in to watch the various nobles find their way inside. Most entered without much fanfare, but between Hrig, Kyren, and me, we were able to identify almost all of the family colors and crests. Others were announced as they entered, typically with an overlong list of titles and honors. One particularly egregious example was the entrance of "Lord Benjamin Gledron-Hamilton Bressington Esquire of the Verdant Peaks and Whitecastle Lakes by the Fives Great Oaks III. Son of Duke Benjamin Gledron-Hamilton Bressington Esquire of the Verdant Peaks and Whitecastle Lakes by the Fives Great Oaks II, and father of Master Benjamin Gledron-Hamilton Bressington Esquire of the Verdant Peaks and Whitecastle Lakes by the Fives Great Oaks IV." By the end of his entrance, I swear most guests had managed to finish an entire drink.

Eventually, enough guests had arrived that the party began to start in full. Entertainers of various types started to file in. Musicians playing music that managed to somehow be loud enough to follow you throughout the party, but soft enough to be easily spoken over. Acrobats dancing across silk ribbons that glided about everyone, and even fire breathers and sword jugglers performing their arts to the delight of easily entertained nobles.

Hrig and Stone went to sample the various trays of food floating around, and in Stone's case, I expected a rather large tithe to be given to Kyren by the end of the night. Kyren and I began mingling, her with the ease of someone trained for court and me with the stiff manners of someone who knew the rules but rarely used them. I was finishing a light conversation with another man that had worn a suit of armor to the party, Baron Kievan, when I heard a voice behind me.

"Sevald?"

I froze. I recognized the voice, or rather, Sevald did. I nodded at Kievan to excuse myself and turned around. Behind me stood an older woman, with brown hair tinged with gray, wearing the distinct black and gold of the house Senturius. Next to her was a similarly aged man, with steel blue eyes and long white hair swept backward. They each wore masks I had memories of playing with in my childhood, and their clothes were dated, but well-maintained.

"Mother, Father, it's good to see you." I fell into formality with them, just as Sevald himself would've done. Manners were a safe bulwark from which to approach complicated relationships.

"It's good to see you too, Sevald," said Sevald's mother. "We've been hearing a little about your exploits. Dungeon clearing, goblin slaying, and Duke Ellis sent us a lovely letter about you."

I nodded, and we stood there awkwardly for a few moments. I was lucky Sevald was already awkward around his parents, or it probably would've been suspicious. "I'm surprised to see you here."

"We were surprised, as well, but we received an invite from the king himself!" Sevald's father beamed with pride. "He said that some noble houses shouldn't be kept from the capital simply because they lack funds, especially one with as storied a past as ours."

"That's very kind of him." I looked around. "Are my brothers here, as well?"

"No, they're still at the estate. They never really had the same taste for travel that you did."

The term "the estate" brought memories of a dilapidated castle that barely stood and the meager five servants they could afford for its upkeep. When a family has more sons than servants, there's typically an issue with priorities. We continued standing; they took small sips of the drinks they were holding and nibbled on a bit of food. Finally, Ser Senturius broke the silence.

"Son, I know we're not the best at this..." he laid a hand on my pauldron, "—but we're proud of you."

I felt the part of my essence that was Sevald roil at that statement, and memories of his began to overwhelm me. His mother helping him onto a horse for the first time, sitting sandwiched between his brothers as his father told him stories of his heritage, holding his youngest brother after he was born, the stern looks of disapproval he got when he left home, the bitterness he felt that his other brother had joined the army and received no such disappointment, but his leaving was somehow worse. I realized I'd been standing still for some time.

"Thank you, Father. That means a lot to me."

And it did. Sevald would have truly appreciated hearing that, and I saw no reason to break his parents' hearts today.

"Well, we're going to mingle a bit more and then retire for the evening." Sevald's mother was flustered—we all were—and she seemed eager to take a break from the high emotions. We exchanged some firm handshakes, and they walked away to talk to some of the other guests.

I began wandering the party, still trying to sort through the new depth of Sevald's memories and impressions that the conversation seemed to have unlocked. Eventually, I found myself watching a fire breather. She was quite impressive. I could actually feel the intense heat of the flames she was blowing out, and she had incredible control over it, holding the flame for what must have been thirty seconds before pausing. She was wearing a simple red mask with flames licking up the sides of it. It beautifully emphasized her golden eyes.

I went still. The woman made brief eye contact with me and smiled before unleashing another wave of fire into the air. I forced myself to take a relaxed stance and then started looking for my companions. Kyren was already approaching me, and I made my way to meet her, moving at what I hoped was a leisurely pace.

"Sevald, I saw someone with golden eyes."

"Me, too. The firebreather, right?"

Her eyes widened. "No, the man with black lion mask." She gestured to a man wearing a silver doublet.

"We need to find Hrig and Stone."

It didn't take us long to do so as they were already looking for us.

"Lad, there's a man with golden eyes serving food."

"And there's one juggling swords near the stairs," said Hrig.

"Kyren and I have each seen one, as well. There's definitely something going on."

Before we could exchange any more information, a horn sounded. We looked to the top of the stairs. Two men stood there with a servant about to announce them. One wore a stunning golden doublet with black accents, his a mask in the shape of a dragon, very similar to my own, except colored gold. The other wore a simpler black outfit and was wrapped in what looked to be a black leather cape. His mask was orange and in the shape of a fox. It matched the color of his hair.

"His Majesty King Caedus the XXXIV, King of Caedun, Ruler of the Middle Kingdom, and his guest of honor, newly recognized Ducal Heir Talen of Cirros."

I clenched my fist and felt the group tense up.

"Ducal heir?" I asked no one in particular.

"He used to fuss about being a royal bastard, but I always thought it was to make himself seem important," said Stone.

"Even if it's a lie, if the king recognizes him, that makes him the duke's son, whether it's true or not," said Kyren.

The king and Talen began walking down the stairs. As they got closer, I was able to see Caedus's face, and I realized his eyes were the same shade of gold as Talen's. Hrig sucked air through her teeth, noticing at the same time I did. Talen flashed a sharp-toothed grin in our direction before he moved to mingle with several guests, though some were giving him dirty looks. Clearly, his reputation had preceded him.

The king headed straight for us.

"Kyren, Hrig, Stone, Sevald, welcome!" he said with a smile

that could only be described as kingly. "Are you enjoying yourselves so far?"

Kyren managed to keep her expression neutral. "Yes, Your Eminence. It's been fabulous so far."

"Good! I'm glad to hear it!" He gave me a once over, stopping at my mask. "It would seem we had the same idea."

"More the artist's idea than mine, actually."

"Well, maybe we should talk about it. Can I borrow you from your companions for a few moments?"

I looked back at them. They didn't seem happy with the idea. I then looked back around the room. At least six children of Aurum at the party. If I went all out, I might be able to take two or even three, but the collateral damage would be massive. Not to mention the fact that regicide was not the safest thing to attempt regardless of circumstances.

"I prefer not to be kept waiting. Or, it's more like I'm simply unused to it."

I nodded at him, and we began to walk through the party. He nodded at various guests, made small talk with a few others. Eventually, we were just strolling through the party together without interruption.

"So, how are you enjoying the masquerade so far?"

"I would've liked for it to be a bit more exclusive. Seems you've invited too much family for other guests to feel comfortable."

He smiled. "You've already killed two of my brothers and cost my sister her little fleet. Seemed stupid to approach you alone."

"It would've been."

He shook his head. "Listen, I think my brother has given you the wrong impression of us. If you'll allow me to explain a few things, maybe we can put a pause on trying to kill each other."

I looked over at my companions. They were still grouped

together, trying to position themselves in such a way that they could come to help me if I needed it. "Go ahead."

"Thank you. We children of Aurum are not bloodthirsty monsters. Well, some of us are, but that's kind of my point. Being a child of Aurum simply makes us more of what we already are, gives us a chance to be something greater."

"What does it actually mean to be a child of Aurum?"

"It's exactly what it sounds like. Our father is Aurum. Not our direct father, mind you, but he's our ancestor. He left little pearls of essence in all of those descended from him, though not all of his descendants are capable of accessing them. Only those who have potential as his heirs."

"His heirs?"

"Yes, those of us capable of taking the place he once held."

"Which is what, godhood?"

"That's the general idea. The point I'm making is that while Talen may be your enemy, I'm not."

"You seem to have just given someone you know to be my enemy quite the gift. Forgive me, but that makes me suspicious."

"That's certainly fair, but I had to give it to him. It's a compromise of sorts. You don't need the details. What I'm trying to tell you is that I'm the more reasonable of us." He looked over to my friends, his golden eyes twinkling as light touched them. "They don't know what you are, do they?"

"No," I lied.

"That's all I needed to know. Just know I'll protect them from Talen. I may need their help to rid me of him, after all. All I need is for you to get out of the way."

"What are you talking abo—"

He placed a hand on my back, and I felt an incredible pain shoot forward from his palm through me. I looked down and realized I was in some kind of arcane circle, draconic runes lit up. They had been mixed into the ornate rug so thoroughly that they'd been entirely invisible before they'd begun glowing. I felt incredible pain and suddenly found myself opened. The seams between my armor, my faceplate—all of it was separated as far as it could go, the void within me visible to everyone that surrounded us.

"Monster!" yelled Caedus, backing away from me.

Talen threw himself at me shoulder first, and I clattered across the hall even as I started to pull myself back together. The party devolved into chaos.

I gritted my metaphorical teeth and pulled myself together. Talen stood across from me, a silver-handled sword pointed in my direction. I launched myself at him, but was suddenly struck by a sword with such force that it actually pierced my side. A sword juggler with golden eyes flashed me a smile as he readied another throw.

Hrig didn't let him get the chance. She slammed into him in a tackle and brought him to the ground. She was unarmed, but she managed to take a sword from the juggler's own kit before he pushed her off of him.

Kyren and Stone moved to face the juggler, but the fire-breather chose that moment to put a wall of flame between me and my companions.

"Wait, wait!" Caedus yelled at them. "Spare them; they knew not that their companion was a monster."

I doubted anyone else could see him through the flames, but I saw him choose that moment to wink in my direction.

Talen lunged at me with his sword, and I didn't have time to draw my own sword through the peace knot, so I removed the sword from my side, bringing it up just in time to stop him from running me through.

"You will pay for what you did to my brother," said Talen through gritted teeth, his golden eyes shining in the firelight.

I pushed him back. "Why do you care? You didn't seem to care much about the green one."

He stabbed at me multiple times, forcing me back as I parried. "The green one was only a brother to me through Aurum. Donyin was a brother to me through Aurum and through bloodshed. We raised each other up, helped each other survive. I don't expect a monster like you to understand that, though."

I threw the juggler's sword at him, but he dodged it as it embedded into the pillar behind him. I noticed that despite the king's words, Hrig, Stone, and Kyren were still locked in combat with the other children of Aurum, even though they seemed to be focused on simply keeping them away from me.

Talen launched himself toward me, and I wasn't able to dodge, feeling my already damaged essence recoil as his sword buried itself in my breastplate where a heart would have been. I was hurt, and there was no way I could defeat Talen and his allies in the state I was in, but there did seem to be a way I could at least save my companions. I grabbed Talen by the shoulders and pulled him closer, hearing the sound of his sword tearing my steel skin, and I headbutted him. He took a few steps back and released his grip on his sword, giving me the space I needed.

I ran and jumped through the fire toward Kyren, who was the closest to me. She held out her hand to help me up. I grabbed it, twisted her around, broke the peace knot on my sword, and held it to her throat. I squeezed her hand two times, the same signal we'd used to indicate poison.

"Stay back!" I yelled.

The two performers hesitated, and the guards that had been trying to intervene got closer, but kept some distance. Hrig and Stone looked over to us, confused expressions on their faces. I began backing toward the nearest window.

I whispered to Kyren, "I don't know any other way we can survive this aside from this one. You have too much to lose; there are too many children of Aurum here for us to defeat, and even if we win the fight, we'd still lose everything else. You didn't know I was a monster and neither did Stone or Hrig. I'm going to make a run for Usulaum." I looked for a moment at Hrig. "I will return."

I reached the window, my back clanging against it. Kyren gave my hand a squeeze and began muttering in elvish.

"What did you do to my son, you monster!" yelled Lady Senturius, her voice cracking as she did so. Ser Senturius was holding her back, keeping her from running at me.

That hurt worse than anything Talen had done to me. It was deserved, though.

"He was too strong for me to leave alive, but he made a fine meal," I yelled to her, hoping that playing the villain might allow them some peace. I saw Talen and Caedus standing next to one another. Talen was smiling with a cruel look in his eyes, and Caedus gave me another wink.

"I'm sorry, but we have to make sure they believe it," whispered Kyren, unleashing a blast of holy energy.

I was thrown through the window in pieces. I felt myself fall as each of my different parts, then felt myself land as each of them. The effect proved disorienting, the damage I took severe. I had just enough time to reassemble myself before I heard the approach of guards. I checked my internal compass, removing Talen's sword from my chest as I did so, and started running east.

31
HUNTED

As I began running, I started to process a new emotion. I felt like there was a fire rising up out of me, one that wanted to explode through my skin. I'd felt a lesser version of it before, but a deep ravine existed between anger and fury. Caedus had used me as a tool and had taken the time to make sure Sevald's parents would be in the audience, and Talen had trapped me. The two of them together had separated me from my friends. I wanted to turn around, fight my way back up through the palace, and kill them both, but that wasn't an option. At least not yet. Instead, I channeled my rage into making my way out of the city as fast as possible.

It wasn't long before I reached the first wall. There were guards, of course, but things seemed relatively lax. I assumed I was a little ahead of the news about me. I moved straight through the main gate, bowling over a few late arrivals to the masquerade as I did so. From there, I had to start weaving through the central district, trying to stay ahead of any pursuit or any potential lockdown.

Unfortunately, as I was weaving my way through an alley, I heard the ringing of a loud bell. It started from the palace and was picked up by additional bells being rung at each wall and gate. I arrived at the gate for the second wall just as it was being closed. The guards looked me over.

"Sorry, ser. That bell means things are going to be shut down. Likely some stupid thief at the masquerade."

"It's alright, I suppose. Plenty of fun to be had on this side of the wall."

I did my best to adopt the air of a flighty noble and walked away. I wanted to avoid a fight in my weakened state. I was lucky that the only thing that could be conveyed by a bell ring was to close the gates. It would be very inconvenient if they had some system of rings that specifically conveyed "kill or arrest the walking suit of armor."

As soon as I was out of the sight of the guards, I found one of the stairways that led up to the top of the wall and bolted up it. There were guards on the stairs, of course, but they were ill-equipped to stop me from running up to the top of the wall and flinging myself off of it.

I crashed through a roof, landing in what the naked couple in the bed indicated was someone's bedroom. I nodded at them and jumped through their open window into the street. From there, it was more running through alleys and doing my best at taking a direct route toward the eastern gate. When I reached it, I wasn't surprised to find another closed gate with guards mustering near it. Unlike the smaller interior wall gates, this one had bars that were a bit further apart. Rather than go around, I started calmly walking toward it.

The guards saw me, and one of them moved in front of the others, holding out his hand. "Ser, I'm afraid that the city is locked down."

I simply kept my pace, moving toward him and closing the distance. Just as he began to draw his sword, I drove my fist into his face, knocking him to the ground.

The others began drawing their swords.

I started running toward them, reaching the first of them before he drew his weapon. I slammed a steel fist into his gut, and he doubled over. Before the others could reach me, I bowled him into the nearest grouping of them. Two more began to swing at me with their swords, but I didn't bother dodging. There was no reason to pretend anymore.

One strike simply glanced off my helmet, but the other managed to dig a bit into my chestplate, expanding the stab wound I'd received from Talen. I grabbed the blade and ripped it out of the guard's hand before smacking him with an open hand and sending him into the street.

The other guard raised his sword for another strike at my head, but I brought that same palm to his face, breaking his nose and sending him to the ground. Before the other guards could rally, I squeezed myself through the bars, just as I had in the pit at the Wyrwind estate, and began running at full speed down the main road.

I felt bad for having to hurt the guards. They were just doing their jobs. The majority of those I'd hurt so far had been people attempting to hurt me or my fellows, or trained fighters. I decided not to give those thoughts much attention and instead focused on putting as much space between myself and the capital as possible. Eventually, the news of what happened would overtake me, and I'd find myself surrounded, with men on horses behind me and men at guardhouses in front of me. Hunting hounds were another possibility, but I doubted they'd be much use when it came to tracking me by scent.

After running on the main road for a long stretch, I began making my way into the more hilly and forested areas the road weaved around. I paused for a moment to fold the cape my companions had given me and store it within myself. Then I did the same with my mask. Both were a bit worse for wear, with scuffs and tears, but I liked them and wanted to make sure the damage didn't get any worse as I ran through the forest.

I started moving again. Occasionally, I'd blow through a camp or jump over a deer, but I never paused long enough to say anything aside from "sorry," though I don't think the deer really cared all that much about how apologetic I was.

The unfortunate thing about not needing to exert myself when I ran was that I could think while I was doing it. I thought about the situation I'd left my companions in, but no matter how many times I ran through things, I couldn't think of any better options than the one I'd taken.

I'd created an opportunity for them, and that was all I could do. The king didn't think they knew what I was, which meant they could pretend to be horrified that they were ever working with me. If he decided to have them killed, it would also have negative political and social implications for him. I'm guessing that was why he wanted to determine what they knew before he attacked me. That, or simply because they saw Talen as an enemy, something I got the impression the king shared with them.

Talen himself was another story, particularly after Stone went through so much effort to dismantle his power in Cirros. Still, even his enmity toward me might not have been transferred to my companions to the same degree. He might even have preferred the idea of me losing them and them feeling betrayed to simply killing them. For now, I had to assume that they could handle themselves and keep putting one foot in front of the other. It was time to become aggressive.

First, I'd go to the Eastlands to see if I could locate a certain orcish sea captain, and from there, I'd head to Usulaum and try to find any usable information. Even if I didn't find it, though, it seemed like bringing the fight to them was going to be my best option. Though whether or not I should involve my friends, especially with a king being a part of the conspiracy, was something I'd have to leave up to them.

After three full days of running, I was starting to get close to Buryn. I'd stayed off the main roads for the most part and so had avoided any patrols or pursuers. I imagine it wasn't too difficult to track a man through the forest leaving a trail in full plate, but it would definitely be difficult to keep up with him if he can run at full speed day and night.

Rather than approach Buryn directly, I started to take a long trek around the city to the north. It would take me longer to reach the coastline, but I'd likely need to hurt far fewer people in the process.

Unfortunately, it seemed some people were eager to be hurt.

I began hearing sounds of pursuit about halfway to my destination. They were closing in on me from multiple directions, probably having predicted my path to the sea. I wasn't exactly being secretive about it.

The first thing to reach me was the dogs, roughly a dozen of them. They were massive beasts with thick fronts and stubby ears, not dogs meant for tracking so much as dogs meant for war. I managed to dodge around two of them as I moved, but one was directly in front of me. He leapt up at my chest and bit at what on a human would've been the throat. I heard his teeth scrape against my gorget, but rather than slow down, I simply kept running with the dog latched to my throat. Animals trained to go after vital points was a solid idea; unfortunately, I didn't have vital points.

I grabbed the dog by the scruff and tried to remove him from me as I kept running, but he seemed only to latch on tighter. While I was focused on him, I failed to notice the men lined up in front of me. They pulled a rope up from the ground just as I reached them, and the dog and I found ourselves rolling through underbrush, at which time he finally ceased his death grip on me and tumbled away.

I picked myself up just as the men approached me with spears. The first one stabbed down at me, hard, but he struck only dirt as I rolled to the side. Another man threw a net over me before I could stand. The net was heavily weighted, the wires of it razor-sharp and digging into my skin as I tried to move. I stood in spite of it and narrowly managed to bat away another spear thrust.

I grabbed at a hole in the netting and began to tear it off myself. It would've sliced a normal man's hands to ribbons, but for me, it simply meant I needed to give myself some repairs. Two men approached me with spears as I was extricating myself, but I dropped low and rolled out of the remnants of the net before they could reach me.

I began running again, but one of them placed himself in front of me. He was a bear of a man, easily seven feet tall, and he swung the spear back and forth in order to keep me from getting past him. I could tell they were all playing for time until the rest of their group arrived. It was possible that with enough nets, rope, and men, they might actually be able to capture me. I didn't want to hurt him, so I opened my faceplate and fired all the rations and food I'd stored for travelling with my companions directly at his face.

He screamed and fell backward in surprise, and I jumped over him and continued my sprint for the ocean. As they faded behind me, I could hear more dogs starting to catch up. I was beginning to resign myself to the fact that I might need to kill some of them, when I broke through the treeline. I'd reached the coast. There was a short stretch of beach, and from there, I saw the ocean spread out in front me, the sun still high in the sky.

I ran directly into it, letting the water wash over me and feeling the waves crash against my chestplate. The sand slowed me down, but by the time my pursuers reached me, I was already up to my neck in water. Once my head was under, I knew they'd have no chance of catching me.

Once I got past the sandbar, it felt once again like I was in another world. The silence that came from entering the ocean, along with the way the light was filtered, and the incredible variety of sea life, made it hard to believe I was still on the same plane. There was a massive system of what looked like plants made of rock that was spread as far as I could see. The rock was all types of different colors, the sea life that seemed to make it their homes equally diverse.

Out of curiosity, I diverted my path a bit to approach one of the smaller groupings of rock plants. I saw a small shelled creature that looked to be a cross between a shrimp and a crab with thick armor and large claws, but also a longer body ending with a fat front. I reached out toward it, and it shot itself backward in a barrage of bubbles. Curious, I went to touch another of the same creatures, but it did the same, launching itself backward.

I opened my faceplate and began taking in water, careful to keep it from touching any of the other items I'd stored. I then opened myself up a bit at the joints of my shoulders and those behind my legs and shot the water out.

I launched myself far more quickly than I could control and slammed into one of the piles of rock plants. I shook myself off and batted away a few fish that were attempting to drive away what they clearly thought was a predator. After I got a little ways away from them, I tried again.

This time, I went slower and was able to turn a short hop in a long jump. I tried again, this time managing a great leap. It wouldn't exactly let me fly through the water, but I had a feeling my journey to Usulaum just got cut in half.

32
SUNK COST

By what I believed to be the following afternoon, I had developed a bit of a system. I'd leap, using the water I shot out to propel myself as far as I could, then I'd land, walk as I refilled, then leap again. It likely wasn't as fast as being on a boat with the wind in its sails, but certainly better than simply walking, particularly as it allowed me to jump over several incredibly deep canyons that dotted the underwater landscape.

I finished another leap and found myself standing above what looked almost like an underwater forest, with large plants in neat rows along the forest floor that went on for miles. The plants themselves were blue with thick leaves that had small clusters of pods randomly distributed along them.

I leapt down for a closer look, landing as far into the forest as I could manage. I got what I was looking for, but I was surprised to also see a woman standing just a few steps away from me. She had light green skin, her hair short and green, reminding me of grass. She stood there for a few moments, her mouth agape and showing several sharp teeth. The most surprising thing about her appearance was her tail. It was long and ended in two fins. The scales of it were mostly silver with hints of blue and purple occasionally peeking out.

I'd heard of mer-folk and knew objectively that they lived in the ocean, but seeing them was rare. They didn't speak any language people on the surface could understand, and they also didn't seem keen on interacting with us to begin with. I was incredibly lucky to have encountered one, though it was also an encounter I was well-suited for.

We both stood there for a few moments, staring at one another. I raised my gauntlet and waved in what I hoped was a universal signal for hello. She returned the awkward gesture, and I realized that she was holding a small woven net, which held clusters of the tree-pods. I looked closer at one near me and realized there was something swimming inside it, something with numerous appendages and big black eyes. They were eggs. I must've been in the middle of some type of farm.

The mer-woman began to approach me slowly. I elected not to make any sudden moves. She poked me a few times, and I could tell even from that that she was immensely strong. Her arms were heavily muscled, likely from working on such a massive farm.

I waved again and began walking eastward, but she grabbed me. I fought the instinct to pull away and instead looked at her. She let me go and gestured for me to follow her. I felt an urgency to continue my journey, but I was concerned that refusing her might lead to more problems than simply going along with her would.

We walked through rows and rows of plants at the slow pace I could manage walking. Eventually, I made a little leap to show her I could move faster, and she smiled a shark-toothed smile before we began making much quicker progress.

A particularly large leap landed me outside of the farm, and I found myself suddenly on the edge of an underwater city. The entire place seemed to be built of the same rock plants I'd seen on the Caedun coast. Most of the buildings were dome-like structures, but a few larger towers stretched to such a height that I couldn't see the tops of them.

The mer-woman shook me from my reverie and gestured for me to keep following. I decided not to make any more jumps as the area was so populous and busy, concerned I'd land on someone. There were mer-women, men, and children, as well as numerous other undersea creatures that all seemed to be living in harmony. The city itself was lit by numerous small jellyfish with bright orbs of light inside of them. I even saw several mer-folk riding what looked to be a giant version of the crab-like creatures I'd seen a day earlier, though they weren't launching themselves as I'd seen the smaller ones do.

As I was noticing them, they were noticing me. Heads turned, and people started to follow us as we made our way to a structure in the center of the city. By the time we'd reached our destination, we were leading a procession of something like a hundred mer-folk.

On entering, I got the immediate impression that I was in something equivalent to a palace or estate on land. Decorative carvings in all of the walls, precious gems lining almost everything, and I started to see pieces of wood used as decoration that could only have come from sunken ships. That made sense upon reflection. Wood would be rarer than gold underwater, particularly wood that had been worked.

I entered a large atrium and realized that the procession that had followed us had stopped doing so at the entrance. The atrium was full of the kind of treasure that would make Stone salivate. Chests full of gold and silver, beautifully cut gems that sparkled in the jellyfish light that illuminated the room, and weapons and armor in their own corner.

In the center of the room was a large mer-woman flanked by two smaller mer-men. My first thought was that they were guards, but judging by the way they lounged against the woman's tail and chest respectively, I amended my impression to courtesans.

The mer-woman who led me there bowed and gestured to me, and I responded by waving. That led to a kind of trill of delight to come from the large woman, who I decided must be their queen or whatever equivalent they had.

The queen floated over to me and began to poke and prod me in the same way the original merwoman had, and they engaged in a conversation of low and high trills as she did so. By the end of it, the woman who had led me there bowed, waved to me, and left the room. After that, she began to make a series of gestures to me. I got the impression she wanted me to jump, so I made the largest one I could in the confines of the room and heard a trill of delight.

She pointed to me and then pointed out an opening in the building toward some of the crab creatures and then did what I assumed was a laugh. I laughed, too. I could definitely see why they'd think I was similar to that creature. I'd learned my method of underwater locomotion from it, after all, and we both had nice, sturdy shells.

The queen then gestured for me to come near a pile of armor and weapons she had in the corner. Not sure of what she wanted, I followed, and she grabbed me and placed me toward the center of the pile. I started to walk out of it, but she wagged a finger back and forth at me. I stepped back toward the center, and she gave a positive noise in my direction, then she returned to her courtesans.

I realized then that I was meant to be a part of the collection she had here. That was not good. It was flattering, to a certain extent, but considering how much rust and old wood was also being collected, I didn't feel like my new keeper's tastes were very refined.

I decided to wait and think. I didn't have much other choice. I had a feeling I could fight my way out of the immediate room, but the city in general was very populous, and if enough of them tried, they could definitely stop me from leaving. My best chance was to wait for them to sleep, but I had no idea when that would happen or even if they all slept at the same time. Still, it was the best option I could see available to myself.

I waited and watched, doing my best *not* to watch when I got a firsthand demonstration of how mer-folk copulated from the queen and her consorts, but unfortunately, I couldn't close my eyes since I didn't have any. Eventually, they finished and settled into a post-coital rest. Their eyes were still open, but unfocused, and even while sleeping, they maintained a kind of slow, steady movement around the room.

I moved carefully, slowly extricating myself from the corner I'd been placed in. I had to step around piles of rusty old iron in order to avoid making unnecessary noise. Aside from trying to be quiet, I also wanted to make sure I didn't move too quickly, as I assumed they'd have some way of feeling movement in the water, even at a distance.

One glint of shiny metal in the pile of rust around me stood out. A sword, with a long, curved blade and an ornate black hilt. Despite being under a mound of rusted equipment, it was clean and undamaged. I decided to risk grabbing it and slid it slowly from the pile it lay in. After a slight crashing noise, I went completely still as the queen momentarily stirred, but she quickly drifted back into the sleep-like state she'd been in before.

I stored the sword through my faceplate and kept going, working my way toward the opening in the side of the building that led to the giant crab creature. Once I was there, I started speeding up, but not risking any leaps. I figured the amount of water it stirred up might wake my captors.

I made it outside and looked around. There weren't any mer-folk nearby, though the city was still active with other less sapient creatures. I took in water and started making leaps, bounding through the streets as fast as I could. Once I made my way out of it, I turned east, hoping to put as much distance between myself and the city of the mer-folk as I possibly could.

Unfortunately, they could swim much faster than I could jump. Three reached me just as I was coming over a crevasse. They slammed into my back, and I had to scramble to keep from falling straight into it.

Instead, I managed to land against the edge of the other side and pull myself back up. A merman was there to meet me. He jabbed at me with a spear, and I wasn't fast enough under the water to stop him. It almost knocked me back over the cliff-side, but I managed to regain my balance. I sucked in more water and launched myself directly at him. My speed surprised him, and I could feel something break as I crashed into him.

I returned to my feet and saw the other two approaching me more warily. They began to swim quickly around me, prodding me with their spears and never staying still long enough for me to grab one or launch myself at them. Realizing that they didn't know anything about me or what I was, I simply decided to collapse and play dead.

They moved closer, and as soon as I felt one of them put his hand on me, I grabbed it and pulled him into an embrace. He struggled, actually shifting me several times, but I squeezed until I felt something snap, and he was out. The final one didn't give me a chance to stand and immediately began stabbing at me with his spear. I shot myself upward with a burst of water, catching his spear as I did so. I then yanked him toward me and punched him with force amplified by shooting water out of the seam behind my elbow plate. He was launched several yards before his body settled onto the ground.

I approached the one that I'd killed. I'd have preferred not to have needed to kill any of them, but I was in their territory, and I couldn't hold back the same way I was able to with my land-based opponents. The dead one also represented a rare opportunity. No one had ever been granted the chance to learn more about the mer-men in the way I had, and it felt right to take this chance to learn more. I hesitated for a moment before giving in, then opened myself to consume him.

This time felt different. I felt a brief rush of incredibly alien thoughts and emotions, but rather than feeling overwhelmed as I had previously, I was in control. I felt all of the partial essence I'd eaten crash against me, but it quickly fell in line like a wave crashing against a rocky beach. I was able to go through and analyze what I'd absorbed rather than integrating directly into myself.

I gained an immediate understanding of the mer-folk language and culture. It was matriarchal and caste-based, with a focus on pleasing those who ruled. The one I'd eaten was born and raised to be a warrior from a young age, blindly following the queen without ever having many thoughts of his own beyond how he might serve her. The city I'd seen was one of many scattered along the ocean floor, each with its own rulers and cultures, many of whom the young mer I'd eaten had fought against.

I wanted to keep sorting through the essence, but not wanting to wait for more pursuers, I began continuing my trek east. I made a mental note to avoid this part of the ocean on my way back. Even if I could speak the language, I doubted I'd have any serious chance at diplomacy at this point.

33
INTERLUDE: DORSIA

The Randid sisters were the last remaining worthy competition in town. Their business was smuggling, prostitution, and crushed weir bone. Often, those three things would intersect, with women and young men being smuggled in and weir bone being sold as a cure for impotence, though its narcotic effects were also highly sought after. It was nothing Dorsia had a problem with on its own. The only issue she really had was that the majority of the men and women they smuggled in weren't there by choice.

Dorsia sat, her rapier at her hip, a small cup of spiced tea in her hand. The Randid sisters sat across from her. Despite their cruel reputation, they were pretty girls, relatively young, and all smiles. They wore their hair in tight buns with golden hair pins holding them in place, and were dressed in gaudy black leather armor with gold etching, picking their teeth with stilettos. It was a cute act. Unfortunately for them, Dorsia saw right through it.

They were as new to Buryn as she was, and their rise had been almost as meteoric. They were ambitious, but in Dorsia's opinion, they lacked style. They favored quick, violent solutions over guile and had no real code or rules, which made them bad to deal with. Even if she didn't shut them down, eventually, their own lack of tact and strategy would lead to their downfall. In a way, Dorsia was offering them a controlled fall, though she doubted that was how they'd see it.

"You want us out? I thought this was a negotiation," said Cyn Randid. They were twins, but Cyn seemed younger.

"It is. You can leave and give your operation over to me, or I can kill you and take it."

"We're also comfortable with meeting you in the middle. We'll beat you bloody, and then you leave," said Jade calmly, standing at Dorsia's right, flexing her clawed fingers menacingly in the Randid sisters' direction.

She'd taken to the role of enforcer quite well. Dorsia herself was no slouch when it came to combat, but Jade had the kind of "can beat" attitude that really helped things to move smoothly. She also had a sense of honor that meant she was able to keep both subordinates' and clients' respect.

"You come into our territory, our bar." Wynne Randid pointed at the sign above the bar. It read "A Randy Place," which Dorsia found tacky. "And threaten us? Everyone here is ours. All you've got is your enforcer. Now, can we stop the dick measuring and get down to actually figuring things out? Let's just draw out each other's territories and leave one another alone. There's money to be made while we sit here jawing."

"I'm afraid that wasn't an option I offered. Though I appreciate that you're clearly the smart one." Dorsia had known that Wynne was the greater threat right away; her gift let her immediately gauge a person's threat level, and she'd been honing it even further since arriving in Buryn. Her initial method of money-making since she'd arrived had been betting on the coliseum fights, an area in which she had a particularly unfair advantage.

"Alright, that's enough. Let's just kill them," said Cyn, and at that moment, the rest of the bar rose from their chairs, drawing daggers, clubs, or putting their hands through brass knuckles.

"Agreed," said Wynne, pulling a shortsword from its sheath.

Dorsia found their confidence interesting. They believed that she would show up alone with only Jade as protection and make no other backup plans. How insulting that they assumed she had nothing up her sleeve.

She kicked the table that was between her and the Randids, threw her scalding tea into the face of the nearest brute, and flipped backward out of her chair, kicking a man with a dagger in the face as she did so. She landed with her rapier drawn and slipped her buckler over her arm.

Jade vanished from where she'd been standing and appeared behind Dorsia, her claws slashing across the face of a man preparing to strike her with a club.

Dorsia lifted her fingers to her mouth, gracefully avoiding the hilt of her rapier, and whistled. On that signal, a massive woman with blond braids slammed through the front door and into the mêlée. She was wielding an axe and made a wide swing as she entered, slaying a half-dozen of the Randids' crew before they even knew what was happening.

Dorsia and Jade took that cue to focus on the sisters, who were still picking themselves up from under the table. Dorsia smashed her buckler into the face of a woman approaching her from the left and used her forward momentum to disarm two more opponents with swift strikes to their hands, which left them with too few fingers to hold their weapons any longer.

Jade used her height and speed to her advantage, laying into the tendons and arterial clusters on legs that she could easily reach. She left a trail of thugs behind her doing their best to stem the bleeding, or in one enterprising case, swiftly using their belt as a tourniquet.

Dorsia watched the Randid sisters grow more panicked as the bodies between them and her fell. By the time she reached Wynne, there was only desperation left in her eyes.

Wynne swung her shortswords in a wild combination of lower and upper strikes, trying to trip her or catch her throat, but Dorsia read her moves before they even began. When the combination stopped, she simply extended her sword, stabbing straight through the leather armor and into Wynne's heart. They held their pose there for a moment before Dorsia let the body slide off her blade and onto the floor. She pulled a red handkerchief from her pocket and cleaned the blade, casually noting the destruction she and her companions had wrought.

Jade had killed Cyn. Her body, pale from blood loss, lay cold on the floor. The runes on Jade's skin that had been lit bright were slowly losing their glow. Hrig was standing among a pile of bodies with a wild look in her eye, viscera hanging from the edge of her axe.

Hrig had joined them just a week prior and had been keen on helping with this particular operation. She seemed in desperate need to blow off steam, and Dorsia was glad to provide it for her. Things moved fast with a woman like Hrig's help.

There were a few men groaning on the floor, either dying or so injured they wished they were, but Dorsia ignored them. She returned the handkerchief to her pocket, put away her sword and buckler, and went behind the bar. She found a surprisingly good bottle of gin and poured three glasses. She sniffed her glass, enjoying the delicate juniper scent before taking a long sip. Hrig and Jade joined her at the bar and took their glasses, mirroring her long, calm sips, and letting themselves relax.

"Well, we now own Buryn. The underworld, at least, which

is my favorite part anyway," said Dorsia with a wry smile on her lips.

"I hope you understand that, at this point, I feel my obligation to you is fulfilled," said Jade.

"Your obligation for me saving your life? Certainly. Your obligation as my friend? I don't think so."

Jade sighed. "Well, from here on, I at least expect to be paid. I like the work, but I expect my cut."

"Maybe I'll arrange another opportunity to save you. Could be worth it in the long run."

Jade rolled her eyes.

They sat in silence for a while after that, well, silence aside from the groaning and dying men and women that surrounded them.

"So...you still haven't told us what happened at the palace. Would you like to speak about it?" asked Dorsia.

Hrig finished her gin and wiped her face with the back of her hand. "Sevald saved us," she said with a touch of bitterness in her voice.

"The rumors I've heard were that he attacked you," said Dorsia.

"He wouldn't do that," responded Jade.

"I'm not saying he would; I'm just saying what the rumor is. Those two things rarely coincide." Dorsia poured another glass. "He is a monster, though? That part rang true, though 'monster' doesn't feel like the right word. A non-human? Though I guess that applies to Jade, as well..."

"He's not human, no, and not dwarf, elf, or orc either. He's a hollow suit of armor, but alive."

"Interesting. That explains why he appeared so strong to me." She looked at Jade and noted her complete lack of surprise. "You knew, didn't you?"

"I did."

"You knew?" asked Hrig.

"I did. He wasn't exactly subtle."

"Why didn't you say anything?" asked Dorsia.

"I promised him I wouldn't tell as a way to fulfill my obligation to him. No point in hiding it now, though."

"I'm hurt you didn't share that with me." Dorsia put her hand over her heart mockingly for a moment, then turned her attention back to Hrig. "I still want to know what actually happened at the palace."

Hrig poured herself another glass. "Things started fine. We mingled, ate good food, and watched some performers. Sevald had a run-in with the real Sevald's parents, but aside from that, it was looking to be a pleasant evening. Unfortunately, we soon noticed at least four children of Aurum were at the party."

"Four of them? Like Donyin?" asked Jade.

"Five. I heard Talen was there, as well," said Dorsia.

"Six, actually. The king was one of them."

Dorsia's eyes widened. "The king?"

"Yes. He insisted on speaking with Sevald alone, and Sevald didn't think he had much of a choice. He walked with him a short way and then there was a flash of light and Sevald seemed to be coming apart, or maybe 'leaking' is the right word. Pure blackness was showing at his joints, and his helmet was open, showing nothing inside. Talen lunged at him, feigning at protecting the king, and we went to help Sevald. Unfortunately, the other children of Aurum held us back. Sevald eventually fought Talen off and made his way to us. That's when he took Kyren hostage—"

"What?"

"He didn't really, just kind of. Kyren explained that he told her it was the only way he could think to keep us safe. If he pretended to be a real monster and we pretended we didn't know, then the king would have a harder time justifying getting rid of us. Kyren is the scion of a noble family that the king had just expressed warm feelings toward, I'm well known here in Buryn and Ellis would likely take umbrage at the king having me killed, and Stone has a lot of favors that would be called in if he died. Whether or not the king believed us, he let us go and even shut down several attempts from Talen to have us arrested. Though I have had a few run-ins with some of his cutthroats since then."

"How unfortunate for them," said Jade.

Hrig smiled. "That it was."

"It makes sense that the king would try to keep things stable. With all the posturing at the elven border, his growing the military, it seems like war is coming. He wants to keep as much cohesion as possible."

"That's what Kyren said. At least, it's what she figured out before I left."

"Where is everyone now?" asked Jade.

"Sevald went to Usulaum to find out what he could at the university. Obviously, we don't have contact with him, but he was heading east, and last we heard, he'd escaped to the ocean. Kyren stayed in the capital. She's undergoing training and dealing with priestly bureaucratic nonsense, trying to discover what she can that way. Stone is calling up contacts across the country to put together a clearer picture of the king and Talen's plans. We're just trying to do whatever we can, however we can."

"Well, I don't know about the king, but I was planning on giving Talen a hard time either way," said Dorsia. "Now that he's running things from the light and the darkness in Cirros, things are getting desperate for people. He's been forcing debtors into the king's army, then selling the right to not be drafted to the nobility and merchants, all while having deserters killed. He's got absolute control there."

"What are your plans, Hrig?" asked Jade.

"Well, aside from helping you with Talen, I was also interested in maybe calling in the favor you owe me."

"What do you need?"

"Your tattoos. Would you be able to put those on someone else?"

Jade hesitated. "Possibly, but why do you want them?"

"I need to be stronger. I've been training since the fight with Donyin, trying to bridge that gap between me and him, but no matter how hard I work, I can still see it. I need more than what I can do so far. Also..." She took a deep drink of gin. "If I'd just been stronger, maybe Sevald would've fought. Maybe we could've made it out of there together."

Dorsia looked at Hrig closely, relying on that special sense Krish had given her that let her size people up. She *was* stronger. Much stronger than she'd been at the tournament, but she was also right. Donyin was a monster, and if the other children of Aurum were as strong as him, she'd need to go even further.

Jade stared into her cup for a moment. "I can do it, but you have to understand that there's a cost."

"What cost?"

"Pain, mostly, and once the runes are in place, they cannot be removed. They also likely won't be as powerful for you as they are for me."

"Why won't they be as powerful?"

"For one, the runes will be in ancient dwarvish, which isn't your language."

"Could you do them in common?"

"No, the human language is too diffuse. The more people know a language, the less powerful the runes of that language become. Ancient dwarvish is rare; it holds mystery and power, and so its runes are more powerful. Aside from that, your body won't be able to handle as many runes as mine can."

"Because I'm not a dwarf?"

"Partially, but also because you don't have the knowledge of them that I do. My family has passed down the magic of the runes for generations. We are born to use them, and our abilities with them are in our blood."

"But you can give me some."

"I can do two on you, possibly three, but anything beyond that may kill you. We'll have to choose words that you embody, ones that are the core of who you are. You'll also need a place to rest and recover. It's likely you'll be out of commission for a while after each rune."

"Don't worry about that part. I'll take care of it," said Dorsia.

Hrig nodded and poured herself another glass of gin. "When can we start?"

34
THE EASTLANDS

I managed to avoid any additional encounters with the mer-folk. For the rest of my journey, the majority of what I encountered was blackness, strange creatures, and emptiness. When I did start to feel the land tilting upward and saw plant life begin to be more colorful, I felt immensely relieved. The cold darkness had left me with nothing but thoughts of Aurum and my companions. Nothing but dark thoughts in the dark. I gave a few large leaps and quickly approached the nearest sandbar.

A peek above water revealed that it was a rainy and miserable day on the surface. A small fishing village sat on the coast ahead of me, and I could see a few smaller vessels nearby being manned by orcs wearing their patterned wool sweaters and casting nets.

I maneuvered myself to ensure I wouldn't be caught in the nets and walked to the rocky shore. My emergence from the water was greeted by a flurry of curse words and looks of fear from two older orcish men sitting on the docks above me.

I gave them what I hoped was a jaunty wave and walked the rest of the way onto the shore. They both looked at half-empty bottles in their hands, poured them into the water, and started stumbling away.

A third orc who hadn't reacted at all continued to stand, or rather sit, his ground. I watched him pull his line back in, add a particularly squirmy grub to his hook, and cast it back out. He was clearly older, with gray-green skin and white hair. His eyes never left the water where he'd cast his line.

"Hail," I said, approaching him.

"Hail," he grunted back, not bothering to look in my direction.

"Any luck today?"

"No."

"Does the rain make the fishing easier or harder?"

"Neither, so far as I know."

"Can I ask where I am?"

"Eastlands."

"Can I ask for a more specific answer?"

"Ballyton."

I looked around. Ballyton was as unimpressive up close as it had been from the water. Lots of simple wooden buildings, a shared dock, and what looked like a rudimentary longhouse. Still, I could feel a kind of charm about the place: the rain, gloom, and disrepair gave off a kind of consistent melancholy that felt romantic in a way. "Nice place."

The man snorted.

"I'm looking for Carntuff. Meeting a friend there."

"North, along the coast."

"Thank you." I looked out at his line. "Good luck with your fishing."

He nodded, still not taking his eyes off the water, and I started making my way north. Carntuff was where Lythia's partial memories told me I might find Vash. Chances were, she was looking for me already, considering both Caedus and Talen knew I'd headed east. If I struck first, I could avoid having her following me and possibly get her to reveal more about their plans.

A little ways from Ballyton, I found a road heading north and started along it. I decided to bulk myself up a little to look more like I was being worn by an orc. I didn't have any plans to hide what I was anymore, but a lone human figure might draw attention that could slow me down interminably, and I was already playing catch up.

The road itself was more of a simple dirt path. Around me were large grass hills with occasional patches of stone. The soft rain created an almost barely perceptible ting as it hit my armor, and between that sound and the simple trail, I found myself enjoying the change of scenery. Certainly, the depths of the ocean were likely something only I and the mer-folk had really experienced, and it contained sights unimaginable to the average person, but could that beat a really green hill? I mean, it could, but when you've been walking through the spectacular for too long, it tends to become mundane, and the mundane you haven't seen in a while becomes spectacular.

After cresting a particularly green and wonderful hill, I saw a small town, the place bustling in spite of the rain. Orcs moving from building to building, boats coming and leaving at the docks, carts arriving to load and unload. It seemed like a place that saw a lot of movement, which made it the perfect place to look for someone.

I entered the town without any trouble, though I did receive quite a few looks. Adventurers were less common in the Eastlands, the head clans would handle requests from villagers involving monsters, and in general, orcs tended to be more capable of handling their own issues to begin with. Still, they had a few, and the majority of the town seemed to assume correctly that I was one.

I made my way to the center of town and found the "Tuff Nuff Tavern." It was busy, with orcs of all kinds sharing drinks, talking, and doing business. Aside from the orcs, I also saw several dwarves and an elf with the look of a sailor. I sat at the bar and waited for the barkeep to finish pouring a drink for another patron before turning his attention to me.

"Ale?"

"Yes, please." I'd up to this point not met a bartender who would answer a question without me buying a drink first.

"Three coppers."

I pulled out the copper and set it on the table. He picked one up and squinted at it.

"Caedun coppers?"

I had not considered the problem that I had only foreign currency. I rarely considered the problem of currency at all. "I, uh, did a job for some Caedun merchant or another recently. That's what he paid me."

"Did a 'job' for a Caedun merchant, eh?" The bartender gave me a smile that showed off his impressive orcish canines. "We've got a lot of folks who do 'business' with them." He nodded at a table, and I saw a tough-looking group of orcs at a table who gave the impression that the business he was talking about was piracy. "I'll take your coin, don't worry. We're used to men coming back from sea with it. It'll just be one copper extra; their coins aren't as heavy as ours."

I nodded and placed another coin on the table in front of him. He went back to the spout and poured me some ale. I took a sip and placed the mug back down.

"So, I'm assuming, given the armor and such, that you're an adventurer."

"I am."

"Well, there's only one reason an adventurer would come to

a tavern, so go ahead and ask." He held out his hand expectantly.

I sighed. The tavern keeper and adventurer relationship was tried and true, but somehow, the bartender's straightforwardness about it made me feel a touch bitter.

"I'm looking for someone."

He simply smiled and gestured to his hands with his eyes.

I took out a single gold and handed it to him.

"Caedun gold coins are also lighter than Eastland's coins."

I slowly dragged my gauntleted hand across my face, wishing I had temples to rub, and grabbed another gold coin to hand to him. I didn't need money, but I also wasn't a fan of being taken advantage of.

He smiled and palmed the coins. "Who is it I can help you find?"

"Vash. She used to be a captain operating out of here."

The bartender's expression turned from affable to venomous in an instant, and he spat on the ground. "That clanless dirt?"

I nodded. Her being clanless is what had so impressed Lythia about her. A clanless captain was almost an impossibility. A clanless captain of four vessels had never happened before.

"Since she got two of my clansmen killed, she's run off to the highlands. Last I heard, she's calling herself the 'Queen of the Highwaymen.' I knew we should never have let some clanless wench lead a vessel. The best they should hope for is to be allowed to clean the decks."

"Where in the highlands is she?"

"Last I heard, she was picking people off on the eastern road, between here and the desert."

"Is she working alone?"

"No, she's been exiled by all clans. She's beyond clanless now, an outcast. Those working with her are outcasts, as well."

"Thank you for the information."

The bartender nodded. "Are you planning on killing her?"

"Probably."

"One of the clans hire you?"

"No, it's more...personal. She tried to kill me once."

"Ah, well, good luck to ya. We'd all be better off with one fewer outcast."

I nodded and stood to walk out.

"You gonna finish this ale?"

I ignored him and continued walking, feeling conflicted. Vash had tried to kill me, but from what I'd seen, her crew had trusted her. Whether or not that trust was deserved, I didn't know, but they likely wouldn't have wanted her to lose what she'd worked so hard to earn because of their deaths. Besides that, their deaths were technically my fault rather than hers. Though the kraken was the one truly at fault.

I made my way out of town and got onto the main road that headed east toward the desert. The Eastlands had once had a large central province, but due to some kind of agricultural mistake in the distant past, it had turned into a massive desert. That had driven all the orcish clans to the coasts and turned them from farmers to raiders and fishermen. The desert was now inhabited by naga and lizardmen tribes that had seemed to sprout from nothing once it had formed.

Aside from Usulaum and the university, there was nothing of value there for most civilized people. Usulaum itself was an independent city founded by Rubrus the Great, a great wizard of some kind. He built a tower and created an oasis in order to study in peace, and eventually, others flocked to the tower until it turned into a city in its own right. Exiled dwarves, outcast orcs, and mages hungry for the knowledge of Rubrus had settled there. Shortly after founding the university, Rubrus vanished, but the city has stood strong as a place of acceptance and learning since then. I wondered if Stone had ever been—the city generally seemed like his kind of place.

All of this history from Pebble flooded through me as I walked the eastern road, a pleasant distraction from the thoughts I'd been avoiding and the rage I could still feel simmering. Were my companions okay? Were the children of Aurum making any more big moves? Was it safe for me to be away from them? Now that I was done going over the history of the Eastlands in my head, I had nothing else but those questions to plague me. What I really needed to help clear my head was a fight.

It was early evening when I got exactly what I needed. Two orcs on horses rode down the path in my direction at full speed with lances. I decided, rather than wait for them to meet me, I would charge them right back.

I loosed the greatshield from my back, pulled my new sword from my helmet, and ran toward the one on the right. Just as I was about to hit their lances, I dropped low and angled the shield in such a way that rather than crashing against me, the horse tripped and fell, tumbling with its rider for a dozen yards into a small rocky outcropping.

The other rider continued past me, but then turned his horse around to charge me again. This time, rather than meeting him, I hefted my new curved blade and threw it, sending it spinning in the rider's direction. He ducked under it, barely avoiding being beheaded, and continued toward me.

I prepared to take a blow to my shield when I realized that the sword I'd just thrown was still in my hand. I sidestepped the horse at the last minute and struck at its rider with my blade, using his own momentum to bisect him diagonally. Half of him sloughed off the other half, and the horse simply kept running, the rider's legs eventually falling onto the side of the road.

I looked at the sword in my hand. It was the same one. I was certain I'd thrown it, so I went to where I had done so and found the sword I'd originally thrown embedded in the dirt. I picked it up and held it for a few moments before it faded and disappeared.

I turned my attention to the original sword and, grabbing at the hilt with both hands, I pulled another copy from it. I then stuck the copy in the ground. I did this about twelve times, and by the twelfth time, the first sword faded, followed by the others.

I held up the curved blade. I'd apparently stumbled onto a second enchanted item without even looking for it.

After I was done experimenting, I walked over to the corpse left by the orc I'd bisected. Aside from the damage I'd done to it, the horse had also trampled the body into a pulp. I consumed what I thought was his head, sorted quickly through the memories and impressions I was able to obtain. He'd respected Vash as a leader and preferred living with a group of other outcasts rather than living alone. Beyond that, I gained nothing of import, not even the location of the camp.

I approached the area I'd seen the other orc and his horse tumble into. The horse was dead, its neck snapped, but the rider was alive and cursing in orcish, his legs broken. His cursing grew louder when he noticed me, and he started trying to push out from under the horse.

"Having a bit of trouble?" I asked in orcish.

The man spat out a slew of vile epithets about my mother while spitting in my direction.

"I don't actually have a mother." I lifted up my visor, revealing the nothingness of my face.

The man went pale and stopped yelling in the middle of a particularly gruesome description of what he intended to do to my ancestors' graves.

"That's better, thank you. I'm looking for your boss, Vash. If you tell me what I need to know, I won't kill you. I'll even carry you to her."

"Kill me, then. I ain't selling out the queen."

"You didn't let me finish. If you don't tell me what I need to know, I'll cut off your head and eat it, and that'll tell me what I want to know anyway, except you'll also be dead."

The orc thought for a moment, grimacing from broken bones and a need to think beyond what he was likely used to. "The first one. I'll lead you to her."

"Thank you." I moved over to him and lifted the horse off of him. It wasn't too heavy, but it was unwieldy to lift, so it took awhile to position my feet in such a way that allowed it. I then tore off pieces of the saddle and made a rudimentary splint.

"I can either carry you in front of me or behind me. In front may be easier on your legs."

"Behind, please."

"Suit yourself." I bent down, and the man climbed onto my back. I hefted him up and heard him inhale sharply, but he managed to keep from screaming.

I was glad I'd already sized myself at orc height. The man was small for an orc, but if I'd still been Sevald's height, I'd have been dragging his feet along the ground as I carried him. I began walking along the road.

"Where to?"

"About a mile up the road, and then we'll make a turn."

"Alright."

I saw the man reach for a dagger and slam it into the gap

between my shoulder plate. I chose not to react and simply keep walking. "The pain made you forget there's nothing in here, huh?"

He sighed. "Yeah."

"So, what's your name?"

"Burias."

"Well, Burias, since I'll be carrying you a ways, why don't you tell me about yourself? Though I suppose you could keep trying to kill me, as well. Either way, I'll be entertained."

35
QUEEN VASH

Burias was not much of a conversationalist, but I did manage to learn that he was a clanless outcast. His family had lost their connection to their clan when his ancestor resorted to cannibalism to survive a particularly harsh winter. Vash's camp was made up mostly of outcasts that she'd been joining under her banner since she herself was forced to join their ranks.

When the camp first came into view, I was surprised to find that it looked more like a military installation than a bandit camp. There was a small pit dug around it, guards at the entrance, and orderly rows of tents. The guards began yelling and passing messages as I approached, and by the time I got to the gate, I found myself surrounded by roughly a dozen orcs.

"I believe this is yours," I said, gently lowering Burias to the ground. I gave him some space, and an orcish woman carefully approached, hefted him up, and helped him through the gate.

"Not a smart move, removing your only leverage," said a particularly large orc with a scar across his eye. He was holding a massive hammer loosely in one hand and seemed to be placing himself so I'd be within reach of it.

"I was hoping you'd take it as a gesture of goodwill. I'm here for Vash."

"I'm afraid she doesn't speak to dead men." The scarred man moved quickly, slinging his hammer at my helmet. I decided to let it hit, my head flying into another orc and knocking him to the ground.

"Was that really necessary?" I asked from my now disembodied head.

The orc holding it screamed and dropped me to the ground.

My body strolled back and placed my head in its rightful place. The entire group just stood there, dumbfounded. I walked back to the orc with the hammer. "My turn."

I punched him in the side of his head, and he crumpled. I then drew my sword and placed it at his throat as his companions began closing in. "Since you seem to insist on me having a hostage, bring me Vash, or I'll do to this orc what he did to me."

A few orcs broke off and went back into their camp. I stood where I was and maintained what I hoped was a relaxed pose while I held my sword to the downed orc's neck. It was nice not trying to hide what I was anymore. Things moved a lot more quickly, and I could take advantage of strengths I wasn't able to use when I was pretending to be a man.

After a few moments, Vash made her appearance. She looked much the same as she had when we'd met on her ship. Her teeth were particularly sharp, her skin the color of charcoal, and her eyes shone like gold coins. She was dressed differently now—all black leather armor covered her, with iron gauntlets on each hand. She had two of the hook swords she'd used on me before at her waist, and when she saw me, her hands went to them.

"You're bigger than the last time I saw you," she said.

"You look different without a ship underneath your feet."

"What do you want?"

"Information." And her head, but I'd start with a different priority.

"Why?"

"I'm not sure I can answer that without you telling your siblings what I asked and inferring things I don't want them to infer."

She spat. "Damn my siblings, damn my father, too. Come into the camp. I'll tell you what you want to know."

I returned my sword to its scabbard and fell in behind Vash, leaving my hostage behind. Now that I was near her, he wasn't necessary. This was going far better than I'd expected, so I naturally became paranoid and stayed ready to start fighting at a moment's notice.

There was some grumbling from the other orcs when I passed by, but a look from Vash shut them right up. She escorted me through to a large tent in the center. The inside was more spartan than I expected, with just a small hammock to one side, a large table in the center with some chairs, and two chests to the side. I'd grown used to the children of Aurum having much more expensive tastes.

She poured herself a cup of water and sat at one end of the table. She had to sit sideways in order to keep from sitting on her tail.

"So tell me, monster, what would you like to know?"

"Just like that? No trading barbs, or sword fighting, or killing someone before you'll answer anything?"

"Nope. Just ask me what you want, and I'll answer as best I can."

I stayed still and thought for a moment. "I guess my first question is why?"

"Why what?"

"Why aren't you trying to kill me? Why are you making this so easy?"

"Because I no longer wish to be a part of my family. I think the world would be better off without them, and I'm guessing you're seeking answers on how to make that a reality."

"What happened?"

She sighed. "*You* happened. You cost me everything. All that I'd worked to accomplish ended all because I thought I could use a favor from Talen to further my own goals. I lost my ships, the dignity I'd earned despite being without a clan, and worst of all, the lives of my crew. Though I didn't fully understand how terrible that loss was until later."

"What do you mean?"

"Imagine growing up as nothing. An outsider in your own society. Then imagine you say and do the right things long enough to create a place for yourself, a ship in my case. Then one day, you feel something new. You hear a voice, and that voice tells you that you have the power to do anything you want. You're part of a family that is of the noblest bloodline imaginable. All others around you exist only for your advancement or your pleasure. The voice not only promises this, but delivers immediately on those promises. You think more clearly, move more quickly, are stronger, and often the exact words you need to say become clear before you even need to say them. Now all your dreams are becoming real, and even better, you are a part of a clan greater than anyone else's, something you'd been denied your whole life."

She paused to take another sip of her water.

"Two members of your new clan are killed by a monster, but they were lesser members, not valuable like you were. A brother offers you a favor for killing the thing responsible, and you accept. You let the gears turn and start spinning a plan that would lead to something grand, a fleet, an admiralty, perhaps even godhood. You fail, miserably. The status you gained is wiped out in an instant, and you realize people were always waiting for you to fail. They were hungry for it. Without that status, the clan you were a part of sees less of a use for you and ceases communications beyond attempts to order you around like a servant. At a certain point, you realize that the status and power had less meaning than the crew you had with you, the people who trusted you with their lives in spite of what you were born as."

I listened to her quietly, taking in her story at first with a grain of salt, but as she continued, I found myself believing her in spite of myself. I wondered if it was Lythia's residual feelings, but I couldn't tell. When she was done talking, all I could think to say was, "I'm sorry."

"I don't need your sympathy."

"You have it anyway."

She grunted. "Your questions, what are they?"

"Aurum, what is he?"

"A god, or something as powerful as one. Beyond that, I'm not sure. He's got something to do with dragons, though, if my tail is any indication."

"That's all you know?"

"Yes, he doesn't talk about himself so much as what he can do for you."

"What does he want in return?"

"He says he does it in order to see his descendants prosper, and that whoever prospers the most will be his heir."

"He'll make them a god?"

"That's what he tells us."

"You're skeptical?"

"The gifts he gives, they do come with a price. The initial ones, the increased strength and knowledge, those felt more like something being unlocked. This—" she gestured at her tail, "—felt like he took something from me and replaced it with a piece of himself. He's always offering more, too. Even now, I'm hearing whispers of claws that could rend your armor, fire that could melt you, or wings to fly away."

"He can see what you're doing?"

"Yes, and he almost never stops talking."

"Does he tell other children of Aurum what you see?"

"No. We can communicate through him, but he doesn't give us any advantages like that over one another. He wants us to compete and not cooperate, unless it's against mutual enemies. Like you."

"What do you think his ultimate goal is, if not to choose an heir?"

"To do whatever he wants."

"What?"

"He only wants to indulge himself. Wine, women, blood, riches, games, fights—he wants all of it."

"Do you know how to stop him?"

"No. Even if you killed all of his current children, I'm sure he could find more descendants and start over. He's spread himself across the world."

"He's letting you tell me all this?"

"He's not 'letting' me, but he isn't trying to stop me either. If I had to guess, he likes you."

"He likes me? Didn't you just refer to me as a 'common enemy' to be fought?"

"You're creating pressure that didn't exist. You and your friends. He likes what it's doing to us."

I paused at that. I didn't like the idea that I was helping him, but I also didn't know what I could do except for stopping as many of his children as I could. "Your brothers, Talen and Caedus, do they suspect Aurum may be deceiving them?"

"No. They're royals; they think to a certain extent that they were always meant to be gods anyway."

"Talen's a genuine son of the duke, then?"

"He's as genuine as a bastard can be. His maid mother whispered all the grand things he was meant for into his ears from the day he was born. He can't see past his idea that he deserves godhood and power, and so he hasn't questioned anything our father has offered."

"Any idea what they're up to now?"

"A vague one. They're both working to create opportunities with two of my other brothers on the border of Sylfen. After that, I assume they'll be going after each other."

"Do you know..." I hesitated, not sure if asking the question would reveal too much, but I decided with all she'd freely shared, she could be trusted. "Do you know if my companions are okay?"

"They're alive, and free, but they're being watched. I think Caedus believed that they didn't know what you were. Either that, or he thinks they'll be useful somehow anyway."

"Thank you. For all your answers."

She nodded and finished her water. "Where are you headed now?"

"Usulaum. I still need more answers on the exact nature of Aurum, and of dragons in general, and I feel like I'll find them there. I almost feel like I'm being pulled in that direction."

Vash smiled. "Sounds like you're a puppet, too."

"Almost certainly, but I don't think I take as much offense to it as you do. It's a role I was made to play. How about you? What are your plans?"

"I'm going to rob, pillage, and fight until I can give everyone here the thing they've always been without."

"What's that?"

"A clan."

"Is that possible? To create a new clan?" I searched through Pebble's knowledge, but found little on the subject. All the orcs he knew in Usulaum were outcasts that had been removed from clan politics for generations.

"It hasn't happened for five hundred years, but it is possible. I'll just have to make the right people bleed."

I stood and considered all she had said. It was possibly true, possibly a lie, and probably a mixture of both. Whatever the case, I didn't feel I could risk leaving someone so dangerous alive, and my fury at the golden eyes in front me wouldn't let me.

I drew my sword and slashed at her neck with as much speed and force as I could manage.

She brought up her tail just in time to block the blow and rolled with the force into the edge of the tent, knocking it down around us. I cut my way through the canvas just in time for her to bring two of her hook blades down on my shoulders. They dug in, and she used their leverage to throw me.

After I landed, I stood up and found myself surrounded by orcs. Two of them attacked, swinging swords at me, but I blocked one with my sword and caught the other. I pushed both of them back and went to slice into their chests.

"No!" I heard Vash yell, and suddenly, she was between me and my attackers. There was a spray of blood, and I heard people cry out all around us.

Everyone was looking at her with deep concern on their faces, and dozens of warriors were closing in, only hesitating for fear of what I might do to Vash. I also noticed for the first time that there were children in the camp as well as men and women who definitely weren't warriors. They were people that could only be a liability to her.

I lowered my sword. Vash was still on her feet, but I'd cut her deeply. It was likely that if she hadn't been enhanced by Aurum, she'd be dead. I put my sword in my sheath and walked away.

Some warriors went to attack me, but I heard Vash weakly mutter, "Let him go."

These people needed her, and I had no right to judge someone who was doing their best to be better. Vash's people stared daggers at me as I walked through the camp. I realized I'd accidentally torn down several family tents and saw small orc children staring at me in fear. Vash may have been a monster in a way, but like me, she had people she cared for and who cared for her in return. I'd give her the same chance I was given.

I made my way out of the front gate and headed east, toward the desert.

36
INTERLUDE: ELLIS

"Why war!? We haven't had so much as a border skirmish with Sylfen in more than two hundred years! Have we even tried to negotiate? To try and avoid it?" Duke Ellis was red in the face as he spoke, his usual calm demeanor totally lost at the news he'd just received.

"It's the will of Caedus himself. The recent troubles with the Twin Kings have created more problems on the border, and he wants to take the initiative before Sylfen themselves strike," said Fybarn.

"Oh, they're the 'Twin Kings' now? We're to show them respect for their rebellion that's going to plunge us into war?"

Fybarn sighed. "Listen, I know you are unfamiliar with war. No one in Caedun but those along the northern border that face barbarians every winter has experienced anything even resembling it. Look at it another way: this is an opportunity to grow our borders. There hasn't been such a chance in whole lifetimes. As a duke, if you throw your full participation behind this, you could grow your family to heights it has never seen before."

"And all it will cost is the lives of thousands of young men and elves, right? Is that what their lives are worth?"

"You used to revel in the coliseum fights. Why the sudden distaste for a little blood?"

"That was sport, it was limited, people almost never actually died. It's impossible to compare the scale of those two things."

"I'm through arguing with you, Ellis. I simply came to tell you to prepare for what's coming. The king and the majority of us in the nobility want this war. We've justified it, sold the peasantry on it, and stand to gain from it. Fall in line or don't; in the end, it will affect nothing." Fybarn stood up from the dinner table and left, stomping up to the room Ellis had, out of courtesy, provided for him for the night.

Ellis picked at his food for a moment and took a small sip of his wine before giving up on eating. Instead, he sat there, stewing and thinking of what he could do. He controlled a good portion of Buryn along with a couple small towns and more than a dozen villages. He could seek an exemption for his people, try to keep them from having to serve in the military, but that could easily be overruled. Besides that, he was certain the young men would seek to join the military anyway. He'd already had more than three servants leave in order to sign up for the promise of adventure and spoils.

Duke Ellis was not like the other nobility. He'd never isolated himself from those without noble blood and had in fact preferred their company. He tired easily of intrigue and words with double meanings, which meant that the simple, straightforward nature of the common people was more appealing to him. It also meant he actually gave a damn what happened to his people.

One of his servants approached him and bowed. "Ser, I'm sorry for interrupting your meal, but there's a Mr. Stone here to see you."

"Stone Tangled in Roots, or Stone in the River Bed?"

"In the River Bed, ser."

"Bring him here, but quietly. Make sure none of Fybarn's servants are aware of him."

"Yes, ser." The servant bowed again, and left. A short time later, he re-entered the room with Stone in tow.

Stone looked different from the last time Ellis had seen him. His normally graying beard and hair were dyed solid black, and he wore heavier leather armor than he'd last seen him in. He also had an additional belt across his chest covered in what looked like round metal balls with short pieces of rope sticking out of them. His usually jovial expression was more neutral, more subdued.

"Stone, welcome. Would you care for something to eat?" Ellis gestured to the opposite end of the table where Fybarn's chair sat empty.

Stone nodded and climbed up to the chair with minimal fuss. "Fybarn's still here, right?"

"Yes. He retired to his room after giving me some news and sharing several opinions I didn't agree with."

Stone nodded, ripping a small loaf of bread in half and generously buttering each side. "The war, I assume?"

"Yes, the war."

"I understand. Two of my grandchildren were drafted. One was foolish enough to sign up for herself, though." Stone took a large bite of the bread he was holding, chewed for a few moments, and swallowed. "How would you like to do something about that?"

"About your grandchildren? I may be able to make sure they're as far from the field as possible, but even that would be difficult now that I've made my feelings about the war clear to Fybarn."

Stone smiled, and he immediately looked a lot more himself wearing the expression. "I appreciate that, that's a real kindness, but I meant more doing something about the war."

"There's nothing I can do. I've tried talking to the other nobles and even speaking with the king, but it accomplished nothing."

"Lad, there's always something you can do. From peasant to duke, there are always options."

"What do you suggest?"

"Well, I'd start by blackmailing your friend Fybarn. I have some rather damning documents detailing his debt at a little place called 'Estelle's House of Unearthly Pain.' As a man that advocates for the removal of all such establishments, including those that are considered temples, I think such a thing would be damning."

Ellis chuckled. "It would be, but it's honestly a rather open secret among the nobility. He's never been that impressive at hiding it."

"What about the fact that he's been going there with Count Valk's daughter for the last four months?"

Ellis raised his eyebrows. "Count Valk would challenge him to a duel immediately if he knew that."

"And he'd kill him quite handily, too, wouldn't he?"

Ellis smiled. "He would, but what would we even ask of him?"

"Little things at first, and bigger things as he becomes further involved with us. The eventual goal would be for him to openly oppose the war."

"I doubt Fybarn's opposition would make much of a dent."

"We wouldn't be stopping at Fybarn. Aside from you and Kyren, I've already found a number of nobles against the prospect of war with Sylfen. People whose families have intermarried with theirs, who trade through their territory, even a few like you who disagree with there being a war on principle.

If we can gather enough of them, we may be able to stop things, or at least slow them down long enough for everyone's blood to cool."

"Would it matter? The king's word is absolute. Even beyond his heritage, he's beloved by many, and the war itself is proving very popular."

"It's easy to rule justly when you've never been challenged, when things always go smoothly for you. Let's see how beloved he is when people see how he behaves when things aren't going his way."

Ellis made his way into his family's mausoleum. Since Hrig had left, he'd been making more frequent trips down there. Part of it was due to what he saw as a failure of management. If he'd been keeping a closer eye on things, it was possible he would have avoided the undead incursion that had briefly disturbed his estate.

The other part was that now that he and Hrig had finally had a chance to talk, he no longer felt the same pain at visiting her siblings, his adopted family. He made his way down to their tomb and lit a few of the candles he'd placed on a small altar in front of them. He then said a short prayer and placed a bundle of flowers from the garden on the altar, as well. He took a letter from his jacket and unfolded it.

"Your sister has been writing to me lately. I thought you'd like to hear how she's been doing with Dorsia." He cleared his throat and placed the letter on the altar. "She didn't write it herself. She was never great with penmanship. Hard to blame her, though; she really only spent time with the tutors to make sure you were both paying attention."

He smiled. "She's still training hard, big surprise there, and she's been active in working with some allies to disrupt Talen's trade with Buryn and trying to hurt his businesses in Cirros, as well. She mostly seems to be doing that by being pointed at issues and breaking them until they aren't problems anymore. Well, you know how she is. She's planning on visiting, along with Dorsia and Jade, but doesn't know when she'll get the chance. That was pretty much it. I just thought you'd like to know how she's doing."

Ellis left the candles burning and made his way back out of the tomb, stopping for only a few extra moments to leave more flowers on his parents' grave. Once out of the mausoleum, he took a deep breath and let the sun warm him, driving the chill of the tomb from his bones.

A servant approached. "My lord, Clara is here to see you. She's taking tea in your study."

"Thank you, Tillis. I'll head that way." Ellis made his way across the grounds and into his manor. He entered the room to find Clara, seated and enjoying tea. She was tan, with a tangle of dark hair that had been forced into the latest style, her eyes light brown with flecks of green.

She smiled and stood as he entered, giving a slight bow. "My lord."

"You don't have to do that. It's not as if we haven't worked together before."

"You'll have to indulge me. I'm so used to dealing with adventurers, I'd really like to flex my courtly manners a little. I rarely get the chance."

"Fair enough." Ellis had found Clara to be a bit of an enigma. She was of low birth, but was smart and capable. She craved the taste of nobility in the same way he had craved the simplicity of common folk.

She curtsied and sat back down. "So, what can I do for you, Duke Ellis?"

"You've heard of the war coming, I presume?"

"Hard to avoid, I'm afraid."

"Is war good for the adventuring business?"

"It is at first, as the young men leave home and places become easier prey to monsters and bandits, but eventually, there's not any money to pay them, and those that would work for free start to not have enough money for equipment, and that tends to lead to their downfall. Some join the army, of course, but they are rarely suited for it. They'd made their way on small teams or as individuals. Those with an adventurer's disposition typically lack the ability to conform necessary to excel at war."

Ellis smiled. "Is that lack of conformity ever trying?"

"Constantly. They often go around my back, or take jobs without negotiation, or even disappear. Managing them is exhausting."

"I'm not surprised to hear that." He paused. "It sounds like you'd prefer to avoid war if possible."

"Absolutely, yes."

"What if I told you I had a way we could do that?"

"I'd say I want to hear it, but I'd also like to know how I'll be involved."

"Stone and I have put together a large group of benefactors. We want to hire something like fifty adventurers."

"Fifty? I only manage seventeen."

"But you know other fixers, right?"

"I suppose... But what would you do with those fifty adventurers?"

"It's simple. We'd end the issue at the heart of the war before it even starts. We're planning on taking out the Twin Kings."

"What?"

"The Twin Kings house noble traitors from our kingdom, and Sylfen believes we're planning on annexing their territories into our own. That's the whole impetus for the war. If we remove the Twin Kings from the board, and take those nobles out, as well, we can stop things before they begin."

"Sylfen itself hasn't been able to bring them in line. What makes you think you can with fifty adventurers?"

"Sylfen moves slowly. It's their longevity, keeps them from risking immediate action. A small group of individuals can move quickly, and a strong group can strike hard. Sylfen is considering and planning and plotting while Caedun escalates things in anticipation of them doing the same. We can get ahead of both of them."

"And it'll be up to me to assemble this group?"

"All but three of the fifty, yes."

Clara sighed and smiled. "Do I need to guess which ones?"

"No, you don't."

"Well, you get me the money, and I'll get you what you need. From there, it's on you."

37
ACROSS THE DESERT

Walking across a desert usually takes a lot of preparation. Water is the most important factor, followed by transport, navigation, and even defense from the many monsters that hide amongst the dunes.

Luckily for me, these were not issues I needed to concern myself with. I didn't need water, I didn't need transport, I had an internal compass to point me where I needed to go, and defense came naturally to me.

It had been a lonely trip so far. There were no caravans active this time of year due to the intense heat and sandstorms, but occasionally, guides would move people across the desert for the right price. So far, though, I had encountered no one.

When Pebble had looked out at the desert, he'd always been comforted by the desolate beauty of it. I felt much the same as I walked, scanning the dunes. It was my fifth day of travel, and I found myself wishing I had more landmarks or indications that I was close to the city, but unfortunately, all I ever saw was sand and the occasional half-buried building that looked much the same as every other half-buried building.

I was surprised when, upon cresting a dune, I found myself

completely surrounded. I hadn't noticed them at first because their scales were the same color as the sand and their graceful movements made no sound. I was struck by their beauty and grace almost immediately, all seven of them. The naga had a kind of proud bearing that radiated from them, and the blending of human and snake features proved very handsome. They were each holding weapons, but they seemed hesitant to get too close to me. A mixed group of males and females, I could tell all but one of them were warriors, though.

I searched my memories for any words in their language, but could find little aside from something Pebble had picked up from an old adventurer that had told him he'd escaped from a naga cavern.

"May the light of Serpa warm your scales." It came out awkwardly as a series of hisses.

The naga's eyes widened in surprise. They hissed at one another and then back at me.

"I speak only common, orcish, dwarvish, elvish, some undercommon, and maybe...draconic." I named each language in the language itself, hoping for some recognition.

A female, the one who didn't have the look of a warrior, took a step, or rather a slither, closer to me.

"You can speak the language of the enemies, but greet us in the way of our people?" she asked in common.

"I suppose I do, yes. How do you know common?"

"It is my responsibility as the storyteller to know all languages in which our story may appear." She looked me up and down. "You are strange."

"I'm aware of that."

The female naga weaved her head side to side, deep in thought. "Is your strangeness the reason you are not dead?"

"Probably, but why do you think I should be dead?"

Her tongue flicked out and tasted the air. "We have been

following you for some time. You entered the desert with no water or food and have not stopped walking for several days. We were intending to simply wait until you collapsed and take you to our young to be eaten."

"Ah, well, normally, that would be a great plan except..." I removed my helmet. "I doubt that your young feed on steel."

All but the closest naga backed away, hissing. The female, however, let out what I assumed was a laugh.

"It would seem we have wasted our time."

"I'd apologize, but you were planning on eating me, so I don't feel I should."

She smiled. "I am Syrene. As you have nothing to offer us and have greeted us with respect, we shall allow you to pass through our desert unharmed."

"I appreciate your practicality."

She nodded. "We can afford to be nothing less."

"Can I ask how far I am from the city?"

"Two more nights, and you shall reach it. Be wary, though. The followers of the wyrm have many patrols in that area."

"Lizardmen?"

"I believe that is what you call them, yes."

"Thank you." I placed my helmet back on.

Syrene cocked her head. "Are there many like you outside the desert?"

"I'm the only one, as far as I know."

"An oddity, then. I look forward to telling our people about you and adding to our story."

I nodded, not fully understanding what she meant, and resumed my trek toward Usulaum. Before I'd even gone ten feet, they'd all vanished back into the desert.

Pebble would have been ecstatic at the encounter I'd just had, though if he'd experienced it himself, he likely would've been eaten. He would've gotten to see naga up close, learn a little bit about them culturally, and actually interact with them directly. He could've written entire papers on what I'd just experienced.

I continued making my way through the desert, mentally composing the paper he would write, as it seemed as good a method as any to keep myself distracted from the growing monotony of my walk through the sand and the persistent thoughts regarding my friends and their situations. I was so deep in thought that I completely forgot I needed to be watching out for lizardmen and was taken by surprise when they attacked.

They burst from the sand behind me, and two of them immediately hurled large javelins in my direction. One skimmed my shoulder plate, and the other slammed into the tower shield I had strapped to my back, shattering into splinters.

Instead of pulling out my usual longsword, I took my new multiplying sword out of my mouth and divided it into two. The lizardmen rushed me as I did so. The nearest one leapt on powerful hind legs, bringing down a massive club covered in what looked to be shards of sharpened black glass.

I stabbed upward before he could bring the club down and ran my sword through the creature's chest, using his own momentum against him. I dropped him, along with the sword, and created another one that I threw at a lizardman that was readying a javelin. It struck him in the leg, severing it, and he collapsed to the ground in pain.

Two more approached me swinging their clubs, but I turned and absorbed their blows on my shield, feeling it sap their energy. I then swiftly twirled with my sword outstretched and slashed them across their stomachs, sending a spray of blood across my armor.

I then started toward the remaining javelin thrower. He made a final throw, but I batted it away with my swords and started running toward him. He eyed his fallen comrades and ran. I pursued him for a few moments, but his feet were made for running on the sand, and my boots were not.

I turned my attention to the lizardmen behind me, or lizardfolk, I thought, realizing that the differing sizes and coloring indicated at least two females among the dead. They wore no clothing. The males had stood a foot taller than I had at orc armor size, and the females were even larger. Their scales were shades of blue, red, or even light purple, but they wore some kind of warpaint that camouflaged them. It was the same coloring that the naga had naturally.

I felt a little guilty at slaying them, but they hadn't given me a chance to talk like the naga had, even though I suspected their intentions were much the same. I stored a few of their strange clubs, which I realized were bladed with obsidian, making them more akin to swords. I considered burying them, but decided the desert would likely take care of that for me.

I initially began walking directly for the city, but hesitated. This was a learning opportunity much like the one I'd had with the mer-folk. I approached what looked to be the most intact of them, and consumed him. I was able to read through his essence much like I had been with my last snack. Part of me missed the overwhelming sensation I used to get, but this was certainly more practical. I saw images of massive underground cities with tunnels spread across the world. Two species locked in combat across these tunnels, where the only peace came from both being too damaged to continue. Massive icons of lizards made of pure gold lined walls of intricately carved flowers of gemstone. The memory that radiated the strongest, however, was a simple one, of lying in a massive pit, the sun coming down, surrounded by my people, warming ourselves in the light, and feeling the heat of it sink into my scales.

They seemed an interesting people, just not one very interested in speaking with outsiders. There was a feeling of superiority the lizardman had, as well as an in-built insularity. I continued to parse through the memories and impressions as I made my way through the desert.

By nightfall, the tower of Usulaum came into sight—an enormous red spire that extended far toward the heavens. The rest of the city sat much lower, but no less grand in its own way. High walls of sandstone, buildings reaching almost half the height of the tower, and all of it lit in such a way that if the desert were flat, it would've been visible for miles.

It took me several more hours to reach the walls of the city. There were no gates, and instead of gatekeepers, I had to find a sand shaper. It took quite some time for me to locate one and even more time to gain his attention, but once he saw me, he moved himself to a portion of the wall, placed his hand above it, and a doorway appeared, allowing me entrance.

I walked through halfway and found the way behind me and in front of me sealed off and a hole above me opened, down which looked the sand shaper. He was pale, likely from working the night shift, had dark eyes, and a shaved head.

"Get drunk and fall out of the walls, or were you one of the escorts that took some students to explore the dunes?"

"Neither, I'm just a visitor."

The man squinted down at me. "From where?"

"Caedus."

"Alone?"

I made a show of looking around the small opening I had. "Seem to be, don't I?"

"I'm going to level with you. That's the most suspicious thing I've ever heard."

"Is it really?"

"Well, I once had a woman tell me her husband didn't mind me spending evenings with her. Turned out that was true, but her boyfriend had a problem with it." He looked me over. "Eh, whatever. I'm supposed to let everyone in except lizardmen and naga, and even that has exceptions. I'm not paid enough to care about this."

He moved, and I felt some energy in the air followed by my way into the city being opened back up.

I made my way through and entered the city proper. There were no planned roads like there had been in the capital of Caedun, and no set gate from which one was meant to enter the city, so I found myself immediately in the night market. The streets were lit by floating paper lanterns that drifted lazily over the various stalls and food vendors. The smell of cooking meat and strong spices filled the air.

It was less busy than it would've been during caravan season, but the large number of students and day laborers that lived in the city were doing their best to keep things alive. Some were chatting outside of food carts, others bartering with merchants for alchemical ingredients, and some even sitting on benches reading, enjoying the company of the market, but not willing to engage with it.

I felt an immediate sense of comfort here. This was where Pebble had grown up, after all, and all of it was familiar to me through his memories. I recognized several of the merchants, including one who'd once swindled Pebble into spending an inordinate amount of money on what he thought was a traditional naga headdress, but was actually something he'd stolen from an artist.

While I had no need to eat, I did spend some time tasting

the various foods as I passed by, noting the spices, types of meat, and the garnishes used by each vendor. Syven would have been ecstatic at the opportunity to learn more about Usulaum food.

I wanted to make my way directly to the university, but I realized that at this time of night, it was likely closed, or at least partially closed. Rather than go and wait outside the library, I wandered around the market, looking at various baubles being sold and occasionally making polite conversation with students who wandered over to ask me about being an adventurer.

In the middle of one such conversation, I heard what sounded like an explosion come out of a nearby restaurant. I ran inside, passing by several customers who were coughing and walking out to find a man desperately trying to put out a fire with a large cloth. I moved in front of him, removed a gauntlet, and jettisoned the water that remained in my armor to douse the flame, revealing a heavily charred lizard. I returned my gauntlet to my hand and turned my attention to the soot-stained man who had been trying to put out the fire. I tasted the air.

The man next to me was a wide dwarf with a short-trimmed beard, the style for dwarves in the hot Usulaum sun, wearing an apron and a concerned expression. He turned to me. "Oh, thank you, ser! I was worried my restaurant was going to burn to the ground."

"Did you try to season this with fire salt?"

"What— Er, yes, ser, I did."

"How much?"

"Three pinches."

"Three!? I'm surprised you're still alive."

"I just followed the recipe given to me by the day chef."

"Describe them."

"Er, she's a half elf, dainty woman, big personality."

"Did you think that maybe a pinch for her is a bit smaller than a pinch for you?"

The man looked down at hands with fingers as thick as sausages. "Oh."

I shook my helmet. "Well, at least you're okay. Watch the fire salt next time, alright?"

I began making my way back out to the market.

"Wait! Do you know anything about cooking?"

I turned back to face him. "I know a fair amount."

Thanks to Syven's years of practice, I knew far more than all but perhaps the cooks that served royalty.

"Would you, well, would you be willing to help me out for the night? The night market is just getting started, and I really need the business."

"I don't know..." I said, but looking at the man, I felt a fair amount of concern that without my help, he would kill himself.

"Please, I'll pay you well. My night chef quit yesterday. I thought I could just follow the recipes and it would be fine, but..." He gestured vaguely at the mess of smoke and soot all around us.

I sighed, which was for show, of course, but that didn't mean I didn't feel it. "Fine, I'll help you."

The man smiled and took off his apron, handing it to me. I tied it on.

"Are you going to remove your armor, ser?"

"Considering the kitchen you left me looks like a battlefield, I think I'd be safer wearing it."

38

INTERLUDE BRUIS/KYREN

Bruis poured Kyren another drink, her tenth of the evening. As usual, the only indication that she'd had any was the slightly larger than usual smile she was wearing.

That day, her smile seemed strained. Bruis had been doing his best to help her relax and put her mind at ease, but she'd been throwing herself into rising in the church with such force that she was exhausted. She had dark bags under her eyes from not sleeping, and she'd been fasting most of the day.

Bruis had asked his grandmother, Kyren's mentor, what exactly she was doing, but he'd received a swift slap on the back of his head for his trouble, along with a stern lecture on asking after church secrets. Luckily, he had other sources. A chat with a priestess of Jeiri had let him know that Kyren was at this point in constant commune with Sidi. If she could maintain the level of focus and dedication she had been, then she would reach a new stage of priesthood both within herself and within the church.

Next to Kyren on the bar sat Old Osric, a gray tabby cat with black stripes and green eyes. As far as most were concerned, Old

Osric was the cornerstone on which the church in the capital had been built. There had always been an Old Osric, even before his grandmother's time, and his line had produced an unbroken chain of Osrics for as long as anyone could remember. He was a source of comfort for all those seeking their vestments, and he'd been particularly close to Kyren since she'd begun her rededication to the church.

Kyren finished her ale, and Bruis poured her another.

"So, have you learned anything?" he asked.

Kyren looked around, making sure the bar was empty. "Have you ever wondered why the gods aren't as active here as they used to be?"

"What do you mean? We experience the gods every day."

"We experience them through priests, through visions, and some of us through direct conversation, but they aren't 'here' in the way they used to be."

"You mean, not walking among us?"

"Exactly. In histories and stories, the gods would physically appear. They would influence things directly. They'd even have children with mortals."

"Is that what you learned? Why they stopped?"

Kyren sighed, exhausted. "No. The only thing I learned was that the question exists. I have a theory, or maybe just an inkling of what happened, but it's on the edges of my awareness, never solid enough for me to grasp. I know it's important, though, and I know it will help me find the answers I seek."

Bruis thought for a moment, absently scratching behind Old Osric's ears. "Do you think it's that the gods don't live as close because they won't, or because they can't?"

Kyren perked up. "What do you mean?"

"I mean, are we assuming that they don't want to be closer, or is it that they can't be? Is something keeping them from here? If so, what could stop them from doing what they wanted?"

"Well, for one of the major gods, it would likely take two or more to fully restrain them. Though there are some gods that are more major than others."

Bruis took her now empty mug and put it to the side for cleaning. "What about an agreement? Something between all of them."

"That would be possible, but why? What would make them limit themselves?"

Bruis shrugged. "I'm not sure."

He'd spoken with enough drunken clerics to have picked up the skills needed for a philosophical conversation, but he rarely had answers to questions. Even if he did, he was fairly certain the questions were meant to be rhetorical.

Kyren rubbed her eyes and yawned. "I should try and get some sleep. Thank you for the ale, and the conversation."

"Anytime," said Bruis.

Kyren got up and went to her room. Bruis had upgraded her from the communal room she'd shared with her companions to a small suite of her own. Aside from two short trips she'd taken to and from her estate, she'd basically made it her home. Bruis was happy to have her company, but he was worried about her. Men had been into the bar multiple times asking about her, wanting specifics on whom she'd spoken with and where she was going. Luckily, he was able to be honest thanks to the care Kyren was taking, but what he'd been able to infer made him scared for her. He'd prefer to pretend he wasn't involved even as he was actively assisting it by assisting Kyren.

"She's getting very close to some real answers. It's quite impressive."

Bruis startled, looking around for the source of the voice, but he saw no one. "Hello? Is someone there?"

"Nope, no one's here," said a voice behind him.

Bruis jumped and whipped around, but saw only Osric

perched on the top shelf behind the bar, the top shelf being where cats naturally belonged.

"Osric?"

"That's me," said the voice, but Osric's mouth didn't move.

Bruis thought for a moment. Talking animals weren't unheard of. He'd even met a talking dog once, though it didn't have much to talk about aside from the joys of herding sheep. Still, he'd known Osric, or Osric's dad, for his entire life.

"Osric, are you talking?"

"Not technically, no."

"Uh, huh... Then what would you call what you're doing?"

"Telepathy."

Bruis leaned on the bar. "Am I hallucinating?"

"I wouldn't know."

Bruis took a deep breath to collect himself. The cat could talk, and it had an attitude. "Could you always ta—er, use telepathy?"

"Yes. I can also talk, but not in this form."

"This form?"

"Yes." Osric stretched and leapt down to the bar. "Though I'm unable to change shape at the moment, too risky."

"Well, if you could always talk, why haven't I heard you do so before now?"

"I talk quite frequently actually, just not usually to those outside the mysteries."

"You mean, you only talk to those in the high clergy?"

"A few of them through history, none recently."

"Well, why are you talking to me now?"

Osric began cleaning between the toes of his left foot. "Because I see an opportunity with our mutual friend."

"Kyren?"

"Yes. She is young, and brave. I think she may be just the

one I need to move the church, or at least some of it, into motion."

"Into motion of what kind?"

"Open conflict with the crown, and others."

Bruis blinked, shook his head, left the room, splashed some water on his face, returned, and gave himself a pinch. "What was that?"

"Open conflict with the crown, and others."

"I think I may need to go lie down."

"I'm afraid I need you to sit down and listen."

Bruis found himself doing just that, and wondering why he was planning on leaving in the first place.

"Good, thank you. Now, what I'm going to need you to do is take this." Osric pushed a small bundle of plants that hadn't been in front of him before into Bruis's hand with his nose.

"What's this?"

"Godroot."

"What do you want me to do with it?"

"Put some into the next drink you serve her."

Bruis went red. "I would never serve a patron a drink with something they didn't agree to in it."

Osric's eyes flashed. "Listen to me, little man. You putting that into her drink may be the difference between my freedom or my death as well as the death of thousands of others. You will serve it to her."

Bruis found himself cowed by the small old tabby in front of him. "What does it do?"

"It will completely restore her energy and allow her to briefly channel the god whom she's closest with directly. This is the last piece in existence. It's been extinct for quite some time. Humans apparently took it until it was gone from this world."

"How will that help? Kyren can already talk to Sidi."

"She can commune with her. Channeling is completely different. To channel a god is to become them."

"Gods! Why would she need that?"

"She's in danger. The kind she needs divine intervention to save her from."

Bruis inhaled. "It won't hurt her?"

"No, in fact, she'll feel better than ever."

"Is there some way I could help to protect her? Why don't we just warn her?"

Osric shook his head. "She won't trust me when I communicate with her, and I can't play my hand that way. There are limits to what I can do, and even this is stretching them. This is the only way."

"Why doesn't Sidi interfere herself, or talk to her?"

"Sidi is limited in what she can do here. You and Kyren already figured out why. This is a way to very temporarily bend the rules, one I've saved for a thousand years."

"A thousand!?"

"Yes."

"Why didn't you just put this in her drink yourself?"

"The intent matters with an ingredient like this. She needs to trust who gives it, and the one who gives it to her needs to do so out of benevolence."

Bruis looked at the plant in his hand. "Fine. I feel like you're telling, or thinking, me the truth. I'll do it. I don't know if I'll be able to lie to her when I give her the drink, though. She knows me well. She'll probably realize something is up."

Osric licked his paw and began cleaning his face. "Don't worry about that. Now that I have your agreement, I'll make it like we never talked. You'll perform the action you've agreed to without even realizing it."

"Wait, what?"

"Thanks again. You're saving lives by doing this, mine most importantly."

Kyren felt strange. Not bad strange, good strange. She'd been exhausted for the last several weeks as she went through a cycle of fasting, meditation, and prayer with only brief breaks that weren't nearly enough to allow her to recover.

Today, though, she felt as if all of her energy had been restored. More than restored, in fact; she felt better than ever. As if she could tug at the very essence of the power she borrowed from Sidi and send it out of her hands as raw energy. She chose not to test it, but she was tempted.

The tasks set out to her by her mentor were complete, and now was the time to present herself to the leaders of the temple and hear their determination as to whether she would be welcomed into the high mysteries. Even before she started feeling better this morning, she'd already begun to feel a new level of closeness with not just her goddess, but the world around her, as well. The contemplation she'd lost herself in had made her feel like she was beginning to understand questions that tugged at the foundational elements of the universe. It was just a feeling, of course, but it still felt like progress.

She arrived at the temple a little early, taking the time to scratch Old Osric under the chin as she passed him. Some initiates nodded or waved at her as she passed, and when she reached Serah, her mentor, they shared a brief bow to one another.

Serah looked her over. "You seem in remarkably good spirits."

Kyren nodded. "It's strange, I feel very refreshed. Is that typical for disciples when we reach this stage?"

Her mentor laughed. "Absolutely not. I was so tired and hungry at this point that I told one of the priests at my review to go jump off the roof."

"Really? You?"

"I was a fiery young thing once, Kyren. Not all of us are born with old souls like you."

Before she could respond, a man in a grey robe opened the door and gestured them inside. The room was made up of a semicircle table at which sat four chairs. Serah left Kyren's side to go sit at one of the chairs while Kyren took her place in the middle.

Aside from Serah was Iomed, a priestess of Jeiri, Jun, a priest of all gods, and Priyap, a priest of Krish. They varied widely in age, with Serah being the oldest and Jun the youngest, all as different a group as was possible. Priyap was a half-elven man with a shaved head, tan skin, and sharp features. Jun was a young dwarf with no beard, but long lustrous brown hair and a kind smile. Iomed was a middle-aged human woman with a small wine glass in her hand and curly hair that tumbled past her shoulders. Her eyes were nearly closed, and she'd clearly been in her cups. Serah was wearing her usual white robes with nothing out of place. Her dark skin was wrinkled with age and her hair was gray, but long and well-maintained.

Kyren bowed and waited. It wasn't her place to begin the conversation.

Jun stood. "Kyren, welcome. We are gathered here today to discuss whether you should be allowed access to the higher mysteries of our temple. In order to honor Dur, we of the council prefer to have the discussions in front of the supplicant in order to give her the chance to defend herself in honor of fairness."

"I understand."

"Excellent. From here, we'll be moving along the table giving our votes and why we believe they are justified. Priyap?"

He stood as Jun sat. "Good morning, Kyren. It's a testament to your will that you are not shaking right now. I know that when I was before the previous council, I was trembling from the lack of food and spiritual preparation."

"Thank you."

"I vote to allow her access to all sacred knowledge. Unlike many among the clergy, she has spent her time out in the world, and I believe that experience will be invaluable and that she has rightfully earned a place among us."

Priyap sat, and Serah stood. "My vote is the same. Kyren's dedication to Sidi is equal to my own, and her work has always reflected the will of our goddess."

Jun stood. "I'm of the opinion that Kyren needs the access more than anyone else. As I've been advocating to the rest of you, I believe now is the time for the church to take a more active role, particularly with the information that has been coming to light. I vote to allow her access." He then sat.

Iomed stood, took a sip of her drink, and gave Kyren a long look. "I have said it time and time again. We should not be involving ourselves in the affairs of state. I have kept us from this precipice dozens of times, and I intend to continue doing so. I vote that Kyren not be allowed access to the mysteries. I believe she'd be disruptive and could damage the reputation of all members of the clergy. If we were to be more active, I would not be surprised if priests are barred from towns, their assets seized, and perhaps even their lives taken. We need to consider what acting against a king would entail, not just for us, but for all priests and clerics across the country."

That surprised Kyren. Iomed had been on her side in the past. Still, she had a chance to argue and chose to take it. "I would think that now more than ever, the church should be involved in what's going on. We stand at the brink of war, and there are powers at play that directly involve us."

"Powers that you know nothing about. Just what you infer."

"Which is exactly why I'm here. To learn the truth. I just want to know about Aurum, about why we put out the edict to hunt dragons. Why are there prayers to him in old books? What was his place in our church? I don't even need access to all the mysteries; I just want the truth."

"The truth?" Iomed smiled, and her inebriated state seemed to abruptly end. She opened her eyes fully, revealing discs of gold. "The truth is that a new god is coming. One who will be real on this earth even while the other gods fester in the ether. I tire of playing church politics to keep you fools from interfering. Now, you die."

Iomed began to glow with golden light, growing in size and even seeming to grow younger. Heat emanated from her, and she inhaled, clearly intending to bathe the room in fire.

The priests all began quick prayer spells, and Priyap drew a blade and lunged for Iomed, but it was clear they would all be too late. All of this passed in front of Kyren in slow motion, and she felt herself drift completely out of her own body as it happened.

Suddenly, she felt a sense of enormous calm and warmth. It reminded her of reading under the old sycamore tree on her grandmother's estate. The feeling filled her, expanding her into something that could house it, and suddenly, she was not herself—she was Sidi.

She lifted her hand, and all the heat that had been building faded immediately. She waved her other hand dismissively at the others in the room, cancelling their spells and teleporting Priyap back to his chair.

"You will not prevent the church from doing what it is

intending to do, Iomed. No matter what Aurum promised you, it is all for naught."

Iomed screamed, building energy again, but Sidi stopped it with another dismissive wave. Iomed then began shifting and struggling against invisible restraints, her body contorting. She sprouted fangs, a tail split from her dress, and her body covered itself in scales, but nothing could break the grip Sidi had on her. Finally, all sanity left her eyes, and she grew silent for a moment before her body burst into flame.

A voice spoke from her that was not her own. "It won't matter, Sidi. You have banished yourselves in order to keep from becoming like me, but I'm still here, and there will never be another like me. My will can exist on this plane even while you attempt your petty interference from the outside. I won't be denied."

After that, the fire burst upward, incinerating the body completely.

Sidi turned her attention to a window through which sat Osric, watching the scene. "Your interference is noted. I forgive you this time, as it was in service to my purposes, but tread lightly."

Kyren felt her goddess thank her for the use of her body, and found herself alone in her body, in control once again.

39
THE UNIVERSITY

I rolled out another dish, hollering at Granite to take it out to the customer. While my initial agreement to help him had been only for the night I arrived, it had quickly extended into an offer for me to be the night chef. This suited me, as the library was closed during the night, and I had no need for sleep. I was finding kitchen work to be incredibly rewarding as all of the time I spent cooking left me absorbed in Syven's memories and that made me feel, in many ways, whole.

I was also damn good at the job. Aside from Syven's experience as a cook, I also had many advantages that were helping me to excel. I could taste things from a distance, I required nothing protective to handle hot things, and I could hold a spoon and spin my gauntlet to mix things far more quickly than would be necessary by hand, though I only did that when I was sure I wasn't being observed. I began preparing some blackened chicken with creamy terok sauce for the next dish.

While I relied on Syven's skills during the night, Pebble's were guiding me during the day. I'd been spending all of my daylight hours immersed in whatever texts I could find involving dragons, gods, and Aurum. I'd so far learned from older texts that Aurum was, in fact, a god, and a major one. He was the god of dragons, a being of pure whim, who did what he wanted when he wanted with or to whomever he wanted.

There were hints in some texts that the gods had worked together to stop him, but what exactly they did, I couldn't find. If I could, then that might be the secret to stopping him. I also learned that it was the gods themselves that had ordered the church to aid in the hunting and extinction of dragons of all kinds. The reason for that was also unclear, though one interesting thing I found was that at least one dragon had betrayed his kind, helping the church to eliminate his brethren.

At this point, I had reached the end of what I could find in the publicly accessible areas of the library, and the time had come to figure out a way to get into the inner library that existed in the tower. Not even Pebble had been granted access to it during his time at the university. Only scholars officially recognized by the university were granted access. It was rumored to be filled with dozens of forbidden texts and ancient histories that only those acknowledged by the university were trusted to access.

I had a few options. I could break in, but it would likely make it difficult to read and research if I was fighting off a group of enraged wizards at the same time. I could ask someone who was a scholar to do the research for me, but so far, the student connections I'd made weren't yet recognized scholars, and the ones that Pebble had known would likely be suspicious if I approached them.

The final option was to become a scholar myself. That option was surprisingly viable thanks to the inherent corruption of the system. There were a few ways to become a scholar: hard work, bribery, and presenting something unique for study, which is also a kind of bribery, but for bookish types. My funds weren't exactly low, but they weren't enough to buy my way in, and I didn't have time to create and defend a thesis, but I did have two magical items that they might not have seen before.

I wrapped up my shift, handing things off to the dainty Miss Tylen, the day chef. She was a wisp of a woman, dainty even for an elf, but she had a real presence to her. When I'd first started, she'd walked me through a few of Oasis's signature dishes, and I had the feeling that in spite of the fact she'd been quite critical the entire time, she had been impressed with me. I gave her a brief rundown on where we were on ingredients and then made my way down the streets toward the university.

While I had initially been concerned about people questioning my armor, to the point that I'd rehearsed what to say if someone asked, so far, it hadn't come up. Usulaum was a city of refugees and outcasts, so people tended to be less curious about an individual's personal idiosyncrasies.

It had felt good to be there. The familiarity of Pebble's essence with the library and city itself and Syven's life in kitchens had meant my time in the city had fully unlocked their memories and impressions in the same way that Sevald's and Byn's were.

Unlike their focus on family and the approval of their communities, Syven and Pebble sought recognition from within themselves. They had goals that they gave meaning to internally. With all of the essences flowing freely through me, I felt more complete, more capable, and that let me put all my focus toward getting whatever information I could find that would let me take the fight to Aurum.

The university grounds were made up of utilitarian buildings consisting of sandstone and built to cool themselves using the water produced by the red tower at the center of the city. That water also fed a lush garden that gave the entire campus a paradise-like feel. A few of the buildings closer to the central tower were made up of a similar red stone, but none were quite the same shade. Some of them even looked like miniature versions of the central one. Attempts by mages to emulate Rubrus that had clearly fallen short.

Eventually, I reached the administrative building that was built up against the tower and entered. A perky young dwarf girl stood at the counter with pen ink on her face. She smiled and waved for me to approach.

"Welcome back. Here to do more research?"

"Hey, Em. Yeah, though I seem to have reached the limits of what I can discover in the main library. I need access to the tower."

"Ah, well, will you be bribing, registering as a student, or presenting an item for research?"

"You are very open about the bribery aspect."

"You betcha; no reason to pretend half our scholars aren't spoiled nobles trying to look smart."

"That's fair. I'll be presenting an item for research."

"In that case, let me fetch an appraiser." She hopped off her chair and made her way to a back room.

Emerald was a uniquely helpful sort of person, a quality I truly appreciated. Many of the other administrators I'd interacted with had been cold and clearly disdained interacting with anyone outside of what they considered their own elite little group.

Em returned with a gangly older orc man wearing glasses and wrapped in loose-fitting robes.

"Good morning," I said.

"What have you got?" he asked gruffly. It seemed clear that Em had dragged him away from something.

I pulled out my new sword and divided it in two, placing both on the desk between us.

The man grabbed them, holding them lightly in his hand, then he put them back on the desk. His right eye glowed briefly.

"A multi-sword. Mildly interesting, but unfortunately, we've seen a few before. This won't earn the title, I'm afraid."

"I have another item."

"Oh? Two magical items is no small thing. I'm surprised."

"Adventurers like me tend to stumble across these kinds of things more often than most." I pulled my shield off my back and laid it down between us. I was a little concerned about giving it up, considering I had still promised it to Rock if he or a champion defeated me, but priorities were what they were, and they'd return the item after they'd completed studying it anyway.

The orc peered down at the shield, his eyes glowing again as he did so. "Hmmm, this one is a bit more interesting. An energy-stealing shield. Eminently practical for one such as yourself, I suppose." He looked at it a bit more closely. "Unfortunately, we have actually encountered this same enchantment before, though it was used on a monk's punching bag to train their endurance more quickly. I'm afraid this wo—" The orc looked up at me, his eyes still glowing. His jaw dropped, and his eyes widened.

"I see you've found the third magic item."

The man fell backward, out cold.

It took a few minutes, but eventually, Em woke the man by splashing cold water on his face, and I helped him to his feet. He shook his head a few times, as if trying to shake something loose. He looked back up at me.

"You alright?" I asked.

His face lit up, all previous grumpiness dispelled. "Alright!? You may be the most fascinating thing to ever walk into this building."

"Does this mean I can receive the title of scholar?"

"If that's what it takes to allow us to study you, absolutely. I'll need to go to the tower at once to bring some of my fellows to examine you. Emerald, please work on having this entity added to our esteemed ranks."

"Entity? What does he mean?" asked Em.

"Oh, I'll show you." I placed my hands on the side of my head, but hesitated. "Please don't be afraid."

"Why would I be afraid?"

I removed my helmet, revealing the nothingness underneath.

"Oh!"

"Yeah. I'm not human. Not sure what I am, actually."

"Fascinating," said the appraiser, having returned with a few men with interesting facial hair, all of whom were doing their best to look down the hole my helmet left.

"Well, human or not, you've always been nice, so I don't see any reason to be afraid."

I returned my head to its rightful place. "Thanks, Em. I appreciate that."

The orc appraiser, whose name was Tesh, had brought in about a half dozen other men who were staring at me with glowing eyes, taking notes, and occasionally asking questions. I'd convinced them that I could do that while also searching the library with my new credentials as a scholar.

For a moment, I felt guilty that I'd gotten that status so easily when Pebble had worked so hard to earn it, but then I realized that it was Pebble that had earned it. If I hadn't eaten him, I would never have thought to search Usulaum for information on Aurum in the first place.

We walked to the entrance to the tower, passing over a small bridge over the water at its base, and two of the men whispered into the door, which flew open. The tower itself wasn't actually all that large, maybe the size of the atrium of the Wyrwind estate, but it made up for that with height. It was so high, in fact, that there was no way it would be structurally sound without magic. The walls on the inside were the same color as the walls on the outside, though I couldn't see much of them as shelves lined them as far as I could see.

"So, you can store items inside yourself?" asked one of my robed shadows.

"Yes, though there's a limit," I said as I started to peruse the spines of the books on the shelf nearest to me.

"Is the limit what would fit into your armor?"

"No, it's quite a bit more significant than that."

"Fascinating, just like an ancient bag of holding."

"Bag of what now?"

"Ah, they were a type of dimensional storage space. The methods for making them were lost, and all of the old ones were worn out until they disintegrated by the adventurers that favored them."

"The fools," added one of the others.

The first one nodded in agreement. "There are none left now."

"Interesting," I said. Perhaps my master had used the methods that created part of those bags as part of my construction. It would be nice to get some answers to what I was on top of what I was searching for relating to Aurum.

After I'd amassed a relatively large stack of books, I sat down and started reading, letting the researchers continue to poke and prod me as I did so. Within only a few hours, I was finding answers to questions I'd spent days searching for, along with answers to questions I didn't even know I had.

Dragons were hunted to extinction by the church in order to curb Aurum's power. Some books theorized it was because the dragon's belief in their god was making him stronger, but the oldest of the books had a darker theory. They posited that Aurum was not born a god, but instead became one by devouring other dragons, gaining their power, and growing stronger in the process.

Aurum had destroyed cities, laid waste to empires, and acted indiscriminately all while having liaisons across the continent. The other gods banded together after using the church to weaken him and joined their powers to strike him down. In order to prevent such atrocities from occurring again at the hands of the gods, they removed themselves from the world.

One book I skimmed theorized that the reason powerful magicians and sorcerers were no longer commonplace was because the absence of gods and dragons had lessened the magic in the world. Which was interesting, but unhelpful.

I found myself at a loss. I had searched through multiple libraries and travelled across the globe to find the information I sought, but while I now had all the answers, I didn't feel like I was any closer to knowing a way to stop what was happening. I had been a fool. I trusted in the sensibilities of those I'd eaten rather than in what the base part of myself understood from the beginning. I had to kill them, and keep killing them until it was done.

I cursed whatever force had pulled me to the tower, but I decided to at least finish looking through the library to its peak. I stood up and began walking up the stairs, making one last check to see if there were any books that still may contain anything useful. I found nothing of use, plenty of other valuable information on magical theory and technological innovation, but nothing that suited my purposes.

When I reached the top, the group of scholars studying me was panting and wheezing from climbing the stairs. The top floor had no books, only a small reading and studying room with a large portrait hanging against the far wall.

The man in the portrait was young and handsome, wearing a bejeweled outfit in a red color that matched that of the tower. He had long burgundy hair, and his eyes were bright gold. I clenched my fist.

"Who is that?" I asked the scholar nearest to me.

He panted a few more times, wiping sweat from his brow before looking at where I was pointing. "That would be the only surviving picture of Rubrus, the mage that built this place. Our esteemed founder."

I looked back at the picture. It was my former master. The hair was longer, the clothes slightly different, and the eyes were not the red I remembered his were, but it was him.

"I'll be leaving now," I said. "I have the answers I need, and other questions I need to resolve immediately."

"But we have not yet finished our inspection of you!"

"What have you learned so far?"

"Well, only a few things. The magic is very complex, you see. Between the armor and the void within is a wall of runic magic, but rather than in dwarven or elvish as is common, this appears to be in draconic. We've already sent for a translator."

"Even with a translator, it sounds like it'll take quite some time for you to find out anything significant."

"Well, the nature of magic is that it's complicated."

"I'm afraid that while the magic is complicated, I tend to be quite simple. I don't have the time to wait around. I'm leaving. Thank you for your help."

"No! You cannot leave! The insights we could gain from you... They're immeasurable."

"I'm afraid you can't stop me." I leaned over the wizened man, growing myself a few inches to add a bit more intimidation factor.

One of the scholars behind me gestured with his right hand, and four daggers made of pure force slammed into me. I grabbed the man in front of me and threw him hard into the one who threw the daggers. They slammed into a wall and collapsed.

The two remaining scholars made more gestures. One of them sent a wave of fire at me through his hands, and the other cast a spell that lifted several of the chairs in the room into the air, and began throwing them at me with his will.

I let the flames wash over me and rolled under one of the chairs, cutting through another before it could hit me. I moved toward the fire thrower, dodging some bolts he threw until I was standing right in front of him. I stood still long enough for the other scholar to throw a table, which I ducked under, letting it slam into his companion. I moved on the last one quickly and rammed my gauntlet into his stomach before he could make another incantation, knocking the wind from him and sending him to the ground.

"You guys weren't half bad for people who've never been in a real fight. If I have the time, I may come back to let you study me, but please be more polite in the future."

I took some time putting out a dozen small fires to make sure the tower didn't end up aflame and made my way back downstairs. I was glad I'd been training a replacement night chef; it didn't seem like I'd be working there anymore.

40
INTERLUDE: STONE, HRIG, KYREN

Stone returned to the forest, holding up five fingers to indicate how much time was left. Kyren and Hrig nodded, and they made their way back to the rest of the group. Waiting for them were four other adventurers: Saldin the Bold, Krishka the Reaper, Slate the Unconquered, and Phyl. Stone and Krishka approached the main wall and began spinning their grappling hooks, waiting for the signal.

The explosion went off exactly as Stone had timed it, and after the guards at the top of the wall moved to investigate, the team's grappling hooks went up. It wasn't difficult for them to find purchase on the citadel's walls as they were made up of tree roots. Kyren and Hrig were the first up, followed by Saldin and Phyl. Slate and Stone needed to be hauled up in order to keep the team moving quickly.

From the top of the walls, they could hear fights breaking out across the fort as other adventurers entered from multiple directions. The fort itself was lightly defended, with most of the kings' troops engaged in protecting and securing the borders. Hard to approach with an army, but easy with smaller, specialized groups of adventurers.

All the entrances were being stormed at once, and the ranged fighters of the groups were sending crossbow bolts, arrows, rocks, and bolts of energy over the walls. The group took the nearby staircase down, with Hrig in the lead and Saldin close behind.

They encountered the first set of guards at the bottom of the stairs. Three elves dressed in the living wood armor common to their people, wielding long, elegant swords. Hrig and Saldin rushed them before they could call for help. Hrig's axe crashed through the armor of the nearest one, sending him flying into the wall in a shower of splinters. Saldin brought his bastard sword down on the head of the second, killing him instantly. The third turned to flee, but a dagger flew into the base of his neck, severing his spine before he could take two steps. Krishka twisted her wrist, and the dagger flew back into her hand before she sheathed it.

The team moved the bodies out of the hallway, Stone taking the time to loot them, and then began moving through the fort. The interior of the fort was opulent, but in a distinctly elvish way. There weren't any grand portraits or works in silver and gold, but tremendous and beautiful sculptures of wood, tapestries woven from leaves and moss, and wooden walls in which were carved intricate histories of the fort and those that had lived there. The team didn't have a solid idea of the layout, so they worked their way from the outside in, sweeping room to room in search of their targets, the Twin Kings.

All throughout their search, they heard their compatriots fighting along the outer walls. They'd occasionally stop more elf warriors from heading that way, but they did their best to avoid combat where they could. The plan generally relied on two things: the distraction provided by the teams at the main entrances, and the group on the inside finding the Twin Kings isolated and taking them out.

The team reached a hallway with a series of rooms. They began systematically searching them with Hrig taking point. The first two rooms were food storage, but the third was a kitchen. Hrig entered the room to the surprised gasps of three servants. Two of them went to run, but were cut off by Phyl, and the third lunged at Hrig with a kitchen knife. She grabbed him by the wrist before he could strike and quickly broke his arm.

Phyl corralled them, and he and Stone began tying them up.

Kyren approached the one with the broken arm and placed her hands onto it. They glowed gold briefly, and his arm began to mend. "Your kings, where are they? Byren and Percy, as well."

The man whose arm she was healing spat at her.

Kyren stood, wiped her face with her sleeve, and looked over to Hrig. "Undo the healing I just did please."

Hrig smiled and grabbed the man by the arm. He just looked up at her defiantly.

"Wait!" said another of the kitchen staff, an older man. "Trayzen and Faden are in the central courtyard, and Percy and Byren are confined to their quarters. You can reach the courtyard if you continue down the hallway, and the guest rooms are on the other side of the fort, opposite of where we are now."

"Traitor," hissed the one with the formerly broken arm.

"Quiet, son. You may be willing to be killed for them, but I'm not willing to watch it happen."

"How long have Percy and Byren been confined to quarters?" asked Stone.

"Since they arrived," responded the third worker, a middle-aged woman.

"Have they been in contact with the kings?" asked Kyren.

"No, they were sent directly there and haven't had visitors or been let out since. We're not even supposed to talk to them when we deliver meals."

"I guess that they'd overestimated how grateful the kings would be," said Hrig.

"That means they won't have any useful information," said Kyren, smiling.

They finished binding and gagging them and then started toward the courtyard per their direction. The interesting thing about elvish construction was that it was actually quite difficult to tell where the inside of a structure began and ended. With walls made of tree and covered in foliage, it was hard to recognize when you'd made it outside.

The team was several steps into the courtyard before Slate looked up and pointed out the stars. The group tensed up, and everyone strained their senses looking for the kings. Unfortunately, the kings found them first.

An arrow slammed into Saldin's back from above, knocking him to the ground. The group started to turn toward the direction it had come from, but before they could turn, a man landed in their midst and lashed out with two thin blades, slashing Slate across the face and Kyren across the arm.

The king in front of them was dressed in ironwood armor painted gold and etched with images of fallen leaves. He wore a helmet in the shape of a hawk's head, and the thin blades he wielded were ringing from the impacts they made, making the same sound the elyrium bars in the Wyrwind basement had. The bowman was nowhere to be found.

The group scattered, readying their weapons. Saldin managed to push himself up and behind a small bench just before a second arrow buried itself into the ground behind him.

The attackers didn't give anyone time to regroup. Arrows began to rain down on everyone, forcing the more lightly armored combatants to take cover, and the dual wielder began striking at the front-liners, keeping them unbalanced.

Rather than take cover from the arrows, Hrig moved to position herself between the swordsman and the arrows and attacked him with her axe. The man danced delicately around the strike and followed up with two strikes of his own, but Hrig managed to deflect those easily, following up with a kick that the swordsman only barely managed to dodge around.

Kyren stepped out from her cover behind a tree and released a spell with a flourish of her hand. As she did so, an arrow broke in front of her as if stopped by an invisible force. "I've shielded you all from arrows!"

The rest of the party emerged from the trees and started throwing attacks at the golden armored swordsman. Saldin's bastard sword swung, but hit nothing but air as the figure danced backward, slashing across Phyl's leg as he moved. Krishka's daggers were batted aside or ignored as the figure moved between everyone, leaving cuts with every flick of his wrist.

The arrows had ceased, and a figure in black armor landed behind Saldin and kicked at the arrow in his back, sending the point through his gut. Saldin screamed, and the figure danced back, wielding a hammer and a curved sword, a quiver half full at his back. His armor was the shadow of his twins, looking like rotting wood with a raven helmet.

Stone leapt forward, his boots letting him launch himself quickly at the black-armored figure, and he managed to land a blow with his sledgehammer right on the figure's helmet. He went for a follow-up, but the figure danced away, moving as fluidly as his golden ally had.

"Are the Twin Kings known to be expert fighters?" asked Phyl as he attempted to swing his massive two-handed club at the golden fighter, and missing.

"I'd thought they were just spoiled nobles," replied Slate, wiping blood from his face before raising his shield to block two swift cuts.

The black-armored figure's helmet had cracked from Stone's blow, and from that crack, Kyren saw a single golden eye peeking through. "They're sons of Aurum!"

She sent a flurry of what looked like birds made of golden light that exploded across the black-armored twin and threw him away.

"Hrig, Kyren, we'll focus on goldie. The rest of you on the other one!" yelled Stone, and the group neatly divided and started their assaults on their respective targets.

Hrig slashed, Stone swung, but the golden twin dodged neatly around them.

"You really think it'll only take you three to stop me? I'm hurt," he said in a faux pouting voice.

"You don't know hurt yet, but you will," said Hrig, starting a flurry of blows.

He dodged two strikes and deflected the others, his thin swords managing to withstand the full weight of Hrig's blows despite their thinness.

Stone joined in with her, aiming his hammer at his legs as Hrig aimed most of her strikes at his head. They weren't able to break his defense, but he wasn't able to launch a counterattack either.

"Did Caedus send you?" he asked, deflecting a particularly heavy blow from Hrig's axe before jumping just out of the reach of Stone's hammer.

"The king sends his regards," lied Stone, using the conversation to back away and take a breath.

His eyes went blank for a moment. "Liar."

Stone shrugged. "Worth a shot."

Kyren released the spell she'd been building, and golden chains wrapped themselves around their foe and brought him to his knees.

Hrig brought her axe down at his shoulder, but instead of a rain of blood, there were only sparks.

He laughed. "Feels familiar, doesn't it?" he asked, his voice full of mirth.

Hrig smiled. "It does."

She raised her axe back up, and symbols began to light up against her skin. One on the back of her neck, one on her right arm, one on her left, and one on her lower back. She brought her axe down in an impossibly fast strike in the same spot as before. There were still sparks, but also plenty of blood this time as well as the axe embedded itself halfway through his chest.

"Trayzen!" yelled the black-armored warrior.

He moved with incredible speed, slashing across Slate's neck, leaving him clutching his throat. Krishka tried to block him, but he smashed his hammer across her face, sending her to the ground. He leapt up at Hrig, but before he could bring his weapons down on her, she sidestepped him with incredible speed, her runes still glowing.

He looked surprised when he hit nothing but air, and he was even more surprised when Phyl slammed his massive club straight down on his head, knocking him prone. Faden rolled and threw himself back up onto his feet.

Hrig's runes faded, and for a moment, she wavered on her feet. Kyren was already working to heal Krishka, leaving only Stone and Phyl in the proper shape to keep fighting.

Faden roared, and the split in his helmet widened and broke as his elf-like features twisted into a dragon-like shape, the rest of his body growing larger.

"I'll kill you for what you've done!" he said before opening his mouth in Stone and Phyl's direction.

Heat started to build, and Phyl launched himself at Stone, pushing him out of the way just in time for him to avoid being barbecued by Faden's fiery breath. Phyl himself was not so lucky and lay clutching his side in pain.

Faden turned toward Stone, his mouth opening for another blast, heat building around his mouth. Just before he released his breath, Stone grabbed one of the black orbs from his chest and threw it, landing it straight in Faden's mouth as he released his breath. His head exploded, sending viscera all throughout the courtyard.

Hrig moved to Stone's side, using the grass of the courtyard to clean off her axe. "What was that you threw?"

Stone smiled. "It's called a bomb."

After Kyren had healed the injured, all except for Slate were in good enough shape to get moving. Hrig carried Slate on her back, and they worked their way through to where they'd been told Byren and Percy were being held. At this point, it was probable that a message had gotten out to the former king's soldiers in the field, and the adventurers would all need to scatter and head back for the border. Stone broke off from the group with Krishka to look for any documentation regarding the kings' activities.

It only took a little bit of searching before the rest of the group found Percy and Byren locked in a suite. They were sitting at a table eating dinner. They looked tired, but had clearly been kept in luxury.

"Sister?" asked Byren as Kyren entered the room.

She nodded at him. "Byren, Percy, you're looking distinctly unwell."

Percy backed away. "What are you here for? Are you taking us back to Caedun? I refuse to be hauled back in chains."

"I don't think that will be an issue," said Kyren, a small smile on her face.

"Of course not. Obviously, Kyren intends for us to be a source of information. We'll cooperate in any way we can," said Byren.

"I'm afraid that the only thing we need from you two is your heads," said Hrig, placing Slate down gently and hefting her axe.

Byren smirked and turned his attention to Kyren. "Come now? Would your goddess really approve of that?"

Kyren's small smile stayed on her face. "I'm certain that Sidi and I agree," she said, a halo of light appearing around her. "Leaving you two alive wouldn't be very wise."

41
FIFTH MEAL

My trip back to Caedun was much less eventful than my trip to the Eastlands had been. I made no pauses, let nothing distract me, and didn't bother trying to make anyone I encountered feel more comfortable by acting human. I ignored a field of sunken ships, a strange ruin covered in arcane runes, and a skeleton working a field of wheat. Those mysteries would normally intrigue me, but there was only one mystery I could focus on, the mystery of me.

I arrived much further south than Buryn, my destination being Entden, the place where my adventure had begun. I relied on Lythia Irontooth's navigation skills and Myphos the merman's understanding of underwater typography to arrive just south of Cirros. I felt a distinct urge to make a short jaunt into the center of the city and make my way to Talen, but my drive for answers overrode that urge, and I began heading southwest.

It took me the better part of a day and a half to arrive at the wooden walls of the town. It was night, and rather than wake a gate guard, I climbed up a nearby tree and leapt over the walls, rolling as I did. The streets were mercifully empty, and I made my way to the headman's office, rapped my fist against the door twice and waited.

I heard some clunking followed by a bit of cursing and a deep breath at the door before Jusuf opened it. The smile he'd managed to summon up before opening the door dropped immediately when he saw me, but he recovered quickly.

"Ser, it's good to see you again." His voice trembled a bit as he spoke, which confirmed that news of me had reached all the way down to Entden.

"The head. Where did you bury it?"

"Pardon, ser?"

"The head we gave you to show we'd completed the job you'd requested."

"I, uh, that is we, buried it just outside the walls. Marked it with a stake."

"Where specifically?"

"Out the front gate and a little north. It's there just before the forest."

"Thank you."

I walked away and heard his door slam closed, some furniture dragged to blockade it. I had considered tying him up or doing something to silence him, but I didn't want to hurt the poor man, and I also didn't feel I had the time. I was too focused on finding answers.

I exited by quickly climbing up the lead up to the walls and leaping down to the ground below. I moved north along the walls and found a tree with a single stake driven into the ground in front of it.

It took a bit of digging, but eventually, I saw the darkened yellow coloring of a skull. I lifted it up and brushed some of the dirt off of it. It had been picked clean, and I was surprised to find that it was covered in draconic runes, almost like someone had carved it with a small knife. I tied the skull to my waist as I wasn't ready to consume it just yet.

I made my way into the forest, toward my old home. When I reached it, I saw a few goblins cooking outside of it, roasting what looked to be a kobold over a spit. I didn't bother stealthing—I simply drew my multi-blade and went to work. It wasn't artful; I found no real challenge from them as I carved my way through the dungeon. It was simply butchering.

When I reached my former master's hall, I found a chieftain dressed in Rubrus's red garments. They'd been torn and belted to fit him better, but the effect was comical. He threw a large rock at me and cursed at me in undercommon. I ignored his attacks and lifted him by his robe.

"Where body clothes on?" I asked in barely passable undercommon.

The goblin bit my hand, so I shook him and asked again. He cursed a little, causing small globs of spittle to land against my faceplate, but this time, he pointed to what I assumed was supposed to be his throne. It was made up of bones, mostly human, but a few goblin and one kobold skull. I snapped the chief's neck and went to gather the human ones. Almost all of them were covered in the same draconic runes I'd found on the skull; those that weren't, I put to the side.

With the amount of time that had passed and the decay that had occurred, I wasn't expecting to get all the information I was looking for, which was why I'd done my best to gather as much of Rubrus together as possible. I was glad I'd been able to insulate myself from the essences I'd eaten. The idea of becoming like him after what I was about to do made me distinctly upset. I gathered all of him in front of me, opened myself, and ate him.

———

I was shivering. The room was cold, and I'd only been given a scrap of a blanket to sleep in. Calling it a "room" was also not exactly accurate. It was more of a barn corner. I whispered a few words and managed to summon a small, soft flame. It didn't give off enough heat to provide significant comfort, but it was better than nothing, and since I wasn't sleeping anyway, it made sense to get a bit of practice in.

I moved the flame left to right, then up and down. I concentrated on growing it larger, then shrinking it down to the size of a cinder. I summoned a second one, then a third, and made them all rotate slowly. I heard a bang against the barn door, and snuffed them out.

"No practice without my supervision! You could burn the place down."

I sighed. "Sorry, master. I was just cold."

"A disciplined mind can ignore such things. Get some sleep. You'll be cutting firewood early tomorrow."

"Yes, master."

Trying once again to get as much of myself as possible under the tattered blanket, I heard him walk away, back into his warm house full up on the fresh firewood I'd provided, with the recently cleaned chamber pots, and freshly plucked chicken. Damn him. Damn magic. Damn this cold.

This was the way of things, though. If a young man wanted to learn magic, there were two choices. One was to join the church and hope a god deigned to provide you with what you wanted, or you served under a master and learned. I'd heard that some masters were kind, let their apprentices live in the house with them, and worried about their wellbeing. Most masters, though, were like mine: cruel, vain men who saw an apprentice as nothing but a servant. Who dangled power just out of reach, feeding them crumbs of knowledge to keep them under their thumbs.

I was tired of it, but I couldn't stop. Magic was everything I'd ever wanted. I wanted to be able to throw fire, lift objects with my mind, and bend the ground itself to my will. At the rate things were going, though, I'd work myself to death or freeze before I reached that level.

What if you didn't have to?

That would be nice, but it's a useless thought.

Not a thought, more of a question.

I started, sat up, and looked around, but there was no one nearby.

You won't see anyone. I'm speaking directly through your soul.

Master?

Not the one you're thinking of. I doubt he has the kind of power to do this.

Then who?

I am Aurum, God of Dragons.

But, aren't you dead?

Only physically. I left a bit of myself here in the world, scattered among my descendants. That's how I'm speaking with you now.

Does that mean...?

Yes, congratulations. It's really quite the honor to be among my bloodline.

Uh, thank you.

Back to my original question. What if you didn't have to suffer? What if I gave you a way to gain what you desired instantly, perhaps even tonight?

I'd take it.

Granted.

I felt my entire body shift. There was no pain, but I could feel parts of myself rearrange and change. Suddenly, I was no longer cold. I also no longer felt tired or sore from all the work I'd done. I also had something else. A spell of sorts, though perhaps it was something more like an ability.

I stood up and made my way out of the barn. The snow seemed to melt under my feet before my skin could touch it. I walked around to my master's house. I could feel the warmth coming from it. I had a bitter memory of sneaking to the door so I could sleep somewhere where the warmth was leaking out, and my master waking me with a savage beating. I opened the door. My master was so focused on his meal and ale that he didn't initially see me come in, but he shivered when the cold entered and turned around.

"What are you doing in here, boy!?" He grabbed his staff and stood brandishing it at me. "I've told you that you are not allowed in here!" He approached and swung it at my head, hard.

I caught the staff with one hand and slammed my fist into his ribs with the other.

He backed away and started muttering a spell. I could feel power building within him, but I backhanded him before it could reach its apex, cancelling the spell. I lifted him by the collar and placed an open palm against his face.

His eyes widened when they met mine. "Your eyes!"

I smiled and used my new power. I felt his soul and mind rip from his body and into my own. I discarded all of him that was useless to me and kept all of his knowledge of magic, integrating it into myself. When I'd finished, I was holding just a husk that I let fall to the ground. I gestured at the door, and it closed for me.

The next day, I left with a pack full of food, a nice red tunic my former master no longer needed, and a map. I exited the house, and once I'd made it a few hundred feet, I turned around and threw a large ball of fire at it. The explosion was satisfying, and I took a few moments to enjoy watching the barn I'd used to sleep in slowly burn to a crisp. I could faintly feel Aurum's approval in the core of myself as I turned around and started to head for the nearest road.

I considered heading for the city and finding some use for my new spells, but I didn't think I was ready. I'd heard of another hedge wizard relatively close by from my former master, and I was still so very hungry to learn.

I felt my awareness return slowly. I was still standing in the dungeon, a dead goblin chief nearby. That memory had been as intense as when I'd eaten full meals in the past despite only eating what I could find of his bones.

I tried to focus on the essence and pull out more memories or thoughts, but found I couldn't. That was odd—if I'd been able to extract such a strong memory, why couldn't I feel any more of them? I focused again, trying harder, but still nothing. I had travelled back across the world, and it had gained me only the smallest sliver of useless information.

I wanted to scream in frustration, but I couldn't. I tried to move and realized my limbs weren't responding either. Then my arms moved without my direction, and my hands brought themselves up to my faceplate. I couldn't stop them, or even wiggle a finger.

"Oh, now this is interesting," said Rubrus, his voice coming from my helmet as if it were my own.

42
HARVEST

My fingers flexed again, and my body moved around the room. There was some awkwardness at first, but soon, it was moving as smoothly as if I myself were in control. It then moved to a wall, clutched its fist, and slammed it into the wall, causing a large crack to form where he'd hit it.

"I can work with this. Now let's see." My finger snapped, but nothing happened. My arms began moving while Rubrus whispered in draconic, but still there was nothing. Finally, he clapped his hands together and separated them, and an axe I had stored popped into his hand. He flicked his hand up, and it disappeared. Then he traced some arcane runes into the air, and my body took on a shimmering quality.

"Huh, so I can't perform external magics, but those that affect me or summon from your void can be utilized. I'll miss my fireballs, but this is certainly better than being dead." He looked around. "You really let the place go, didn't you? Or, wait a moment."

I felt him probe within, but I resisted.

"Interesting. I can't view your thoughts and memories

directly. You must have developed some control. I guess I'll have to let you speak."

I felt the probing stop and tested speaking. "Please go back to being dead."

Rubrus laughed. "I don't think I will." He started walking through the dungeon, checking the state of traps and kicking corpses out of the way as he walked.

"How are you doing this? How'd you take control?"

"Well, I had a bit of a trap etched into my body and soul. It wasn't actually meant for you, but happy accidents."

"Who was it meant for?"

"Oh, an ancestor of mine. I didn't really feel like being a puppet."

"You mean Aurum?"

He stopped in his tracks. "How do you know that name?"

I would've smiled then if I could. I had leverage. "I'll tell you if you answer a few questions of mine."

"Hmmm, you seem to have evolved quite a bit. My own genius is coming back to bite me. Classic wizard problem; you see it all the time."

I felt the probing sensation again, but this time, it wasn't focused on my mind, but instead my body and void.

"Wow, you may have advanced a lot socially, but I'm distinctly unimpressed with what you've discovered about yourself."

I felt something inside me click, and I felt a portion of the void within me reveal itself. It was filled with steel bars, fine food and drink, clothing, jewelry, even furniture.

Rubrus snapped, and a goblet of wine disappeared from my void and manifested in his hands. "Hmm, your taste is slightly different from mine. This is a bit more bitter than I recall."

"What did you do?"

"This is the part of you I was using to store my things. I had it behind an extra layer of protection. Did you think the things I summoned came from nothing?"

"I did."

"That is possible, but exhausting. Using you was much simpler."

"Is that what I'm meant to be? Storage?"

"How about this. I'll provide you with an answer, then you provide me with one. Deal?"

I mulled it over. It wasn't like I had much choice. "Deal."

"You are mainly meant as storage, yes. Don't worry, though, I never meant for you to strictly exist as a walking closet. You can store anything. Objects, memories, enchantments, souls. Some things are harder for you to store than others and you more eat than store them, but it amounts to the same thing in your case. You're a unique creation. You're also meant to protect what you store."

"Why was I created?"

"Tut tut, it's my turn, remember? How do you know of Aurum?"

"I've read about him."

"I sense that's only a partial truth. What book would tell you enough to recognize that Aurum is my ancestor? Please, the whole truth, and I'll allow another question."

As we spoke, I could feel Rubrus taking inventory even as he began removing corpses and trash from the dungeon.

"I have fought several children of Aurum. Killed two." I could feel the smile Rubrus couldn't make when I mentioned I'd killed them.

"Glad to know my creation can handle his. It feels nice to be able to compete with a god. Still, things are on the move, how unfortunate. I'll have to make a real effort to secure this place." He gestured to his chest, and I felt the few scrapes on my armor from the goblins' seal themselves, though this time, I could see that the metal my repairs used was coming from the steel bars that were stored within me. That was interesting.

"Why did you create me?"

"To use as storage. What a waste of a question."

"It wouldn't be wasted if you answered it truly and fully as I did yours."

"Fine, I have one more question I want to ask, so I'll clarify. I created you to store part of myself, to shield me from my father's influence."

"Is that why your eyes were no longer gold? And why'd you use me to slay those adventurers?"

"I'll give you those for free. Yes, it was, and no tool should serve only one purpose. I intended to be here for a long time. Using you for entertainment was simply a good way to pass the time. Now for my final question. What have you been doing since I've been dead?"

"Adventuring."

"Really? Adventuring?" I could feel his contempt. "You could've become incredibly powerful with the abilities I imbued you with, and you've used it adventuring?"

"Absolutely."

"I find that incredibly disappointing. That's enough from you. I have work to do."

I felt my ability to speak shut off. I watched him work for a few moments. He wrapped up cleaning out the corpses and was starting repair work on the traps. I could tell he was annoyed at having to do things manually, which I took marginal comfort in, but my overall feeling was one of frustration. The only thing I could think to do was attempt to probe him in the same way he'd probed me.

I reached out, finding walls of will holding me back, but I kept at it. I tried to be subtle, to look for any small break I could find. Eventually, I found one.

The lightning bolt bounced off my shield and into the wall behind me. I stifled a yawn, lifted my hand, and sealed the opposing magus' body in rock. He screamed and struggled, but it was a useless gesture. I approached him and placed my hand on his face. He was a paltry meal, and as I removed my hand from the husk that remained of him, I was disappointed to find nothing new. I sighed, wiped my hand clean on my robe, and started descending down the wizard's tower.

Well done.

Thank you.

Aurum always approved when I took something I wanted, but this time, I felt unsatisfied. I hadn't had a good meal in a hundred years. I'd eaten my way through all of the great wizards in Caedun, Sylfen, the Eastlands, and even the northern tribes—what a cold, miserable decade that had been.

I stepped over a few collapsed columns and shattered golems. The gains had been steadily declining over the years. The wizards seemed to be weaker than those I'd begun with, and there were also fewer to eat. It had taken me the better part of five years to find this one, and it had been worthless.

I was the problem. I'd figured it out after the last two I'd eaten in Sylfen. I'd eaten too many, and now, there were none left to teach new students who would then become wizards capable of teaching. I'd glutted myself, and now my favorite meal was extinct.

I leaned against a tree that had been bisected by a wind-cutting spell I'd thrown. I needed a new plan. Something more sustainable than what I'd done so far. I considered trying to further things myself, but immediately found that idea incredibly off-putting. I was a grand wizard, and the descendant of a god. I was more comfortable with taking than creating myself.

I found myself back outside of Rubrus's memories. I looked to see what he'd been up to. I couldn't tell how much time had passed, but the dungeon seemed to be repaired, and a few goblins tied together at the waist were scrubbing the floors clean. Rubrus was carving runes into a nearby wall. Draconic for nil and friction. I felt him send a fraction of his will toward the rune, and the nearest goblin slipped and fell, bringing his fellow prisoners down with him.

"Seems like I found another avenue for magic. More prep than I'd prefer, though."

He didn't seem to have noticed I'd been gone. I noticed he'd made several changes to my form, ones I hadn't realized would be possible. He'd shaped the top of my helmet into a crown, added claws to my gauntlets, and teeth to my faceplate. I didn't much care for the changes, though I had to admit they were intimidating, and the clawed gauntlets would certainly have their uses.

I watched him for a little longer before deciding to look for another break. This time, it proved easier. There actually seemed to be a number of hairline cracks all throughout the wall he was using to protect his essence. I couldn't tell if they were new, or if I had simply gotten better at finding them. I went to the nearest one and slipped my awareness through.

This year's crop was looking promising, I thought as I walked through the university's grounds toward my tower. There were several students with innate gifts and a few hard workers I was confident would turn themselves into something worth consuming.

I nodded and smiled at the students as I passed, doing my best to be genial. It was easier for me if they liked me rather than feared me. I'd found that they tended to work better this way, and they were more willing to share their progress with me, as well.

My idea had been brilliant. I'd eaten all of the mages of value, so now it fell onto me to cultivate a crop of my own. I built a tower in a desert, played the role of the powerful, wise wizard, and waited for those with the drive to get to me to begin appearing. I'd had to protect them from the occasional naga or lizardman incursion, but that hadn't been too difficult, especially since I'd trained the first few sand shapers.

The city that had grown around me was a nice bonus. I could find good food, drink, or company with relative ease, and I liked the eclectic nature of the people that had gathered. Exiles and refugees tended to be a particularly interesting group.

I made my way into the tower and sealed the doors. I had a meeting with a new scholar who I was certain was dying to meet me. After a quick climb up the stairs, I entered the room to find a young woman seated in a chair in front of my desk. I made my way gradually around, to my desk, trying to keep a dignified bearing despite the excitement I felt.

"Scholar Luda, correct?"

"Yes, ser," she said through her orcish teeth.

"First of all, I wanted to congratulate you on becoming a scholar."

"Thank you." She gave a wide smile, which I returned.

"I'd also heard something very interesting about you. A special magical ability of yours?"

"It's not too special. Technically, it's come about in the Deadeye clan many times." Her voice turned bitter at the mention of Deadeye.

"Describe it to me."

"Well, if I focus, I can determine someone's intentions toward me."

I widened my smile, stood up from my desk, and sat on the edge of it closer to her.

"Try it on me."

She smiled and obliged. I felt a peculiar energy flow through her. Her eyes widened.

Before she could move, I grabbed her head on both sides and consumed her. Aside from the new ability, I also tasted a few subtle variations to shielding spells, a welcome garnish. I activated my new ability.

Well done.

At Aurum's words, the ability activated. I collapsed to my knees. The intentions I felt from him were the same as those Luda had felt from me.

43
ORIGIN

I came out from the memory to find my gauntlets embedded in a man's chest, the life leaving his eyes.

Rubrus threw him, and the body crumpled against the wall. Aside from the man he'd just killed, there were a half dozen others dead around the room and three still standing. The remaining three looked terrified: one held a bastard sword, the other two daggers, and the third was notching an arrow with a narrow head, clearly meant to pierce armor.

Rubrus moved before they could regain the courage to fight. He walked quickly to the one with the bastard sword, deflecting a blow with a glimmering shield and grabbing him by the throat. He snapped it in a mirror image of when I watched Aurum slay that man on the boat.

The man with the two daggers lunged and slammed his daggers into my neck.

Rubrus reached back with inhuman flexibility and grabbed him before throwing him over his back, sending him into the wall. There was a crash as he impacted, and he ceased moving.

The archer had turned around and was running, but Rubrus

placed my gauntlet on the ground, and glowing runes lit the path she'd taken. She lost her balance and crashed into the wall.

Rubrus barked some orders in undercommon, and several goblins in mismatched armor came in and hacked the archer to pieces. After that, they started to clean the room. They seemed much more compliant than the last time I'd seen them.

I could feel his attention turn to me as he went to sit on a throne in the middle of the room. "You're back! Where have you been? Searching through old memories, I presume? Trying to distract yourself from your fate?"

I felt him unlock my ability to speak at the end of the question. It seemed he wasn't aware it was his memories I'd been searching through.

"What happened?" I asked, a knot in my nonexistent stomach.

"Ah, just some thugs. They say they were sent by a man named Talen to look for you. They weren't much of a threat to me, though I assume they wouldn't have been difficult for you to deal with either. My assumption is that they weren't actually meant to engage you, but oh well."

I felt a measure of relief. I was worried that he'd just slaughtered a group of adventurers just trying to keep the town safe, but Talen's thugs were another story. They did create their own problems, though. If Talen and his men had found me, it meant that my companions may, as well, and I had no idea what Rubrus would do to them.

I turned my attention again to Rubrus's essence. The cracks were wider this time. I wasn't sure if what I was doing was weakening his defenses or if perhaps because the spell he'd weaved to keep from being eaten wasn't meant for me and was ill-suited for it, but it meant he was weakening. It meant I may be able to regain control.

"You're hiding something from me, aren't you?"

I paused. "Of course I am." An outright lie seemed pointless.

I felt his essence probe around yet was surprised to find it wasn't my own essence he was probing, but my void.

"There are things here I'm not reaching. Trying to protect something?"

I felt him push, and as he did, I realized I had been hiding things from him. I'd instinctually insulated my most precious items. The cape, my mask, the elyrium bars, the multi-sword, and the shield.

Now that I was aware I had been defending them subconsciously, I started to actively try and keep the items from him. He felt my resistance and began to push harder. I realized quickly that I wouldn't be able to hold off forever, so I decided on a ploy, slowly giving in enough for him to see the multi-sword and energy-eating shield and then dropping all active resistance, as if that was all I'd hidden.

"Magical items. That makes sense. Let's see." He extracted the items and held them for a moment, then I felt something strange. A kind of movement from the items into me. By the end of it, I had a sense that the items no longer held their enchantments, but I did.

"Useful items, though it's a shame that the sword's enchantment is restricted to swords specifically." He held up his hand, and a perfect copy of the multi-sword appeared as if summoned from the void, but that was impossible, as I could see it on the ground.

"Let this be a lesson. There's no sense fighting me."

I felt my voice lock once again and looked at the increasing cracks within Rubrus's void. Even if it was useless, fighting was its own reward. I slipped into the nearest crack and lost myself to another memory.

It had been hard to abandon my university project, but I hadn't had much of a choice. The insight I'd gained from Luda's ability meant that I was on borrowed time, and this was the only way I could think to survive. Aurum was planning on eating me, or at least my soul, to fuel his return. Every bit of assistance I received from him was paid for by an offering of myself. His urge to live again at my expense was so powerful that Luda's ability had been burnt up from sensing it.

I doubted my soul alone would be enough for him, but it was only a matter of time before he awakened more of his children, if he hadn't already. He was cultivating a power source, raising us up to make us a better meal. He was doing exactly what I had been doing at the university, just on a much more epic scale.

I had continued hearing his whispers since I'd realized the truth, but I'd been able to push them away for now. The last things I'd heard from him had been assurances he was proud of me. He'd apparently needed to do much less work to convince me to follow my instincts for power than he'd expected. The temporary protections I'd put in place were strong, and should have allowed me to maintain control if he attempted to take it directly, but I had a more permanent solution in mind. Creating a space to work hadn't been too difficult. I'd simply taken a cave that already existed and molded it into something more suitable. I'd lined the walls in cold iron to dampen my connection to Aurum enough to keep what I was doing hidden. I had taken all the materials I'd needed before leaving the university.

I etched the runes into the floor carefully, creating four circles of draconic, one for each item I'd involved in the ritual. There was a bag of holding, a suit of armor of absorption in which I'd inscribed thousands of runes, and me. The last circle was a piece of void, something a student had traded to be a scholar. It was a small black marble that was ice-cold to the touch, a piece of the ether in which the gods resided when they weren't on this plane. I could feel it recoil when I touched it; it seemed not to enjoy godly energy, as if nothing was meant to exist within its emptiness, but the gods forced it to accept their presence anyway. The void was the most important piece—without it, I wouldn't be able to store the godly energies within me.

I started the ritual, whispering in draconic. The circles on the floor lit blood red, and energies from me, the bag of holding, and the piece of void swirled into the suit of armor on the floor. I could feel myself being drained, watching as the golden light from my body mixed with the black light of the void.

When the ritual ended, I collapsed. I had taken precautions to reduce the weakness I'd experience as much as possible. I'd burnt runes into my bones and empowered myself with dozens of different spells, but it couldn't compare to the power I felt I'd lost. I felt hollow. Emptier even than I'd been before Aurum had spoken to me. I estimated I was likely at half a soul from where I'd begun.

The suit of armor stirred. I watched as it sat up and stood. Its movements were stiff and unnatural. I forced myself to focus on its face and saw nothing but void. The glamour that was meant to keep people from looking too closely at it seemed to be working well.

I stood and walked over to it. It didn't move or respond as I did, so I placed my hand on its chestplate and extended my energy toward it. I could sense the items I'd had in the bag of holding still there. I told it to walk, and it did so. Jump, and it followed that direction, as well.

I had him stop and dragged myself up to my chair. It was likely it would take quite some time before my energy had restored itself, and even once it did, there was the chance that

Aurum could raise himself. I'd be here a long time. I needed to figure out some way to stay entertained...

I returned from his memories to find myself sitting on the throne at the end of the dungeon. Torches were lit, and the space was exactly as I'd remembered it, though I'd never looked at it from this angle.

"Welcome back once again. You're just in time for the show to start."

I felt him unlock my ability to speak.

"Show?"

"A few brave adventurers are making their way through the dungeon. They're doing quite well so far, too."

That wasn't good. The cracks on Rubrus's essence had widened to canyons, but I still wasn't sure I'd be able to take over, and I was concerned that he might be able to reinforce himself if I didn't succeed the first time. Aside from that, I was still reeling from witnessing my own creation, and it had left me with one question that even up to now I had no answer to.

"Why did I kill you?" I asked. I could feel that the question surprised him, but I also felt that surprise quickly turn to anger.

"Why indeed?" He tapped my now clawed gauntlets on the arm of his chair. He let out an unnecessary sigh. "I have a theory."

I held my tongue. I wanted him to elaborate, but I was concerned he wouldn't if he knew how badly I wanted to know. I also knew that he enjoyed hearing himself talk.

"When I consumed people's essence, it was while I already had a soul of my own. Something that let me control and guide what I was seeing. For you, though, eating an essence was a shock to your system. It fought to survive and adapted. Each essence was another shock, and eventually, you broke. I believe that the souls all became hopelessly entwined in such a way that they became like a soul for you yourself. A monstrous twisted thing. Likely, you ate enough misguided individuals with a penchant for heroism that you were possessed to end me. Had I been paying proper attention, though, it never would've happened. Classic wizard hubris, not even I am immune to it."

I considered what he said. It seemed right, but he didn't have the whole picture. The essences I'd absorbed had given me something similar to a soul, and it had certainly been a monstrous mix at first, but that had changed. I had integrated them, learned who they belonged to, fulfilled their dreams and wishes, and strived to live a life they themselves would've wanted. I'd taken their lives from them, but they'd given me something precious. From what I'd taken, I had created something new. I had built myself. I was as much my own creation as Rubrus's, and I found strength in that thought.

"Ah, the guests are arriving."

I felt my ability to speak locked once again. Three adventurers had entered. A male dwarf and two women. One was massive, wielding an enormous axe already stained with goblin blood. The other wore white robes, her dark hair framed by golden light that surrounded her. The dwarf was in sleek black leather. His beard had been dyed black, but patches of gray were starting to appear, and he had a sledgehammer gripped in both hands.

"Well, now, isn't this familiar?"

44
RESCUE

"A reunion! How wonderful," said Rubrus, rising from his throne. "I've missed you all so much."

Stone stepped forward. "What's going on, lad? Why are you holed back up in here?"

I felt Rubrus curl the pointed teeth he'd used to morph my faceplate into a smile. "Dungeons are where monsters belong. They're the best places to lure in foolish adventurers for a tasty meal."

He emphasized the last word with a rapid opening and closing of his faceplate, making a snapping noise.

"It's not him," said Hrig, gripping her axe more tightly.

"The voice sounds like his master."

I could feel a tinge of annoyance from Rubrus. He clearly wanted them to think he was me. I'd had no doubts that they'd see through it. He had a bit too big of a personality to pretend to be someone else.

Kyren's face hardened. "If his master has somehow gained control of him, he'd want us to stop him."

"Aye."

Hrig didn't answer, but her face contorted in rage, and I saw a glow begin emanating from runes on her skin. She pressed forward, moving more quickly than I'd thought she was capable of. Rubrus barely had time to dodge as her axe sliced his throne in half and glided a foot into the stone below.

Before Rubrus could recover, Kyren sent out three bolts of holy energy in quick succession. He managed to dodge the first two, but the third one slammed into his chest, knocking him back.

The bolt damaged me and Rubrus both, and our essences recoiled from the holy energies as they washed over us.

Rubrus touched the floor, and runes lit up across it. Hrig and Kyren slipped and fell as they were closing the distance, but Stone managed to leap at the last minute and close the gap between them. He brought his sledgehammer down across Rubrus's shoulder, removing his hand from the runes and freeing Kyren and Hrig to move.

Rubrus slashed at Stone with a clawed gauntlet, but he deftly dodged away before slamming at Rubrus again with his hammer.

The hammer bounced off an invisible shield, and Rubrus summoned a multi-sword copy into his hand to slash at Stone. He caught his hammer with only a glancing blow, but the sheer force of it sent Stone reeling away.

Hrig slammed her axe into Rubrus's side, and the shield he'd cast over himself cracked but held firm. He began swinging at her wildly with his sword, but Hrig was too skilled and deftly dodged or deflected each of his blows. Clearly, his focus on eating mages over warriors had a few drawbacks while he was in a body unable to cast spells his usual way. Against an opponent like Hrig, he wouldn't be able to rely on brute strength.

Rather than continue engaging her, he rolled out of the engagement and placed his hand against the wall. Suddenly, draconic runes across the ceiling lit, and small bolts of fire started raining down.

Kyren extended a bubble of force around herself, deflecting the orbs. Hrig dodged and ducked, trying to make her way closer to him, but failed to make any headway, and Stone jumped and dodged as fast as he could, but was clipped by several of the firebolts.

Stone took a small metal orb off of the strap across his chest and lit the wick on a descending firebolt before slinging it across the room. Rubrus caught it deftly with one hand, and looked closer at what he'd thrown for a moment before an explosion sent him flying across the room and slammed him into a pillar. The firebolts ceased as soon as the explosion occurred, and Hrig and Stone quickly closed the distance between them.

Kyren unleashed a burst of energy, and the edges of Hrig's axe and Stone's hammer were lit with holy light.

Rubrus brought his arms up, thickening the armor on them as much as possible as Hrig and Stone started to bring down their weapons again and again. I could feel every blow, and I knew it was just as damaging for him. I saw his essence crack even further.

Suddenly, he activated something, and I could sense the energy from Stone and Hrig drain into me. Their blows began to weaken, and Rubrus slammed forward, knocking them on their backs. He went to leap onto them, gauntlet claws extended, but at that moment, chains of light extended from the wall and wrapped themselves around him. They yanked him back into the wall. He strained against the chains, trying to place his gauntlets against the wall where runes were already beginning to glow in anticipation of him activating them, but the chains gave him nothing.

Hrig approached, the runes on her body lit like miniature suns. Her eyes were filled with tears as she raised her axe.

It was now or never. I slammed my essence into Rubrus's.

The games had been fun. The armor was proving its worth even beyond the expectations I'd had when I'd created him. It didn't quite make up for the loss of power I'd incurred when I stored the power Aurum had given me within him, but it was a fine consolation prize. I was curious how well the traps had done this time. I sensed that three of the original adventurers had survived so far, an impressive majority of them. That would make things oh so satisfying for the finale.

The group entered. I could tell there had been some injuries, but their overall health surprised me. What surprised me the most, though, was how much blood was on the armor. He'd participated far more in the battles up to this point than he had in the past.

"I see you made it to my inner sanctum." I swirled the wine in my cup. "I'm impressed."

I watched them regard me, attempting to size me up. I luxuriated in it for a moment.

They fanned out, readying themselves for a charge. I didn't like that; I had hoped for a bit of banter. It just wasn't as fun when they decided not to play.

"Nothing to say? Not 'stop killing villagers?' Or 'we're here to end your reign of terror?' Come now, I've been terrorizing this area for years. I'm sure you could come up with something!"

I saw some glares, and the dwarf approached me, thinking he was in my blind spot.

"Oi, I've got something," he muttered, doing his best to look intimidating with his hammer. It was adorable.

I smiled, hoping he'd engage in a bit more back and forth, but he disappointed me.

"This!" He charged, raising his hammer to strike.

I sighed but didn't move. The hammer fell, cracking the throne, where I'd been, but I'd long since blinked away from there to stand behind him. I drained the goblet I held in my hand, crushed it using strength enhanced with magic, and threw it aside.

"Fine. We'll skip to the part where I kill you."

The big woman jumped at me with her axe high in the air, but I raised my hand and sent her back with a blast of force from my palm. The dwarf followed, swinging his hammer, but he lost his footing when I had a pillar of earth rise up at his feet and launched him into the air.

After that, the armor made its move. We'd had a simple routine down at that point. I'd dodge his downward blow, the one to my right, and a shield bash, staying just out of his reach each time. I let out a dramatic yawn, winked at him, and tapped his armor, letting him throw himself backward.

I was suddenly engulfed in white light. The pain was excruciating, and I could tell from its signature that it was holy. I'd been particularly susceptible to that type of damage since I'd found myself with half a soul. I turned my attention to the holy woman and started approaching her as she prepared more spells.

I was surprised when the big woman and the dwarf both struck me at the same time. The hammer had bounced off my shield spell, but the woman's axe had left a small cut.

"That's enough!" I yelled and sent a wave of force to knock my attackers backward. I then sealed all three of them into stone coffins, restricting their movements.

The armor rose and charged me with a scream. It was an excellent bit of theater. I almost felt like he was genuinely upset. I raised my hand, and he went still. We were at my favorite part of the performance.

"You cannot defeat me, warrior. I'm too powerful." I pretended to crush him with invisible force, and he complied by crumpling himself slightly. "Do you wish to live?"

"Yes...I do," he said in what I assumed was his newest voice.

"I shall let you live...on one condition," I responded with a wide smile.

"Anything," he said just loudly enough for the adventurers to hear.

I was quivering with anticipation. This part was always so deliciously wonderful. "Kill your companions."

He looked over at his false allies. The big woman and dwarf's faces were twisted up in fury, but the holy woman was incredibly calm.

"Do it," she said.

I unwillingly let my expression shift from one of contempt to surprise.

"He'll kill us all anyway. There's no shame in saving yourself."

This wasn't part of the script!

"She's right. Do what you need to do," said the big woman. "I already owe you my life for earlier."

"As do I, lad. Do what you need to do," said the dwarf.

This was awful. A complete waste of a dramatic performance. I took a moment to consider what horrible way I could afflict them for ruining my entertainment, dropping my shield to prepare a spell I hoped would turn them inside out.

Pain exploded in my side as a sword ripped through the small wound in my stomach up through my spine. My eyes widened in surprise as I turned them to the armor.

This wasn't supposed to happen. I still had so much more to do. I'd done so much to survive.

My vision narrowed, I felt blackness surround me.

I woke to the sound of gentle droplets hitting my armor. I wondered for a moment if it was rain before the eyes staring down at me came into focus. I was in Hrig's lap. I could feel a deep rend in my armor through my shoulder and across my chest.

I heard sobbing and realized Stone was standing on the other side, crying along with her. Kyren put an arm around him. She was the only one managing to hold back tears, though I could tell they were welled up in her eyes.

I sat there for a moment and did a quick inventory on myself. I was damaged, possibly more than I ever had been before, but it was only physical. My core, the essence I'd made my own, was mostly unharmed.

I let myself sit there for a moment, enjoying how warm Hrig's lap was against my helmet before I decided I should seal myself up. I began to close the gash across my chest, sealing in the black ichor leaking from me with a shield spell, and drawing material from the steel bars I had stored within me. As I did so, I started reshaping myself, returning my body to the form I was used to.

There were gasps, and Hrig stood quickly, grabbing her axe. Stone and Kyren similarly took a defensive stance.

I sat up slowly, careful to keep my hands at my side.

"It's me," I said.

"How can we be sure?" asked Kyren.

"I don't think it would be possible to be completely sure," I responded.

Stone chuckled. "That sounds like Sevald. I'd think an evil sorcerer would likely attempt to be a little more convincing."

Hrig dropped her axe and crouched down to hug me, wiping tears from her eyes as she did so.

Kyren laid a hand gently on my shoulder. "Welcome back to Caedun."

45
RETURN

We all sat there for a while longer. I sorted through Rubrus's memories and discarded everything in his personality. There was a part of me that admired his sheer brazenness, but I couldn't risk how that would impact me.

While I sorted everything out and focused on repairing myself, Hrig, Kyren, and Stone explained to me what they'd been up to in my absence. They'd slain three children of Aurum, removed the cause of a war, and generally made nuisances of themselves. I found myself proud to call them my friends.

"Unfortunately, removing the reason for the war has only slowed things down," said Kyren. "The church has been moving to preach against it, and has done everything they can politically to slow things down, but the king's grip on power is strong. If they'd started sooner, they may have been able to do more, but they'd been held back by Iomed and her faction."

Stone nodded. "We've had similar issues using the nobility angle. Duke Ellis and some other brave or blackmailed nobles have been up in arms about the conflict, actively slowing things down wherever they can. Unfortunately, people's blood is already up. Rather than seeing the assassination of the Twin Kings as a reason to cease hostilities, many say that since it was Caedun that solved the problem, we're entitled to their territory. Phyl the Fire-Touched even told me he'd heard some fresh recruits to the military say they want to slay some elves just like we adventurers did."

"Dorsia, Jade, and I have been more focused on Talen. While at first it seemed he was intent on supporting Caedus, what he was really doing was creating a portion of the army that was loyal to him. He was subtle at first, but since things have been slipping, he's been slowly growing more antagonistic toward him. The worst part is that he's managed to build a small army of mercenaries as well on the backs of his illicit operations in Cirros."

"Caedus and Talen are using war to compete for a prize that doesn't even exist. Aurum has promised his children godhood, but the only thing they're doing is feeding him. He's just using them to pave the way for his own return," I said, and followed up by explaining everything I'd learned in my talks with Vash, my time at the university, and what I'd learned from consuming Rubrus. By the end of it, I was feeling fully recovered.

"We need to take the fight to them," said Stone.

"I agree. We can't play at politics or worry about the repercussions at this point. Aurum is pushing this conflict because he knows it will lead to his resurrection, and I feel like he's close to it. Though I don't have any proof."

"I believe you. The gods themselves are pushing us in this direction. I can feel it," said Kyren.

Hrig smiled, and I realized she hadn't let go of my hand since I'd regained control of my body. "Kingslayer. Now there's a title I wouldn't mind having."

After we finished talking, we made our way out of the dungeon. It was clear to me that while the party had had a difficult time their first time through, this time, they'd cleared it masterfully. Dead goblins were everywhere, cleaved in twain, broken into pieces, or scorched by holy fire. There were two dead trolls similarly afflicted and a cave drake twice the size of the last one with its head two yards from its lifeless body. The traps had been expertly dismantled or simply smashed, as well. My friends were much stronger than when I'd first met them. I was excited to show them the tricks I'd managed to pick up myself.

We made a trek a few miles from the dungeon, careful to avoid the main path, and made camp with a small fire. Stone went to cook, but I shooed him away. I wanted to show them what I'd learned in the kitchen at Usulaum and brought out the spices I'd stored in myself for easy access when cooking and took the meat Stone had started to prepare.

By the time I was done, I'd managed a solid approximation of a traditional orcish soup that had been given a spicy twist in Usulaum. Stone and Hrig were red in the face as they ate, but didn't seem able to keep themselves from eating spoonful after spoonful, and Kyren managed to finish three bowls herself. Elves tended to have a strong preference for spicy food in my experience, but Kyren's enjoyment was on another level.

At the end of the night, everyone settled in to sleep, and I took the first watch. In spite of everything that had gone wrong, and how much we had left to do, I felt more comfortable at that moment, watching over my companions, than I'd felt in a long time.

After a few hours, I felt a stir and saw Hrig approaching. She didn't bother hiding her presence and sat next to me on the fallen log I'd been using as a chair. We sat together in silence for a while before she spoke.

"What are you planning to do?"

"Keep watch?"

She chuckled. "After that. After Talen, and Caedus, and Aurum. What are you going to do?"

I took a few moments to think about it. I probably wouldn't be able to stay in Caedun, but by the end of things, it wasn't clear whether they'd be able to either. They had friends, though, people they could stay with who could protect them, and connections they'd want to maintain.

"I think I'll travel. I read about a lot of interesting places. Spires higher than the clouds, cities built on ash, islands the color of emeralds. I think I'd like to see them."

Hrig looked thoughtful for a few moments. "Would you like some company?"

I hesitated. "I would've thought you'd want to stay here. You have people."

"The people I had have been gone for a long time. Besides, I don't think they'd want me to stick around for the rest of my life even if they were here."

"Then yes. I'd...really like it if you'd join me. Assuming we survive."

Hrig leaned over and kissed my faceplate gently. "It'll be easy as long as we have a reason to. Tell me more about these places you're intending to take me to."

The rest of the night passed uneventfully, with Hrig eventually falling asleep leaning against my pauldron. I'd removed my cape from my storage and draped it across her. She was snoring gently, a line of drool running from her mouth. I gently picked her up and laid her back on her bedroll. I then began reheating breakfast. It was a long road to Cirros, and I wanted to make sure everyone had a good meal.

Stone and Kyren awoke first, the smell of the food drawing them to the fire. Kyren looked at Hrig's sleeping form, still wrapped in my cape, and regarded me with a raised eyebrow and her usual smile. Stone simply gave me a wink before grabbing himself a bowl of the reheated stew from last night.

By the time Hrig awoke, both Stone and Kyren were on their second bowls. She stretched and pulled a few small twigs from her hair before carefully folding my cape and returning it to me. I took it, feeling a kind of jump in my breastplate as her fingers brushed mine. I stored it and started to break down the camp as they finished their meals.

We planned on taking the road most of the way to Entden before diverting around to avoid trouble, but Stone held up a hand and we started to divert, stopping us.

"D'you smell that?" he asked.

Hrig took a deep breath into her nose. "Smoke."

Kyren quickly climbed the nearest tree. "It's Entden. There's smoke rising from the town."

We drew our weapons as a group as Kyren climbed down from the tree, and we moved toward the town. My first thoughts were of the goblins and kobolds. It was uncommon for them to attack a town, but it wasn't as if things had been typical recently.

The gates to the town were open, but I saw no signs of struggle as we approached. Odder than that was the quiet. No sound of swords hitting shields, or arrows flying through the air.

We went through the front gate and found nothing, the streets clear and quiet. I led the way toward the source of the fire. We found it in the center of the town. A roaring bonfire made up of furniture that must've been taken from the surrounding houses.

Sitting in front of the fire facing us, flanked by a man and woman with golden eyes, was Talen. He was wearing the same black cloak, but no mask. His eyes twinkled in the firelight, and he wore a smile that didn't reach them.

"Sevald, welcome," he said in the tone of a man meeting someone for lunch.

I took several quick steps forward.

The children of Aurum that flanked him stepped in front of him, blocking my path with weapons in hand. One wore colorful blue silk and wielded a long halberd, and the other was in a long overcoat and held a bastard sword in each hand. I'd noticed the children of Aurum didn't favor any armor. I assumed it was because they had no need for it when they could simply ask the ancestor for some invulnerable scales and not concern themselves with what they might cost.

I hesitated. I knew my companions could more than handle themselves at this point, but three children of Aurum was a tricky proposition. It might have benefited them to size the enemy up a little, maybe subtly try to change position.

"What do you want, Talen? Are the people who live here okay?"

"They're fine. I simply asked them to stay within their homes while I dealt with their monster problem."

"Planning on suicide, then?" asked Stone.

Talen grimaced. "I was hoping to have a civil discussion."

"Fine. Talk," I said.

"I'm aware that you hate me, but I think at this point, it's clear we have something in common."

"What's that?"

"An enemy. Caedus. Surely, your vitriol for him outweighs that which you have toward me at this point? I drove you from a single city; he drove you from a country. Seems that the scale of his activity is far above my own, doesn't it?"

"In spite of that, I find that I hate you both in roughly equal measure, actually. What of your own hatred of me? After all, I slew your brother Donyin."

There was a twitch at the corner of Talen's mouth as I spoke, but he only reacted to the first part of my comment. "I can work with equal hatred."

"Get to the point."

"Fine. Forgive me for indulging in a bit of buildup. My proposal is simple. Let's join forces. I have a lot of support at my back, a lot of allies waiting for my signal to act against the king. With your muscle, things could go a lot more smoothly. After it's done, we part ways, and we never need to see each other again."

I chuckled. "Except what you're not sharing with me is that you think that will earn you godhood from your father, after which you believe you'll be able to handle me easily."

Talen tensed, almost imperceptibly. "I see Caedus may have told you a bit more about things than I thought he would."

"He and Vash both. You're wrong, though. It's not godhood your father is promising, but death."

Talen's companions tensed and looked at him, clearly feeling a little unsure.

Talen laughed. "Honestly, even if I'm wrong, it doesn't matter, and I don't believe I am. I want him out of my way, and I want a weak little stand-in to take over so I can run things. Will you assist, or do you choose death?"

I looked around. It didn't make sense for Talen to have only two guards with him, but I supposed it wouldn't have made sense for him to bring in any of his usual thugs. I could play along, pretend to work with him until I had a chance to make a move, but the thought of that made me feel as if there were flies crawling beneath my plate.

"I've been trying to do things peacefully, or work things out, or find some perfect solution to the problems you children of Aurum have been presenting me with since we first encountered you, and you know what I've realized?"

"That it's better to join us?"

"No. The best way to deal with you is to kill you."

46
TALEN

I lunged for the nearest child of Aurum, the one wearing silk, but moved into a roll when an enormous spear plunged deep into the earth in front of me. I was right. Talen had someone else hiding in the shadows.

I summoned a quick shield around myself and closed the distance between me and the silken warrior. She brought up their halberd and swung at me with a horizontal swipe, but I dodged beneath it and stabbed up at her neck. She just barely managed to dodge, and my sword wound up above her face, so I brought the hilt down onto her nose. There was a crunching noise, and she stumbled back, sweeping with her halberd to gain space. Before I could close it, another spear buried itself near me, but this time, too far away for me to bother dodging.

As I fought, I watched Stone, Hrig, and Kyren take on the one wielding two bastard swords. Stone and Hrig had closed the distance quickly—I assumed to keep the spear thrower from risking hitting his companion—and I noticed a shimmering bubble around Kyren. Hrig's tattoos were glowing as she swung her axe, and she'd already left several deep cuts on her opponent. Meanwhile, Stone was using hammer blows to force changes in his footing and stance in order to keep him from gaining momentum, and Kyren was flinging bolts of energy at him every time he managed to break away.

I summoned a second multi-sword into my other hand and began another round of attacks focusing on Talen. The spears had stopped, and that let me give my full attention to the fight in front of me.

Talen was wielding a slender silver blade with a coppery edge and making lightning-fast strikes at me while his ally did her best to keep me pinned with her halberd. She stabbed at me with it, and I caught the halberd with my blade, pulling her and it in front of me in order to block one of Talen's blows, but his sword glided through its haft, my shield spell, and my armor like there was nothing there. His sword was edged with elyrium.

As we continued, my opponents gained an edge, and I started to have large rends carved into my armor. The halberdier had made a few thrusts at me with the remaining haft, but gave up when it broke against me, switching to using large claws I hadn't noticed before, and I found her close-combat abilities to be much more difficult to defend against.

As I fought, I began to repair myself, drawing on my internal reserves. Talen's blade continued to cut me, but as it did, it began producing fewer and fewer tears and getting caught on my armor. Soon, my steel body was laced with lines of bronze from the elyrium I was drawing from the bars I'd stored for Kyren. Talen's every hit was just making me stronger.

As I started to take the upper hand, pushing Talen and his ally back, I noticed that the man dual-wielding the bastard swords had started to push Stone and Hrig back toward Kyren, and he seemed to be focused on reaching her.

Before anyone could press an advantage, there was a crash as three figures slammed into the town square from a nearby rooftop. There was a man with golden eyes twirling a spear, being pushed back by a woman wielding a rapier and a dwarf with long metal claws. Dorsia and Jade had joined the fight. It looked like I had allies of my own.

They looked a bit worse for wear than either myself or my other companions, but they'd held their own against a child of Aurum and had managed to keep spears from slamming into me, so I took that as a victory in their favor. They joined Hrig and Stone in protecting Kyren, and the bastard sword-wielding child of Aurum fell in with his spearman brother.

I managed to break through the daughter of Aurum's defense, slamming a sword into her side, managing to push it through her scales, before immediately dismissing the blade and let her blood flow freely from the wound. Talen slashed at me before I could follow up, but I let his blow hit me and filled myself in with another line of elyrium. Their blows were rattling my essence, but that became less possible as the golden lines across my armor grew.

I heard a cry from behind me and saw that Dorsia had managed to drive her rapier deep into an axe wound Hrig had left on the dual-wielder. The spearman went into a rage, but lost his footing as gold chains sprang up and wrapped around his legs. The silken child of Aurum broke off from me and let out a large stream of fire, sending my companions reeling and giving the spearmen time to break free of his bonds.

That left me and Talen fighting one another alone. I began attacking with empty hands, summoning blades just before they'd strike Talen and then de-summoning them to repeat the process. It distracted him and moved him back, forcing him to watch my every movement.

Occasionally, I wouldn't summon a sword, but he'd dodge thinking I would, and I'd manage a quick punch or kick. I could see that the fight was wearing on him. I'd managed no real blows on him, but his allies were losing in spite of their incredible strength, and I was much more equipped to fight him than I had been after I'd been injured by Caedus. Talen wasn't used to fair fights, and it showed.

He made a mistake, and I pressed my advantage, closing in for what I hoped would be a fatal blow. Suddenly, his cloak whipped around and slammed into me hard, just under my faceplate, sending me flying toward my companions, crashing into Stone. Talen's cloak unfurled, and I realized that it wasn't a leather cloak, but rather large powerful wings that sprouted from him. They started to beat, and Talen began turning around, attempting to make a run for it.

I tapped Stone's boots, absorbing the enchantment within them. "Sorry, don't try to use these for the rest of the fight."

I rolled up and let my companions continue their fight while I ran straight for Talen. He was starting to gain altitude, rising up past the nearest building and starting to fly over it toward the gate. I made it to the building and leapt up onto the roof, the enchantment from Stone's boots allowing me a solid twelve-foot vertical. A few more steps to gain momentum, and I leapt again, this time landing on Talen's back.

He fell a bit, but rather than landing, he angled himself upward and started carrying us high into the air as quickly as possible, trying to shake me loose from him. I shifted the tips of my gauntlets into claws and drove them deep into Talen's shoulders. He screamed, but continued to fly us higher, jerking and twisting the whole way as he did so.

I started clawing at his back, tearing into him, but suddenly, I went from tearing out flesh to only creating sparks. Golden scales began spreading from his back and slowly covered him from head to toe. He dove, directing us toward the forest.

Wind whistled by as the ground came closer and closer to us, and at the last minute, he curved upward. We slammed into the treeline, and from there, it became a test of endurance. Branches and whole trees broke as we crashed into them. When we started to slow down, Talen began rising back up into the air.

The slowdown allowed me to pull myself up and wrap my arms around his golden neck. He put on a burst of speed to launch himself into the air, and soon, we were even higher than we'd been before, almost reaching the clouds. I started to squeeze, putting as much pressure on his throat as I could, but unlike Donyin, Talen didn't panic. He simply stopped flying and let us fall, with me underneath him.

I held firm, not letting up and continuing to squeeze as hard as I possibly could. I solidified the shield I'd put up and extended the boots' enchantment to my entire body, hoping to absorb the fall.

We landed in the middle of the bonfire, sending embers flying across the town and cracking the earth. I held on, still not giving an inch. Talen began to tear across my arms with newly formed talons, but I swiftly replaced the missing steel with elyrium and squeezed harder, adding in the pressure from the shield spell to crush his neck by a few more millimeters. We rolled through the flames as we struggled, and Talen's wings beat, trying in vain to shake or move me. Gradually, his will to resist faded, and I felt him draw his last breath.

I stood slowly, climbing out from beneath him and stood over him, looking down. His eyes flashed open as a white-hot burst of flame erupted from it. I could feel parts of me melt, but I summoned a blade and drove it through his open mouth and through the back of his head. I saw pure hatred in his eyes as his body burst into flame. Another soul added to Aurum's growing collection.

I turned toward my friends. They had acquitted themselves similarly well. The bodies of the three they'd faced were also burning up in intense heat. We'd won the battle, but a part of me felt that by doing so, we'd quite possibly strengthened Aurum himself. Still, it made more sense to focus on the tangible threat his children were at the moment rather than the existential one he represented.

I walked over to them. The town had mostly avoided catching fire, but a few townsfolk had made their way out of their homes in order to put out what small fires remained. They gave us all a wide berth as they did so.

Stone was clutching his side, and Kyren was healing him. Dorsia was on the ground as well, seemingly after having been healed, with Jade holding a waterskin to let her drink. Hrig was leaning heavily against her axe.

She gave me a once over and smiled. "I like a man with scars."

I looked myself over. I was now crisscrossed with threads of elyrium across my entire body. I found that I rather liked how it looked, too, though Hrig was right in calling them scars.

"Is everyone okay?" I asked.

"Aye, lad," said Stone, lifting himself up and wiping the blood away from his now healed side.

Dorsia gave a thumbs-up but didn't move aside from that, and Jade just nodded. The fight had been hard, but this was likely the one group of people on the continent that could manage to survive it.

Stone moved over to Talen's body, took a small gold coin, and tossed it into the flames. He let out a heavy sigh and returned to us. At our questioning looks, he simply said, "Still owed him something, from a long time ago."

I nodded somberly. It was important to remember that before Aurum's influence, many people had been harmless, or at least much less dangerous than they'd become. Stone had described Talen as a middle man when he'd last seen him. With

Aurum's influence, he'd become a duke, a lord of the underworld that ruled with an iron fist and ruthless methods. Donyin had been a beggar, Vash captain of a single ship, and Rubrus a hedge mage's apprentice. Aurum had made them more powerful, but he'd also made them selfish and terrible. I shuddered at the thought of what Caedus was becoming due to that influence. He was already a born king—the powers and influence of a god of sheer will on top of that was a terrible thing to contemplate.

I had to reach him as quickly as possible. With a war on the way and Aurum looming beyond that, I had no time to lose. Luckily, between Stone and Dorsia, I had the perfect group to help smuggle me into the capital.

47
GETTING AHEAD

Rather than taking a direct route up through Cirros, we decided to try and avoid the city whose ruler we'd recently slain and travel along the riverways.

Dorsia and Stone concocted a plan for us to travel as merchants hauling goods. Dorsia played the role of head merchant, donning simple travel clothes and keeping only a small dagger at her side. Stone was our wizened guide, wearing an old worn cloak and boots. Jade and Hrig were haulers wearing heavy cloaks to hide their obvious tattoos, and Kyren was Dorsia's apprentice, having exchanged her white robes for a simple tunic and boots.

I myself played a role I was sure they envied, a part of the goods. I had disassembled myself and been placed in a crate. My companions left the lid open and talked to me when they could, but the small river vessels made that difficult.

Aside from myself, we were also hauling twenty steel bars I'd volunteered, the weapons I'd collected over my travels, and several crates of turnips. Stone and Dorsia had spent an hour arguing about what goods to purchase that they'd most likely see a return on, and then they'd haggled with the farmer they were buying from for a further half hour.

"Why does it matter if we're only using it as cover?" I'd asked.

Dorsia and Stone had both regarded me with offended looks at the question before Stone responded, "It's a matter of principle!"

And Dorsia added, "Also, what kind of trader doesn't do their best to make a profit? It would be suspicious if we didn't put this kind of effort in."

I'd relented, but I still felt like they'd simply wanted the excuse to make a few extra silver.

At the third river transfer, we were approached by several men in armor bearing the symbol of Caedun on their chest. The shortest one led the group.

"Hail, we're performing searches on any cargo passing through here. We'll need to inspect what you've got and ask a few questions."

Dorsia sighed. "C'mon, ser, I don't have a lot of time to get to the next raft."

"Sorry, ma'am. Rules are rules."

"Fine, let's get through this quick. Daph, Dai, open the crates so they can search them. What are your questions?"

"Alright, why are you travelling upriver like this instead of going through Cirros?"

"Taxes have been too high lately. Trying a more roundabout route to Buryn."

The man grimaced. "Well, that's not illegal, but I wish you'd consider the good those taxes would do for the war effort."

"War doesn't keep my family fed, ser."

He sighed. "Well, that also covers where you're headed. Have you seen a man in fullplate, roughly six feet tall, never takes off his helmet?"

"You talking about the monster that attacked the king?"

He nodded.

"No, ser. Saw some adventurers we bought some gear off of, but no one in full plate."

One of the men searching the crates stopped at mine. He reached in and pulled out my helmet. He turned it over in his hands a few times, and I got an up close look at yellow teeth and patchy facial hair. It took serious willpower, but I managed not to say boo. Once he was satisfied, he placed me back in the crate and went on to the next one.

After a few more questions, the guards finished searching everything and left. Unfortunately, they'd taken just enough time to cost us our river transport, so we were forced to spend the rest of the day finding a new one. Still, it would've cost us a lot more time had we been discovered, so I didn't complain.

We arrived at the small central Caedun town of Dulhin late the following afternoon. Dulhin was to the west and a bit north of Cirros. It existed primarily as an interior dock for river boats, its main economy in the building and repairing of those boats, at least on the surface.

The other reason it existed was as an alternate port that could be used to avoid taxes in Cirros and Buryn if one wanted to take things directly to the capital. It also attracted a fair number of smugglers trying to avoid the costly business of dealing with the underworld elements that controlled the ports in Buryn and Cirros.

That led to a certain odd mixture of people. There were the honest boatmen making their way, and the less-than-honest smugglers. They seemed to keep to themselves, and I observed pockets of both groups doing their best to avoid one another as I peered from the crate in which I'd been stored.

Once our crates had been stored in a small warehouse at the dock, Hrig was nice enough to strap me behind her right shoulder next to her axe so I could accompany them to the tavern.

There were two taverns in the town. One called simply "The Raft" and the other "The Drowned Rat." Due to the preferences of everyone, including Kyren, we of course found ourselves in the much seedier The Drowned Rat. It was a dingy place with a sign that showed a mug with a rat tail dangling off the side. The clientele matched the exterior. Scoundrels of all types played cards, bet on a wrestling match in the corner, and gave off an overall impression of "we will stab you for three copper on a bet."

It took the group only about two drinks to completely shift that attitude, though. First, Hrig took me over to the wrestling match. The men fighting were an elf and a clean-shaven dwarf. The elf had reach, but the dwarf was incredibly stable. It was going in the elf's favor for a minute as he struck and danced out of the dwarf's reach, but once the dwarf got him to the ground, it was over in seconds. Hrig and Jade, of course, had to take part themselves, and so I found myself placed in the care of Kyren at the bar.

Kyren began her usual drinking and soon found herself the subject of the other drunks' attention.

"All that ale for you, little lass?" asked one of them, leaning close and gesturing toward the three mugs in front of her.

She gave a small smile. "Since no one else seems to be a competent drinker, I thought I'd lead by example."

He whistled. "Care to have a little competition?"

"Drink 'til one of us pukes or collapses and the other pays for what we had?"

He raised an eyebrow. "How'd you know?"

She raised a mug and held it casually in her hand. "I had a feeling."

After that, I was taken by Stone, who dragged me to a table he was sharing with a few other older men.

"And this is the reason for all the trouble," he said, placing me at the center of the table facing a dwarf with white hair smoking on a long-stemmed pipe.

"This helmet?"

"That's right. This is what was causing all the trouble in my marriage. It's a special helmet, you see. A fey gave it a touch o' mischief, and so it likes to sow a little discord whenever it can. Somehow, it actually found its way into the wall of my house, and whenever me or my wife passed it, it would make a snide little comment in one of our voices. 'It'd be nice of you to cook for a change' or 'that apron gives you the ass of an orc.' It almost brought us to ruin before we figured it out"

The pipe-smoking man shook his head. "I don't believe ya."

"An idiot like you wouldn't," I said, and he nearly fell from his chair in surprise.

"I told you," said Stone, staring at the man with a wide grin.

The man picked himself up, brushing the ashes from his pipe out of his beard. "Can it speak beyond insults?"

"Nope, just curses."

I sent a foul oath in dwarvish in Stone's direction, one I'd lifted from Burias the orc, and I was satisfied to see even Stone blushing a bit by the time I'd finished it.

I traded a few more barbs at the table until Dorsia decided to scoop me up and take me to her card game.

"I'll throw in this helmet," she said, tossing me into the middle.

One of the men at the table, a man wearing glasses, lifted me, turned me around, and gave a solid knock on my head.

"Steel, eh? Alright, deal. I hope you're ready to lose this, though. Luck hasn't exactly been on your side since you sat at this table."

Dorsia smiled and sat back down, eyeing her hand. It was a game of dead kings, with one live one on the table and three down. I could see everyone's hand, and I realized very quickly that Dorsia's ability to sense a person's strength applied to card games, as well. She'd led them on, clearly with the intention of leading them to believe that she was a poor helpless tradeswoman with little talent at playing cards, but even less luck.

After a few more raises, the pot was substantial, particularly when including my own pricelessness. The man to Dorsia's left laid down his hand first, and then they each followed from his left, with a sharp intake of breath when the man wearing glasses laid his hand down and gave a smile.

On Dorsia's turn, she sighed heavily before laying down her cards one by one. With each card she placed, I watched the bespectacled man's smile shrink and shrink as his eyes bulged more and more.

"I believe this will take the pot, gentlemen."

The man stood, drawing the dagger at his belt. "You cheating wench!" He lunged at her.

Just before he made it across the table, she lifted me, and I found myself slammed across his face. I was satisfied to see that using me made the man twirl off the table and onto the ground, missing some of the teeth he'd started his night with.

The rest of the bar stopped what they were doing for a moment while another man from the table took the bespectacled man's pulse and gave a thumbs-up, returning everyone to their revelry. From there, I was picked up by Hrig, who had a few fresh bruises. She placed me back on her shoulder.

"How'd you do?" I whispered.

"Me and Jade won, of course, but we had a bit of trouble with each other. Even without those runes of hers, the woman hits like a brick, and hitting her feels like punching a wall."

"Which of you won?"

"Neither, but Jade would probably tell you she did."

"You seem a little defensive."

Some color made its way to her cheeks. "I'm not! We just disagree on what a victory is."

When we made it to the bar, Kyren was sitting surrounded by men that seemed willing to kill themselves on alcohol to beat her. She herself was wearing her small smile. I hadn't been able to figure it out before I'd eaten Rubrus, but I finally realized how she did it. She was using a spell that cured poison on a low level all throughout her body. I had a feeling she didn't need to use it to beat one or two drunks, but when she got the attention of several, it seemed like a smart way to keep her victory going.

Everyone wrapped up their encounters and shared a drink at the bar before we headed up to the room. Hrig laid me on a pillow next to hers, and before long, everyone was out sleeping.

I wasn't sure what to expect once we reached the capital, but I hope that whatever happened, we'd still be able to have time like this. I knew that that was unlikely; attacking a king to prevent the arrival of a forgotten god didn't seem like the type of thing that people got to have normal lives after, but maybe we'd get lucky. It was possible that the lives of adventurers were a bit easier to maintain after something like that.

48
LONG WAY ROUND

After a few more days of travel, we arrived in Buryn. The roundabout route had taken more time than I'd have liked, but I had enjoyed the extra time I'd been able to spend with my companions. Stone and Dorsia briefly went to the market to see what kind of profit could be made from turnips, which turned out to be surprisingly high this close to where the war effort was being supplied.

Once we were safely ensconced in one of Dorsia's many hideaways, I reassembled myself. Being only a head for so long had been disorienting, but the ease with which it had allowed us to travel had been nice. The team watched me rebuild myself before they spoke.

"That was about the most surreal thing I've ever seen," said Jade as I finished screwing on my head.

"After seeing him eat a ten-foot pole of metal and spin his head like a top, it just doesn't faze me like it used to," said Kyren, sighing disappointedly.

"I'm sorry I've grown so one note. I'll try and find a way to surprise you."

"Please see that you do," she replied with a smirk.

Stone chuckled. "Nobles. So entitled."

Jade looked me over. "Those bronze lines of yours are going to make it even harder to get you into the capital."

"They do stand out a bit, don't they?" I asked.

"Well, hopefully, our contact will have something figured out for us. He's been looking for a direct way to help for quite some time. He's been instrumental in starting to peel off the king's support, particularly among the common folk," said Kyren.

There was a knock on the door, two raps, followed by three more in an odd cadence. Dorsia opened the door, and two rough-looking men walked in followed by a dwarf that wore a cloak over his head. The two rough-looking ones had a brief word with Dorsia, who clapped one of them on the shoulder, put a pile of coins in the other's hand, and sent them out. Once the door was closed, the cloaked dwarf removed his hood, revealing a clean-shaven face.

It was odd to see a dwarf without a beard. Even some dwarven women liked to maintain them. I was used to the close-cut ones in Usulaum, but a bare-faced dwarf was in many ways stranger than a living suit of armor.

"Hello, everyone," said the man in a fatherly tone.

"Hello, Jun," responded Kyren. She looked over at me and Hrig. "This is our contact, in case that wasn't clear. He's the head of the church in the capital and a priest of all gods."

"Well met," I said, extending my hand.

He grabbed my wrist and gave a firm shake, smiling up at me as he did so. "Well met indeed. I've heard a lot about you."

"Don't believe everything Kyren says," I responded, drawing some side-eye from her.

"Oh, I didn't hear it from Kyren."

He didn't elaborate further, though I had a feeling I knew exactly what he was talking about.

"So, you can get us into the capital?" asked Stone.

Jun nodded. "I can, though luckily, I don't need to."

"What do you mean?" he asked.

"The king is about to leave the capital to head for Sylfen's border. He's planning to meet with the forces he's gathered there. I found out just this morning from a courier. It's unfortunate I spent so much time developing a way to smuggle all of you in. The plan had coffins, arson, and even a short trip through some sewers."

"You sound disappointed," said Kyren.

"I haven't gotten to experience the life of an adventurer like you. It was nice to be able to turn my focus to something earthly rather than celestial." He sighed heavily. "The good thing, though, is that it should be easier to get to him in the middle of an army than it would be to go through gates, walls, and guards."

"Relatively, but it'll still be difficult. Any chance we can catch up with him before he reaches his main force?" asked Hrig.

"No, his group is travelling on horseback to get there. He apparently wants to give some kind of demonstration," said Jun.

"I don't like the sound of that," I said.

Jun nodded. "He was also travelling with at least three golden-eyed bodyguards as well as more than one hundred additional men. I have enough contacts in the main force on the border that we can likely slip you into the lines, but getting you all there before the king's planned demonstration is going to be tight."

Between Dorsia and Jun, we acquired two horses each. I had been given a large spotted brown one and a solid black one, both of which I gained an immediate fondness of. Sevald had trained with horses since he was a young boy, and I found myself awash with the warm feelings he'd had toward the creatures as I lifted myself up onto the back of the brown one.

I hadn't ever ridden one—my own ability to distance run and cut across thick underbrush was usually more useful, especially since I was able to do so without breaks. This time, however, we would be travelling straight west across major roads and taking only minimal breaks. With time being a factor, horses were the best option. I also wasn't sure it would be wise for me to travel alone into enemy lines. I was stronger than I'd ever been before, but there were certainly limits to what I could do.

While we rode, I decided to explore those limits. The insights that Rubrus had given me into my own functions had already yielded some impressive results. Knowing that I was using the metal I'd stored internally to repair myself let me strengthen my body with elyrium, and absorbing enchantments meant I could now summon multi-swords at will and absorb energy from people's blows against me. Not to mention that I could absorb and then return those enchantments as I had with Stone's boots. He'd tried to charge me a rental fee, but we agreed to call it even.

I focused internally and regarded the three elyrium bars I had in my inventory. One was missing about two feet of its initial length. I began pulling it, using it to thicken my armor beneath the areas that were still steel while simultaneously layering steel over where I'd already patched myself with elyrium.

By the time I was done, I looked how I had before. I felt a

tinge of vanity, as I'd enjoyed how I'd looked with the threads, but they made me far more noticeable than was desirable now. Aside from that, I'd now be able to surprise my foes with my durability, even if they'd normally be strong enough to pierce steel.

After that was done, I thought about the enchantments I had on me. I focused on the storage space I had and found that I could actually manifest multi-swords within myself. They still faded over time, but I could create them almost instantly since I no longer had to pull them apart and could instead summon them at will. I summoned as many as possible internally as quickly as I could and was able to completely fill the space before the first of them I'd manifested dematerialized. That gave me some interesting options.

My other enchantment, the ability to absorb energy, was not something I could stretch in the same way. It was certainly useful, particularly against my more mundane foes, but against children of Aurum, it had limited uses.

We stopped to water and change our horses and allow everyone a brief meal of trail rations.

"No more scars?" asked Hrig, a bit of disappointment leaking into her voice.

"I thought inconspicuous may be the way to go this time. I'm sure I'll have some new ones by the end of things."

She patted me on the shoulder and went to tend to her horse. I needed to be certain that I didn't discount the way my allies could contribute. All of them were stronger than they had been before, more capable. I could rely on them the same that they could rely on me, but perhaps I could still help them to be even more reliable.

"Hrig, can I see your axe for a moment?" I asked.

"Finally thinking of switching to a true warrior's weapon?"

she asked with a smile, drawing her axe and extending the handle of it toward me.

"Now that swords are built into me, I think they're what I'll stick with. I just wanted to give you a little gift." I held her axe, feeling it become an extension of myself, and I channeled the elyrium from within me onto the edge of her axe, leaving it bronze. I handed it back to her.

"I know you're strong enough now to cut through their scales, but I figured this might help."

Hrig took her axe, smiling as she ran a finger down the edge, drawing a little blood. "I don't think I've received such a nice gift in some time."

Jade and Dorsia approached after that, and I did the same for them, leaving Dorsia with an elyrium-edged rapier and Jade with bronze-colored claws. Kyren and Stone's weaponry wasn't really in need of reinforcement in that way; a hammer still hammers fine without elyrium, and magic was not so easy to strengthen.

"Did everyone thank you for that?" asked Kyren.

"Yes, though a thank you from Jade is usually more like a grunt."

"Well, they seem to have forgotten to thank me," she said with her small smile.

"Thank you?" I thought for a moment. "Oh...right."

She laughed. "Don't worry, I'm not serious. This is more important than the gold those bars might have made me. Besides, the ones I already sold were more than enough to cover the expenses of the estate, and my brothers' heads also helped to make sure I wouldn't have to worry about that kind of thing any time soon either."

I returned to the horses, taking the time to make sure they were in good enough shape to keep travelling. We were planning on riding them hard, but that didn't mean I wanted them to be uncomfortable. Once I was sure they were okay to ride, we all mounted back up and continued on.

We were near the capital and so would need to loop around, using side roads to avoid any patrols or random encounters with those loyal to Caedus. Luckily, the roads were well cleared. Jun had said he'd have a temple holiday scheduled to celebrate with a large feast, which seemed to have had a positive impact on the traffic. Aside from that, I was relatively certain that Caedus was simply no longer concerned about us. He was nearing what he believed to be an ascension. The culmination of dozens of plans and tremendous effort. It was simply a shame all of his work was for naught.

It was early morning by the time we reached the edges of the camp. We lit a metal lantern and opened and closed the front of it three times. A few minutes later, we were met by two young men in what had become the standard soldier's garb of a simple tunic with the emblem of an eagle's claw.

Kyren approached and spoke with them in hushed tones before they led us into a tent on the outskirts of the camp. Inside were some simple beds and a table with a small map of the encampment. The men said a few final words to Kyren, and then they slipped out.

We all approached the table.

"They say that the king plans to begin things here, in just an hour or so. We have a few extra uniforms for all of us, and all the attention will likely be focused on the stage."

"What if we try something now, before he's even up there?" asked Jade.

"The king is already on the stage making preparations. We'll benefit more from striking while everyone is focused on him rather than all the wandering eyes there now," said Stone.

"Less than an hour, then? I suppose we're lucky we got here before it started at all," I said, crossing my arms. "No real time to plan. I guess we'll just get as close as we can and try to stop him. Will we have any help?"

"Jun's people are too afraid to help directly. I'm afraid we're on our own," said Kyren.

"Well, there's no group of people I'd rather do this with."

49
CEREMONY

By the time the king's speech was to begin, we were all dressed in soldier's uniforms. Because of how conspicuous I was, I needed to be on the edges of things. The plan was for everyone else to get as close as possible to the king and then I would act as a distraction to draw attention to myself.

The plan made me nervous. I was, even with all the improvements my allies had made, still the heaviest hitter. In spite of that, I trusted them, and this was the plan that made the most sense. I was also the only one who could potentially keep from killing any of the common soldiers who might choose to get in my way.

It wasn't difficult to tell where the speech was happening. There was a stage erected in the middle of a group of soldiers thousands strong. I could make out Caedus's golden hair and armor even from the outside where I stood. I wasn't sure of where my allies were, but I knew they'd be in places once I began my attempt at distraction.

Around Caedus, I noticed more than a dozen guards, a few I could tell were wearing no armor. I guessed those without armor were likely children of Aurum he'd brought under his sway. I found a position near the top of a hill looking down at the stage, and waited. From where I stood, I could see a force similar in size to our own across a wide no-man's land on which sat the border between Caedun and Sylfen.

Caedus took the stage and began speaking. I wasn't expecting to be able to hear him and so was surprised when he came in crystal-clear, almost as if he were right beside me.

"Hello, my fellow countrymen. Before I begin my demonstration, I just wanted to say a few words to all of you loyal citizens of Caedun."

I saw many of those in the crowd looking around, trying to see where his voice was coming from.

"The elves across the border think I am here to speak to you before calling a truce. They think we are afraid of them, but they don't know the power we here in Caedun hold. I will show them, and you, that power. I want you all to watch closely. The world will build statues of this moment."

Caedus turned away, and I saw a golden light begin to surround him. Runes I couldn't make out lit up in a massive and complex pattern that covered the stage he was on. I could actually feel a vibration in the air as pure power started to condense around him.

It was time for my distraction. I yelled, testing how loud I could actually be for the first time.

"CAEDUS! I WILL NOT ALLOW YOU THIS UNJUST WAR! WHAT YOU DO DOOMS US ALL!"

My voice exploded out of me, and those standing close actually fell to the ground clutching their ears. I saw some of Caedus's guards point at me and heard a few shouts of "get him!", but Caedus himself didn't move an inch, too enraptured in the ritual he likely thought would grant him godhood.

Men nearby mostly parted as I began running toward the

stage, but eventually, enough got in my way with weapons drawn that I was forced to slow down. My strategy for handling them non-lethally was to simply turn on my energy-eating enchantment and keep walking. I'd experimented with it a bit and found that I could actually increase the effect it had if I made a conscious effort.

As men hit me with spears, swords, and even axes, they would simply collapse as I took as much energy from their bodies as I possibly could. Soon, there were more than a hundred collapsed men behind me.

By the time I'd made it halfway, two golden-eyed figures put themselves in my path. I recognized them from the party as the juggler and the firebreather, roles which they quickly lived up to.

The juggler closed in on me and began attacking with three shortswords, always keeping one in the air as he slashed and struck at me. I used two summoned swords to block his blows, but when I went to counterattack, he would dodge away, letting the firebreather unleash her breath at me.

The heat washed over me, but I heard the screams of soldiers around me as they caught fire or were simply incinerated. When the fire stopped, I was struck by two powerful blows that knocked me forward but didn't manage to pierce my now elyrium body.

I twirled, dismissing my own swords to catch the one he had in the air, bringing it down in a smooth arc. My sight was clouded by the fire, but attacks from behind were generally pointless. I managed to cut the juggler across the arm before he dodged away.

I went to pursue him, but the firebreather hit me again, this time with some form of concentrated blast that had all of the force of her previous attack, but focused into a kind of beam. It knocked me down, and the steel I had placed over my elyrium melted away where it hit, but I pushed myself upward. I placed both my gauntlets out to block the beam and started marching grimly toward her. She kept it up, seemingly able to put out the blast continuously, vaporizing the poor men who were hit any time the beam deviated from me.

Just before I could reach her, the juggler reappeared and went to bring his swords down onto my back. I chose that moment to duck. The beam slammed into his chest, leaving him staring down at an empty hole, his expression one of surprise.

The firebreather's roar turned to a cry of anguish as her blast ended. I quickly covered the ground between us, and just as she was managing to recover and send out another beam, I summoned a blade and buried it into her mouth, killing her instantly.

My conflict with them had cleared away a large swath of the soldiers around me, who had taken that moment to cut and run. Up by the stage, I saw my companions locked in conflict with still more golden-eyed beings, as well as dozens of guards. Luckily, their battle had proven too much for the common soldiers, as well, and so all those nearest to the stage had fled. Caedus himself was untouched and continued to stand, exuding a kind of golden light.

I began to run, moving as quickly as I could for the stage. A few common soldiers attempted to stop me, but were knocked out by my enchantment, and in one case, my fist as I continued forward. I reached Kyren on the edge of the battle. She was shooting out bolts of holy light, just in time to intercept a dozen guards, one of whom had golden eyes. Kyren pushed out a wall of force, knocking away four of them, but only slowing down the other two.

I slammed into them, tackling them to the ground before rolling up and summoning a multi-sword. The golden-eyed one launched himself at me, swinging a large axe similar to Hrig's down at me, but I dodged the blow and rolled backward in front of Kyren. I turned my gauntlet into a claw and quickly scratched a few runes into the ground behind me before the golden-eyed axeman reached us.

I jumped toward him, surprising him in mid-air, then spun my body around and slammed him into the dirt where I'd placed the runes, activating them as I did so. By softening the earth with runic magic, I was able to bury him head first up to his feet. I made a few more quick runes and resolidified the earth from there, his feet flailing as he struggled. A few hits from my pommel and a solid kick later, and I'd cleared out Kyren's attackers. She returned her focus to aiding our allies.

With all of the remaining guards occupied, I climbed directly onto the stage without interference. Another golden-eyed figure tried to stop me, but Hrig slammed her axe into his head, throwing him out of my path. While I approached the king, I noticed Jade and Dorsia holding their own against a man with a single golden arm. Stone was hopping between guards, a blur with a sledgehammer knocking them off balance or braining them as he went.

I reached Caedus, summoning a multi-sword as I did, and I swung down. Just before my blade reached him, all of the runes surrounding us flew from the floor onto his skin, covering him in golden draconic. I was hit by an invisible wall of force and flew backwards, just barely keeping myself on the stage.

Caedus was laughing, a roaring, maddening laugh that seemed to vibrate the air around him. I rushed him, swinging multi-swords at his throat. He turned and caught the blades in his hands, still laughing. I looked into his eyes and saw that his golden irises had expanded, turning his entire eye gold, and around his eyes, small cracks were forming with golden light spilling out of them.

He shattered my swords and kicked me, launching me from the stage and onto the ground. He then leapt and landed on me, slamming into my chest. Thin trails of golden energy were flowing in the air toward him, and I realized that it was coming from the children of Aurum my allies had been fighting. They had caught fire, but they continued to fight as everything they were bled into Caedus.

Caedus started slamming his fists into me, hitting me so hard that the ground beneath me began to crack and give way. As he began another rain of blows, I activated a rune I'd begun just before he'd landed on me. A massive explosion sent us both into the air, and I managed to wrap myself around him before we landed.

I began to squeeze on his neck with all my might, hoping that the strategy I'd so successfully implemented with Donyin and Talen would also work here. Unfortunately, it didn't. Caedus's laughing only grew louder as I squeezed.

He launched us into the air and slammed his elbows backward into me, separating me from him. When I stood to face him, I noticed that while his lips were curled up into a cruel smile, his eyes were wide with fear. The cracks on him were spreading, breaking into the runes on his skin, and his flesh was burning away at the edges of it. His siblings that had continued fighting had stopped, the damage to their bodies too much to allow them to continue on. The laughter coming from Caedus's ruined face also seemed to be mixed with sobbing.

He stumbled toward me, more pieces of him burning up as he did so. It seemed as if he were being pulled toward me by puppet strings. I caught him as he fell toward me. I could feel an intense and fiery heat emanating from him, and the air hummed with power. He looked up at me and opened his mouth to speak.

"Help me."

At that moment, all the power that had gathered within him exploded outward, throwing me across the battlefield. My senses were suddenly overwhelmed by golden light, heat hotter than anything I'd ever felt, and the smell of metal. When they returned, I almost wished they hadn't.

Occupying nearly half the battlefield was a tremendous golden form. Its scales shone blindingly in the sunlight, its teeth and talons ivory white, the inside of its wings a deep red, the color of dried blood.

Just as I was beginning to understand the sheer scale and power of what was in front of me, it lifted its head and roared, unleashing flames into the air and shaking the earth itself with the raw force of its bellowing.

Aurum had returned.

50
ASCENSION

I pulled myself to my feet, staring up in awe in spite of myself. Aurum was massive and magnificent. I felt an intense desire to supplicate myself before him that I was only able to fight off thanks to the repulsive feeling of self-satisfaction I could feel emanating off of him.

He stretched luxuriantly, absentmindedly rending large cuts into the ground with his claws. After that, he swept his eyes across the battlefield. He then rose into the air with powerful beats of his wings that produced so much wind, I thought I might be blown away. He flew across the no-man's land between the armies, and once he reached the Sylfen lines, he unleashed hellfire on them, killing thousands.

Once he was satisfied, he turned around and came back, landing where he'd started, the earth trembling. He then swept his golden eyes across the battlefield, eventually landing them on me. He tilted his head downward at me and opened his mouth to speak, revealing teeth as large as I was tall.

"Hail, son of Rubrus, grandchild of mine."

I clenched my fist, looking at the fire in the distance. "Aurum."

"Thank you for attending my resurrection party. It was a little drab, so I decided to do a bit of decorating." He gestured with a talon to the fire blazing on the elven lines. "What do you think?"

"I think you're a monster."

Aurum chuckled. "You're one to talk, grandson. We're two of a kind, you and I. I can feel the power I'd provided Rubrus running through you, powering you, and I can also sense that you've made liberal use of it."

I stayed silent, and began summoning as many multi-swords within myself as I possibly could.

"I'm rather proud of you, actually. You wound up being more useful to me than any of my recognized offspring. You pushed them into giving me more of themselves than I could've hoped. I had initially expected them to compete more directly with one another, but their decision to cooperate turned things glacial. Nothing like a new threat to speed things up."

I remained quiet but tilted my head down. I'd known since talking to Vash that I may have been helping him, but I still felt that I couldn't have simply let his children remain unchecked. I continued to summon blades and readied myself to make quick action. I wasn't sure if my plan would work, but I needed to do everything I could to ensure that it would.

"As a reward for all your help," he continued, "I think I'll let you leave."

That surprised me, and I lifted my helmet back to face him.

He smiled a terrifying smile. "Of course, your allies will have to stay behind. The large woman and priestess should provide some entertainment. Sure, one of them worships Sidi for now, but I'm sure I'll have them both worshipping me before too long."

I pulled all the metal from inside myself and expanded. First the elyrium, then the steel, and finally, the metal from all of the multi-swords I had within me. As I expanded, I drove my enlarging fist right into Aurum's chin, using the force of my expansion to strike him with enough force that he was launched into the no-man's land.

I lumbered after him, moving as quickly as possible to put as much distance between everyone else and the impending battle between Aurum and me.

He managed to overcome his surprise before I reached him, and he unleashed a wave of hellfire that covered me. I pushed through, restoring the metal he melted as quickly as I could by drawing on more multi-swords while also trying to bring up a magical barrier to lessen the damage as much as possible. I slammed my fist into his open mouth, once again sending him reeling, then I gripped one gauntlet in the other and slammed both of them down on top of him, cracking the earth beneath him as I did.

He clawed up at me, tearing out enormous hunks of armor as he did so, and pushed me back. He then stood himself up and leapt at me, knocking me to my back and sending up an enormous cloud of dust. Once he was on top of me, he began tearing and biting at me, each individual blow slamming into my essence and causing black ooze of the void to begin spilling freely from me.

I opened my faceplate and unleashed a continuous spray of multi-swords directly into his face, forcing him off of me. I kept shooting them at him, dismissing them as soon as they struck, only to immediately summon more so I could force him to stay down.

He backed away and roared, unleashing another harsh spray of flame as he did so. The flame immediately melted any incoming sword, and I backed away to avoid it. When I did so, the flame began to narrow, becoming a focused beam like what I'd seen the firebreather use.

I rolled, an inelegant gesture at that size, and managed to avoid it as it crashed into a line of trees in the distance, causing a massive explosion that lit the battlefield. Aurum reared up for another, but I lifted up a gauntleted hand and shot it toward him with as much explosive force as I could muster. It slammed into his golden face, closing his mouth just as his blast was about to leave and causing an explosion within his mouth, but he recovered and leapt at me, using his wings to increase the force of his blow.

I molded my remaining gauntlet into claws and slashed at him, but his wings let him shift his momentum at the last moment to dodge. My other gauntlet returned, and I shaped that one into a blade, moving to close the distance between us as I did so.

Aurum and I began engaging in a fierce trade of blows, slashing, stabbing, and clawing at one another. Before long, I was covered in so many cuts that I could no longer repair myself quickly enough to keep up with it. More black ooze flowed freely out of me, and I could sense my essence fading fast, but I kept pushing, putting everything I had into the fight.

Aurum, on the other hand, seemed completely uninjured. There was rage in his eyes, and I'd landed blows I knew had hurt him, but nothing that had left anything resembling a wound.

I managed a particularly strong blow that turned the dragon god slightly away, and I leapt onto his back, wrapping my arms around him and attempting to cut off his air supply. I pulled with all my might, but as I did so, he began to claw at my arms, eventually removing enough that he was able to free his head and bite the rest of them off. As he was about to throw me off his back, I opened my faceplate, shaping it into rows of sharp teeth, and bit down with all the force I could muster, finally breaking through his thick scales and drawing blood.

Aurum roared and threw me from his back, slamming his tail into me as he did. The combined force of his blows launched me from him, and I landed on my back.

I went to push myself back up, but realized I hadn't been able to reform my arms since he'd destroyed them; instead, only black ichor flowed out. I opened my mouth and shot multi-swords at him as I had before, but it didn't even slow him.

He pounced on me and started neatly carving through my armor toward my elyrium center. I kicked and struggled, but couldn't deter him—I lost more and more strength as my essence was ripped asunder in his attack.

Finally, he reached into the giant shell I'd created and pulled out my now elyrium bronze-colored core. I struggled, but I was too weakened, and his power seemed not at all diminished by our battle. He gently slashed across my chestplate, cutting through the elyrium easily in spite of its durability.

"That was the greatest fight I've ever had with a mortal. You truly are worthy of being considered my progeny. For that, I'll offer you the honor of dying by my hand."

He smiled, and the point of his talon slowly pierced my chest.

I kept struggling, summoning swords to attack the talon, trying to separate and escape, and just pushing back the talon as hard as I could, but it was useless. I felt the claw slide through me, and then there was only blackness.

I awoke in a room. Despite what I had just been experiencing, I felt a tremendous sense of calm. I was in a kitchen, seated at a table, with four others. Two men, a dwarf, and a young woman.

A man leaned over a stove across from us. Next to him sat an arrangement of spices in small bowls, perfectly measured and arrayed. The man started placing each of the spices into a pot, stirring as he did so. Once all of the ingredients were in, he stoked the heat and stirred for a few minutes. He then placed a large wooden spoon into the pot and sampled some of the sauce, frowning as he did.

"Hmmm, still not as good as Sidi's," he muttered, starting to pour generous amounts of the sauce over a dish of chicken and rice. "I followed the instructions perfectly. I refuse to believe that it can only be made perfectly when cooking by 'feel'." He stopped muttering and shook his head, grabbing plates and approaching the table.

He was a severe-looking man, tall and thin, with sunken eyes and black hair touched with gray. He radiated a kind of calm, but it wasn't pleasant. It reminded me of the kind of calm that comes with acceptance that things simply are the way they are. He placed a plate in front of everyone and then sat at the table's head across from me.

They all started eating, and the severe man pointed at a small pepper shaker in the center of the table.

"Could you pass that, Sevald?"

I reached for it, but was cut off by the man sitting to my right. I looked up at him and saw the face of the man who had been my fourth meal. I looked around the rest of the table, seeing Syven, Pebble, and Byn all quietly eating their meals. I looked down at my hands, and instead of gauntlets, I saw only a silhouette of a body, filled up with darkness. When I glanced up, I could see the man at the head of the table looking at me.

"Welcome to my table," he said, and at that moment, I realized who he was.

"Thank you for having me, Lord Dur."

He smiled. "Sidi and Jeiri wanted to welcome you themselves, and Krish has a bit of a crush on you, but I reminded them that I laid claim to you some time ago."

"The oath?"

"That is correct."

"I didn't think that was something I could actually complete. Leaving my armor is a bit of an impossibility."

"You'd think so, wouldn't you? Either way, before we see what happens when you're let out, let's make sure you've honored your end of the bargain." He turned to Byn. "So, how heavy do you feel his sins are?"

Byn finished his food and looked up at Dur nervously. He still looked young, just a boy, but in spite of that, he managed to smile through his anxiety as he looked at me.

"I-I feel, that is to say, I think his sins are light as air. I feel that the good he's done outweighs the harm he brought me, and I appreciate that he did what he could for Dad."

Dur nodded and tilted his head at Pebble.

Pebble pushed the glasses that sat on his nose back up onto his face and scratched at his neatly trimmed beard. "I don't think his sins are quite that light, but I also acknowledge that weighing concepts is inherently—"

Dur cleared his throat, giving him an exasperated stare.

Pebble sighed. "In a metaphorical sense, I feel his sins are lighter than his armor. He's learned so much about the world, and I'm grateful that a part of me has been a part of that. Also, I rather enjoyed him smacking a few of my old professors around."

Dur nodded toward Syven.

"Personally, I feel a bit more sin may have been good for you. You're out there constantly helping people, saving who you can, and even sparing those that try to harm you. You didn't even try to negotiate pay with Granite when you basically saved his restaurant!" She sighed dramatically, but there was a small smile on her face. "I have to sadly agree that your sin is lighter than your armor. I'm very disappointed in you. Maybe if you get back, you and Hrig can work on that by—"

Dur coughed, glaring at her, and she sheepishly put her head down and began eating again, though not before giving me a wink.

"Sevald?" he asked.

The man to my left raised his head and looked at me, his expression hard. "I was in my prime, just getting started at being an adventurer. Since you've killed me, you've lived the life I've always imagined for myself. Slaying goblins, fighting in tournaments, dueling pirates, foiling the plans of evil men." He shook his head. "I wanted all of that, but before I make a decision, I need you to promise me you'll do the one thing every adventurer dreams of, the one thing I wanted since I was a boy."

"What's that?" I asked.

"Slaying a dragon."

I wished at that moment I could smile.

"I'll do it."

"Then in order for a part of me to live my dream, I find your sins to be lighter than your armor."

Dur nodded at Sevald and looked at me.

"Your oath is fulfilled. Keep in mind, when I send you back, it doesn't mean that your victory is assured. It is still a nearly impossible thing."

"Is there anything else you can do to help?"

"Myself and the other gods have already done all we can do."

"In that case, thank you. I'll take it from here."

He nodded a grim smile on his face. Byn, Pebble, Syven, and Sevald smiled, as well, and then I was sent back.

I returned to Aurum's claw piercing me, and extraordinary pain racking my every sense, but there was also something else. The runes that linked me to my armor were gone. I no longer felt any connection to the thing which I'd considered my body for so long. All that was left of me was void, power, hunger, and an amalgamation of souls and essences that held it all together.

I surged out onto Aurum's talon, my blackness covering as much of him as I possibly could as quickly as possible. He jerked back, dropping the hunk of elyrium I'd once been and backing away, but I was already on him, and I kept spreading.

I felt fear from him for the first time as he unleashed a blast of fire onto me, scorching me with intense heat, but I didn't relent. As I reached his shoulder and started spreading out onto his wings, I began eating my largest meal yet.

Unlike the others, it wasn't instant, and it wasn't easy. It was sheer agony. His every scale contained as much essence and memory as a hundred distinct meals would have. I wasn't able to fully shield my core as flashes of thousands of years of experiences rammed into me. His godly nature also burned ferociously as I fought to contain it. In spite of all of that, I dared not relent, pressing harder and harder, eating more and more.

Aurum began roaring and flailing, sending out flames and radiating rage and holy golden light. The sky itself clouded over, and lightning rained down onto us. The earth began to shake, not as a direct consequence of our titanic struggle, but as if the entire world was roiling from what was happening.

I pushed forward more and more, covering the tip of his tail up to his neck in inky blackness. Eventually, I reached a tipping point as I managed to eat more of his essence than I was losing in the struggle. I could feel his will pressing against my own, a god and his desire for life, one that was stronger than that of any other living thing in that moment.

The only thing that was stronger than his desire to live was my desire to end him. I reached his face and eyes, and as he gave one last defiant roar, I flowed down his throat, completely absorbing his essence.

I felt the last of him fade away into me, and for a moment, I was completely alone. Then, the full force of his personality slammed into me, his raw sense of self fighting to be as much a part of whatever we were becoming as possible, but in spite of that, my core stayed strong. I wrestled it down and subdued it, godlike though it was, and found myself fundamentally changed.

I shrank down, alternating between dozens of shapes. Man, woman, orc, dwarf, goblin, dragon, all with their own advantages and connections to who I was, but I knew, even as I started cycling through them, that there was only one possible decision to make.

I landed in the middle of where Aurum and I had fought, my boots clanking as I hit the ground. A longsword sat on my hip, and my burgundy cape flowed behind me. My silver skin was marked in places with scars of bronze.

I looked up to see five figures running toward me. Two short, two average height, and one tall. Hrig slammed into me first, her long legs carrying her farther faster than the others. I didn't have to fall backward, but I let it happen anyway. Shortly after, she was followed by everyone else, and I was covered in a diverse pile of adventurers.

We'd won.

EPILOGUE

Visiting the other gods wasn't exactly the thing I'd prefer to be doing—I had a trip to get underway, after all—but I knew it was necessary.

The ether I was drifting through felt comfortable, likely more so to me than it was to them as I was still, at least partially, made of it. I could sense the other gods ahead of me, behind a barrier of their own creation, but I had no such restrictions. I could feel conflicted emotions on the other side of the barrier, gods afraid of themselves, and afraid of each other, but I could also sense excitement, anticipation.

If they'd had a vote, they might have chosen to remain as they were. Separate from the mortal plane, acting through intermediaries and distant blessing. Fortunately, the decision was out of their hands. As I was the only god outside of the barrier, I was the only one who could choose to bring it down.

I extended my hand, grasping at the threads of the barrier. I could feel the godly magic flowing through it and see their origins, meanings, and the wills that were woven into them. I gripped it tightly, and pulled. It shattered easily in my hand—

there was never meant to be an entity powerful enough to reach it, on the outside of it.

I felt in that moment the energy of hundreds of gods, major and minor, fly past me, eager in spite of their fear to return to the world they'd helped shape. All but three, who instead chose to stop in front of me.

One I recognized as Dur, who had so recently been kind enough to have me at his table. The others were a dwarf, who looked distinctly like Stone, but younger and with a somehow wider smile, and an older elven woman, who had manifested in a chair holding a cane firmly in one hand and a small cup of tea in another. It was she that spoke first.

"Do you think this is wise?" she asked, a wry smile on her lips.

"Hard to tell this soon," I responded.

"Wise answer," said Jeiri. "Let's see how he feels after we've been roaming around for a while."

"That seems fair," said Dur, his expression a mirror of Sidi's.

"Did you three spend all of your time behind that barrier working on this little routine?" I asked.

"Well, not all of it, lad. It took me a couple centuries to get them to agree to it," said Jeiri.

"We were woefully short on preferred company," said Dur with an exaggerated frown.

Sidi took a sip of her tea. "We have all grown quite comfortable with our roles since we were formed. It's not very difficult for us to lean into it. My question is, what role you are going to be playing going forward?"

"Indeed. What domain you encompass will affect the balance of this world," said Dur.

I considered it. I'd had a feeling as soon as I ascended, a connection to abstract concepts I hadn't had before. When I began to speak, I felt certain that I knew what I had become the god of.

"Magic, and change."

Sidi's eyes twinkled. "The thing you were born of, and the thing you've done the most. Fitting."

Jeiri shuffled from foot to foot. "Well, if that's settled, I have some mischief to make and some cavorting to do."

I held up my hand. "I actually have a suggestion for the first thing you could do. I think it's a pretty funny option, if you'll hear me out."

He raised an eyebrow. "I'm listening."

Stone was sitting on a porch when we arrived. He was relaxing, a mug of ale in one hand and a pipe in the other, a satisfied but tired look on his face. A visit from all of his daughters and grandchildren was enjoyable, but he needed to make an escape every once in a while to breathe. He sat up when he noticed Jeiri and me approaching his porch, a smile spreading quickly across his face.

"Lad!" He bounded up and wrapped me in a hug, which I enthusiastically returned. "It's been a few weeks. How're things in the heavens?"

"Not as exciting as things here are about to be."

"Oh, really? You'll have to tell me about it. Oh! You should come meet the family. The grandkids will really get a kick out of you. Stay for dinner?"

"Of course. Can my friend join us?"

Stone turned his attention to Jeiri, noticing him for the first time. "You making other dwarf friends? Am I not enough all of a sudden?" he asked in mock offense.

Jeiri chuckled.

Stone's eyes widened. "That laugh... I know that laugh."

"I have a gift for you," said Jeiri, approaching him.

"Aye, what would that be?" asked Stone warily.

Jeiri stepped forward and smacked Stone in the crotch with the back of his hand.

Stone's eyes widened, and he stumbled backward, cursing.

I winced. This wasn't exactly what I'd had in mind, but Jeiri laughed.

"The one time wasn't enough for you?" asked Stone through gritted teeth.

"Maybe you should make sure."

"What do you..." Stone's eyes went out of focus for a moment. "You cheeky bastard."

Jeiri laughed. "I thought I'd return that."

Kyren had been busy. The theological implications of everything that was happening, on top of the political implications of a dead king and her personal responsibilities, hadn't given her much time to relax.

I felt some guilt for that; the majority of it was my fault. I found her asleep against an old oak tree, an aged tomcat sleeping peacefully on her lap. I could feel that Sidi had been nearby recently. The air had a feeling of calm to it, and there was the faint smell of tea. She stirred as I approached and smiled sleepily.

"You alright?" I asked.

"Great, actually. That was the best sleep I've had in quite some time."

"Seems like being on the receiving end of a sleep spell isn't too bad."

"I suppose not," she said, standing and brushing a few bits

of dead grass off of herself. The old cat hopped off her with a discontented mrrow. "So, to what do I owe the pleasure of a visit from the god of magic and change?"

I winced a bit, projecting the feeling out to her. I'd chosen a form without a face, but I'd found a workaround for emoting.

"Would you prefer Sevy?"

I let out an exasperated sigh. "I just came to check on how things were doing. I wanted to make sure you were alright."

"Well, the gods walk among us again, so things have been a bit crazy at the temples. Politically, things are surprisingly okay. It took the court researchers quite some time to determine who was next in line for succession. The Caedus line had been unbroken for centuries. It turned out to be a branch line that was barely holding on to a viscount title. It's good, though, he's weak, so the nobles who were focused on peace have been able to control him well enough, and he's deliriously happy from the weight of a crown on his head. Sylfen was willing to settle quickly; they were happy for terms that left their borders intact, considering they lost their entire army in a day."

"And the thing I asked you to take care of?"

"Sevald's grand-nephew is doing well. I have no regrets fostering him."

"You think he'll do well for them?"

"With my help, and Ellis', I know he will."

I let out a sigh of relief. "Thank you, Kyren. I know his family still hasn't forgiven me, and my ascension likely leaves a bitter taste. I appreciate you helping me to make amends."

She smiled and wrapped me in a hug. "Of course."

We separated.

"Anything else up?" I asked.

"Well, I don't know if he was able to send you an invitation, but Duke Ellis is getting married soon."

"Really!? Anyone I know?"

"Yes, it's Clara."

I emanated surprise.

"Apparently, they got quite close while planning the attack on the Twin Kings."

"Well, I'll be there. I'm sure Hrig would like to go, too."

"And how's the trip going so far?"

"Pretty well, but I think she's a little miffed. I keep teleporting off the boat."

"Can you blame her?"

"No, but it's hard to sit still when you can be anywhere in almost an instant."

"Well, you should probably be getting back to her. Come visit when things are less busy."

"I will. I just have a couple more stops, and I'm all hers."

"While you're gallivanting about, you may need to think about selecting a few clerics. You're already starting to accumulate some followers. It's important to give them some direction."

"That's actually what the next couple stops are about." I started to leave before turning around. "One more thing before I go, actually."

I moved over to Old Osric, whose fur stood on end as he started to back away.

"I'm not going to hurt you, and you no longer have to live in fear. I'm not going to punish you for what you did. Just go. You're the only one left. Remind people what it's like to see one of you in the sky again."

Osric's scared appearance dropped, and he turned around, walking far enough away for there to be a good amount of space between us. He shimmered, glowing silver and black and expanding. As the glow faded, what remained was a large silver-black dragon, shining in the sunlight. He spread his wings and flew off with powerful wing-beats, heading west.

Vash stood on the edge of a battlefield. She'd won another victory, but the cost was only growing larger. They'd fought clan after clan, pushing them back, trying to force them to negotiate, to come to the table, but they'd been stubborn. They'd preferred to send wave after wave of men after her and her people rather than just giving them what they wanted.

She stood on the dock of a small village, one that had been evacuated by a clan they'd been warring with. She breathed deeply, taking in the sea air. If her strength hadn't failed her like it had, if Aurum's blessings hadn't left her, she might have been able to do more herself, but even without those abilities, her people still depended on her.

She didn't notice me behind her until I made a gentle coughing noise. She spun around, swinging a hook sword at my head, but the blade stopped dead as it hit me.

"Hello, Vash."

"You..."

"Yes, me."

"What are you doing here?"

"Well, I was hoping to help you get what you want."

She spat on the ground. "We don't need your pity."

"My help isn't offered freely. There will be a cost. What I'll grant you won't ensure victory either. I wouldn't want to step on Krish's toes like that."

"What is it you're offering?"

"What you lost when Aurum died. A touch of godly power. As well as some very helpful contacts and a bit of information."

"And the cost?"

"Well... I'm in need of some priests. I thought you might be my first."

Vash laughed. Took a breath. Laughed some more. "Are you an idiot?"

"Sometimes, but I have my reasons for this."

"Which are?"

"I'm the god of change now. You're an example of change. Both within and without, you've been an agent of it. I think you're uniquely suited to being my priest because of it."

"If I refuse?"

"I'll leave you alone. I think there's a possibility of victory for you either way. I'm just trying to push the odds a bit more into your favor."

She looked toward the buildings her people had sheltered in, then back to me.

"I'll do it."

I smiled and sent a portion of my energy toward her. I saw her posture straighten, and her eyes, which had reverted to their natural brown, shimmered in a silvery steel color.

"Now, aside from that, I'd like to introduce you to some people that can make orcish maritime superiority a problem. How do you feel about learning to speak mer-folk?"

My last stop was just outside the capital. It had been several months since I'd seen him, but in spite of what he must've heard about me, Rock still insisted we meet for the duel. I stood across from him in a field, my hand resting casually against my sword. Rock was standing in front of a tent, not yet in armor, which made me hope this might be over quickly.

"You don't have to go through with this, you know. I'm perfectly willing to return your shield to you. It's not like it would be a fair fight."

Rock smiled widely. "You're right, the fight won't be fair, but you won't be fighting me; you'll be fighting my champion."

"Whatever brute you've enlisted to help you, I can't really imagine it'll make much of a difference."

"Oh, really?" he asked.

At that moment, a woman walked out of the tent. She was an elf, with sharp features and red eyes, wearing armor the color of blood, a single long braid of black hair falling down her back. She was all smiles as she approached, and her teeth were pointed.

"Krish! You're his champion?"

She nodded. "I've been wanting to get a good match with you since I got here," she said, cracking her neck as she approached.

Rock was wearing the most self-satisfied expression I'd ever seen on any living creature.

"Shi—"

When I returned to the boat, I was covered in scorch marks and missing large chunks of myself. Hrig looked at me with a raised eyebrow.

"I don't want to talk about it."

She walked across the deck to me and gave me a long kiss on my faceplate. "I already know. Krish asked me permission before she fought you."

"She did?"

"She said it wouldn't be right if she didn't get permission. It sounded more like she was asking to sleep with you than asking to fight."

I sighed. "The gods are all so damned weird."

Hrig gave me a firm pat on the rear. "Don't worry, I'll help you get back in fighting shape." She started leading me back to our cabin.

"How are Jade and Dorsia?"

"They're good. They say they'll part ways at the next port. Otherwise, they've been spending their time in much the same way we're about to."

"I'll be sorry to see them go. I'm also sorry I was so busy today."

We reached our destination and she led me into the bedroom.

"Don't worry, I'm sure you'll make it up to me." She locked the door.

END

THANK YOU FOR READING ARMOR

We hope you enjoyed it as much as we enjoyed bringing it to you. We just wanted to take a moment to encourage you to review the book. Follow this link: Armor to be directed to the book's Amazon product page to leave your review.

Every review helps further the author's reach and, ultimately, helps them continue writing fantastic books for us all to enjoy.

―――

Want to discuss our books with other readers and even the authors like Shirtaloon, Zogarth, Cale Plamann, Noret Flood (Puddles4263) and so many more?

Join our Discord server today and be a part of the Aethon community.

Facebook | Instagram | Twitter | Website

You can also join our non-spam mailing list by visiting

www.subscribepage.com/AethonReadersGroup and never miss out on future releases. You'll also receive three full books completely Free as our thanks to you.

Looking for more great books?

An abused NPC gains consciousness. Now, he wants revenge. Players beware... After a player-led event turns his once peaceful town into a band of ravenous monsters, a warrior NPC named Hirrus obtains a level of consciousness usually unobtainable by non-player characters. It might be a gift of the gods, or a mistake, but Hirrus doesn't care. It means he can track down and find the players responsible and stop them from doing it again. Thing is, players don't like their plans being interrupted. And in this game, there's no resurrection until the weekly reset. Will Hirrus be able to cut a path of destruction across the land to get his revenge, or will the players be able to overwhelm him and bring him to justice?

Get Harbinger of Destruction Now!

On the day of Aiden and Olivia's math final, things take a surprise turn... The end of the world. *During Finals, the worst thing most people worry about is a failing grade. For Aiden and his sister Olivia, they must contend with the apocalypse. But at least there won't be any more math tests! With his trusty pen in hand, Aiden is determined to protect his sister no matter the cost. The future seems bleak as the school warps around them to become a maze of death and otherworldly monsters start appearing. Essence, their one and only lifeline in this new world, changes everything, granting them power to fight back against the tide of chaos. Aiden does what he must to survive and save his sister. In doing so, he begins to uncover the larger picture as a Quest leads them into the great beyond. In a world of magic and monsters, all the cards are stacked against them. Do they have what it takes to work the System and come out on top?*

Get Apocalypse Unleashed Now!

What do you do when your dream job turns into a nightmare? *Warren loves his job. As a Game Master for Fate and Freedom Online, he gets to do everything from piloting World Bosses to helping players stuck in geometry. When he overhears two coworkers plotting to hack the game and endanger players, things go downhill fast. Not wanting to leave a witness, Warren finds himself stuck in the game as a gnoll! He's level 1, aggroing to every player, and unable to call for help or even log out of the game. How could things possibly get any worse? Warren's only hope is to become a World Boss and get back some semblance of regular game UI. Unfortunately, standing between him and escape is a Boss Monster that isn't too keen on letting him level up. With some new friends and a little luck, will Warren escape his digital prison, or will he be stuck as a gnoll forever?*

Get Tooth & Paw Now!

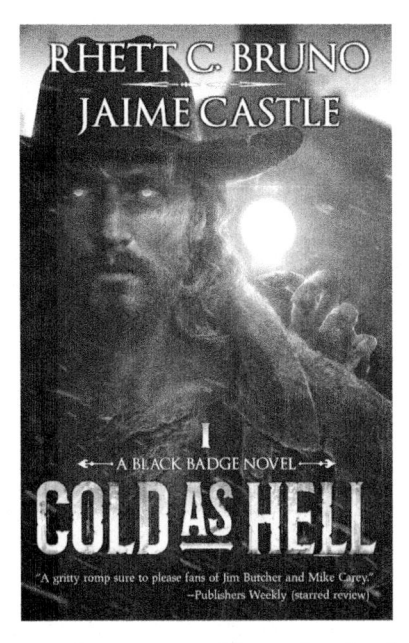

In the West, there are worse things to fear than bandits and outlaws. *Demons. Monsters. Witches. James Crowley's sacred duty as a Black Badge is to hunt them down and send them packing, banish them from the mortal realm for good. He didn't choose this life. No. He didn't choose life at all. Shot dead in a gunfight many years ago, now he's stuck in purgatory, serving the whims of the White Throne to avoid falling to hell. Not quite undead, though not alive either, the best he can hope for is to work off his penance and fade away. This time, the White Throne has sent him investigate a strange bank robbery in Lonely Hill. An outlaw with the ability to conjure ice has frozen and shattered open the bank vault and is now on a spree, robbing the region for all it's worth. In his quest to track down the ice-wielder and suss out which demon is behind granting a mortal such power, Crowley finds himself face-to-face with hellish beasts, shapeshifters, and, worse ... temptation. But the truth behind the attacks is worse than he ever imagined ...* **The Witcher *meets* The Dresden Files** *in this weird Western series by the Audible number-one bestselling duo behind* **Dead Acre.**

GET COLD AS HELL NOW AND EXPERIENCE WHAT

PUBLISHER'S WEEKLY CALLED PERFECT FOR FANS OF JIM BUTCHER AND MIKE CAREY.

Also available on audio, voiced by Red Dead Redemption 2's Roger Clark (Arthur Morgan)

For all our LitRPG books, visit our website.

Printed in Great Britain
by Amazon